# JOURNEY OF THE LIGHTWORKER

SHARI A. HEMBREE

This is a work of fiction. Names, characters, places, and incidents either are the product of the authors' imagination or are used fictitiously. Any resemblance to actual persons, living or dead, events, or locales is entirely coincidental.

*Published by:*
**Shari A. Hembree**
Delray Beach, FL
www.ShariAHembree.com

ISBNs:
Softcover: 978-1-7329016-0-5
Hardcover: 978-1-7329016-2-9
Ebook: 978-1-7329016-1-2



Cover design by Marc Gist

Book design and production by Gary A. Rosenberg
thebookcouple.com

Editing by Carol Killman Rosenberg | carolkillmanrosenberg.com

Printed in the United States of America

*With Love and Gratitude, I dedicate this book*
*To the Angels, who never left my side*
*even when my faith waivered;*
*To my Spirit Guides, who gave me the advice*
*to write this book in the first place;*
*And to my Loved Ones, both living and deceased,*
*who waited patiently for me to make my own journey.*

# Contents

# *What Is a Lightworker?*

A ***LIGHTWORKER*** is any person seeking a spiritual path of enlightenment, self-awareness, and a true understanding of who they really are.

A *Lightworker's* quest begins with differentiating between who they were taught to be through their upbringing, and choosing instead the life they were meant to live.

Step back and imagine:

*A life of self-fulfillment and genuine happiness;*

*A life of incredible bliss without labels, self-created illusions, or fear of the opinions of others;*

*A life filled with love, joy, faith, and inspiration; and,*

*A life in which you know the next step in your journey will divinely appear exactly when you are ready for it.*

A *Lightworker* helps others to understand and honor their lives as an expression of love, not fear, and to unlock their own divine potential. They are an inspiration to those around them by helping others discover what truly brings joy and meaning into their own lives.

A *Lightworker* is believed to have volunteered before birth for their current life purpose. As a *Lightworker*, special gifts from Spirit may have been given to them, such as heightened intuition and spiritual healing abilities. They have learned to follow their instincts even when it doesn't always make sense or follow logic.

And, finally, a *Lightworker* is most often drawn to counsel others, teach, write, or work in the healing arts. A *Lightworker* feels an inner calling to heal others and themselves, or to heal the earth's environmental and social illnesses through their actions and efforts.

Are you a *Lightworker*?

# Prologue

***The little girl was dreaming***. . . and it was a dream she had dreamt many times before. She was standing at the edge of a forest. The majestic pine trees stretched up endlessly into the pale blue sky. So tall were the trees, she could barely see the sunlight above the dense canopy. Squinting her eyes, the girl peered back towards the inside of the forest. It was dark and eerie—and not a place she wanted to go.

Just then the wind began to blow, sweeping the girl's long blond hair across her face and into her mouth. With a tense hand, she brushed her hair away from her cheeks. Struggling from within, she tried desperately not to be afraid. Her heart beat rapidly as fear began to wash over her small body.

For an instant, the girl thought about running far away. But instead, she closed her eyes and took a slow, deep breath . . .

As she inhaled, the fresh air warmed her nostrils, and a soft, gentle pine smell filled her nose. With her eyes still tightly closed, the girl began to realize she could also hear the sound of the pine trees. They seemed to *whisper*, making a gentle whooshing noise, as their long, thin branches danced in the summer breeze. *The trees almost seem to be calling my name*, the girl thought, as she listened carefully to the sound.

She slowly opened her eyes and took another deep breath. The sunlight sparkled as it peeked through the leaves of the swaying branches. The playful dance looked almost *magical*, mused the girl, as she watched the branches rock back and forth in the gentle breeze. Her fear had subsided. She felt calm and peaceful here . . . and then she began to smile.

Casting her eyes downward, the girl saw at her feet a winding path made of gravel, leading deep into the woods. She took a brave step forward and heard a soft crunch, as her foot gently pressed into the small beige stones. She paused for a moment, then cautiously took another step, and began to walk the path deeper and deeper into the woods.

*This path seems to wind on forever*, the young girl thought curiously, venturing even farther into the thick, shadowy woods.

At first the forest had seemed very dark, but the further along she walked, the brighter it became. Her eyes adjusted to the light, and she could see much more clearly now. To her amazement, wondrous creatures came almost out of nowhere to greet her. Deer, mice, rabbits, and even a large unicorn appeared, each bowing its head as if to say hello as she passed it by. All the while, small white birds chirped sweetly just above her head. Their sound offered her ears a delightful melody, as they flew joyfully through the branches. The animals were not afraid of the girl and seemed quite happy living in the forest.

As she continued on her way, she came across a most enchanting scene of tiny fairies darting in and out of the trees. Their miniature orbs of light sent purple sparkles shimmering through the air, as they whizzed by her. They giggled as they zipped by, and she giggled too, wishing she could fly with them on their dizzying voyage.

"The forest *is* magical," said the girl, and her heart filled with delight.

She continued to follow the path as it wound its way around a clear blue, effervescent stream. The water was cool to her touch and felt good, and she dipped her hand in to pick up a small heart-shaped stone. Following along the edge of the bubbling brook, the girl eventually came upon an unexpected vista—an expansive grass-covered meadow. Wildflowers of every imaginable color grew in the grass, adding playful patches of white, pink, blue, orange, and bright yellow to the lush green landscape.

The girl skipped across the meadow, but then stopped suddenly, awestruck by what lay beyond the outer edge of the colorful field—a massive, endless body of water. She eagerly approached the water's edge. She stopped to watch the rippling waves sweep across the expansive shoreline—and then splash onto the sand, making a soft crashing sound. The girl had never seen a body of water so large, and the shoreline completely disappeared off into the horizon.

By now, it was almost evening, and the rising full moon brightly reflected its glowing light upon the moving waters. The girl glanced upward at the serene, darkening skyline. She reached her hand up, and thought if she could touch the sky, it would feel like soft black velvet. A million white diamonds twinkled in the dark skyline, as she gazed up in awe at the heavens. Standing there silently, her heart felt like it would burst with immense joy at this perfect moment in time.

The girl excitedly stepped onto the sandy shoreline and began to play in the warm, salty water. As she splashed and skipped about, tiny water nymphs danced with delight in the waves, destined only seconds later to crash down upon the soft, wet sand. She thought she could hear the nymphs squeal just before the waves hit the shoreline. The girl laughed and felt so happy to be in this amazing place.

She continued playing in the warm water, skipping and picking up seashells, examining each one in the radiant moonlight. Suddenly her intuition ignited a strange feeling, and the girl realized she was not alone. Startled, she swung around to look behind her.

There stood a strikingly beautiful woman. Her bare feet were planted firmly in the sand, just steps away from the child. She had long flowing hair that cascaded down her shoulders, and she wore a gown that seemed almost ancient, but somehow familiar to the girl. Her hair and gown were a brilliant silvery-white, and the woman seemed to *glow* with light as the girl looked up at her. A gentle, slow smile spread across the woman's face, and her eyes filled with love as she gazed down upon the child.

"Who *are* you?" asked the little girl, looking up at the woman with innocence.

The woman knelt down beside the girl and with an expression of pure love replied, "I am your Guide, little one."

"My Guide?" asked the girl puzzled. She didn't quite understand.

"Yes," replied the woman. "We have spent many lifetimes together, and you are a part of my soul family."

The girl thought about that for a moment, and liked the way it made her feel inside. She then asked curiously, "Why are you here?"

The woman stood up, her hair and gown shimmering, and she turned toward the girl to face her directly. Looking deeply into the curious child's eyes, she answered softly, "To help you remember, little one."

And with that, the woman took the little girl's hand, and they began to travel up, up, up into the brilliant evening stars . . .

Part 1

# Life in San Francisco

# 1

Kyra woke up and looked at the alarm clock on her nightstand. It was 3:33 am again. "How many nights have I woken up *exactly* at this same time?" she asked herself in frustration, throwing a pillow over her head. The insomnia that plagued her seemed to coincide with her promotion to Senior Vice President at Vortex, a global company, two years earlier. Since then her mind seldom rested, and sleep had become a luxury. As she lay awake, her mind wandered aimlessly, and she tossed back and forth in a futile attempt to fall asleep again.

Kyra's thoughts drifted off to her move to San Francisco. *Has it really been five years now?* she wondered. *It feels like a lifetime ago . . .*

She had made the move originally to advance her career, but much to her surprise, she instantly fell in love with the city. The sweeping vistas on every hilltop, the romantic charm of the glorious sunsets, and the spectacular cultural events of theater, ballet, and opera, all enlivened her senses. Even the crazy, eclectic people who lived there made Kyra smile. She vividly recalled her first visit to San Francisco and the comforting feeling she had somehow "come home." *It was such a strange but familiar feeling, even though I'd never visited the city before*, Kyra remembered fondly.

Yes, San Francisco was a vibrant mixture of art and culture. But it also offered world-class shopping and fine restaurants, and its nearly idyllic Mediterranean-type weather was certainly famous. A lover of year-round outdoor activities, Kyra thrived on the incredible variety of the microclimates in the Bay Area. On any given day, the weather could range from cold fog rolling off the spectacular Twin Peaks on the west side, which made her shiver, to the gorgeous sunny warmth down east in the Mission District. The pleasant mild temperatures just north in

Sonoma Valley always filled her heart with joy, but the strong winds rippling across the stunning Half Moon Bay, just south of the city, fully enlivened her.

She turned over in her bed again, and Kyra's heart warmed as her thoughts turned to deep appreciation. *I am so blessed to live here, and San Francisco has so much to offer. How amazing is it that I live where most people only dream of visiting?*

The most unique aspect of the city, and what Kyra loved best about California, was that it offered her the Pacific Ocean. Even as a child, she was indescribably drawn to the ocean, despite not having grown up near a body of saltwater. She loved to drink in the strong, fresh smell of the salt air in the morning when she visited the beach, and the hypnotic cries of the seagulls above her head would always bring a smile to her lips. She adored the power of the wind on her face when the ocean breeze would sweep her hair off to one side, and her heart would fill with delight as the peaceful waves rolled in and crashed upon the shore.

As Kyra lay in bed, she imagined her toes scrunching in the sand and instantly felt grounded, as if she were really there walking along the shoreline. The ocean had an amazingly calming effect on her and made her feel vibrant. *Unlike that cold office building I work in,* she thought, cringing for a moment and wrinkling her nose in distaste. *No, I definitely prefer the magic of the ocean.* As she stretched out on her bed more comfortably, Kyra reflected on the feelings of tranquility the ocean offered her.

Although the majority of her week was spent working twelve to fourteen hour days, every Saturday morning, Kyra made a fifty-minute trek north to Stinson Beach just to spend an hour there. She'd then return home to run errands and work the remainder of the weekend.

The cozy, laidback town of Stinson Beach was so picturesque with its gorgeous three-mile expanse of sandy shoreline—it seemed to stretch on forever. She often gazed off into the horizon, taking time to reflect on her life.

Feeling right at home among this mostly mellow surfing community, Kyra always wore her most comfortable faded jeans shorts, along with her favorite navy sweatshirt. And, because the beach could be very windy at times, she'd pull her hair back into a simple ponytail to keep her hair from blowing too wildly across her face.

Kyra cherished the serenity of wiggling her toes in the sand and gazing out into the deep sapphire water. Her mind would wander as she watched the waves roll in. At times, she'd close her eyes and just listen to the sound as each wave crashed upon the shore. She never grew tired of sitting there, and the ocean seemed to feed her soul.

Taking a deep breath, Kyra turned over in her bed, trying not to think about the early morning hour. She remembered when she sat at the beach, she totally ignored her watch and simply lived in the moment. *The ocean makes me feel so positive and uplifted. It's almost as if God is there for me,* she reflected, adding a silent prayer of gratitude. She pictured her precious moments of silence at the waterside and how easily she could slip into meditation once she was there. Truly, it was her special time with God and the Universe to simply give thanks and feel at peace with the world.

Kyra stretched out again, having given up on tossing and turning any longer. She stared up at the white bedroom ceiling, and her thoughts gently shifted to her second most favorite outdoor pastime. When her schedule allowed, she would make an extra stop on her way home from the beach to the nearby Muir Woods for some easy hiking. There were six miles of trails with half-hour loops, so depending on her Saturday work schedule, she could choose how long to spend there. The forest was so beautiful and mysterious, always eliciting a feeling of childlike wonder. Kyra was in awe of its magnificent testament to living in harmony with nature.

"It truly *is* God's country," she said aloud, envisioning the peaceful feeling of walking among the trees.

The redwood forest was also unique in that it was home to some the most ancient and largest trees known on the face of the earth. Some of the trees had diameters close to 20 feet, and many reached dizzying heights of nearly 400 feet tall. Kyra closed her eyes and imagined stretching her neck back to look up at the tall forest ceiling. She recalled, too, gazing down at the forest floor and how her heart would skip a beat whenever she'd catch a glimpse of a tiny mouse or squirrel scampering off into woods. Each time she was caught by surprise, her heart filled with immense joy to momentarily spy the tiny creatures that lived there. Muir Woods was most simply a peaceful sanctuary with its captivating beauty and serenity. *I always feel in total harmony among the trees,* she thought.

On the surface, Kyra's life seemed perfect. She lived in a charming two-story condo on Hyde Street in the prestigious Russian Hill district. Her neighbors in the hilly residential neighborhood were mostly like her: young, successful, and hard-working professionals. Laid out in a grid pattern, Russian Hill was also famous for having some of the steepest grades in the city. Small portions of the streets were completely blocked off to car access due to the elevation and featured instead beautifully landscaped walking lanes and steep winding staircases.

Kyra was pleasantly surprised, and even taken aback at times, by the dazzling mix of architecturally attractive homes, trendy restaurants, antique shops, and stunning views of Alcatraz Island and the San Francisco Bay. She enjoyed the vibe of the city, despite having spent her childhood in Chicago. San Francisco somehow felt like it had always been home to her.

Taking a deep breath, Kyra smoothed out her bed covers and lay on her side. She looked around her bedroom and thought back to how incredibly blessed she felt to have stumbled serendipitously on her condo. She recalled her first house-hunting trip with excitement. It had just come on the market the same day she had gone out with her realtor. With very few units available for sale in that building, they might have missed it completely, but on a whim, Kyra had introduced herself to one of the residents in a hallway. She was a young woman about Kyra's age.

Looking a little frustrated, Kyra boldly approached the attractive woman. "Hello," she said, trying to sound calm. "My realtor is showing me around, and I'm interested in buying an apartment in this building. If you don't mind my asking, do you like living here?"

Her future neighbor replied with contagious enthusiasm, "My husband and I have lived here for nearly three years, and we love it! It's a quiet building and close to great restaurants and shopping. It's the perfect location for us. I think you'd really like it here."

The woman had gone on to tell them both that she'd just heard that the model unit had been foreclosed on recently. "It should be back on the market sometime soon, and it's the nicest unit here actually. You should definitely keep your eyes open for that one," she said eagerly, giving them some details about the interior.

"Thanks so very much for all of your help! I hope this building does work out for me," Kyra said, giving her a warm and friendly handshake.

Her realtor immediately rechecked the listings in the building and *voilà!*—the unit had just been put on the market that morning. It seemed to Kyra that the Universe had intervened on her behalf, and she felt blessed for having listened to her intuition.

When Kyra stepped over the threshold and into the condo, she gasped for a moment, taking a deep and excited breath. "I can't believe this. . . . It's *exactly* what I've always dreamed of," she'd said with surprise. Her realtor beamed in agreeable excitement, "Oh my . . . this is perfect!"

The unit had undergone a complete renovation three years earlier; it had shiny dark hardwood floors, a remodeled kitchen with brand-new appliances, and updated bathrooms with new fixtures and marble flooring. The walls were freshly painted pale yellow, and intricate crown molding topped off the ten-foot ceilings. Clearly, no expense had been spared, and the effect was simply stunning. Kyra made her decision to buy it on the spot. And, being it was a foreclosure, the bank closed quickly to get the expensive property off their books.

Kyra moved in immediately following the closing and took enormous pride in decorating her new home. Choosing an eclectic mix of transitional-style furnishing, she added many contemporary touches, such as soft suede beige couches to the more traditional-style interior. Huge mirrors framed in dark wood accented her walls, and throw pillows in a bold pattern of cream, bright yellow, and dark brown added contrast to the otherwise neutral palette. In the end, her place had a simple, comfortable, but trendy feel to it.

Kyra looked around her bedroom with sleepy eyes, and the moonlight streamed in through her bedroom window. *Yes, how blessed am I to live here?* she thought again, as gratitude settled into her heart. Fate had indeed orchestrated her finding this place. In fact, everything had just fallen into place when she relocated to San Francisco for her job at Vortex.

From a career standpoint, Kyra had always been driven, and many would consider her the quintessential image of corporate success. At only thirty-five years of age, she was also the youngest Senior Vice President at her company. Given that she was a petite, attractive woman with shoulder-length blond hair, she was particularly proud that her intellect had won out over any preconceived notions others may have about her leadership capabilities. She'd earned her promotion to Senior Vice President through much hard work and unrelenting perseverance.

At Vortex, Inc., like a lot of technology companies, men still heavily dominated the executive ranks. Kyra had worked unbelievably hard to achieve the respect of her male colleagues, but while the hard work had paid off with rapid promotions, the long hours and stress had surely taken their toll on her. She was exhausted and feeling slightly burnt out.

The peaceful memories of the beach and the woods were now gone, and Kyra lay awake in bed, more agitated than before. She began tossing again, and disquieting thoughts washed over her: *I've sacrificed so much these past thirteen years. Eighty-hour workweeks, very little social life, a part-time boyfriend, no husband, no children. I don't even have time for a dog!*

She groaned, as her mind shifted gears, and she thought about her upcoming workday. She had six meetings scheduled with her staff, two international conference calls with suppliers, and a presentation to the Board of Directors on the recent quarter's financial results for her business unit. Revenues were down, as was consistent with her competitors. Nevertheless, Kyra had good news to share with the Board. She had reduced costs substantially, and the next quarter looked to be on a positive trajectory. She felt confident in her abilities to keep improvements underway.

Kyra often relied heavily on her sharp, intuitive skills in her business decisions, instead of always using cold, hard facts. In fact, she'd recently used her carefully honed gift to avoid a disastrous deal that would have cost the company millions of dollars. She had argued her point for hours in a meeting, finally winning over the president's support. She could still hear his concluding words, "Your business sense has always been right on target, Kyra. So despite the logic that we should move forward with acquiring Integra Corporation, I'll agree to hold off for two weeks. You better not be wrong since it will not bode well for the company . . . or for you."

*And in less than one week,* Kyra remembered with much satisfaction, *our deal fell completely apart when the financial scandal hit the Wall Street Journal. What a nightmare when Integra saw their stock plummet more than fifty percent in one day. My intuition was right on target!*

Kyra sighed as her mind struggled between pride over her business accomplishments and the reality of her exhausting work schedule. She thought about sleep again and tried desperately to find a quiet space inside her mind. Occasionally, when she drifted into a deep sleep, Kyra awoke the next morning and vaguely remembered a dream she'd had as a child. It was a familiar dream, like a special place she had visited many times before . . . and she knew she always felt happy in the dream. But the details of it completely escaped her now, and when she awoke, she'd quickly forget her dream. Sprinting through her hectic workday distracted her from everything else.

Kyra looked at the clock again; it read 4:44 am. *Argh . . . I have such a long day planned at the office tomorrow.* She closed her eyes and finally drifted off into deep slumber and began to dream. And, in the dream, she was standing at the edge of a forest and the wind was blowing her long hair across her face . . .

# 2

The alarm clock blasted at 6:00 am, signaling the start of Kyra's workday routine. She moaned, turning the alarm off with one hand, almost knocking it completely off the nightstand. Stumbling out of bed, she made her way to her large marble master bathroom. Once showered and dressed in a simple, dark, tailored suit, she then tossed back two cups of espresso and gulped down a small cup of yogurt.

By 7:15 am, she stepped outside and briskly walked a few blocks to wait for the Powell/Hyde Cable Car. Part of her morning routine was to take the cable car when the weather was nice, or the subway when the weather was rainy, to her downtown office building. This morning, the day was especially beautiful. Kyra boarded the cable car, traveling down scenic Hyde Street and crossing over to Powell Street, where she exited and continued on her morning commute. Of course, Kyra could have driven her car to work every day, but she took pride in supporting public transportation. This was her way of "going green" and helping to reduce carbon omissions in an already overstressed city environment. It brought her much joy and a sense of accomplishment to be environmentally conscious with small steps like these.

She arrived at her office promptly by 8:00 am, with a full schedule of meetings ahead of her. But today, at exactly 9:00 am, the president unexpectedly called her into an impromptu meeting. Kyra asked her assistant to clear her morning calendar, and she next headed to the boardroom.

The President of Vortex, her direct supervisor, sat down and invited her to take a seat as well. It was just the two of them, which Kyra viewed as a bit unusual.

"Kyra," he began matter-of-factly, "I have some difficult news. Profits have plummeted this past year, and we are struggling to cut costs. There is no easy way to tell you this, but we are eliminating your position. It's not a reflection of your work."

Kyra felt herself go ice cold and stiffen as he continued, "You've done a stellar job these past five years, but we've decided for cost-reduction reasons to consolidate your division into another line of business. We've scheduled a meeting with your staff later this afternoon to announce the changes. Of course, your severance package will include a year's salary and full benefits. I'd be happy to be a reference for you as you look for a new job . . ."

The president continued speaking for another five minutes, explaining details of the press release and the severance package, but Kyra didn't seem to hear his words. When he finished speaking, she stood up and quietly composed herself. She simply replied, "Thank you. I understand." But inside her heart was racing.

She shook the president's hand and walked back to her office to pack her belongings. She had learned the art of keeping her composure in any business meeting, despite the severity of the situation. And, she knew there was no point in negotiating or trying to convince the president to reconsider his decision—It was business as usual at Vortex.

By 10:30 am, she was back on her normal cable car route heading home to her condo, but this time toting along her office belongings. Kyra had been given a portable carry cart with two small boxes. She sat quietly on the cable car as it slowly moved forward, almost bursting into laughter at the irony of the situation. *Everything I accumulated in my five years at Vortex conveniently fits into two small boxes! How sad is that?!*

At 11:15 am, Kyra found herself standing in the middle of her kitchen with the boxes sitting atop her shiny black granite countertop. She rarely drank during the week, much less during the day, but the morning's shock required some numbing of her frazzled nerves. She fixed herself a generous vodka tonic, plunking three ice cubes into her glass. As the chilly liquid washed over her lips, the alcohol seemed to have barely any effect on her. Her muscles were rigid and tight, and the tension made her skin feel clammy and cold.

"After all the crazy hours I've worked and all the amazing results

I've achieved—how could they do this to me?" Kyra angrily complained aloud to her kitchen.

She felt the numbing emotions of shock and anger transform suddenly into embarrassment. She had *never* failed at anything before in her entire life. She continued speaking aloud, "And how am I going to tell my friends that my position was eliminated—as if what I did wasn't good enough?"

As Kyra looked around her kitchen for an answer that she'd never find there, it began to dawn on her that it would take time to digest everything that had happened that morning. She knew she'd be okay financially with her savings, investments, and the very generous severance package she'd been given—but she also realized her pride was greatly injured.

Kyra sipped her cocktail. "I'll have plenty of time to get a new position," she told herself. "But *ugh* . . . I need to think this all through. For starters, the next time around I'll definitely work for a president who actually appreciates my work!"

Kyra put her drink down and picked up her cell phone to call Steve, her boyfriend. They'd been dating for a little over a year now. Her mood shifted, as she thought with affection back to the night when they'd first met. It was Valentine's Day, and Kyra had reluctantly agreed to attend a charity ball at the Ritz Carlton on Stockton Street.

Normally Kyra didn't attend many charity events, but her friend Emma had bought her a ticket and insisted they go together. Kyra's own charity giving consisted mostly of writing checks, as her crazy work schedule left little time for actual volunteering, even though she loved the idea of helping others directly.

Emma had tried her best to be persuasive. "Kyra, darling," she'd said, "we will have so much fun at the ball. It's about us girls getting dressed up and having a fun evening—while supporting a good cause of course. Who cares if we meet any guys!"

Emma's slight southern drawl was quite charming to the opposite sex; men were simply drawn to her. She had long dark brown hair and bright blue eyes that illuminated when she spoke. Kyra laughed at

Emma's antics, falling under her friend's spell as well. After two weeks of encouragement, her friend's enthusiasm had finally rubbed off on her. And despite its being Valentine's Day—a day that Kyra typically avoided when she wasn't dating someone—she'd graciously conceded, telling Emma, "Okay, okay, you win!"

But much to Kyra's surprise when the date drew closer, she'd actually found herself excited to attend the formal event. *I am really looking forward to getting dressed "to the nines" for a much-needed change of pace!* she thought enthusiastically. After searching through her closet and wondering what she'd wear, Kyra had decided a shopping spree was in order.

The night of the ball, she'd stood in front of her bathroom mirror, taking an inventory of herself.

Kyra had been blessed with a petite frame and athletic body. Her light blond hair and olive complexion came from her mother's side of the family, but her deeply set dark brown eyes definitely came from her father's side. It was a striking combination, which easily drew compliments from men and women alike. A naturally beautiful woman, Kyra typically downplayed her attractive looks at the office with minimal makeup, a simple ponytail, and dark conservative business suits. To further accentuate her business persona, she used her razor-sharp mind and serious demeanor to hold her own with the executive men in her industry—not her looks.

That night, however, with Emma's advice, she'd decided to let loose and drop her guard a bit. She'd chosen an off-the-shoulder black lace silk gown by Gucci, and to complement her style, she'd swept her hair up and off her shoulders. She'd even taken the time to have her makeup professionally done at her local salon. The result had been simply stunning.

When she and Emma had stepped into the party room, all eyes turned toward them. Kyra had been entirely unaware of the effect she had on the men, but Emma had whispered, "Look how many eyes are on you, darling."

"I'm not the only one they're looking at," she'd said with a blush, flashing her friend an awkward smile.

The Ritz Carlton had been splendidly decorated that evening. In the courtyard attached to the Terrace Room, tables were covered in soft white linens, pale pink candles, and elegant china awaited the guests. Centerpieces of vibrant red and pink roses completed a setting that radiated romance and *amore,* as Emma would say.

Emma had chatted excitedly, as she always did, filling Kyra in on her most recent trip to the south of France, as the women approached the bar. Kyra's mind had wandered for a moment, and she'd glanced across the room. As if drawn by a magnet, her eyes had immediately locked on to Steve's. The chemistry between them had been palpable, and she'd felt her skin tingle when she realized how handsome he looked in his tuxedo.

He'd quickly made his way across the crowded room and stopped just a few feet away from Kyra. "Excuse me," he'd said politely, but firmly. Emma's voice trailed off then, and she'd put her attention fully on the man in front of them. "I couldn't help but notice you two very lovely ladies." The women smiled acknowledging his greeting and he went on, "My name is Steve." Then, turning more directly to Kyra, he'd added, "Have I met you before?"

Feeling a bit tongue-tied—not at all her normal self, especially given all of her experience speaking at corporate boardroom meetings—she had slightly mumbled her response. Her dark brown eyes were fully dilated, giving her a deer-in-the-headlights sort of look. "Uh, I don't think so. I'm Kyra. . . . It's very nice to meet you. *Steve*, did you say?"

Steve had smiled at her awkward response and took her hand firmly in his. "I'm so glad to meet you. This may be a bit forward of me, but I think you are just adorable."

Kyra had blushed at the compliment. Anywhere else, she might have considered being called "adorable" a bit too bold, but in this splendid, romantic setting, it had seemed appropriate—especially coming from such a handsome man. Steve's tanned complexion and dark blond hair deeply complemented his sparkling blue eyes and very white teeth as he stood there, smiling at her.

*Charm and sophistication*, Kyra noted now, *were the two characteristics that immediately drew me in . . . .*

Emma had promptly diverted her attention to another close-by handsome man and began flirting with him, while Kyra and Steve spent the remainder of the evening chatting. Shortly following the charity ball, they began dating—quickly falling into a routine that worked for both of their schedules.

Kyra and Steve spent most weekends together, alternating between whose place they'd stay at in the city. Every Friday night, they'd have dinner together, sparing no expense and often eating at the finest restaurants in the Bay Area. Every Saturday, they ran errands separately or even worked all day, but met back up again for dinner on Saturday evenings. On Sundays, they each worked a full day at their respective offices.

*We never get together during the week,* Kyra reminded herself, but she'd chalked that up to their hectic work schedules. Like Kyra, Steve was a successful Vice President at his company, and he often had to travel extensively for work. She understood why they didn't see each other during the week, but what she didn't understand was why Steve rarely called her during the week just to catch up. Instead, his communication with her was usually limited to a text message in the morning, reading something like, "Hey Gorgeous! Kick Butt Today!" or "Knock 'em Dead, Baby!" The message would brighten her day for a moment, but the feeling would quickly fade as she sprinted off to her own hectic workday.

Kyra looked down at the cell phone in her hand. It was a Tuesday, May 27, and the middle of a workday. She usually didn't call Steve during the week either; he had set that precedent, and she had accommodated him. But today was different, and she needed to talk to him. She hesitated making the call and then stopped to reflect more on their relationship.

At thirty-seven years old, Steve was close to her in age. He was a tall, handsome man with a deep, husky voice who oozed sex appeal. Despite the incredible chemistry between them, Kyra had slowly come to the realization that Steve may very well be emotionally unavailable. And she often overlooked his slight arrogance and selfishness. When they traveled together for vacations, they shared expenses, and Steve rarely did thoughtful things such as buying Kyra flowers or a gift for no reason.

*He barely remembered my birthday this year,* Kyra sadly reminded herself.

Despite Steve's flaws, Kyra had fallen hard for him, so much so that her usual response to his morning text message was "Have an awesome day! Love you!"

As the months rolled by, Kyra began to realize that Steve likely would never marry her. She tried to rationalize that their intense chemistry was enough, but deep down, she knew what she truly wanted in a relationship: someone who would always be there for her.

Not once had Steve told Kyra that he loved her. One time, when she had pressed him on this issue, they'd nearly broken up. After taking a three-week break, Kyra decided to let it go, and they'd started dating again. Steve fulfilled her need for companionship, and although in her heart she wished she could change him, he was not "the one" she envisioned spending the rest of her life with—unless something changed drastically.

Kyra's thoughts returned to the day at hand. She took her drink and cell phone, and settled down in the middle of her living room floor. Dialing Steve's cell phone number, the phone rang four times and rolled over to voicemail. She left a message: "Hi, Steve. It's Kyra. Please give me a call as soon as you get this message. It's very important. I need your help . . . I really need to talk to you."

As she ended the call, she cringed slightly, wondering if she'd sounded too desperate and needy.

Kyra downed the last of her drink, gulping the ice-cold liquid in one quick swallow. She got up off the floor and went back to the kitchen to pour herself a second one. She sipped this drink more slowly, and her mind wandered back over the past thirteen years of her life.

*How did I end up here?*

# 3

With time on her hands for the first time in a long while, Kyra settled down at her kitchen table to reflect on her life. She placed her cellphone and cocktail in front of her, and gently leaned her elbows on the glass tabletop. She momentarily thought about changing out of her suit, but simply slipped off her shoes instead. Her mind drifted back to her life in Chicago, where both of her parents had been born.

With an ironic half smile, she mused, "My parents couldn't have come from more different backgrounds."

Her father, Robert, had grown up in the prestigious Gold Coast neighborhood on the north side of Chicago—a wealthy neighborhood known for its opulent mansions, elegant townhouses, and sleek high-rise apartments. His side of the family had lived in Chicago for more than a century. Her great-grandparents were Roman Catholic and had immigrated to the U.S. from Ireland. Dirt poor upon their arrival here, it was the next generation—Kyra's grandparents—who had made it big. They'd pursued their passion in the publishing industry. With unwavering hard work and devotion to achieving success, they had become incredibly wealthy. Retiring about twenty years ago after selling their empire, they now spent the majority of their time traveling abroad. By stark contrast, Kyra's mother, Sarah, had grown up in the predominately Jewish community of West Ridge, also on the north side of Chicago. Her side of the family was clearly middle class. They were "salt-of-the-earth" kind of people, very religious, and super practical. Originally from Israel, Kyra's maternal grandparents had arrived in the U.S. shortly following the end of World War II. They had lived very modestly, rarely enjoying the luxuries in life, choosing instead to save nearly every penny.

Kyra took a sip of her drink and looked around her lavish kitchen.

*Hmmm . . . I did manage to inherit the best qualities from each of you,* Kyra thought, raising her glass in a toast to her absent parents. "To you, Father, for giving me your brilliant mind and drive for success, and to you, Mother, for blessing me with your lovely good looks and trusting demeanor."

Kyra put her glass down on the table, making more of a loud bang than she'd intended. Her parents were certainly an interesting, but unusual, union. They had been in their early to mid-twenties when they'd met at the bank where Sarah worked as a secretary to the president. A young investment banker, Robert was instantly drawn in by Sarah's pale olive skin and silky light blonde hair, which perfectly highlighted her flirty, sparkling blue eyes. She was a naturally beautiful woman who dressed well for her position. Robert, a handsome, tall man with thick black hair and deeply set dark brown eyes likewise attracted Sarah.

Kyra chuckled. *Oh yes, the cliché that "opposites attract" was most definitely the case with them.*

As the story went, her parents had begun dating almost immediately and married two years later. Robert's family had vehemently opposed the marriage because Sarah was Jewish—not Catholic—and from a very modest financial background. Sarah's family, of course, had intended for her to marry a "nice Jewish boy" to ensure the children would be raised in the traditional Jewish faith. In fact, the couple would have married even sooner if they had received either family's blessing more quickly.

Eventually, both sides did give in, and Kyra's parents had a small ceremony officiated by a Justice of the Peace at Robert's parents' mansion with a few close friends in attendance.

A deep sadness enveloped Kyra just then, and although she brought her glass to her lips, she didn't take a drink. Her parents were gone now. She put the glass on the table. Her father—a chain smoker—had died five years earlier of emphysema at the young age of sixty. And her mother—a chain drinker—had died only two short years later from cirrhosis of the liver at age sixty-two. Kyra had already been living in San Francisco when her parents had passed away, and their deaths had proven to be very difficult for her.

*Losing you both so young and so close together made me feel more alone than I'd ever felt,* she quietly lamented.

Kyra had mourned their passing privately, never once showing her emotions at the office. Sometimes, though, when she was alone in her condo, she would mourn the family life they'd never really had.

Kyra recalled the last time she had been at her parents' house in Chicago when she was making final preparations to put the home up for sale. A chill ran up her spine. *It was early evening,* she remembered. *And with most of the furniture gone, the house felt so empty. I missed you both so much, Mom and Dad. I felt so lonely, and I wished you could have been there for me. . .*

Almost as if it were yesterday, she could see herself standing on the first floor of the nearly empty Chicago house and glancing up the staircase. She could have sworn she saw her father walk by in the hallway—just like he used to do when he was getting ready to leave for work. With her heart racing, she had run up the stairs and called out his name . . . but, of course, he wasn't there.

This time, Kyra did take a sip of her drink, and then she spoke directly to her absent father, "But maybe you were there Father? I thought I could smell your cologne lingering in the air. And I could almost *feel* you around me. If you did visit me at the house that day, what were you trying to tell me?"

She actually waited a moment for a response, but then settled her mind on the intense drive for success she had inherited from her father. In fact, at the young age of twenty, she had graduated at the top of her class with highest honors, summa cum laude, from Northwestern University in Chicago with a double major in Finance and Marketing—a full two years earlier than her peers. She then went on to complete her MBA at twenty-two from Harvard University in Boston.

*What's made me so incredibly driven?* Kyra wondered, searching her memories of some long-ago counseling sessions she'd had with a psychologist. She had learned in the sessions that what lay beneath the surface of all her successes were the fears she had developed during childhood.

Her father was always at work, making business deals and striving for success above all else, while her stay-at-home mother lost herself every afternoon in her gin-and-tonic cocktails. As Kyra grew older, she spent as little time at home as possible, avoiding her parents' dysfunction. She chose instead to pour herself into her schoolwork and keep herself busy with extracurricular activities. Then, once she started college, she rarely returned home, except for Christmas and Easter.

After graduation, Kyra quickly excelled in the corporate world and took great pride in her rapid promotions. When the opportunity presented itself eight years later to work for Vortex, she had gladly accepted the promotion and moved to San Francisco. But her eighty-hour workweeks left her little time to enjoy the city or even the ocean for that matter. Her drive to succeed at work overshadowed everything else, and she totally immersed herself in her work.

*I learned the fear of failure from you, Father. And just like you, I spent the majority of my time building my career. . . All I really wanted was your unconditional love. What were you trying to tell me that day on the staircase? That you loved me, even if you didn't say it very often?*

The psychologist had suggested to Kyra that she'd carried this fear forward in her relationship with men, since she sometimes sought their approval without expecting unconditional love in return.

She took another sip of her drink and got up from the table. *Hmmm,* she thought with a wry smile, *it's starting to make more sense to me now.*

She made her way back to the living room and plopped lazily down into her soft suede couch. The sunlight beamed in through the large bay window, and she could see the lovely sapphire waters of the San Francisco Bay from where she sat.

She stretched her legs across the couch and glanced up at the celling as she continued to think. Without close family ties, Kyra had become very dependent on her friends for emotional support. She sought their approval almost to a fault because she feared not being liked or accepted by her peers.

*Yes, sometimes I try too hard to fit in and be accepted,* she thought, perhaps a bit too harshly about herself.

She let out a huge sigh, as she thought back again to her counseling sessions. On a few occasions, she and the psychologist had discussed Kyra's overwhelmingly strong need to always look her best—well, perfect actually. She knew she could be a bit obsessive about her clothing, which made her laugh now, because the truth beneath the surface was that she really preferred wearing just a plain pair of jeans and a t-shirt.

Her smile slowly faded as she thought of her parents again. Yes, they had chosen to live such unhealthy lives. Her father's life had actually been relatively easy earlier on, but her mother's life had always been a difficult one. Kyra was glad that her father had shared some of her mother's story, giving her some insight into her mother's drinking problem.

As Kyra recalled the story, her mother, Sarah, had been six years old when Kyra's grandmother had asked her husband for a divorce. Being Orthodox Jews, divorce was virtually unheard of, but her poor grandmother felt there was no other choice. Every evening and weekend, Kyra's grandfather drank at the bars, squandering away the money from his weekly paycheck, which was desperately needed to pay for rent, much less food. Her grandmother—*Nana*—as she was better known to Kyra, had a baby to raise, and she was determined that her daughter, Sarah, would have the best possible life. This included a stable home life and good schooling. Nana made the wise decision to move in with her parents and eventually took a job as an accountant to support herself and her daughter.

Although the divorce was never granted, Kyra's grandfather, Avi, had met his untimely demise when he stumbled out into a street following a heavy night of drinking. Tragically, he was hit by a car. The driver tried to swerve to miss Avi, but he never saw the car coming and died instantly.

A simple funeral was held the next day, as was the Jewish tradition to bury the dead as quickly as possible after death. Only a handful of people attended the funeral services, and as time passed, he was never spoken of again.

Sadly, Nana chose to not remarry, but she did adapt well to her new life with the support of her family. Kyra's mother, Sarah, however, did not. She never recuperated from the shame of the rumors of the divorce nor the circumstances of her father's death. Her own alcoholism began when she and Robert started dating. By age thirty-five, manic depression ruled Sarah's world, making it difficult for a young Kyra to be around her. Robert knew his wife had a serious problem but had been much too proud to check her into the expensive alcohol treatment center in Chicago, instead pouring himself into his career and avoiding the problem altogether.

Kyra stood up from the couch, looking around her living room, and walked over to the bay window. She gazed out over the tranquil waters. *Despite your issues, I was so blessed that you were my parents, but I need to let go of the past. . . .* She felt tightness in her heart as she reflected on her intension, but just then her stomach let out a loud grumble. Kyra realized her body had signaled the need to make a sandwich to offset the alcohol she'd been consuming.

Back in the kitchen, she gathered the necessary ingredients from her refrigerator and placed them on the countertop. As she sliced up the Swiss cheese, her mind settled upon a perplexing question: Why had she spent so little time with her father as a child, despite the fact that she truly wanted to be with him?

As an adult, Kyra had come to realize just how dominant her father's family had been in her young life. Because they were wealthy, her paternal grandparents were adamant that Kyra be raised in their faith and attend church. This likely heightened some of the friction between her parents. Ironically, Kyra never developed a close relationship with her Catholic grandparents, who spent most of their time traveling internationally. She could recall only brief Christmas dinners at their lavish house in Chicago, and each year a birthday gift would arrive in the mail from some exotic location where they were vacationing.

Kyra took some slices of ham and laid them across the bread as she continuing to ponder her family history. On the other hand, her maternal grandmother, Nana, was a breath of fresh air and the closest thing to a real mother she had ever known. Nana was so named because, as a young child, Kyra kept stumbling over the word *grandmother,* pronouncing it as *Nana-Nana.* Nana had been so delighted with the nickname that she decided to keep it, instead of the more traditional grandmother, or *savta* in Hebrew. Kyra's lips curved up in immense happiness as she recalled Nana telling her that story again and again.

With a smear of Dijon mustard and a pickle on the side, Kyra's sandwich was finally complete. As she placed the plate on the kitchen countertop, a genuine smile spread across her face, and her heart filled with love, just thinking about Nana. She recalled telling her grandmother many years ago, "Nana, you are the one person in my life I can always count on. You never judge me, and you always love me no matter what. I love you so much."

Kyra took a huge, hungry bite of her sandwich, and as she was eating she realized what she adored most about Nana: her positive outlook on life. Despite her hardships, she always looked on the bright side of things. She was not the stereotypical overprotective, smothering Jewish matriarch of the family, as some of Kyra's friends might have assumed. No, Nana was sweet, funny, and always offered Kyra the best advice. They had spent many Saturdays together when Kyra still lived in Chicago, having lunch and chatting. Occasionally, they even spoke about her mother, but Nana had a rule to speak only positively of other people, so most often they spoke about other things.

Nana and Kyra had so much in common that they seemed more like sisters in many ways despite their difference in age. Both loved to shop, although Nana was more of a spectator, supporting Kyra's elaborate taste and style. The pair also loved to visit art museums together, taking in the colors and warmth of the paintings, and sharing their feelings about the artwork.

Kyra took another large mouthful of her sandwich and bit into her pickle. Quickly swallowing both, she looked around her kitchen and spoke aloud now, "Oh, Nana, how many times have I suddenly thought of you, only to have you instantly give me a call? How *did* I know you were thinking of me? Oh, but I'd do anything for a phone call from you now."

She wanted the phone to ring, but Nana was currently in Israel visiting her younger brother, Saul. Kyra knew the time difference made it a little late for a long conversation. She sighed, and then finished up the remaining portion of her sandwich. Her face softened as she thought back on the weekly lunch dates she used to share with Nana. Her grandmother always chose a casual restaurant with home-style foods over the high-end restaurants, which Kyra could easily afford. Since her move to San Francisco, they called each other at least once a week just to chat and catch up. Kyra so deeply treasured those conversations.

Nana had a slight Israeli accent from spending her younger days in Jerusalem. And although she often spoke softly, she was very firm in voicing her opinions. Kyra always looked forward to Nana's advice, adoring her wise perspectives on life.

Leaning a bit on the countertop, she recalled some of Nana's best sayings now: "Honey, if you don't like something, change it—or God will change it for you." And "Honey, you can learn your lessons the hard way or the easy way. The hard way is when you hit rock bottom, then work your way back up because you didn't pay attention to the signs. The easy way, which looks hard at first, is when you decide to do something different—despite your fears—and it becomes easier for you as you go along. Everything turns out beautiful, honey, because you followed your heart. *Ani ohevet otach.*"

Despite her sweetness, Nana had a tough side as well. She had always been a fighter and smart as a whip, and she didn't take nonsense from anyone—all of which Kyra greatly admired. Nana had such a unique way of making her feel uplifted and joyful, no matter what was going on in her life. The memories of her were so incredibly vivid right now, Kyra felt almost as if her grandmother were standing in the kitchen with her.

But Nana would be in Jerusalem for another month and a half. She had left early in May and would be there until the end of June—the start of the hot summer season in Jerusalem. She took a trip to Israel every year to reconnect with her family there. Kyra laughed. She felt so proud to have a grandmother who was still traveling at eighty-seven years old!

*My sweet Nana, I could really use your advice,* she thought wistfully.

And that's when the phone call came in from Jerusalem. Kyra looked at the clock. It was 11:55 am in California, but 9:55 pm in Israel. Her great uncle Saul's voice responded to her hesitant "Hello?"

"Kyra, I have some very bad news for you." He wept on the other end of the line for a moment before he could speak again. As Kyra waited, she felt her heart clench.

Her uncle's voice was strained, and his heavy Israeli accent was harder than usual to understand. "I don't know how to tell you, dear Kyra, but Nana is dead."

# Part 2

# Journey to Israel

# 4

Kyra felt herself go completely numb. She could barely hear her great uncle's words as he continued to speak, and her mind raced uncontrollably.

"Your grandmother took a nap after dinner and passed away in her sleep—there was no pain, no suffering. She just never woke up."

As his words slowly sunk in, Kyra shivered from a sudden adrenaline rush, and she thought back to the last time she had seen Nana alive.

Uncle Saul interrupted her thoughts and continued, "Kyra, we need to make a decision on the funeral services." He spoke slowly so that she would understand the seriousness of his words beneath his heavy Israeli accent. "Most important, we need to decide *where* to bury Nana. It's our tradition to bury our loved ones immediately after death—normally within a day or two."

"I understand," Kyra replied, her heart pounding wildly. *Could this really be happening?* her mind cried. She desperately wanted it all to just go away.

Saul continued to carefully explain the situation. "With your grandmother's dual citizenship, we have two choices, dear child. We can either bury her here in Jerusalem within a day or two according to our tradition, or we can transport her back to Chicago to be buried in the same cemetery with our parents. But that choice could take over a week to accomplish."

Kyra listened apprehensively as Saul further weighed the second option. "In the morning, I will contact the U.S. Bureau of Consular Affairs and the local U.S. Embassy to begin the process of bringing her home to Chicago. But the paperwork can take up to five days to complete, and there's also the air transport too. . ." He paused, waiting for her reaction, before he finished, "Let us pray that things go smoothly should we decide to go that route." He concluded, giving her some time to think.

Kyra tried to clear her mind, but her voice was barely a whisper when she spoke. "I'm not thinking too clearly right now, Uncle Saul. . . . Truthfully, I don't know what to do. I just can't believe that Nana is gone . . ." Kyra sobbed gently.

A moment of silence passed before he offered a suggestion, "Kyra, *if* you are able to book a flight to Jerusalem, leaving tomorrow morning and arriving the following day, we can have the memorial service and burial the same day. You can stay with me, and we'll sit Shiva at my house. Family and friends will come to offer their condolences and mourn with us. We do have a lot of family here in Jerusalem to support us, and they can attend the services as well. I'm not trying to tell you which decision is better. . . . Perhaps you can look at the flights, and we can figure it out from there?"

Kyra understood the logic of her uncle's request, but hesitated when she answered, trying to keep her voice steady, "I don't even know if I can get a last-minute flight. But I do want to do what's best for Nana—and the family."

Saul paused before adding, "Yes, family is important during difficult times like these, and we do have very strong roots here in Jerusalem. You could meet our family, too. We all loved her so much," he said, his voice trailing off.

After another moment of silence, he continued more calmly. "I know your nana didn't speak much to you about your grandfather, Avi, did she? Let me fill you in a bit and tell you their story. It may help you understand our strong family ties here in Jerusalem," Saul suggested.

"No, she didn't talk much about him at all," Kyra replied, her curiosity piqued. Her grandmother rarely, if ever, made reference to her late husband and often avoided the subject completely. Kyra curled up on the couch eager for Uncle Saul to fill her in on some of her family's background.

He first explained that her great-grandparents had arrived in the

United States in the late fall of 1945, just months following the end of the World War II.

"You don't have to be Jewish to know what a difficult period this was in our history," Saul said. "*Palestine*, as Israel was known back then, was under British rule as a territory. And while we weren't directly involved in the war or Hitler's Holocaust, Jerusalem had been seeing such an escalation in violence and political unrest, which included many protest bombings against our British occupation. Living here was very dangerous, and so our parents decided to leave Jerusalem for a new life in the United States—a life in which we would be safe. I was only fifteen years old, a boy really, and it was a sad and difficult decision to leave the rest of our family behind. I really missed everyone after we left."

Kyra suddenly saw her uncle in her mind's eye as the handsome young boy she remembered from old photographs. Her heart felt his pain, and she wanted to reach out and soothe that young boy's fears and concerns.

Kyra pulled a soft, cotton throw over her legs to warm her skin and to get more comfortable as she continued to listen.

"Back then my sister was promised to marry Avi—and through a traditional matchmaker I might add." Saul chuckled slightly, since he knew the concept was likely foreign to Kyra and he wanted to add a little levity to their conversation.

"They were both so young—barely eighteen, and our parents urged them both to join us on our journey to the United States. We, of course, had no way of knowing that only three short years later the independent State of Israel would be formed when Palestine gained its independence from Britain. If Avi and your grandmother had known that would happen, they may have stayed here instead. But fate had such a different plan for them."

"If they had remained in Jerusalem, Uncle Saul, I wouldn't be here," Kyra said, adding a little humor of her own. For a moment, she was simply enjoying a conversation with her great uncle instead of focusing on their grief.

"Ah, very true indeed," Saul acknowledged before he continued.

"First, I should tell you, your grandparents were married in a small ceremony here in Jerusalem just before the five of us made our passage to the U.S. I remember Avi and my sister sharing their eagerness for the promise of a new life in the United States—a life without bloodshed or political turbulence. I don't know what came over Avi after our arrival in Chicago. He almost immediately turned to drinking, and this brought great sadness to all of us, but especially to my kind and loving sister. And their marriage ended such a short while later with Avi's untimely death."

"I do remember Nana had mentioned his death to me, but she never told me the full story, Uncle Saul. I never knew any of this," Kyra shared.

She recalled that the majority of her family had stayed in Israel, and that Uncle Saul returned home at the age of twenty-six after becoming a rabbi. He married Esther in Jerusalem, and there they started their own family. Meanwhile, Kyra's grandmother was living with their parents in Chicago and barely making ends meet after her grandfather's passing.

"Ah, but despite the distance," Saul said proudly, "my sister always called me once a week to stay in touch. I will dearly miss speaking with her. . . ." His voice trailed off again.

Kyra agreed. "I dearly loved my conversations with her, too. I'm not sure how I'll get by without seeing her again." Kyra's eyes filled with tears, but she kept her composure.

"That's how I felt when I first moved back to Israel, dear child. I missed her so much, but we were fortunate in that I was able to come back to the U.S. periodically to visit our parents and my sister. And I even managed to spend some time with you—before you got so busy with your career," he added.

Kyra cringed silently on the other end of the phone, realizing it had been years since they had last seen each other.

"Of course, once your grandmother retired, her annual trips home were such a wonderful treat for me and the rest of our family. Her retirement didn't allow for many luxuries, but each year, she saved every penny she could to make the journey home. She so dearly loved her family here, Kyra. Israel always remained her first home, and it was so very special to her . . . but now my sweet sister is gone."

Kyra spoke gently as her uncle went silent, "I have always appreciated Nana's loving and positive attitude in spite of the challenges life gave her. Truthfully, I wish I'd told her more often how much she meant to me. . . . I . . . I miss her so much, too, Uncle Saul."

Kyra's voice became choked with emotion, and silence ensued. Finally, taking a deep breath, she continued, "I know that Nana was considering moving back to Israel—especially with my having left Chicago and her friends becoming fewer and fewer with each passing year . . . I think burying her in Israel is a good decision. . . You are right. It was her first home and closest to her heart."

Saul let out a sigh of relief. It seemed to Kyra that he had been waiting for her to come to that conclusion, and she was glad she finally did.

"Call me back once you know more about your flights, and I will make the arrangements? *Ani ohev otach.*"

"I'll get right back to you, Uncle Saul," Kyra replied, then added, "and I love you too."

After ending the call, Kyra took the vodka tonic sitting beside the couch and gulped down the remaining liquid. After taking a moment to weep, she crossed the room, setting her empty glass down loudly on the large walnut burl wood desk in the living room. Plopping down into the soft leather chair, she powered up her computer to begin researching flights to Israel.

She gritted her teeth in frustration, and her arm muscles were tense, causing her fingertips to hit several keys at once. She tried again. Fully expecting her laptop screen to reveal no available flights to Jerusalem on such short notice, she closed her eyes for a moment in prayer, and then she looked at the screen again.

*The angels must be with me,* she thought, when much to her amazement, she'd found a flight leaving San Francisco early the next morning with a connection in New York at JFK Airport, and arriving early the following afternoon in Tel Aviv. Blinking again to make sure she was not imagining things, Kyra quickly booked the rather expensive flights and called her great uncle to confirm her arrival time.

When they spoke for the second time, Saul further explained the services to be held for Nana. Kyra noted the tension in his voice. "The Memorial Prayer Services will be held just before sunset and officiated by both me and one other rabbi. You will arrive in plenty of time to refresh yourself at my house, and then we will leave for the cemetery about an hour before sunset. As I mentioned, Kyra, Shiva—the traditional weeklong period of mourning—begins immediately after the burial of a loved one. We will sit Shiva for seven days at my house to allow family members and friends to come by and offer their condolences. You are welcome to stay for one or all seven days. You can decide how long to stay after you arrive of course."

Feeling grateful, Kyra said with sincerity, "Thank you so much, Uncle Saul, for taking such wonderful care of Nana all these years, and now for taking care of these arrangements. I know this is a very difficult time for you, too. If I can help in anyway, please. . . please let me know. I will be there as quickly as I can."

"I appreciate your offer, dear child, and I will see you soon. *Laila Tov*," Saul said.

"Yes, good night, Uncle Saul," Kyra responded and ended the call.

Her head began spinning with the details, and she found herself dreading the long trip ahead of her. A traditional Jewish burial was done as quickly as possible after death, but this was much more complicated with her being so far away. Kyra hoped the plane would arrive on time. Deciding she should begin packing right away, she headed upstairs to her bedroom to locate her large black suitcase.

Her mind still racing, Kyra randomly grabbed whatever clothing she came across: a dark suit, a hat, a scarf, and some sweaters. Unable to think clearly, she overpacked to avoid making any mistakes. It was late springtime, so the weather in Israel would be in the low eighties during the day, but evening temperatures could be in the low sixties—actually warmer than San Francisco. Tucking her passport into her purse, she checked her wallet for cash and decided she would need to stop at an ATM in the morning, just to be sure she had enough money on hand.

After finally changing out of her suit into a comfortable pair of jeans and t-shirt, she picked up the phone and called Emma, feeling the need to be comforted by a close friend. Kyra climbed into her bed when her sweet friend answered, expecting they'd be on the phone for a while.

Her voice was ridged and her vocal cords strained as she filled Emma in on the details of her grandmother's passing and her upcoming trip to Jerusalem.

Emma's voice had a more serious tone than usual, but her soft Southern drawl was warm and comforting. "Kyra darling, I am so very sorry for the loss of your grandmother. I know how much your nana meant to you. Please do call me *anytime* if I can be of help to you or you just want to talk. I'm here for you day or night, darling. When you get back, we'll get together for a girls' night out." Emma's voice trailed off for a moment, and she then she added again, "I'm so very sorry, Kyra."

"I'm so lucky to have you as a friend," Kyra responded with gratitude. "It's been a rough day for me overall. My position at Vortex was eliminated today as well."

Emma gasped. "Oh my girl! What happened?"

Kyra didn't want to focus on that aspect of her life right now and simply replied, "It's a long story, and I'll explain the details another time. But, yes, when I get back Emma, some girl time will definitely be in order."

After the hour-long call, Kyra was feeling a little more settled, but the earlier adrenaline rush had still left her nerves frazzled. She headed back to the kitchen and poured herself a third vodka tonic, and then called Steve again. The call went straight to voicemail. She spoke with urgency, "Please give me a call. It's very important, Steve."

She laid her phone down and thought angrily, *How busy can he possibly be?*

For the remainder of the afternoon, Kyra sat on her living room floor with several boxes of old photos that she had never taken the time to digitize on her computer. She looked at the yellowed, faded pictures of her grandmother as a young girl, including one of her and Great Uncle Saul as young children. The crumpled aging photographs felt nice to hold in her hands.

She found several photos of Nana as a young woman—*Perhaps when she'd first moved to the United States?* Kyra wondered. A few of the black-and-white photos included Nana with other unknown family members, but the last photo she found was of her grandparents' wedding.

Nana had a warm, soft smile in all of her pictures, instead of the more serious expression so common in the photographs of that era. Even Avi looked happy in the pictures, she noted.

"My goodness, Nana, you were such an amazingly beautiful woman—inside and out. I am so blessed to have had you in my life," Kyra said to the photograph.

And, at that moment, she felt tremendous warmth fill her heart. The feeling was overwhelming and indescribable, but somehow very familiar. She turned back and looked over her shoulder.

"Nana? Are you here?" she asked aloud. No one answered of course, which saddened Kyra for a moment. She let out a small sigh at her silly hopefulness, but her sigh died in her throat at the sound of a loud thump from across the room.

Startled, Kyra immediately jumped up off the floor. A small crystal teddy bear had fallen from the desk to the floor, but miraculously, it had not shattered. Light streamed in from a nearby window, reflecting off the crystal bear, casting a small rainbow across the floor. One of Nana's favorite things to look for after a terrible storm was a rainbow.

Kyra's eyes watered, and she tried not to burst out crying. "Oh Nana, it *is* you!" she said, retrieving the crystal bear from the hardwood floor. She had received that bear from her grandmother on her sixteenth birthday and had treasured it deeply ever since.

She held the small bear in her hand for a long time, savoring the moment as she felt her grandmother's love. She then placed the bear back on the desk and returned to the living room floor, opening another box of photos from her own childhood. Kyra spent the remainder of the afternoon and well into the evening trying to focus on the good times she could remember with Nana and her parents.

She slowly shuffled through the pictures, choosing her favorite one. *Ah, this photo is so very special to me,* she thought as she gazed at the photo of her six-year-old self with long blonde hair in a pink party dress.

Nana was dressed in her simple, dark clothing. It was her grandmother's birthday celebration, and they were hugging each other.

*What an amazing influence you've been in my life,* Kyra thought. *And I spent my time consumed with my career instead of spending more time with you.* Her heart ached with regret, but she tried to keep a positive focus.

By early evening, Kyra finished her last cocktail and dragged herself up the stairs to her bedroom. She undressed quickly, set her alarm, and then quietly slipped into bed.

Early the next morning, the loud buzzing of the alarm woke her up, and Kyra let out a moan. *I will get through this day,* she assured herself.

Almost as if on autopilot, she promptly got up, showered, and dressed in comfortable cotton dress and a lightweight sweater for traveling. Once finished, she lugged the heavy suitcase down the stairs and checked her watch. It was exactly 5:55 am when she stepped outside to meet the waiting taxi.

Upon arriving at San Francisco International Airport, Kyra checked her suitcase, to which she had tied a large purple ribbon. She easily wound her way through security since it was early morning, and the airport was less busy than usual. Soon, she had settled into a chair at her gate, juggling an espresso and a blueberry muffin, along with her purse.

Munching on her muffin, Kyra took a moment to check her cell phone again. There was no phone message from Steve. She felt her temperature flash hot, as frustration and anger filled her inner core at her boyfriend's thoughtlessness. She put the espresso down and stared at her phone for several seconds. Then, with purpose and a clear intention, she quickly typed Steve a text message: "I'm at the airport headed to Jerusalem. My grandmother passed away yesterday, so I'm flying out for the services. My position at Vortex was eliminated, so I don't have to worry about missing work. Please don't bother calling me back Steve. I wish you the very best."

And with that, Kyra was no longer dating Steve. Much to her surprise, she felt a huge wave of relief.

The flights were long, but relatively smooth. First, she arrived at JFK where she had an hour layover before boarding her next flight to Tel Aviv. She glanced at the small, uncomfortable-looking seat and was immediately thankful she'd brought along a sleeping pill for the overnight flight.

*I've been spoiled,* she thought ironically, recalling the many business trips she had taken, enjoying the luxury of first-class seating. Today, she was relegated to business class because her flights had been booked so last minute. She settled in, slipped in earplugs, and pulled a navy blanket up over her legs, falling asleep in less than twenty minutes after takeoff.

It seemed as if she had just left JFK when she realized the plane was preparing for landing. The captain announced they were arriving at Terminal 3 at Ben Gurion Airport, and only ten minutes past their scheduled arrival time.

After patiently exiting the plane, her next destination was Passport Control, where she answered questions about the purpose of her visit to Israel. She kept her answers short and simple, explaining that she was attending her grandmother's funeral and she would likely be in Israel for about a week.

"Is this your first trip to Israel?" the agent asked her.

Kyra was taken aback by how hard this question stung her. "Yes," she replied, as redness began to flush across her face. It only now occurred to her that she had never taken the time to visit Israel before today. Immense shame washed over her body at not having made the trip with Nana while she was still alive.

Kyra tried desperately to keep a straight face, hoping to hide her shame from the government agent. He gave her a quizzical look, but said nothing. And, after answering a few more questions, the agent finally gave her an entry permit sticker for her passport.

"Thank you," Kyra said simply and continued on with her journey.

# 5

*This isn't at all what I expected* was Kyra's first thought as she began making her way through the international terminal of Ben Gurion Airport. The inside looked remarkably modern and secure, not matching her expectation of a much older, less sophisticated airport. Armed security guards and police throughout the airport lent a serious tone to the atmosphere, and Kyra could immediately sense how committed the Israelis were in combatting terrorism and ensuring the safety of their travelers.

Aside from the armed guards, the airport seemed relatively normal with restaurants, coffee shops, and even a small shopping mall for passengers to browse and make purchases while awaiting their flights. It was midday now, and the terminal was bustling with people. Kyra walked slowly down the long corridors, taking in the sights and sounds to keep her mind off her reason for being there, and finally arrived at the baggage area to gather her suitcase.

*Uncle Saul's cousin Amos will be picking me up soon to take me to Saul's home in Jerusalem. It's about thirty miles from the airport, I think. . . Fifty kilometers actually,* Kyra thought, reminding herself to think in the metric system now that she was out of the U.S. She knew the drive would take slightly less than an hour depending on the traffic.

Kyra's stomach churned, and she brushed her hand across her belly. She felt apprehensive about seeing her uncle again and facing the reality of her grandmother's services. "I *can* do this," she said aloud to reassure herself as she approached the luggage carousel. She glanced at a young Israeli woman to her right, who gave her a polite nod and smile, as if to confirm that thought. Kyra politely smiled back and silently added a small prayer, *God, please help me get through this.*

Kyra pushed her hair back from her face and reminded herself to take a slow, deep breath as she waited for her luggage. To her relief, she saw her large black suitcase with the purple ribbon coming around the carousel bend, and once it was directly in front of her, she deftly pulled it off the belt despite its heavy load. Her arm had strained a bit as she retrieved the suitcase, and it dawned on her that she was still running on adrenaline. *I think I'm a bit nervous too,* she realized.

Rolling the suitcase behind her, Kyra stepped outside to the passenger pickup area where she was met by the crispness of the dry Mediterranean air. It felt nice on her face and momentarily reminded her of home in San Francisco, bringing a slight smile to her face. She stood on the curbside slightly lost in her thoughts, just as Amos walked up and waived his hand to her in recognition.

He was a tall, lanky man in his late sixties. Being a Haredi Orthodox Jew, he was dressed in a long, black overcoat with a matching wide-brimmed black hat. A thick bristly beard covered his chin, and long curled sidelocks spiraled down each side of his face. This, Kyra had learned was the traditional dress of the strictest Orthodox Jews and had not varied much in many centuries, from what Nana had shared with her. *He looks like he's from a whole different era*, Kyra thought.

Despite his rather austere appearance, Amos wore a sincere smile upon greeting her. His dark eyes sparkled when he spoke, his accent expectedly heavy, "*Shalom,* Kyra! And *Tzohora'im Tovim!* That means *peace* and *good afternoon* in Hebrew," he clarified. "It's nice to make your acquaintance, despite our sad circumstances. I am Amos." Kyra noted a slight formality in his tone, as he continued, "I've only seen photos of you from your uncle Saul, but I can say that you have your grandmother's demeanor and graceful face. I am so sorry about her passing. She was greatly loved by many here for her generous heart and kindness to our community."

Kyra immediately felt comfortable with Amos and replied, "Thank you, Cousin Amos, for your very thoughtful words." And with much relief and gratitude, she gently wiped a tear from her eye.

Amos lowered his head for a moment to give her some privacy, and then said, "Let's go to my car."

Kyra followed Amos to his small Hyundai economy car but was briefly taken aback when she saw the vehicle. "Cousin Amos, I am so very sorry, but I may have overpacked. I wasn't thinking too clearly when I left San Francisco. . . . I'm embarrassed to say I'm not sure my suitcase will fit in your car," she said a bit panicked.

Noticing her concern, Amos waved her away and skillfully lugged the heavy bag into the small trunk. He added in a reassuring tone, "Don't worry, cousin, I'm here to help you."

"Yes, thank you for coming here today. . . . I can't tell you how much I appreciate it," Kyra said, exhaling a sigh of relief as she spoke.

As the car began its journey, Kyra could not help but glance back toward the airport, watching it slowly fade away. She was a bit nervous and didn't know what to expect, but they were now heading southeast on Highway 1 toward one of the most ancient cities in the world—Jerusalem.

Amos may have been a little nervous himself—or perhaps uncomfortable with the silence in the car—and to Kyra's surprise, he began to speak almost nonstop as he drove.

After exchanging some pleasantries, Amos said, "I know this is your first visit to Israel, and there is probably a lot about our country that you do not know. May I fill you in a bit about our wonderful homeland?" He had asked the question with great seriousness and pride.

"Yes, I'd like that very much," Kyra responded warmly. She was glad for the distraction, but also eager to learn more about her grandmother's first home.

Amos zealously continued, which almost sounded to Kyra like a scholarly professor, "Well, let me start by saying that Israel is a *very* diverse land with a rich and complicated history. But I think what's more important, cousin, is that Israel is also a land of many contrasts. We have the ancient to the modern. We also have Jews, Christians, and Muslims. And although we are religiously diverse, this has created much conflict here, as I am sure you are aware."

Kyra responded, "Uncle Saul and I were just discussing the long history of turmoil in Israel. It was the reason he and Nana left Israel and moved to the U.S." Her voice trailed off for a moment as she thought of her grandmother.

"So let me talk of less serious matters for now and tell you about the beauty of our land," he said, gently switching the subject to ease his cousin's sadness.

Kyra listened intently as Amos painted a picturesque image of Israel's geography. With excitement, he described the land as both beautiful and diverse and talked about many activities such as day hikes through the lush green hills of Mount Carmel in the springtime, to swimming and boating on the tranquil waters of the Sea of Galilee. "I know you really enjoy these things," Amos said, glancing over at her.

Kyra gave him a quick look of surprise.

"Your grandmother spoke of you often," he explained. "There is much I know." Amos looked back toward the road and continued speaking, "And, just like San Francisco, we too have our wonderful mild Mediterranean weather in both Tel Aviv and Jerusalem. But, in contrast, I should tell you, we also have our harsh, dry weather in our deserts to the south."

Kyra thought about her home in San Francisco again and how she did indeed love the weather there. She had never been to a desert, and so this piqued her curiosity.

"The desert is also home to another unique landmark—the Dead Sea. Tourists who visit there enjoy the indescribable experience of floating in its dense, salty waters. But more important, of course, is the historical significance of the Dead Sea Scrolls!" These last words were spoken with great enthusiasm, clearly reflecting Amos's passion for the earliest known written version of *The Torah*.

Kyra laughed for a moment, feeling lightness surround her. Her cousin was making the drive pleasant and enjoyable, and the temporary diversion from her grief was welcomed. "Please do go on. I am learning a lot today," Kyra said with appreciation.

Amos next began to enthusiastically described places to visit in Israel, but his voice became tense—and even sad—when the topic turned to the violent and turbulent history of the West Bank and the Gaza Strip.

Noticing his discomfort, Kyra asked about the history of Masada and what it meant to Israel. "I've heard about it from Nana, but I don't fully understand its significance," she explained.

Amos's face lit up again, and Kyra could almost feel the heat of the desert sun on her skin as Amos described the ancient fortress. "Of course you will want to visit this site in the Negev Desert of Israel overlooking the Dead Sea," he said with enthusiasm. "It truly is one of our people's most cherished sites. Masada is where King Herod built a fortress on top of a steep cliff, and seventy-five years after his death, a group of Jewish rebels fought their Romans enemies and took their own lives rather than surrender. They chose death over slavery. It's become our national symbol of courage. A bit like your Alamo in the United States."

Kyra noted the pride in his voice and was beginning to see why he felt proud to live there and why Nana had wished to return here year after year. "Israel is *very* different from what I imagined," Kyra said with a lighter tone. "There is so much more to see, do, and experience here than I realized."

"Ah then, let me tell you a bit more about the religious significance of Israel—which I think you will also find interesting," he added, seizing the opportunity to share his passion about a topic near and dear to his heart. Kyra smiled as she was really enjoying her cousin's lecture. "I know you were raised a Christian, but I also sense that your Jewish heritage is important to you. Either way, here in Israel, we have some of the most important religious sites of both Christianity and Judaism." Amos paused for a moment and then added thoughtfully, "Perhaps for a future visit, my dear cousin, when we are not mourning the death of a loved one."

"Yes, I would like that very much, Amos," Kyra responded, the reality of her loss rising to the surface once again. After reflecting for a moment, she added, "I'm curious to hear more . . . for my future visit, of course."

Amos appreciated the encouragement and went on, "There are too many important sites to cover during this short ride, so let me talk about a few that you may find significant. The first is Mount Zion, where King David's Tomb lies; this is important to the Jews, but it's also the location of 'The Room of the Last Supper' where your Jesus is said to have spent his last day with his disciples. That is important to Christians, of course."

Kyra nodded, and he continued, "Mount of Olives is an important site to both religions, too. It has one of the oldest Jewish burial grounds, which has been in use for over three thousand years! Ah, the history! It is also a sacred site because of its proximity to the Valley of Jehoshaphat, where our people believe the final judgment and resurrection will occur."

He paused for a moment to give that statement due respect, and then went on, "But back to Mount of Olives. According to your Christianity, it's also where Jesus taught his disciples the 'Lord's Prayers' and the place where Jesus is believed by Christians to have ascended into heaven."

Kyra was appreciative that Amos could discuss the Christian significance of the sites, despite its not being his own core belief. She was intrigued by the conversation and grateful for his kindness. "I've never fully appreciated the religious significance of Jerusalem to *both* Christianity and Judaism," she said. "I just never paid enough attention to it during my years in Catholic school."

"Ah, I'm glad you are enjoying our talk!" Amos said, as Kyra smiled and continued to listen with careful attention.

"From a Jewish significance, I should also tell you about the Western Wall in Jerusalem," Amos went on, "which you may also know as the Wailing Wall. Jews come from all over the world to pray here, and for many, it's a very sacred pilgrimage made only once in a lifetime. But the most important aspect is that it's the western portion of the walls that surround our holiest of sites called the Temple Mount. In Hebrew, we call it *Har HaBáyit.*"

Amos carefully enunciated the Hebrew words, and Kyra repeated them. He seemed pleased with her pronunciation.

"The Temple Mount is important to all three major religions: Judaism, Christianity, and Islam. But for Jews and Christians, the Temple is believed to be the site of all creation, and the place where Adam—the first man—was made from dust. It's also the site of the destruction of two of our most important temples, and the site where a third and final temple will be built. This is one of our most holiest sites in Israel for Jews."

Kyra could feel Amos's immense love for his homeland. "What do you mean by 'will be built'?" she asked, shifting slightly in the passenger seat.

Amos responded with poignancy, "The third and final temple is prophesied in the Book of Ezekiel. It will be an eternal building and permanent place of *HaShem*—or God, as you may say—on the Temple Mount."

Kyra admired Amos's deep passion for his religious views. Again, she appreciated his kindness in explaining the Christian aspects of the sites as well. *What a blessing it is that I come from both religions,* she reminded herself. Her thoughts then shifted, and she admitted to Amos that she was embarrassed to know so little about Israel. "It truly is an amazing country, Amos. I wish I'd taken the time to visit when Nana had invited me all those years ago. . . . I just can't believe she's gone and I missed that opportunity." Deep regret and sadness enveloped her, and her heart sank even further.

Amos seemed to notice her internal discomfort and said with much kindness, "We have a saying in our family, Kyra. One does not come to Israel unless *HaShem* invites him." Amos paused for a moment to be sure Kyra understood. He then continued, "Despite the sad circumstances of this visit, I hope you will come back to experience the homeland of our ancestors. Your nana would have liked that very much."

Kyra eyes filled with tears, as she looked outside the car window at the lovely countryside her grandmother had once called home. *Yes,* she thought, *Nana would have liked that indeed.*

Kyra continued to gaze out the window as they continued along Highway 1. The road began a gentle climb upward as they approached the hills of Judea. The air felt drier, and the temperature was dropping. *Hmmm. This is totally reminding me of San Francisco,* she thought and briefly wondered if her affinity for San Francisco had something to do with her family ties to this land.

Keeping her gaze on the passing landscape outside the window, she felt almost as if they were entering another world. Gone now was the urban feel of the airport, replaced with lovely hills in a rich shade of green. Mediterranean oaks, olives, and pine trees dotted the hillside, with gorgeous oleanders in pale pink, fuchsia, and white adding delicate springtime color. Centuries-old stone terracing gave the land an aged feel, looking weathered and rustic, almost crumbling. She felt the ancient richness of the land. *It's all so overwhelming . . . and beautiful,* she thought, as her eyes drank in the loveliness of the late-spring landscape.

Amos and Kyra had fallen into a comfortable silence. Fields of barley billowed in the light breeze, and fig trees were beginning to bloom. The land was abundant with flowers and fruit, just before the heat of summer would set in and dry up much of the vegetation.

Kyra could almost hear Nana's sweet voice saying to her, "It's always best to visit Jerusalem in the springtime, Kyra! It's the most beautiful time of year."

Amos roused Kyra from her daydream. "We will be arriving in Jerusalem shortly. Our major cities, Tel Aviv and Jerusalem, are vastly different from one another. Do you know much about them?"

"I must admit I know very little, but tell me more?" Kyra replied with curiosity. She recalled the airport was located more than 15 kilometers in the opposite direction from Tel Aviv. She had not yet actually seen the city.

Amos was more than happy to explain. "Tel Aviv, my cousin, is a city known for its modern architecture and contemporary lifestyle. It's similar to many U.S. cities with art museums, galleries, symphonies, and even the theater. Like other cosmopolitan cities, Tel Aviv is known as the 'City that Never Sleeps.'"

Kyra laughed, immediately thinking of the nightlife in New York City and Las Vegas. Amos assured her that Tel Aviv did indeed have a reputation for late-night dancing and bars that stayed open "'til sunrise," as he put it.

"Jerusalem by contrast is one of the oldest cities in Israel, steeped in a very rich history and much more traditional." He continued with an easy smile, "It's the capital of Israel of course—and a place of many religious traditions. Although we have cultural venues, restaurants, and nightlife here, many restaurants and bars close at sunset on Friday, the Sabbath, and remain closed until after sunset on Saturday. The cities are 'polar opposites' as you might say in America." He chuckled at his own comment.

The imagery brought a smile to Kyra's face. "I can't imagine any bars or restaurants staying closed from Friday night to Saturday night in the United States," Kyra mused. "They'd go out of business."

"It is our tradition, our way," answered Amos with a serious tone.

Kyra nodded that she understood.

"To further clarify where we are heading, the area of Jerusalem where Saul and I live is called *Mea She'arim.*" Again Amos pronounced the Hebrew name very carefully. "It's where the Haredi Jews live, and one of the oldest and most traditional neighborhoods in Jerusalem. While Mea She'arim lies outside the Old City Walls of Jerusalem, inside the Old City of Jerusalem is actually *four* major religious quarters: Jewish, Muslim, Christian, and Armenian. Each religion has its own quarter with a unique look and culture."

"Fascinating," Kyra responded, giving Amos time to finish his thought.

"Surrounding the Old City of Jerusalem are the more modern areas of Jerusalem, with the exception of course of Mea She'arim where we live. . . . Ah, we will soon be heading downtown and just slightly north of Zion Square to reach your uncle's home."

Kyra had thoroughly enjoyed the experience of getting to know her cousin and learning about his homeland, and she wished it could have been under better circumstances. *I can see why Nana made this trip every year and why she was thinking of returning here permanently.* "I'm so happy we've had this time together, Amos," Kyra said with sincerity. "I have learned so much. I appreciate your thoughtfulness."

As they approached the outskirts of Jerusalem, Kyra was astonished by the city's strong impression on her. It was indeed a blending of both old and new, as Amos had described—but some how still different from what she had expected. Off toward the horizon, she could see Jerusalem's Chords Bridge, which struck her as both modern and magical.

"It was fashioned after our great King David's harp," Amos explained, noting the bridge's resemblance to the musical instrument. "Perhaps it looks somewhat like San Francisco's Golden Gate Bridge?"

"Oh my, yes, it most certainly *does,*" Kyra responded, delightfully becoming more aware of the synchronicities between the two cities.

The highway was now ending, and they were just entering the city limits. Kyra took note that parts of the city were relatively modern with three-lane roads and heavy traffic, but other areas looked ancient. The buildings themselves were all attractive structures built with the unique Jerusalem stone, giving everything a uniform appearance and style. The limestone seemed to cast an enchanting glow over the city in the strong sunlight, which fascinated Kyra.

All types of people—from university students and couples holding hands to families with baby strollers and children rambling slowly behind their parents—walked along the busy sidewalks.

*It all looks so normal . . . like any other city*, Kyra thought, not quite sure what she had been expecting. Next she noticed the Haredi Jews in their traditional black dress also walking the sidewalks, contrasting sharply with some uniformed soldiers—their automatic rifles securely draped over their shoulders. Despite the somber demeanor of the soldiers, the city had a calm, safe feel to it, which surprised her.

"We are now entering the Mea She'arim neighborhood in which Saul and I live," Amos explained, as he made a sharp right turn with the car.

Kyra instantly felt as if she had taken another step back in time. *This looks like a city within a city,* she reflected, taking in the sights. Thinking back to her childhood history books, Kyra was reminded of the old turn-of-the-century photographs of cities that had become modernized beyond recognition. But before her now were those same narrow streets, some even made of cobblestone. Low three-story buildings, old and rustic, dotted the streets—many with stores on the first floor and family quarters on the levels above.

The women wore scarves to cover their heads and black stockings to cover the small portion of their legs that peaked out from their dresses, which fell well below their knees. They also kept their arms completely covered. "All of this is done to display modesty, Kyra," she could hear Nana's voice telling her.

The men, of course, were dressed in the traditional wide-brimmed hats and black overcoats, which matched Amos's attire. They also wore thick beards and long curled sidelocks that spiraled down the sides of their faces, contrasting with their otherwise short, conservative haircuts.

Kyra was reminded of the Amish people she had seen as a child in Pennsylvania. . . . *but perhaps a little more Eastern European in influence?*, she thought. She observed with some humor that modern technology had not been shunned by these folk, however, as many of the Haredi Jewish men freely talked on their cell phones and drove their automobiles to destinations unknown. Clearly, this was a unique blending of cultures, which to Kyra seemed almost like a strange science fiction movie.

As they drove closer to Uncle's Saul apartment and down one of the main streets, Kyra could now see grocery shops, barbershops, clothing boutiques, and dry-goods stores. A wall along the sidewalk displayed news for passersby to read, and an overhead PA system gave out information in Hebrew. She wondered what they were saying, but didn't bother to ask.

Next Amos turned down one of the side cobblestone streets and parked the car in front of Saul's apartment building. Kyra looked up at the very old, simple beige concrete building, realizing with deep sadness, *So this was the last place my grandmother had been.* She tried hard not to cry and sternly gained her composure.

Not sensing any apprehension in his cousin, Amos immediately jumped out of the vehicle, as Kyra stepped out onto the street as well. He prepared to walk her to the door, but first said with great sincerity, "Welcome to Jerusalem, cousin." Next Amos helped unload the heavy suitcase onto the sidewalk, and just as they as they were approaching the building, Uncle Saul promptly opened the front door and called out, "*Shalom,* dear Kyra. *Tzohora'im Tovim.*" Kyra realized it was the same phrase that Amos had used to greet her earlier at the airport. "Hi, Uncle

Saul. Good afternoon to you too." She looked at him pensively, trying hard to keep her voice from cracking. "It's so nice to see you . . . despite the circumstances."

Amos waived to Saul and then turned to Kyra, saying softly, "I will leave you with Saul, but I will see you both later today at the services."

Kyra reached forward to hug her cousin in appreciation for the safe transportation to her uncle's home and for the wonderful overall experience. But Amos simply bowed his head instead. In the Haredi Jewish tradition, men did not touch women who were not immediately related to them. Kyra understood almost instinctively and lowered her head to acknowledge his goodbye. She silently thought, *Yes, I am at peace, cousin, and you have been amazingly kind to me. Thank you for being there when I needed you.*

She then wheeled her suitcase toward her uncle, their eyes meeting for a long while in silent understanding of each other's pain. Together, they walked into the building with Kyra carefully dragging her suitcase up the steps to the small second-story apartment. Like everything else she had so far experienced, she had no idea what to expect next.

# 6

"I trust your trip went smoothly," Saul said once they were inside the cozy apartment. His Israeli accent was thick, but had a warm tone to it. "I wish you were visiting under different circumstances, dear child," he added, his voice breaking slightly as he strained to say the words.Kyra noticed that her uncle had left the front door open. Upon seeing her inquisitive, but respectful, look, Saul explained that it was customary to leave the door open when men and female guests were in confined quarters. Kyra acknowledged his explanation with a nod of her head. He had already explained to her during one of their phone conversations that he would be staying the nights at a neighbor's apartment during her visit, assuring her it was not an inconvenience; it was simply their custom.

As she rolled her suitcase out of the foyer, she paused for a moment, then said, "I apologize for not visiting sooner." Her voice was filled with emotion, and she tried not to cry. "Please forgive me."

Saul did not reply, but gently looked her in the eyes to comfort her. "Let me show you my apartment and where you will be staying."

Very simple, but nicely furnished, the apartment had two bedrooms and two bathrooms. Nestled between the buildings in the back was a small garden area. It was decorated with pots of brightly colored flowers and a wrought iron bench, giving the place an air of charm. As her uncle explained, his wife, Esther, had particularly enjoyed the outdoor patio before her passing many years earlier.

"Your great aunt Esther and I moved to this smaller place once the last of our six children had left home. We just didn't need such a large place, and we were blessed when this apartment became available."

Kyra nodded in understanding. "Do you get to visit with your children often?" she asked.

"Oh, yes," he replied. "Some stayed here in Mea She'arim, and some moved to neighboring cities. It's so comforting to have family close by, Kyra, especially during times like these. I know your grandmother would have appreciated your being here, as I do. Of course, now you will get to meet the family—*your* family, I should say."

In that moment, Kyra was stuck by how much she always envied Nana's close-knit family. *So very different from my experience of a mother and father who barely spoke to each other—or even to me, for that matter.* Her thoughts quickly shifted when she realized that she was starting to feel so much more at home here than she had ever felt in Chicago.

"Come, let us have a cup of coffee," he offered after showing her the guestroom.

Kyra was travel-weary and welcomed the hot beverage. After Saul opened the kitchen door as dictated by his customs, they took seats at the small kitchen table to discuss the services.

"Prayer services begin a half hour before sunset tonight at the cemetery—around 7:00 pm. Family members and close friends will join us. Then Shiva will start at the house immediately afterward. As you may know, Kyra, *Shiva* means 'seven'; it's our tradition to mourn for seven days after the death of a loved one. Family and friends will come to comfort us and allow us this time to grieve."

"I know a little about Shiva, but not a lot," Kyra said, as she sipped her coffee. "Truthfully, I've never actually sat Shiva before. . . . I wish I had paid better attention in the past when Nana had explained it to me." She felt a bit ashamed for not being more familiar with the customs.

If Saul noticed the flush in her face, he politely ignored it. He simply nodded and then went on to explain the details of the actual services so that Kyra would know what to expect. He even told her the names of many close family members who would be attending. "But don't worry about remembering everyone's names, Kyra. They will all be pleased to meet you," Saul assured her.

Kyra thanked him for the family information. "I will stay for the entire seven days, of course," she said with certainty. "And I know the circumstances are not ideal . . . but I am looking forward to meeting the family—*my* family."

Saul smiled at her and stood up. "Come then, help me prepare for the mourners."

Kyra joined her uncle in the solemn act of covering the large mirrors in the hallway and bathrooms. Saul offered an explanation: "We are not concerned with our appearance while mourning, so mirrors are covered. Vanity is not a consideration during mourning."

It dawned on Kyra that for the next seven days she would not look in a mirror. She found the idea intriguing. *When have I ever done that?* she wondered, and she quickly answered her own question: *Never*. Her desire to "look perfect" would take a backseat this week, and the idea of it felt a bit freeing.

Saul further noted the additional steps to prepare the apartment: "We will unlock the front door to allow people to enter and leave quietly as they wish. And a pitcher of water will be placed outside the front door so visitors can wash their hands before entering the house. This symbolizes separating ourselves from the impurity attributed to death, and we wash our hands after leaving the cemetery. We will also place low benches in the living room for the mourners, and the dining table will be covered in a tablecloth for food that friends will bring to us. A memorial candle will be lit as well."

Kyra walked around the apartment, taking cues from her uncle, and by the time they were finished preparing for Shiva, it was late in the afternoon.

The caffeine from the coffee wasn't strong enough to counteract Kyra's travel-induced weariness, so with Saul's urgings, she stood up to excuse herself. Jet lag was beginning to set in, and she desperately needed to rest before they left for the cemetery.

Kyra gratefully slipped off to the guestroom. She first chose a suitable long-sleeved black dress and black hose from her suitcase to replace the cotton travel dress and sweater she was wearing. She laid the black dress across a chair, and then climbed on top of the comfortable bed.

Within moments, she felt herself slip into a dream-like state, and she had the vague feeling she was back in Chicago in her old apartment. It was a Saturday early afternoon.

"Kyra, it's time for our lunch date. Where shall we go today?"

Kyra's eyes shot open. She had heard her grandmother's voice as plain as day. At first, she didn't realize where she was—or even *when* it was. As her eyes adjusted to the light in the room, her disorientation faded, and it slowly dawned on her what lay ahead.

She quickly grabbed the black dress off the chair, and as she slipped it over her head, but stiffness in her body protested. *Thanks to that uncomfortable airline seat!* she thought with some frustration.

She ran a brush through her hair, slipped on her stockings, and settled her feet into a pair of flat Tory Burch shoes. She was dressed, but apprehensive, and inside her heart raced. At 6:00 pm, she met Saul in the foyer.

"Kyra are you ready?" he asked solemnly.

Kyra simply nodded. She held back her tears as she followed her uncle outside to the car. They drove to the cemetery in silence.

They arrived exactly one-half hour before the services were to begin. After making sure everything was in place and meeting the other rabbi, Kyra watched with a solemn face as family members and friends began to arrive.

Most were Haredi Jews and dressed similarly to Uncle Saul or her dear Nana in simple dark clothing that modestly covered their skin. The men wore their wide black-rimmed hats covering their heads, and the women wrapped scarves around their heads. In accordance with tradition, the men and women sat on separate sides at the gravesite.

Kyra settled down in her seat among the other women. She counted the attendees, and by the time service began, she estimated there were about eighty-five people all together. *You were loved by so many people, Nana!* she realized, and a comforting warmth spread through her body. She was truly amazed by how many lives her grandmother had touched.

Although Saul was Nana's only living brother, he was now the generous age of eighty-four. He and his wife, Esther, had six children, who in turn had given them numerous grandchildren. Then, of course, there were the cousins, with Amos among them, spanning many generations. Kyra's mind spun as she tried to figure out the relationships between first cousins, second cousins, and third cousins. She wasn't exactly sure how she fit in, but she was glad for the temporary distraction from her sadness. And like Saul had suggested, she barely remembered anyone's names throughout the quick introductions.

The memorial service began promptly at 7:00 pm. Per the custom, the right side of the blouse and shirts of the closest family mourners—which in this case was Uncle Saul—was torn by the rabbi. This step was performed as a sign of mourning.

Kyra knew to expect the tearing of her great uncle's shirt lapel, but flinched when the rabbi performed the Kriah. She felt her heart tear, too, as she thought of her grandmother and saying her final goodbye.

Nana's body, wrapped only in a plain white linen shroud, was carried on a simple stretcher to the gravesite. There were no flowers, and everyone listened in silence. Saul led the mourners in prayer alongside the other rabbi. He began by reciting scriptures, and the services continued with the Hesped, or eulogy.

Overall, Kyra felt that the service was a lovely tribute to her grandmother. Many of the mourners took turns speaking about how Kyra's grandmother had cared for them during her annual visits to Jerusalem. While most of the eulogies were spoken in Hebrew, some were in English, which touched Kyra's heart.

Her grandmother's close friend, Maya, reflected with bittersweet admiration, "She helped me cook meals for the poor . . . and what a difference it made to those families we helped."

Making sure she also spoke in English so that Kyra could understand her, Cousin Naomi kindly shared, "She was such a blessing in my life and always so positive, offering me verses from the Torah for inspiration whenever I was struggling with something."

This intrigued Kyra. Her grandmother had offered her much wisdom over the years, often reciting verses from the Torah, since it was part of the Old Testament and didn't conflict with her Christian upbringing.

She felt fortunate not to have missed out on this aspect of her grandmother's experience.

Daniel, a young friend of the family, offered a heartfelt tribute: "I simply don't know how to say goodbye. . . . I am forever grateful for her kind spirit and loving help to all those she encountered."

Kyra found it incredible that her grandmother had meant so much to so many people and had formed such strong bonds during her stays in Israel. It gave her great pause, as she reflected on her own life—and realized she herself hadn't made time to help others.

*Oh, Nana,* she thought, *I admire you even more than I did before. It had always been my intention to help others, but I just never made it a priority. I wish you were with me right now. I need your wise advice and unconditional love.*

Thoughts such as these continued silently in Kyra's mind as she listened to the kind and loving words of her grandmother's friends and family.

When the eulogies concluded, her grandmother's body was lowered into the grave with no casket. Kyra found this a bit disconcerting, but understood and respected the simplicity of the custom. The mourners came forward, one at a time, to cover the grave, all partaking of the custom to place a few scoops of dirt into the hole with a small shovel. Kyra noted that the shovel was not passed from person to person, but rather placed back in the earth for the next person to pick up. As Uncle Saul had mentioned earlier, "This symbolizes not passing on one's grief onto the next person, thus allowing them to lift the shovel anew from the ground."

Uncle Saul concluded the services with the Kaddish—a special mourning prayer. While the prayer was in Hebrew and Kyra couldn't understand the words being spoken, she could clearly see the expression of love on Uncle Saul's face as he cited the words. She reflected on his face and thought, *Thank you, Uncle Saul, for taking such good care of Nana.*

As the crowd of mourners made ready to leave and head back to Saul's apartment, Kyra was introduced to even more family and friends. Feeling a bit overwhelmed, she politely acknowledged each person she met, until they each left the cemetery, and then when everyone was gone, she and her uncle headed back to his apartment.

During the drive, Saul filled Kyra in once again on the customs of Shiva. "Each visitor will quietly enter the house; they will not greet us—the mourners—until we initiate a conversation with them. We can choose to speak or not speak to anyone who stops by. It is our choice. It is considered a great *mitzvah,* or a moral deed of kindness, for a friend to pay a visit to the home of the mourners and to bring food. And, if we want to be silent, there is no disrespect in doing so."

"I'm sure I'll speak to everyone," Kyra said, unable to imagine herself not engaging in conversation with others. "I'm glad we can spend this time with the family. I truly appreciate this opportunity to remember my grandmother. . . . I, I loved her so much." With that, Kyra felt her heart fill with regret once again that this was her first visit to her grandmother's beloved homeland. She gently wiped a tear from her eye, trying to hide her deep sadness from her uncle.

When they arrived back at the apartment, several family members including Saul's children and a few close friends were already there to offer comfort and their condolences.

Kyra and her uncle spoke quietly to the visitors. The mood was solemn and respectful. Again, Kyra was impressed by the fondness and thoughtfulness with which people spoke of her grandmother. She was particularly taken with Nana's friend Edna.

"Oh, so you are dear Kyra!" Edna said with great affection. "Oh my, your *savta* was so proud of you. Always telling me about your accomplishments in your career. Vortex is it?"

Kyra nodded yes, feeling now was not the time to disclose that her career with Vortex was over.

Edna went on, warmly holding Kyra's soft hand in her aged one, "It's so nice to finally meet you, though I wish it could have been under different circumstances, dear. Just the other day, the day before she passed in fact, your *savta* was telling me how much she used to adore those special lunches you had with her back in Chicago. She loved you very much you know."

Kyra's eyes widened in surprise, recalling how clearly she had heard her grandmother's voice earlier in the bedroom. Her heart melted, and she was only able to reply after a few moments of silence. "Edna, I truly appreciate your kind words. . . . We should have met much sooner than this." Her voice cracked in an effort not to burst into tears. "Thank you for being here."

Visitors continued to come and go well into the evening, and while Kyra was tired, she felt truly welcomed into this loving circle of family and friends. Hirsch, a cousin of Saul's, was the last one to leave that evening. He turned at the door and, speaking in Hebrew, offered comfort with the melodic sound of his words: "*Hamakom y'nachem etkhem b'tokh sha'ar avelei tziyon viyrushalayim.*"

Saul translated his words for Kyra once Hirsch was gone: "May *HaShem* comfort you among the mourners of Zion and Jerusalem." He further explained, "It's a common phrase we use here in Israel, and you may hear it often as the visitors leave our home."

"It is a lovely saying," Kyra replied, thinking a little comfort from God was greatly appreciated right now. As she spoke the words, she immediately felt her energy level drop, realizing how drained she felt. In a quiet, tentative tone, she said, "Uncle Saul, thank you for your kind advice and for making this possible. I am glad we made the decision to have the funeral here."

Saul nodded, the sadness over the loss of his sister playing across his face. Kyra's looked down for a moment out of respect.

"Despite the circumstance," she added, "it has been wonderful to meet so many of the friends and family that Nana held so dear in her heart. I'm in no rush to return home to San Francisco." A small yawn inadvertently escaped her lips. "I must admit, though, I'm about to tip over in exhaustion. Would you mind if I slip off and go to sleep now?"

Saul stood up and crossed the room to leave. He asked Kyra if she needed anything else before retiring, and she shook her head no. His kind eyes settled on her weary face, his love for her palpable, and said, "Thanks, dear child, for making the long trip to Jerusalem," he said. "*Laila Tov, Ot Nehmadim.* Good night and sweet dreams."

With that, Kyra excused herself. The clock in the guestroom read 11:03 pm. After the long journey and the incredibly emotional day, she expected to fall right to sleep, but sleep did not come easily.

When she finally did drift off to sleep, she found herself dreaming of the Redwood Forest in California. But in her dream, she felt much smaller, almost child-like. With some confusion, she realized that the idea of going into the forest frightened her. In fact, her fear felt overwhelming. Even in her sleep state, she could feel her heart racing. *But I love that forest,* she told herself.

Yet somehow, this dream felt familiar to her—as if she'd had this dream before. . . .

# 7

Kyra awoke early the next morning after just a few hours of sleep, but her uncle had not yet returned from the neighbor's apartment. She quietly prepared a pot of coffee and took a cup down to the small garden. The air was quite chilly. The fragrant scent of honeysuckle mingled with the delicious-smelling breakfast foods cooking in a nearby apartment, giving the fresh morning air a uniquely sweet and spicy aroma.

*What a pleasant start to the day,* Kyra thought, momentarily releasing some of her pain. *How much I wish you were here with me, Nana, enjoying this beautiful morning.*

She slowly sipped her coffee, enjoying the solitude after last night's gathering. She guessed the second day of Shiva would bring many, if not more, visitors to Saul's home.

Kyra's thoughts drifted back to the last time she had been with her grandmother. They had just finished a shopping spree in downtown Chicago. Kyra had dropped Nana off at her apartment, and they were saying goodbye. Even now she could almost *feel* her grandmother's hug. She was smiling as she spoke. "Honey, I truly enjoyed our day together and thanks for treating me to this beautiful sweater!" She paused before adding, "And remember, I'm always with you—even when we aren't together. Just think of me, and I'll be there with you. *Ani ohev otach.*"

Kyra thought it was an odd statement at the time, but now she wondered if Nana had somehow known it would be their last experience together. Looking back, she'd give anything to hug her grandmother just one last time.

Putting the cup of coffee up to her lips, she took a sip and glanced down at the ground beneath her feet. Kyra almost spat her coffee out in disbelief. There was a single freshly cut Gerbera daisy lying on the ground, slightly hidden beneath the wrought-iron bench she sat upon. She stared in disbelief and quickly set the coffee cup down to pick up the flower.

Gerbera daisies were Nana's most favorite flower. "Oh, Nana, did you leave this flower here for me? Or is this just some strange coincidence? . . . I don't know the answer, but I can't thank the Angels enough for putting it here in front of me today. *Ani ohev otach*—I love you, too."

Kyra wept softly, quietly holding the flower next to her heart. She closed her eyes, drinking in the memories of the wonderful times she and her grandmother had spent together.

When she walked back to the apartment, Saul had returned and greeted her. He had just woken up, but seemed slightly upbeat. "*Boker Tov,* Kyra. Did you sleep well last night?" he asked.

"Good morning," Kyra responded, flashing him a bright smile that contrasted with the emptiness she felt inside. "I wish I could say I slept well . . . but the truth is, I barely slept at all. . . . I just miss Nana so very much."

Uncle Saul spoke up, glancing at the flower in her hand, "Dear child, we will get through this period of mourning together. I know how much you miss your grandmother. I miss her deeply as well. But now, we have each other."

He opened a cabinet and took out a bud vase for the flower, which he filled halfway with water. He silently handed it to Kyra, and she quietly placed the flower in the vase. The pair simply admired the flower for a moment before Uncle Saul broke the silence. "Let's fix a hearty breakfast and start our day off well. We will need our stamina for the day ahead."

Kyra happily agreed, and she and her uncle began preparing a large breakfast side by side, the cheerful Gerbera daisy looking on. The food from the night before had been neatly arranged on the shelves by some of the women for easy access, and they quickly gathered what they needed. They cut up a melon and sliced a few bagels, opened a tub of cream cheese, and arranged a couple slices of lox, or smoked salmon, on a plate. Lastly, they prepared a tomato-based stew with simmered eggs called *shakshuka*. This was a dish that needed to be freshly prepared.

As they stood there side by side preparing the food, Kyra quietly reflected on how she would have given anything to share such an experience with her father when he was still alive. Instead, she lovingly acknowledged that she now felt grateful to have this opportunity with her uncle Saul.

When they sat down to eat, Kyra found herself thoroughly enjoying the variety of flavors and textures, comparing them to her usual quick breakfast of yogurt. There was something truly comforting about this food, which she had so enjoyed preparing with Uncle Saul.

"This *shakshuka*—it's different from anything I've ever tasted," Kyra noted, scooping up a large spoonful. "It's delicious. I see you have learned a few cooking skills—maybe from Aunt Esther . . . or from Nana?" Kyra offered lightheartedly, trying to brighten the mood. "I remember what a skillful cook Nana was."

"Yes, perhaps I *did* learn a few things, but not until after my dear Esther passed on. And, yes indeed, it was your grandmother who insisted on teaching me a few kitchen skills . . . since I'm alone now. At first, I didn't want to cook at all for myself," he added.

Kyra could tell by the look on Saul's face that Esther's passing still deeply saddened him. She felt thankful that her uncle had his children around to look after him. She wanted to reach out her hand to touch his, but instead simply said, "I envy the amazing marriage you had with Aunt Esther. I hope to be so lucky someday."

Saul smiled and nodded in affirmation.

Kyra briefly thought of her newly single status, realizing that breaking up with Steve was an amazing gift to have given herself. Now, at least she felt there was a chance for true love in her future. She quickly dismissed any thought of Steve, not giving it a second thought that he'd returned her phone calls much too late, and with breakfast over, she cleared the dishes and cleaned the kitchen. The pair then retreated to get dressed and make final preparations for Shiva.

Kyra wore the same black dress and no makeup. This was an unusual experience for her, but she respected the tradition. She felt closer to her Jewish roots, and even Nana in some ways, she slowly began to realize.

Around 11:00 am, visitors began stopping by to pay their condolences, and the home was once again filled with family and friends coming and going all day long.

Many of the visitors brought food, including more platters of smoked salmon and other smoked fish, which looked to Kyra like pickled herring. Various breads and bagels were piled high in baskets. As was the Jewish tradition, hard-boiled eggs had been brought the first night, symbolizing the cycle of life. Family members also supplied more traditional foods such as fruit, nuts, and baked goods. The dining table soon overflowed with a huge assortment of delicious foods, but Kyra had little appetite, forgetting to eat anything much past the hearty breakfast she had enjoyed with her uncle.

The mourners greeted each guest as they arrived, again speaking in quiet, respectful voices. Kyra could only converse somewhat, depending on how much English the guest knew. She had learned a few key phrases in Hebrew from Saul such as *Boker Tov,* meaning "good morning"; *Tzohora'im Tovim,* meaning "good afternoon"; and of course *Shalom* meaning "peace"—which was easy to remember and could also be used as both *hello* and *goodbye,* just in case she stumbled over her words.

After a long day of greeting visitors, and just as the evening sky began to darken, a young couple and their son arrived. The boy hid shyly behind his father's leg until he was properly introduced.

"Kyra, I'd like you to meet some very special friends," Saul told her. "This is David and Leah."

David greeted Kyra warmly with "*Erev Tov,* Kyra."

Kyra responded, "Good evening to you, David. It's nice to meet you."

David continued, "We are so sorry for the passing of your grandmother. *Ale-ha Ha-sholom,* which means 'May Pease be Upon Her.' I do want to say that your grandmother was such a wonderful influence in our lives."

Kyra noted that David's English was quite good and that he only had a slight accent.

David turned toward the woman beside him and said, "I'd like to introduce you to my wife, Leah, and this is our son, Moshe. Moshe is actually *Moses* in English and a fairly common name here in Israel."

Moshe looked up at Kyra, and his face beamed. He appeared to be about seven or eight years old with soft brown curly hair and huge dark brown eyes.

Leah stepped forward and gave Kyra a slight hug and simply said, "*Shalom*" and added, "I'm so sorry for your loss."

Kyra was touched by the family's warmth, but couldn't help a curious glance at their clothing. It was obvious that David and Leah did not have much money, as their mourning shoes were considerably worn and their clothing a bit frayed.

David went on, "It's also nice to finally meet you, Kyra. I feel as if I already know you; your grandmother spoke of you often. She invited us over for many dinners here at Rabbi Saul's apartment when she was staying here. Your grandmother was an excellent cook, and we greatly enjoyed our meals with her . . . not to mention her wonderful sense of humor. And she always offered us the best advice."

Kyra noted the affection in David's eyes as he spoke of her grandmother. She smiled politely, imagining her grandmother offering her love and generosity to these lovely people.

David paused for a moment and thoughtfully added, "I recall her reciting Psalm 1:3 to us often: *And he shall be like a tree planted by streams of water, that bring forth its fruit in its season, and whose leaf does not wither, and in whatever he does he shall prosper.* She reminded us that prosperity is meant for everyone, despite the hard times we sometimes face. Oh, but let me say, we met your grandmother through your uncle Saul before Moshe was even born! We feel truly *baruch*—blessed—for having known her, and we would like to tell you again how sorry we are at her passing."

Kyra held back her sorrow and replied, "I can't thank you enough for your kind words. I always appreciated my grandmother's advice to me as well, and your words are very touching . . . more than you may realize."

Just as Kyra finished speaking, she turned around and glanced over at Moshe, who was now standing at the edge of the dining table overflowing with food. Kyra blinked, wanting to be sure that what she was seeing was accurate. The small boy appeared to be carefully wrapping up food in cloth napkins and hiding them in his pants under his loose shirt.

*Very odd,* she thought—and felt rather disturbed that this boy was stealing food from her uncle's home. David and Leah had moved on, not noticing their son's actions, but Kyra kept her eye on him with growing disbelief and astonishment. *How can a child take food without asking permission*? she wondered, *And from a house of mourning?* Kyra was in complete shock.

After Moshe finished filling up his pants, he carefully slipped out the back door. Kyra swiftly moved to a window and watched him skipping down the alleyway, hurrying off somewhere in the early evening darkness. With all of his bouncing, one of the bundles slipped out from his pants, and he quickly bent down to retrieve it.

She suddenly felt the full impact of the child's actions. And perhaps the gravity of the last several days had weighed too heavily upon her, because at that very moment—Kyra snapped. Tension filled her body, and her face flushed with her anger.

She rapidly made her way across the room and waved her hand in front of Amos to interrupt him in mid-conversation. Amos turned around, and Kyra said in a serious tone, "Amos, I need your help please." She whispered so no one nearby could hear her. "Can you accompany me for a moment? It's very important."

Amos looked a little startled and replied in a semiformal tone, "Yes, of course, Kyra. How may I help you?"

She waved to Amos to follow her quickly, and they both hurried out the back door and downstairs into the same alleyway to follow Moshe.

Kyra's steps became faster and faster, as they both rushed down the dark alley to catch up with the boy. Moshe had been skipping rather carefree, so Kyra was able to quickly catch up with him. She lunged out her right hand and grabbed the boy on the shoulder. The child swung around swiftly from the unexpected hand, and Kyra faced him squarely in the alleyway, looking directly into his face. His brown eyes were huge and a look of complete shock covered his young face.

Kyra tried to control her anger, and paused as she took in a deep breath before she spoke. "Moshe, I must admit I'm a bit upset—*disappointed,* I should say—that you would run off with food from a house of mourning. Who put you up to this? Was it your parents?"

Moshe spoke very little English, so Amos stepped in to translate. The tall man looked at Kyra for a moment with some discomfort, but carefully repeated what she had said in Hebrew, speaking slowly so the child would be sure to understand.

Kyra detected compassion mingled in with Amos's serious tone when he spoke to Moshe, though she could not understand his words.

The boy looked wide-eyed at Kyra as Amos spoke, and his face then softened with innocence.

Amos translated his response: "I was not stealing. I was bringing food to my friend Eli. We go to school together, and Eli's father is not working right now. I have been taking him food from our dinner each night, but tonight we did not have dinner at home. We came to Rabbi Saul's apartment instead, and we brought food for the Shiva. Your grandmother always told me to help others when I can. She said it was important to give to those in need. I was only taking a small bit of food so my friend would not be hungry tonight. We—Eli and I—call it is our *secret.*"

Moshe had carefully enunciated the word *secret* in Hebrew—*sod*—putting his small index finger over his lips and making a soft "shushing sound" to show he could properly keep a secret. To Kyra, the boy's eyes looked like pools of dark well water as he spoke, and his innocent intention permeated the veil of his youthful appearance.

Kyra's heart instantly melted at the realization of what the boy had intended to do. Yes, Nana would have wanted him to take food to his friend in need. She was stunned by her reaction and assumption. *How could I have possibly misjudged this beautiful child?* she wondered.

Amos translated her response as she bent down to the boy's level to speak directly to him, "Moshe, I am so very sorry I misjudged you. Yes, you are right. My Nana would have wanted you to help your friend. . . . Can you please forgive me?"

Moshe reached out and hugged Kyra to comfort her, as she fought back her tears. Finally, he looked directly into Kyra's eyes and spoke slowly, so Amos could once again translate his words, "I was taught in school that the Torah is God's greatest gift to us. We learned the Eighth Commandment 'Thou Shalt Not Steal.' I'm sorry I did not ask for permission to take the food to my friend. Your grandmother always told me to be kind and help someone whenever I can. I was only trying to help my friend." He cast his eyes downward when he finished speaking.

Kyra hugged the child, and Amos translated her words once again: "Yes, you have done a very good deed for your friend, Eli. Please, please do forgive me for not seeing you as the beautiful child you are! I am so very sorry I misjudged your intentions. I . . . I have been in a kind of bondage—trapped really . . . I think sometimes that I've forgotten *how* to trust and be kind to others. I'm afraid it may have something to do with what I learned at my old job. . . . I am so very sorry, Moshe."

Kyra realized the boy wouldn't fully understand what any of that meant, but Amos gave her a comforting look, seeming to understand her internal struggles.

Moshe gave Kyra another hug, and then he stepped back and spoke again in Hebrew. Kyra kept hearing the Hebrew word *matana* when Moshe spoke. Amos translated: "Your grandmother told me in the Torah it says it's important to be giving and kind—it is a *gift,* she told me . . . of the heart. She would always tell me the story of Exodus 22:21 and that we should be kind to widows and orphans. But she would stop for a moment and laugh when she said it. She said it was really she, the widow, who was being kind! That was her *gift,* she said. She always laughed when she told this to me. I was giving food to my friend Eli. And that was my *gift* to him from her, but I should have asked your permission first. Again, I am very sorry."

Amos wore an expression of immense compassion as he conveyed the boy's words to Kyra, and Kyra's own face filled with fresh feelings of grief, shame, and gratitude as she listened to her cousin translate on behalf of the boy.

Moshe added, "I would like to give you a *gift,* too . . . my heart. I loved your grandmother very much, and you remind me of her."

When he finished speaking, Kyra watched him put his hand first on his own heart and then motion toward Kyra's heart, as if to transfer his gift from his heart to hers.

Amos added his own thought to the translation: "In Hebrew, *matana* is the word for *gift*. Moshe is offering you the gift of his heart."

Suddenly, Kyra began to weep as she had never wept before. The child's sweet gesture had broken down a wall she had been building for years around her heart. It was suddenly as if a dam had burst and the floodwaters were flowing unimpeded and freely. For the first time in many years, Kyra felt the full impact of her emotions. She felt the unconditional love of a child, she felt the sadness of her grandmother's passing, but most important, she felt hope for the first time that her life could be different.

Amos and Moshe watched her respectfully, both understanding on their own level that something significant had shifted within Kyra.

When she finally composed herself, she stood up and said, "You have given me a great *gift* indeed, Moshe." Kyra touched her own heart and put her palm on the boy's heart to indicate her love. The boy shook his head that he understood; no translation was necessary.

The three new friends continued down the alleyway to Eli's home. Moshe quietly dropped off the food through Eli's partially open bedroom window, and then they walked back to the apartment with Kyra holding Moshe's hand, feeling a bond with the boy that transcended any need for words.

Once back inside the busy apartment, Moshe quietly rejoined his parents, while Amos lingered behind in the kitchen to refresh himself with a glass of water. Kyra followed the boy into the living room.

"Where have you been, Moshe? We were worried about you!" David asked, his concern written across his dark features. He had spoken in Hebrew, but Kyra understood the gist of his words. The worried parents looked at her a bit anxiously.

Smoothing her dress, Kyra calmly replied, "Moshe, Amos, and I stepped outside for some fresh air . . . and we enjoyed a most wonderful conversation about my grandmother."

She hoped that Moshe would understand that she was keeping his secret, despite his inability to understand her words.

David seemed to accept the explanation, but Leah said, "Moshe should let me know when he is going outside." She turned to her son and added in a firm voice, *"Ani muchzevet mimcha!"*

Again, while Kyra could not understand her words, Leah was clearly scolding Moshe for his disappearance.

Despite Leah's obvious disapproval, Kyra felt enormously lighthearted. With deep admiration for the young couple, she leaned forward and took Leah's hand in her own. "Your son is an incredible boy," she said. "And he will grow up to be an incredible man. You have raised him well." She offered the compliment with heartfelt sincerity.

The couple smiled proudly at their son and thanked her for her kind words, his disappearance now forgiven, if not all but forgotten.

"Thank you both for being here," she went on. "You have touched me so deeply, especially little Moshe here." Kyra lovingly placed her hand on the boy's head and ruffled his hair, while his parents looked on with a mix of curiosity and appreciation. "Your kindness has meant more to me than you know."

David warmly responded on both their behalves, "We should be the ones to thank you. It's truly our pleasure to finally meet you after all these years, Kyra. Your grandmother spoke of you often and deeply loved you. *Laila Tov.*"

Kyra tenderly responded with *"Laila Tov"* feeling her heart ache as she said farewell to David, Leah, and sweet little Moshe.

The hour had grown late, and most visitors began making their exits. Immensely worn down from the day's events, Kyra excused herself to the guestroom. When the last of the visitors had left, she stepped back into the kitchen to share a few private words with her uncle. A cool gentle breeze filled the room from the open kitchen door.

"How are you doing, Kyra?" he asked her gently, handing her a cup of coffee.

Kyra knew that her eyes were red, and it was clear to her uncle what an emotional day it had been for her. She proceeded to tell him about the evening's events and how she had misjudged Moshe. She shared her astonishment that such a young boy could be so wise and teach *her* about compassion and trust.

"I have learned so much tonight, Uncle Saul. I never realized how much Nana gave to others." Saul affirmed his sister's generosity with a nod of his head, as Kyra continued emphatically, "But I've also learned so much about myself, too." She took a sip of the coffee and sat down at the table across from her uncle. With slight hesitation, she finally finished with a hint of desperation, "I sit here tonight and I wonder, *When did I close my heart off to helping others*?"

"Don't be too hard on yourself, dear child," Saul said with great care and compassion.

Kyra looked into his kind, elderly face, and thought, *You look so much like Nana.* She felt tears welling up in her eyes, but didn't try to fight them back as she usually did. Instead, she allowed her uncle to see the full force of her pain and permitted herself to feel it as well.

Several minutes went by as Kyra cried, and Saul patiently waited for her emotional storm to pass. He kept a comforting gaze upon hers until her tears were completely spent.

She finally looked him in the eyes and said, "I have long forgotten most of the things Nana tried to teach me when I was a child. And, tonight, when I looked into the beautiful face of that child, I realized that I loved Moshe for his innocence and good intentions."

After reflecting for a moment, Kyra continued, "He has the most amazing brown eyes and such a sweet smile. He is a kind, loving, good boy." She felt a lump forming in her throat and swallowed hard. "When I hugged him, I could feel his heart beating rapidly against mine, and I realized for the first time in a long time that my heart *is* full of love."

Saul's features remained soft, and his eyes gleamed, as he listened to his niece speak without any judgments.

She looked back at her uncle sheepishly. "I am deeply embarrassed that I misjudged him. He is a child of God—*HaShem,* I mean—and he was only helping his friend. My heart has been shut off for such a long time, Uncle Saul . . . "

This time, Saul spoke in serious tone. "Don't punish yourself. We've both been under a terrible strain with your grandmother's passing . . . And, yes, Moshe is a *Yeled Tov*—a 'good boy,' as you say in English. I'm happy you made amends for your actions. Children do not hold grudges, Kyra, and soon this will be only a faint memory for him."

"I appreciate your kindness," she replied, but realized that her uncle was being more than kind. "Yes, Nana's passing has been a terrible strain. She was my only true confidant . . . " Kyra's words trailed off. She was suddenly overcome with the desire to share more of herself with her uncle. "May I fill you in a bit on a few things if you're not too tired? I haven't told you everything that happened to me this week. . . And let me share that it has been a difficult week, to say the least."

Saul urged her on with a nod of his graying head. "Of course, of course," he added.

Kyra took a deep breath and said, "I was a very successful executive in a well-known corporation in San Francisco. You know, Vortex. But after five years of incredibly hard work, they 'rewarded' me by eliminating my position—just a corporate decision to save money." Kyra paused, allowing the reality of the situation to sink in once again. "It really stung, Uncle Saul. . . . It was so cold-hearted." Kyra glanced down in mild embarrassment. "It wasn't a reflection of my work, of course," she added to be sure her uncle understood.

"No, no, of course not," he responded, as if to reassure her.

"And to make things worse, I'd been dating a man named Steve, who I probably should *not* have been dating. I knew in my heart that our relationship would never go anywhere . . . and when I needed him the most after you told me of Nana's passing, he wasn't there for me! He couldn't even take the time to pick up the phone to call me."

Saul gave her a sympathetic smile.

Kyra sighed. "I think I've learned an awful lot the last few days about what's most important in life. Nana always told me that I could learn my lessons the hard way or I could learn them the easy way. I think I chose to learn them the hard way."

Saul chuckled slightly but with compassion, and then offered her the same wise sentiment Amos had shared upon her arrival in Jerusalem. "Kyra, we have a saying in our family that I'd like to share with you: One does not come to Israel unless they are invited by *HaShem* himself."

Kyra recalled that Amos had shared the same family saying when she had first arrived in Jerusalem. A corner of her mouth turned up, but she couldn't manage a full smile. She felt so at home sitting across from her uncle, as if her grandmother had orchestrated this new, growing bond between them.

Saul gazed deeply into her eyes for a long moment and then went on, "You have been through so much, dear child, these past five years. You moved to San Francisco from Chicago—both of your parents passed away and you barely mourned their deaths, I might add, before returning to work. Your grandmother had expressed her concern to me about this, you know. And now with her death . . ." Saul's voice choked up, and Kyra waited respectfully for him to collect himself.

She turned her attention to the pool of liquid in her coffee cup and only looked up again when he continued. "We've both been through a lot. And sometimes, in life, you have to make decisions to let go of things that aren't working for you. And, in your case, *HaShem* may have just helped you a little bit." His eyes twinkled slightly, breaking the serious tone of the conversation. "Your job and your boyfriend were not your *Goral*."

"*Goral*?" Kyra questioned.

"'Destiny' or 'fate' is the best English translation for this word," he explained before shifting to a more direct tone of voice. "Let me ask you something important. Are you happy with your life, Kyra?"

Kyra opened her mouth to give him an answer, although she was unsure exactly what it would be, but Saul held up his hand, indicating that she should not speak. "Don't answer me now. We are both grieving the loss of a woman who was very dear to us. But do give it some thought." Saul paused, taking her hand again and concluded, "Perhaps it will be good for you to take some time off from your busy life to reflect on what you'd like to do *differently* with it. Maybe some time away from San Francisco, away from your home, will help you discover who you really are and how you'd like your life to look before you start your life anew."

Kyra recognized the wisdom in his words and almost felt as if she were talking with Nana. She felt her heart squeeze with longing.

"You are welcome to stay here as long as you'd like, of course," Saul suggested, sounding somewhat hopeful. "The answers will come in *HaShem's* own miraculous way. Look for the signs, Kyra, listen to your heart, and then go home to live your life. Think of Moses during the great Exodus. He suffered much hardship and made the difficult, but courageous, decision to lead our people out of Egypt. Moses never made it to the Promised Land, but forty years after he led the Jews out of Egypt, his dream was fulfilled: his people entered the Land of Israel again. Home, dear child, is where your heart lies. Take some time to find your heart again."

"You're so much like Nana," Kyra said. "Good advice must run in our family." They both chuckled, as she went on, "I will think about taking some time to reflect on my life. . . . But please know, I will come back to Israel someday to fully experience the land of my ancestors and experience its rich history and amazing beauty." *Israel is now in my heart,* she added silently to herself.

With that, she stood up to wish her uncle a warm goodnight. He gazed affectionately at her, and she loved how it felt to have a "grandfather" figure in her life. She took that warm feeling with her when they each retired for the night.

Each day of Shiva passed in much the same manner as the days before. Kyra's bonds grew deeper with those who had loved her grandmother, and she knew she would always feel at home in this place and with these people. She felt a true kinship with Saul's children, their spouses, and their many children.

Saul expressed his heartfelt delight over the developing relationship between his niece and his large family. He assured her that his children and their children would always be there to welcome her—even when he passed.

Kyra certainly didn't want to face the thought of losing someone else, but she knew that Saul was getting on in age. She wouldn't try to pretend it was any other way. She thoroughly enjoyed her time with him, despite the sad circumstances, and stayed present so that she could remember every detail of their shared experience.

On the seventh day, when Shiva concluded, Kyra felt much more at peace and grounded than she had upon her arrival in Jerusalem. She shared emotional goodbyes with her uncle and the extended family, who had come to see her off and wish her well. They all expressed interest in having her return someday soon so that they could "celebrate life as it is meant to be celebrated."

Kyra sincerely looked forward to that day. For now, however, she was on her way back to the U.S. Cousin Amos had graciously agreed to drop her off at the airport chatting non-stop the entire way, which made Kyra chuckle inwardly.

When they arrived at their destination, she said cheerfully, "Well, it's time for me to decide what to do next with my life, cousin."

"May you experience much success," Amos said with sincerity, adding with the slightly formal tone she'd grown accustomed to, "*Laila Tov,* Kyra. I look forward to your return, but for now, safe travels home. *Shalom.*"

"Peace to you as well," Kyra offered with a final wave of her hand.

United Airlines Flight #222 from Tel Aviv took off on time and landed in Chicago sixteen hours later. Kyra headed to her grandmother's apartment where she took her time getting Nana's affairs in order. She donated the majority of her things to Goodwill, but packed up a few boxes of sentimental items to ship back to her home in San Francisco. The apartment felt empty—empty of her grandmother's spirit—and Kyra realized that if Nana's spirit were anywhere, it was back in Israel . . . along with a piece of Kyra's heart.

Five days later, Kyra boarded her flight at O'Hare International Airport and made her way home to San Francisco. It was a foggy, cold morning when she landed in California, but her heart felt warm and her head felt clear.

# Part 3

# Journey to Spain

# 9

Kyra opened her eyes and looked at the alarm clock. It was early morning—1:11 am to be exact. *How strange*, she thought. *I've been waking up to triple digit numbers! When I worked at Vortex, it was always 3:33 am.* She briefly wondered about the significance of the sequence, recognizing it was becoming a more frequent occurrence. Tucking away a mental note to research the meaning later, she stared into the darkness as her mind turned toward other things.

Kyra had slept for nearly three full days once she'd arrived back in San Francisco. Taking care of her grandmother's belongings in Chicago had been a bittersweet time. *I miss you so much, Nana,* she thought sadly. *How lucky was I to come across that photo of us at your eightieth-birthday celebration?* In the picture, Nana was blowing out the candles on her birthday cake, and Kyra and her mother were standing on either side of her . . . both wore big smiles on their faces. It had been a much happier time.

She turned over on her side and tossed one of her pillows to the floor. There was no denying that the events of the past two weeks had completely drained her. Sleep was her body's way of coping with the stress, and she quickly dozed back off.

At 11:30 am, she woke up to start her day—something she had never done before in her entire life. It was Monday morning, and just a few weeks ago, she would already have been at her office and halfway through a productive workday. "*Arrgghh,*" she groaned. "I still can't believe I'm not at Vortex . . . but truthfully," she reassured herself, "I don't miss it there at all." Flinging her legs over the side of the bed, she planted her feet firmly on the ground and vowed, "I'll put more thought into finding my next role soon, but for now it can wait."

She dragged herself fully out of bed and headed down to the kitchen. After carefully pouring water into her espresso machine, she flipped on the switch. Her favorite morning beverage began to brew with a loud *hiss*, and while she waited, she enjoyed a small container of strawberry yogurt. Kyra licked a spoonful of the creamy mixture as the late-morning sunlight poured in through the kitchen window, warming her face. She closed her eyes when the bright light temporarily blinded her.

*Mmmm, it feels like being at the beach*, she reminisced. She could picture herself there now, in the sand, where she often sat with her eyes closed when the sun was very intense. Drinking in the delicious feeling of the toasty sunlight on her face, she imagined the ocean spray refreshing and cooling her skin.

Kyra opened her eyes slowly and realized with surprise that there was nothing on her agenda at the moment. Other than spending the next few days unpacking the boxes of mementos from her grandmother's apartment, she had no plans. *How funny to have an entire day with nothing to do,* she reflected with irony. After spending years on a tight corporate schedule where every minute of every day was so carefully planned out and accounted for—having a totally free day felt incredibly strange to her.

Taking a sip of her steaming hot coffee, she gradually headed up the stairs for a late morning shower. She was almost to the top of the landing when her cell phone rang loudly. It was still sitting on the shiny black granite countertop beside the espresso machine where she'd left it. Kyra swung back down the stairs to retrieve the phone from the kitchen.

"That's strange," she said, glancing down at the phone. It was a foreign number, but she recognized the city code of the incoming call. Barcelona? Who in the world is calling me from Spain?

"Hello?" she answered hesitantly.

The woman on the other end spoke perfect English, but with a slight Spanish accent. Kyra recognized the bubbly voice immediately. It had been a few years since they last spoke and a heartfelt smile spread across her face.

"Kyra, it's Gabriela! I heard from one of our old Harvard friends that your grandmother passed away. I'm so very sorry, *Chica* . . . I wanted to reach out and say hi. How *are* you doing?"

"What a nice surprise!" Kyra responded. "I can't believe it's you, Gabby. It's been much too long since we've last spoken . . . and thanks for being so sweet and thoughtful. To be honest, it's been a very rough couple of weeks, and I've had a lot of changes in my life. I'm doing okay—but I'm actually taking a little time off right now to decompress."

She proceeded to fill her friend in on all the recent happenings, beginning first with her downsizing at Vortex. Gabby responded with a shocked gasp, but Kyra continued without missing a beat. "I also broke up with my boyfriend, Steve, who I'd been dating for about a year. I knew all along it wasn't the right relationship for me, but I was too absorbed in my career. I just kept letting things slide with him. I should have noticed the red flags and broken up with him much sooner. You know, looking back at it now, it was just a convenient relationship. I didn't want to put the effort into meeting someone new. How sad is *that?*"

"Don't punish yourself for the past mistakes," Gabby responded emphatically. "Vortex—and Steve, I might add—clearly did not appreciate you! And you *should* take some time off to refresh yourself. You deserve some fun after working all of those *locas* hours at work. I'm here for you—day or night. Call me anytime you want to talk. I've missed you, girlfriend!"

Kyra's eyes filled with tears, feeling deeply touched by her friend's concern. "You have always been such a dear friend, Gabby. . . and we shared some super-crazy times together in grad school, didn't we? I've missed you. Thanks for being here for me now—exactly when I need you the most." Kyra quietly composed herself to stop from bursting into tears.

Gabby responded with an emotional "*Awww*" to acknowledge her friend's sentiments, but quickly continued in her bubbly voice, keeping the conversation upbeat. "You know, I've made some serious changes in my life since you last saw me. You remember I started working at that global consulting company in Boston right out of grad school? Well, I also worked those same preposterous hours you do there in the U.S.

*¡Que ridículo!* But after eleven years, I was burned out from the heavy workload and travel schedule."

Kyra knew what it meant to feel burnt out and sympathized with Gabby. She smiled inwardly at her friend's constant interjection of Spanish into their conversation. It had become a private joke between them during grad school and a quirk that Kyra adored about Gabby's personality. *She's still trying to teach me to speak Spanish after all these years,* she thought affectionately. *Someday I will get up the nerve to properly learn a second language!*

Gabby went on to say that her firm had offered her a chance to relocate to Barcelona, her native home. "At first I wasn't too thrilled with the idea of moving back here," Gabby admitted, "but I gave it some serious thought and realized I wanted to make big changes in my life. The timing seemed perfect! Nothing was holding me in Boston, so I decided that moving home would put me closer to *mi familia,* and I really liked that idea. I feel so blessed to have my family around me now—and they are so crazy. *¡Totalmente locos!* But they love me, and they are always there for me with their help and support. Plus, I work fewer hours in Spain, so I now take time away from work to enjoy life. We have so much more holiday time here than you do in the States. It's simply our culture here in Europe."

Kyra loved the idea of a more balanced work-life schedule and felt happy for her friend, but she couldn't help but feel a little envious that Gabby had a large immediate family to turn to.

"Ah, but last, and maybe *most important,*" Gabby said with a giggle, the way she used to do when they were in grad school, "I met Alejandro a year and a half ago. You will so laugh! I had been in Spain for only about six months, and I really wasn't looking to meet anyone. I was still unwinding from the exhaustion of my former job, but then some dear friends invited me to meet them at the theater for a show one weekend. I showed up and they had invited Alejandro as my 'blind date' and *Voila!* . . . the rest is history, as you say!"

Kyra chuckled. "You always manage to make me laugh! I'm so happy for you both. I'd love to see you again someday . . . and, of course, meet this amazing man who has captured your heart—*Alejandro,* did you say?"

Gabby paused for a moment, then replied, "You know . . . if you have time and want to make a trip to Spain, I can take a little time off from work, and we can have some fun together. Barcelona is right here on the Mediterranean coast. Ah! But there's also Madrid, our capital, which is located in the central part of Spain. You'll want to visit there, too. Not to mention the magnificent Andalucía region in the Southern part of Spain—you must see the quaint cobblestone streets and horse-drawn carriages. Oh there's so much to see and do here. You'll love it! . . . Hmmm, there's even a cool place called San Sebastián, a very nice city in the Basque Country to the North. Now those Basque are *muy locos* and even speak their very own language!"

*A trip to Spain?* Kyra thought. The wheels in her head began turning.

"The weather is beautiful this time of year," Gabby went on, her enthusiasm rubbing off on Kyra, "and it's the start of summer vacation here. You can stay at my apartment and travel out across the country as you wish. Stay as long as you like! Who knows, I can likely get some of my crazy *familia* to be tour guides. What you do you think, *Chica*?"

"I very well may take you up on that offer!" Kyra said, the excitement clear in her voice. "I would love to see you again—and meet Alejandro—and your crazy family, too. Let me look into it and get back to you in a day or two. Does that work for you?"

Gabby giggled. "Whatever works for you is *maravilloso* for me. We can even make plans for this coming weekend. Just get back to me with the details, and I will see you soon! *Muwahhh!*"

Kyra smiled as she ended the call, and it was the first time she had honestly smiled in over two weeks.

The hot water cascaded over Kyra's smooth skin, invigorating her senses. As she lathered her hair, she thought of her call with Gabby, and she could feel her heart jumping in anticipation of her potential trip.

Tossing her head back, she let the steaming, sudsy water slowly wash away the anxiety of the past couple of weeks.

Following her shower, she dried herself with a soft beige towel and took time to fix her hair and apply a little makeup. She slipped into a comfortable pair of jeans and a white T-shirt—much nicer than the same nightshirt she had worn for the past three days.

Kyra soon found herself in the soft leather chair at her large walnut burl desk, opening her laptop, which sat squarely in the middle of the desk. She thought of Great Uncle Saul for a moment and could hear his advice to her as plain as day: "*Perhaps it will be good for you to take some time off from your busy life to reflect on what you'd like to do differently with it. Maybe some time away from San Francisco . . .*"

She spoke aloud as her fingers danced across the keyboard, "Yes, Uncle Saul, you are exactly right. I do need some time off to think."

Kyra looked again at her computer screen to verify her flight leaving Friday, June 20th from San Francisco, California, at 8:30 am, and arriving in Barcelona, Spain, the next day at 8:45 am. The keyboard made a gentle *click* as her finger hit the "confirm" key on the laptop keyboard. The one-way flight was now booked.

*How funny to have no itinerary for my trip,* Kyra pondered. She was planning to just "wing it," which was totally new territory for her. *This will be an adventure indeed. I need to just go with the flow . . . and not be in control of everything for once.* With that thought, Kyra firmly flipped her laptop closed.

With her flight booked and feeling more at ease with the immediate future, she jumped into her white Mercedes convertible and made her way to a nearby local bookstore to purchase a travel guide for Spain. Then, with the guide in hand, she drove the nearly one-hour drive north to her place of solitude—Stinson Beach.

It was late Monday afternoon now and quiet at the beach. The usual weekend crowd would be nowhere to be seen on a workday. Kyra lazily plopped herself down in the soft, moist sand, feeling the ocean breeze softly kiss her face. The sunlight was golden, and she closed her eyes, letting the warm light gently caresses her eyelids. She savored the moment before opening her eyes to fully drink in the beauty of her surroundings.

*Despite the circumstances, I am so lucky to be here, right now,* she told herself. She gazed out at the ocean and scrunched her toes into the sand, delighting in the carefree calm that now enveloped her. Soon, she turned her attention to the travel guide and began to flip through the pages. For a change, she was in no particular hurry. She took note of the places she'd like to visit, knowing full well that Gabby would be giving her lots of advice, too.

Mesmerized by the solitude and the serenity of the day, Kyra's mind drifted off. She looked up from the guide and silently thought, *Thank you, God, for this amazing day and for all the blessings coming my way . . . By your grace, I can't wait to see what good comes from all of this!*

Just then a flock of seagulls flew overhead squawking loudly, seeming to acknowledge that a new chapter had arrived in Kyra's life. With that sign from the Universe, she stated aloud with clear intention, "Thank you also for this opportunity to be here today and to think about how I'd like my life to look going forward. Thank you, God, for the wonderful abundance I've created in my life. Thank you for my incredibly good health and for allowing me the opportunity to take even better care of myself with more sleep and less stress. And thank you for all my many wonderful friends, for Great Uncle Saul, but most importantly, thank you, God, for allowing me to have had Nana in my life."

Kyra gazed out with teary eyes across the magnificent white rolling waves atop the surface of the deep sapphire blue ocean. Her travel guide all but forgotten, she remained still and silent for quite some time, simply basking in her feelings of gratitude and peace.

When she returned home early in evening, she spent the remainder of the night putting away the contents of the boxes she'd packed at her grandmother's. *Ah, Nana, you lived such a wonderful life,* she reflected, fondly recalling the many good times she and her grandmother had spent together over the years.

She plucked an old postcard from Barcelona out of one of the boxes. Flipping it over, she saw that it was to her grandmother from her parents.

*How funny, Nana, that you kept this postcard all these years . . . Long before my parents had even dreamed of having me.*

The next morning, after a restful night's sleep, Kyra called Gabby to confirm her trip. Gabby's enthusiastic reply filled her with happiness. "Oh, *Chica*, I'm ecstatic! We are going to have a blast!"

Kyra felt her level of anticipation growing, but she took her time getting everything in order for her upcoming absence. How long would she be gone? Two weeks? A month? She had absolutely no clue. And, with regard to her old life, the absurdity of not knowing made her laugh.

Over the next few days, Kyra carefully made her preparations for her trip. First, she scheduled her monthly bills and mortgage for two months of auto payments, just to be on the safe side. Next she asked a neighbor to keep an eye on her place, giving the kind woman a key for any emergencies.

The neighbor had cheerfully responded, "You will have a lovely trip for sure! I wish I were going."

Kyra thanked her, then paused for a moment before adding, "I'm very grateful to have someone as thoughtful as you . . . so close by that I can trust."

She secretly wished she had taken more time to get to know her neighbor. In the future, she would indeed take more time to make friends. Promptly returning home, she finished her preparations by wheeling her large suitcase out of the closet and began to pack for an extended stay.

Unlike her trip to Israel when she'd tossed clothes randomly into her suitcase, this time she packed slowly, carefully choosing each piece of clothing. As she folded her evening dresses, she imagined herself on a night out on the town at a fancy restaurant. She also chose several of her most favorite casual dresses with summertime in mind. Next she added evening pants and a variety of blouses, shoes, and jewelry. Mostly, though, she packed lots of skirts, jeans, and T-shirts, and of course tennis shoes. She even threw in a pair of hiking boots. *I'll be ready for whatever comes my way!* The thought made her feel adventuresome and ready to try something new.

As Kyra zipped up her suitcase, it occurred to her just how thrilled she was to be taking a long vacation. Had she *ever* gone on a vacation when she didn't work too? Other than her many work-related trips—and many to exotic locations—there were only a handful of extended weekends away with Steve or some of her girlfriends. *What a great sense of freedom having absolutely no work to do. For the first time in my life, I can focus on myself for a change.* A few weeks ago she would have cringed at the thought, but now she saw it as a new and welcome change.

"How amazing and freeing is all of this?" she confirmed her thoughts aloud, carefully dragging her heavy suitcase down the long flight of stairs. She felt as if she was descending into a deeper level of her life and ready to explore the possibilities.

# 10

Kyra waited patiently at Gate 33, sipping an especially strong espresso and munching on her traditional blueberry muffin. Normally she made only the healthiest food choices, but this was her sweet indulgence to enjoy while traveling. Only crumbs of the treat were left when an elderly man and woman sat down beside her to wait for the flight.

Kyra noticed how tightly the couple held hands. The woman caught Kyra's eye, and the pair exchanged a smile. "We are celebrating our wedding anniversary with a trip to Spain—Barcelona actually," the woman explained, striking up conversation. "Where are you headed, my dear?"

Kyra looked into the woman's beaming blue eyes. Her delicately lined face was framed with soft gray hair, and her affectionate demeanor drew Kyra in. "I'm also heading to Spain," she replied. "Considering we're waiting for a flight to Philly, it's quite a coincidence that both our final destinations are Barcelona."

The elderly man joined the conversation. "Have you ever been to Spain before? It's quite beautiful . . . and an adventure," he said with insightful eyes.

"Oh no," Kyra replied, "but I can't wait to take this vacation and to see my friend of course . . . Anyway, congratulations on your anniversary. You look like such a happy couple. How long have you been married, if I may ask?"

The woman's blue eyes twinkled as she softly replied, "Albert and I are celebrating our *second* anniversary, my dear . . . Love can come to you anytime." She chuckled, as if sharing a private joke, and tightly squeezed Albert's hand.

Kyra's heart melted as she admired the couple. She could clearly see the love they had for each other in their eyes. And she couldn't help but be touched by their happiness. *Yes, that's exactly what I want!* she told herself privately—*Genuine love and happiness.*

She and the couple exchanged a few more pleasantries, but soon it was time to board the plane. Kyra was actually looking forward to the flight, unlike when she used to travel for her job and spent the majority of her airtime reviewing contracts and answering corporate emails. Today, however, she had several e-books neatly loaded on her tablet that she'd planned to read, but had never found the time. She'd also brought one paperback, too—the travel guide—which was full of sticky notes marking different areas she was interested in visiting.

After she settled into her seat and the plane had reached cruising altitude, she slipped the tablet out of her purse. It occurred to her that the look and feel of a paperback just couldn't be replaced by an e-book, despite its convenience. Holding the tablet in her hands, Kyra wondered, *Am I perhaps a bit old school?* She loved owning hardbound books too, and, in fact, she had a whole wall of them in her condominium—everything from collectibles to silly romance novels. She opened her first e-book and settled back, reclining her seat to a comfortable position.

The five-and-a-half-hour flight was smooth, and by the time they landed, Kyra had completely finished her first novel and began reading *A Tale of Two Cities* during the two-hour layover in Philadelphia. *Dickens hit the nail on the head,* she thought, as she turned the first page. *It was the best of times, it was the worst of times . . . it was the season of Light, it was the season of Darkness. How appropriate for this trip . . . and life in general.*

After her layover, Flight 303 to Barcelona departed exactly on time at 6:30 pm. Once the in-flight food service was completed, Kyra took a sleep-aid for the overnight flight and slept most of the way to her destination. She had done this many times for her international travels and knew this was the best course for an overnight flight to help adjust to the time change at the other end. In this case, it would be an eight-hour time difference. She slept soundly, but woke up abruptly when the flight attendant tapped her on the shoulder to ask her to prepare for the final descent.

Kyra rubbed her eyes and stretched comfortably in the upright chair, realizing that she was finally starting to relax and feel more at ease. A short time later, the wheels of the plane screeched loudly as they touched down on the runway. The pilot announced, first in English and then in Spanish, "Passengers of Flight 303 we have just landed in Barcelona and will taxi on the runway for several minutes before arriving at our gate. The weather looks to be perfect this beautiful Saturday morning with a temperature of around 19 degrees Celsius. We've very much enjoyed having you on board, and we hope we made your flight as comfortable as possible. Have a pleasant stay, but most important: Welcome to Barcelona!"

Some of the people on the plane clapped, but Kyra cheered inwardly. *I can't believe I'm in Spain and I'm off to see Gabby! . . . For the first time in more than ten years, I think.* Kyra suddenly felt a bit worried that Gabby might think she had changed. *Will she think I look older? Or that I'm a completely different person? Life has taken me on such a different path since our grad school days. . . awww, but I can't wait to see her.*

When she arrived at the luggage carousel, Kyra turned on her cell phone and the message indicator light instantly flashed. The first message was from Emma in San Francisco: "Kyra, darling, I'm so proud of you! I can't wait to hear about your adventures in Spain. Miss you, girlfriend!" *How sweet*, Kyra thought, pressing the send button with a lighthearted response: "Yes, I can't wait to catch up with you too! Miss ya. K." A second message was from Gabby of course: "¡Buenos días! I will meet you at the passenger pickup area at the airport shortly. Look for me in a red-and-white striped BMW MINI Cooper."

Kyra giggled. Red was so Gabby's style and fit her personality perfectly. She easily spotted the car once she'd stepped outside into the crisp morning air with her suitcase trailing behind her. Gabby immediately jumped out of the car and rushed toward her.

Kyra made a mental note of how stunningly beautiful her friend still was, with her thick dark hair in long loose curls pulled back slightly to show off her striking features. Her flawless olive complexion complemented her dark almond-shaped eyes, and her white teeth sparkled between lips in a bright red lipstick, which perfectly matched the color of her car.

"Oh my, Gabby. You look exactly the same!" Kyra exclaimed affectionately as her friend neared.

"Ha!" Gabby said unpretentiously, "You are much too kind, my dear friend. *Te ves preciosa!* Oh and welcome to my hometown—Barcelona!"

Kyra was somewhat startled as Gabby embraced her in an affectionate hug and planted a proper Spanish kiss on each cheek—making a *muwahhh* sound with each kiss. She had completely forgotten about her friend's warm greetings. Kyra hugged her back and felt excited to be spending time with her again.

With their greetings behind them, both women hoisted Kyra's heavy suitcase into the MINI Cooper's trunk. Gabby gasped at the weight of the suitcase, struggling to help lift it into the car. "Did you pack a dead body in here?!" she exclaimed.

Kyra flushed in mild embarrassment. "Hmmm, I may have overpacked a bit . . . And, yes, it's true this isn't the lightweight suitcase I took on all those *thousands* of business trips!"

Both women chuckled. "Well good for you, *Chica.*" Gabby said with a laugh.

Kyra's ears perked up at the use of her nickname. "You know, Gabby, you are the only person in the world who calls me *Chica.*"

"Ah, but you earned that nickname on our crazy adventure in Puerto Rico." Gabby burst out laughing. "And it's a well-deserved nickname that's stuck with you ever since!" They were unmistakably happy to be in each other's company again and hopped in the car for the drive to Gabby's apartment. It was just like they were back in grad school and nothing had changed. Kyra let out a sigh of relief as Gabby drove quickly away from the airport.

On the way to downtown Barcelona, Kyra gazed outside the car window and couldn't help but admire the beautiful, warm sunny morning. The salty Mediterranean breeze gently rippled across the palm trees dotting the city streets, making the area look both exotic but somehow soothing too.

"Ah, yes, I think I have arrived." Kyra said, as a deeper feeling of relaxation settled over her.

Gabby smiled. "I don't know if both you and your luggage are going to fit into my very small one-bedroom apartment," she joked, and Kyra gave her a knowing smile. "It's very small," Gabby continued, "but it's right on our most fashionable major avenue in the heart of the city, *Passeig de Gràcia.* My eldest brother, Carlos, brought over a small twin bed for you, and we've already set it up in my study. It will be a bit cozy, but it's a great location, and I think you will really love it. Your luggage will have to sleep on the floor though."

"No worries, Gabby," Kyra said with deep affection. "I can't tell you how grateful I am that you invited me and that I'm actually here on such short notice. I'm sure your apartment is lovely. We will have so much fun. I'm really looking forward to meeting your family."

With a mischievous grin, Gabby let her in on a secret: "Well, my friend, that will be sooner than you think. My *mamá*, and you can call her *Carmen*, has already invited us over this afternoon for a huge lunch around two thirty. It's called *la comida* in Spanish. Most of my family will be there, and you'll meet Alejandro later in the evening when we join him and some other friends for dinner in the city. It's Saturday night after all!"

Kyra was thrilled that her friend had taken the initiative to plan out their afternoon, but perhaps a little apprehensive about meeting her entire family so soon. Still the fun night out on the town would be the perfect kickoff for her first day in Barcelona.

"Of course, I'll let you rest up a bit first, then we'll freshen up before heading to my parents' house. Wait until you meet my *mamá.* She is always pressuring Alejandro and me to get married and start a family. I am after all thirty-seven now. *¡Ahí está el problema!* I mean, and there lies the problem! *¡Ay—ay—ay!"* Gabby exclaimed in frustration, but the affection and love she felt for her mother still came through sincerely.

As the car turned onto Passeig de Gràcia Avenue, located in the heart of downtown Barcelona, Kyra was awestruck by the breathtaking architecture. As Gabby had explained, they were now in the area called

Catalonia—and, more specifically, in Barcelona's well-known district Eixample.

Gabby rolled down the car windows a bit, letting in some fresh air. The smell of the salty, crisp, cool air filled Kyra's nose, reminding her of San Francisco. A sudden and slightly odd feeling overcame her as she looked around in wonder. *It feels almost like I've been here before . . . familiar yet somehow different. Hmmm, maybe the Mediterranean air is just reminding me of home.*

Shrugging off the strange feeling, Kyra continued to marvel at the unique buildings lining the city streets, almost nudging her nose up against the car window next to her to see everything clearly. There was a splendid mix of several different architectural styles, just as she had read in her travel guide, but it was even more dazzling to experience in person. The traditional Gothic architecture was both grandiose and intricate, and almost haunting in some ways. *Medieval looking,* she wondered, thinking it looked a bit eerie. On the contrary, the more *Modernista* style of Antoni Gaudí was colorful and whimsical, if not surreal, and appeared as if it were straight from a fairytale.

Two of Gaudí's architectural masterpieces were close to where Gabby lived: Casa Milà and Casa Batlló. When they drove past each of the houses, the buildings mesmerized Kyra with their amazingly bold but uniquely modern design. She instantly made a decision to visit both, since she loved art in all forms and these looked to be most interesting.

"I can't believe Gaudí's modern designs have withstood the test of time—despite being built nearly a hundred years ago," she commented.

*"Sí. Sí."* Gabby replied enthusiastically. "But wait till you see the rest of the city! I have many surprises in store for you."

As Gabby drove on, Kyra became lost in the charming ambience of the city—with its street cafes lining the sidewalks, offering everything from steaming cups of *café* to plentiful plates of *tapas*. Upscale shopping like Chanel, Gucci, Louis Vuitton, Valentino, Hermes, and Prada beckoned shoppers to come inside to try on—and hopefully purchase—their exquisite clothing.

A magnificent water fountain at the southern end of the street elegantly sprayed water into the air, with smaller streams dancing toward the center of the fountain. The water display jarred Kyra's memory of a childhood dream: in her mind's eye, she saw water nymphs prancing in ocean waves. The memory sparked a warm feeling in her heart, and she could almost imagine hearing the water nymphs squeal with joy as the waves crashed down upon the shore. The details of the dream eluded her right then, but the feeling of it made her happy just the same.

"It's so charming," Kyra said with delight. "It's unlike any other European city I've ever visited."

"Now you understand *why* I came home," Gabby said with great pride.

A few minutes later, they were in Gabby's apartment building, lugging Kyra's heavy suitcase into the elevator. The doors opened on the fourth floor. Kyra was eager to see her friend's place, and Gabby seemed just as eager to share it with her. She flung the door of her apartment wide open and stated proudly, "Welcome to my humble home!"

"It's gorgeous!" Kyra said, stepping through the sleek modern doorway.

The apartment was indeed small, but it had freshly finished light bamboo flooring, gray granite kitchen countertops, and mostly white furniture, which contrasted boldly with the bright red walls.

"Your place suits your personality to a tee—and even matches your car!"

Gabby smiled, her eyes twinkling. "Come, I'll show you where you can hang your clothes and relieve yourself of your mammoth suitcase."

Kyra took her time unpacking in the small study she'd be using as a bedroom. She then joined Gabby in the kitchen and sat at the small glass dining table.

Popping her head out from inside the refrigerator, Gabby asked, "*¿Agua con gas?*"

"I'd love a glass of sparkling water," Kyra replied, glad to brush up on her high school Spanish. She was inwardly appreciative of Gabby's constant efforts to subtly teach her Spanish.

The friends chatted nonstop for what seemed like an hour as they caught up on their lives. It had been too long since they'd last seen each other, and soon they were reminiscing about their past.

"Ah, *Chica*, we were so young and idealistic in grad school. Remember summer break when I talked you into taking those Reiki classes with me? We finished the first two levels—and the advanced training, too. I was on a quest for enlightenment back then . . . before I took the consulting job in Boston. Then I quickly realized I didn't have a spare moment for anything else! Enlightenment would have to wait." She giggled.

Kyra began searching her memory as Gabby went on, "But since I've moved back home to Barcelona, I've made some important changes. I'm taking more time for my personal interests now, and I'm even planning to complete my Reiki Master Training next month in England. I'll spend a week in the small town of Glastonbury."

"Glastonbury?" Kyra asked curiously. "I've never heard of it."

"*¿En serio?*" Gabby asked, but then waved the rhetorical question away. "Glastonbury could be best described as a cool, hippy, metaphysical town with some funky shops. And . . . you won't believe this . . . the final Reiki Master ceremony will be held at nearby Stonehenge! Now *that* I know you've heard of. The fellow doing the training has special permission for his students to go into the center of the gargantuan stones once the regular visitors leave for the evening. Normally, it's roped off to visitors and viewed from a distance. How cool is that?"

"That's sounds amazing," Kyra responded. She paused a moment before adding, "You know, I had all but forgotten about those classes. I think I only took them because you encouraged me to go . . . and I also didn't want to go back to Chicago that summer and spend it at my parents' house." She paused again as that thought sank in. "Truthfully before that first class, I thought Reiki was just a bunch of metaphysical mumbo-jumbo. But, honestly, I ended up really *liking* it and the whole concept of energy healing once we finished the series of classes."

Kyra suddenly felt sorry for not having pursued the Japanese hands-on healing technique, which surprised her a bit. Like Gabby, she had let her work life and being a successful businesswoman become her priority instead. "I remember now how much I loved the spiritual approach to healing and how relaxing a Reiki session can be. Back then I even thought of doing volunteer work with Reiki to help others." Kyra unexpectedly felt the stirrings of desire to explore the ancient practice once again.

Gabby nodded and added sincerely, "This may sound a little *loco* to you, but I'm really doing this training for myself. I'd love to get back into more metaphysical type of things. You know, I've always felt more . . . well, *authentic*, I think would be the best word—when I pursued my Reiki interests. Ah, but I have to be a little careful of *mamá.* She is a devout Catholic and doesn't quite understand that it does not conflict with our religion."

"Yes, I do remember that," Kyra recalled, her interest piqued. "We learned that you must have a religious foundation or belief in God, but Reiki itself is nondenominational and open to anyone who is interested in healing."

Suddenly Gabby's eyes lit up, and she leaned toward Kyra. "If you'd like to join me, you most likely can! You already have the required experience, so we just need to make sure there's availability. Plus, it will be a phenomenal trip."

Kyra's heart skipped a beat. Something about the idea really intrigued her. She let out a chuckle and responded, "I don't even know what I'll be doing tomorrow, much less a few weeks from now, but I do appreciate the invitation. Let me give it some serious consideration and get back to you."

A sly look crossed Gabby's face. "We have a saying in our family, '*¡El destino tiene una manera de llegar cuando menos te lo esperas!*' This translates loosely to 'Destiny has a way of arriving when you least expect it!'"

A chill ran up Kyra's spine while she absorbed the comment. She suddenly flashed back to her grad school days, as if she had momentarily stepped back in time.

She was in Boston on summer break. Her long blond hair cascaded down her back, and she was wearing a tattered pair of blue jeans and a short pink T-shirt. She'd been doing a practice Reiki session on one of the other students, Marta. In the middle of the session, Kyra thought she heard a woman's voice. But it was more like a *whisper,* and while she could hear the woman speaking, the conversation seemed to take place only in her imagination. She swore the voice said, "Tell her I love her! Tell her the small gold locket with the photos inside is in the basement near the furnace. Please tell her."

The hairs on the back of Kyra's neck stood on end and a chill raced up her spine. She didn't know what to do, so she quietly finished the Reiki session. Afterward, Marta thanked her for an amazing session and went on to say that Kyra's energy felt quite strong—maybe even stronger than the other students.

Kyra's wasn't clear about what she wanted to do with the strange message she'd received, but she finally decided to be bold. First, she thanked Marta for the compliment and expressed her appreciation for the opportunity to work with her, then added, "I know this may sound a little strange, but did you lose a gold locket with some pictures in it? I think it may be in a basement near a furnace."

The amazed look on Marta's face had etched itself strongly in Kyra's memory.

"I lost a locket that my mother had given me many years ago," Marta explained. "I was just thinking about it the other day because it was the eighth anniversary of her death." The young woman's voice cracked as she went on, "I miss her terribly. I wonder if I'll find it after all these years. Wow, that would be really amazing! I'll give my dad a call to check for it by the old furnace. I'll let you know what happens."

Kyra embraced Marta affectionately and hoped that her information was correct. Despite being taken aback by the idea that she'd received a message from a deceased love one, she felt good to be of possible help to her new friend. A day or so later, much to Kyra's utter amazement, Marta informed her that the locket had been found *exactly* where Kyra had said it would be.

Kyra came back to the present moment with a start. Why had she never told anyone about that experience? Why had she never pursued what could potentially be a special gift? With those questions weighing on her, an image of Stonehenge shot into her mind, and she had an eerie feeling she was indeed meant to go there. Perhaps destiny had arrived after all. She would give Gabby's invitation some serious thought.

"*Chica*, I think I just lost you. And how will you ever learn any Spanish if you don't listen to me? But, seriously, your destiny is not until at least tomorrow, so let me finish my story," Gabby chided her.

The friends continued to catch up on their lives before breaking down into a fit of laughter when they realized they would have plenty more time to chat over the next several days. They decided to part ways for an hour so that Kyra could relax before the big lunch. Gabby helped her put two crisp gray sheets on the portable twin bed and tossed her a lightweight white cotton blanket on top for extra comfort.

Grateful for feeling none of the effects of jetlag, Kyra took a quick twenty-minute catnap, and then opted for a shower to further refresh her. As she applied her makeup in the bathroom mirror, her lips curved up into a big smile. She wondered how crazy the *familia* would be, especially compared to her dear friend Gabriela. *What have I gotten myself into?* she thought with amusement.

Gabby joined her at the mirror and began brushing her hair. "Okay! Let me explain a little to you about my *familia* so you can be prepared," she said with a serious tone, not missing a beat. "My *mamá* is the matriarch of the family—and in Spain, that is the heart of the family. And my *papá* is Eduardo."

Kyra noticed how carefully Gabby enunciated each syllable of her father's name.

"He is very outspoken and opinionated. He will offer you much information on the family history and make you laugh. They have been living in Barcelona for twenty years now, but are originally from Madrid. I have six brothers and sisters . . . Did I tell you my family is Catholic? Okay, seriously! My brother's names are Carlos, José, and Javier, and my sister's names are Mónica, Sonia, and Cristina." Gabby's hands moved like lightning, as she quickly freshened her bright red lipstick in the mirror. She then glanced at Kyra.

"Everyone is married and most have children now. One of my sisters, Sonia, lives in France with her husband and they won't be here today. Oh, did I mention I'm the only one *not* married in my family? Well *Mamá* will fill you in on that one, I'm sure! Anyway, everyone speaks some English—unless they have been drinking heavily. . . . So just enjoy lunch and the conversation will flow. And don't worry about getting everyone's name straight just yet. Are you ready to leave, *Chica?*"

Kyra looked at Gabby in the mirror and grinned a bit nervously. "I'm so looking forward to meeting the parents that spawned you, Gabriela."

# 11

With their high heels clicking loudly on the sidewalk, Kyra and Gabby made their way swiftly to the MINI Cooper. They were heading to an area known as El Gótic—or the Gothic Quarter. It was one of the oldest neighborhoods in Barcelona and originally the center of the city. Kyra was taken aback by how ancient, almost medieval, some of the buildings appeared.

Seeing her friend's puzzled look, Gabby clarified, "You probably know this is one of the earliest known neighborhoods in Barcelona from studying your travel guide. And some ancient remnants here date back to the Roman settlement of Barcelona—if you can imagine that! What you may not know is that the majority of the buildings here are *much newer*—from the thirteenth through the fifteenth centuries." Gabby giggled at her joke, which had not been lost on Kyra, who giggled too.

"It's amazing that these old buildings have survived for so many centuries," Kyra said, the laughter still on her lips. But then she grew more serious. "It almost seems like a metaphor for life. If you have a strong foundation, you can survive the test of time."

Gabby nodded before a mischievous look crossed her face. "In the nineteenth and twentieth century, they did lot of restoration to keep things updated. And we girls know a little restoration work never hurt anyone!" she chuckled. "Pretty impressive, huh?"

"It truly is incredible," Kyra said, reflecting on the ancient beauty of the neighborhood.

"Oh, I should mention too that the old streets in *El Gótic* can be very narrow and much like a labyrinth. It's *very* easy to get lost here and the streets seem to all look alike—be careful if you are out alone. Okay? So what do you think of our city so far?"

"I feel like we've arrived in Gotham City, Catwoman," Kyra said deadpan, and Gabby let out another giggle.

"Oh yes! We very well may have," she playfully agreed.

The drive seemed to take no more than about fifteen minutes, but for the first time in her life, Kyra realized she was not paying close attention to the time. Instead, she was simply enjoying being in the moment as they drove to their afternoon destination.

"Hold on tight!" Gabby said, as she carefully but swiftly slid the car it into a tiny parking space that had just opened up outside the building along the narrow street.

El Gótic took Kyra by surprise. From her place on the sidewalk, she craned her neck to look up at the impressively tall, ancient-looking apartment building. "I feel like Batman and Robin should be pulling up any second now," Kyra said, feeling as if she were really in a movie. "But I'm not sure how they'd be able to maneuver the Batmobile in this crowded part of the city . . . Awesome job, Gabby!"

Gabby flashed a smile of agreement and pulled open the heavy wooden front door of her parent's apartment building. They took the elevator up to the penthouse and were soon inside the spacious apartment. Kyra was immediately struck by how the modern interior contrasted so obviously with the building's ancient exterior design. The walls were stark white with sleek dark dining room furniture and rich brown leather sofas. Red wool rugs added bright color to the dining room and large living room. Bold and contemporary, it clearly was not what Kyra had expected based on her initial impression of the neighborhood.

"*¡Hola, Papá! ¡Hola, Carlos! ¡Hola, Mónica!*" Gabby yelled across the living room to each of her family members, embracing them one at a time in a big hug and planting a proper Spanish kiss on each of their cheeks. It seemed to Kyra as if they had not seen each other in months, but she knew differently.

It was apparent to Kyra that they were a very affectionate—and a very loud family too. *So unlike the family I came from,* she thought. She momentarily felt a sharp twinge of regret and loss for something she'd never had, but quickly refocused her attention on the welcoming and jovial feeling between the family members.

Kyra felt overwhelmingly accepted as she received affectionate hugs and double-cheek kisses from each family member she met. She and Gabby eventually made their way into the kitchen where Gabby's mamá, Carmen, moved hurriedly around the kitchen, preparing the huge meal they would shortly consume. She had just pulled a fresh loaf of bread out of the oven, and its tantalizing scent mingled with the smell of the seafood simmering in a pot on the stovetop, making Kyra's mouth water.

Carmen wiped her hands on her apron and gave Kyra the greeting she'd become accustomed to in just a short time since her arrival in Spain. She could feel Carmen's heart beating rapidly as she squeezed Kyra tightly before letting her go. Her heart, too, was deeply touched by Carmen's genuine kindness in welcoming her to their household.

"*Keeyra*, we are so happy to finally meet you! Gabriela has spoken of you often, and I'm so glad you can join us for *la comida* today." She spoke in English but with a heavy Spanish accent. In the next breath, she shouted into the next room, "Eduardo! Are you getting *Keeyra a copa de vino?*"

Kyra jumped back by the force of her voice, and jumped again when Eduardo, Gabby's father, yelled back, "*¡Sí, sí, sí, Mamá!* She just walked in the door!"

She appreciated that they were partly shouting in English apparently for her benefit.

As Carmen prepared the food, she asked Kyra about her life in the United States. She seemed especially curious about San Francisco. "I've heard San Francisco is *muy hermoso*—I mean, a *beautiful* place to live. And perhaps not too different than our beloved Barcelona. I understand from Gabriela that you too are single? My beloved Gabriela is the only daughter who is not married—and now she is thirty-seven!"

"*¡Mamá! ¡Por favor!*" Gabby interjected. "Things are going very well with Alejandro, but we are not rushing things . . . *¡Ay—ay—ay!*" She tossed her hands in the air in obvious frustration.

Kyra chuckled inwardly as she watched the interaction between mother and daughter. She enjoyed seeing Gabby being put on the spot by her adorable, but opinionated mamá. Not only was the family resemblance amazing, but Kyra could easily see where Gabby had inherited her outspoken personality.

When Carmen had exhausted her questions, she shooed the women from the kitchen, insisting they go relax with the rest of the family. A loud conversation was in full swing, but they all quickly turned their attention to their guest, filling her in on who's who in the big family. Children shouted as they ran about the living room, playing carefree and ignoring the adult conversation altogether.

Carlos, the eldest brother, was married to Maria, and they had three children. José, the second eldest, was married to Marta. They had been married for seven years, but as Marta had put it, they had not yet been "blessed with a family." They were, however, in the middle of the adoption process and hopeful it would go through soon. Sonia, the third eldest, was not at the lunch and lived in France with her husband, Philippe. They had two children. Gabby, as it turned out, was the fourth child—and, as her mamá had so carefully reminded them in the kitchen, unmarried. The fifth child, Mónica, was married to Sergio and their first child, a boy, had just turned six years old. Cristina, the sixth child, was married to Jorge, and she was in her last trimester of pregnancy with their first child. Lastly, there was Javier, the youngest son and seventh child who had married Verónica less than a year ago.

*Whew!* Kyra thought after getting the full rundown. The family background continued to unfold, but Kyra had a hard time keeping everything straight.

"I guess it would be tough to be the only single child in this family," she whispered so that only Gabby would hear. Her friend impishly replied a simple "*¡Sí!*" Kyra smiled as she translated this to mean "*duh!*" in English.

She noticed with some amazement how different Gabby's old-fashioned Spanish *familia*—or at least her mother—approached the idea of marriage. *So unlike the U.S. where marriage seems more of an option, if not almost a luxury, especially if you had a successful corporate career.* She kept these thoughts to herself as she chatted freely with the friendly but boisterous family members.

Almost an hour later, Carmen emerged from the kitchen, waving her hands. "*¡Por favor, por favor!*" she called out, signaling that it was time to take their places at the dining table.

An extra table had been set up in the kitchen for the children, and all of the adults sat in the main dining room. Once the family was seated, Carmen swiftly began placing platters of food on the main table. Carlos, in turn, filled everyone's glasses with wine and several decanters were placed around the table so that the glasses could be kept full at all times.

Kyra had never seen so much food in a single household—not even at the Shiva in Israel. The meal began with an appetizer of Spanish Serrano ham and various cheeses, as well as a savory seafood soup—or *sopa de pescado,* as Carmen had called it. A basket of freshly baked bread made its way around the table and was refilled several times, making sure everyone had plenty. Fresh asparagus drizzled in olive oil and vinegar turned out to be Kyra's favorite among the starters.

"This is simply divine," Kyra said between bites, but everyone was too busy eating to reply. There were just a lot of *mmmms* going around the table.

The main course included *mariscos,* shellfish with a light white wine sauce and white rice and a second dish called *cordero asado,* roast lamb. A salad along with more vegetables was passed around, and when Kyra was sure she'd bust out of her tight-fitting yellow sundress, Carmen served dessert.

She had certainly had *flan* before, a traditional Spanish custard topped with caramel sauce, but she had never tasted such a heavenly version of this decadent treat on her tongue. "Carmen, the *flan* is simply *mar-a-vil-loso* . . . and the best I've ever had!" Kyra said, slightly stumbling over her Spanish choice of words for "wonderful." She realized the free-flowing wine was going to her head and thought that she may want to slow down just a bit.

Following the meal, Eduardo stood up to make a toast to honor Kyra. Having imbibed a good deal of the wine himself, his English came out a bit broken, but Kyra appreciated his sweet effort. "*Keeyra*," he said, "thank you for coming to our *beau-ti-ful* city of Barcelona. We are very pleased to meet Gabriela's American friend after all of these years. *¡Salud!*"

Everyone around the table raised their glasses and said, "*¡Salud!*"

Eduardo then retook his seat, leaned back in his chair, and continued, "Let me tell you a little bit about *la historia de la familia*. It's important to understand where you come from, and our family has a very proud *her-i-tage*."

Gabby glanced over at Kyra with a funny look that read, "watch out," but Kyra couldn't quite figure out the meaning of her warning.

Eduardo continued speaking, "*Nuestra familia*—our family—is rather new to Barcelona, as we have only been in the *Cataluña* region for about twenty years, but moved here from Madrid. We are very *bendecidos*—uh, sorry, blessed to live here, but our ancestors are descended from none other than King Ferdinand and Queen Isabella!"

Kyra looked at Gabby, who rolled her eyes, and that's when her friend's warning began to make sense. She could not wait to hear the remainder of the story and quiz Gabby later about her royal heritage.

Eduardo continued, "You may recall from your history books, *Keeyra*, that King Ferdinand and Queen Isabella were one of the most famous royal couples in Spain's history. They lived back in the fifteenth century. They fought a *diez*—uh, ten—year *blood-i-est* battle with the Muslims in Granada to ultimately create a Christian unified Spain. Our bloodline can be directly traced to this very important couple! This is why our family is so genetically handsome and *inteligente*."

Gabby's sister Cristina let out a soft giggle as her father continued his story, and rubbed her stomach. "The baby is kicking—perhaps in agreement," she joked.

Eduardo wasn't deterred by the interruption and kept on with Kyra's history lesson. "And, of course, you remember that this couple also provided *financiación*—ah, financing—for a very famous sea captain named

Christopher Columbus. And you may recall that this captain sailed his ships across the Atlantic Ocean to discover America . . . but he was actually looking for the East Indies and really was a bit lost. Ah! It also did not end too well for Captain Columbus, because he was arrested and later filed suit against the Crown for compensation he never received. But I digress—that *loco marinero!*"

Kyra looked at Gabby and winked to say, *Now I understand.*

Gabby winked back, stifling her laughter.

Eduardo spoke for another forty-five minutes, and even though Kyra's head was dizzy from the wine, she listened closely as he explained the most recent five hundred years of the family history, including the move from Madrid to Barcelona. The information was interesting—if not entertaining—and Kyra injected an occasional "uh huh" or nodded her head to indicate her attention was fully vested in the conversation.

By the time the patriarch of the family excused himself from the table, it was nearly five in the evening. Now with *la comida* officially over, the men congregated in the living room, and the women gathered in the kitchen to clean up. The children resumed playing, running from room to room.

It was nearly 6:30 pm when Gabby rounded up Kyra, indicating it was time to go. Kyra gave Gabby's parents an affectionate goodbye hug and kiss on each cheek, fully embracing the custom, when they saw her to the front door. "I cannot express in words how much I have enjoyed meeting you today," she said with deep sincerity. "You have made me feel like such a special part of your *familia.*"

Carmen's eyes grew watery. "*Keeyra,* you have been such a delight—and we welcome you to come back to see us anytime, *mi querida.*"

Gabby leaned over to Kyra and explained, "*Mamá* just called you 'my dear' in Spanish." She then turned back to her mother. "Ah, *Mamá,* I love you so much," she said, and offered Carmen her final farewell, *muwahhh!*

Eduardo and the family waved from the doorway, as the women made their way down the hallway to the elevator. Kyra felt warm from head to toe, more from the love she felt emanating from these incredible people than from her many glasses of wine.

"So, is my *familia* crazy enough for you?" Gabby asked once they were back in the car on their way back to her apartment.

Kyra gave her friend a devious smile. "I had a blast, and uh, love your *familia!*" She slurred her words slightly. "I had no idea you came from such royalty either. I bow down my head to you in awe!" She did a mini curtsey with a sweep of her arm and a bow of her head, and in the process banged her forehead on the dashboard, but only barely. "Ouch!" she cried, which she followed up with an uncontrollable fit of laughter.

Gabby began laughing too. "*¿En serio?*"

As soon as they were back in the apartment, the friends promptly took an hour-and-a-half nap. They still had dinner plans to prepare for much later that evening. Kyra had already taken a catnap earlier, and a second nap in one day was something she had never indulged in before. Today, however, it seemed most appropriate. *I am on vacation after all,* she thought as she pulled back the top sheet. Drinking wine in the daytime was not the "norm" for her either. She heard Gabby let out a familiar loud snore as she turned out the light, and she fell fast asleep as soon as her head hit the pillow.

As the women primped themselves in Gabby's master bedroom for their night out, Gabby explained the details of the evening to Kyra. They would be meeting Alejandro and his friend for a light dinner at a restaurant around 9 pm—which would, of course, involve drinking more wine.

The nap had helped Kyra's head, but she wondered if she was even capable of having more food and wine that evening. She didn't voice her concerns and made a pact with herself to just go with the flow.

"*¡Bueno!* Since it's Saturday night, we will go out dancing afterward and enjoy some live music. Of course, you know the party doesn't start here until two am." Gabby watched her friend for a reaction.

Kyra realized how structured her life had been in San Francisco and how staying out past midnight on Saturday was an extravagant exception—especially since she typically worked the next day. "Oh my,

Gabby." she said with a laugh as she brushed her hair. "What trouble *will* we get into?"

Gabby deftly applied more lipstick and smacked her lips. "You haven't seen anything yet," she replied with a huge grin.

Getting into the spirit of Barcelona's nightlife, Kyra chose a tight-fitting red summer dress with gold high-heeled sandals, which complemented her hair. Gabby chose a striking white skirt, a black-and-white striped blouse, and bold red high-heeled shoes with a matching purse to finish out her look for the evening. Kyra thought her friend looked just stunning, and Gabby's approving look at Kyra told her that she thought the same about her.

"Alejandro and Francisco will be waiting for us at *Alkimia* in the *Gràcia Barrio* of Barcelona, so let's get going. It's just a ten-minute drive," Gabby said once they were ready.

Kyra grabbed her purse and followed Gabby out. "How coincidental that Alejandro's friend, Francisco, has the same name as my beautiful hometown."

With a twinkle in her eye, Gabby replied, "Yes, Francisco is *muy guapo*—that's handsome to you—just like San Francisco. You know, a name is very telling. For instance, the restaurant we're headed to is called *Alkimia.* It means 'alchemy' in Medieval Latin. Maybe this restaurant will transform you into gold."

"I think a little transformation is already underway for me. . . . and I *love* the name of the restaurant." Kyra grabbed her friend's arm as they walked to the car.

Once in the MINI Cooper, they headed slightly north to the Gràcia district and parked Gabby's car along a side street not too far from the restaurant. Alejandro and Francisco were already waiting at the bar per Alejandro's text message to Gabby earlier.

When they walked inside, Kyra admired the sleek and contemporary decor of soft beige walls and white tablecloths. A white crescent light fixture hung overhead, contrasting nicely with the red-and-black benches and the bold, colorful artwork hanging on the walls.

Kyra turned to Gabby with wide eyes. "Our clothing matches the restaurant perfectly! What a wonderful coincidence."

Gabby laughingly responded, "Ah, there are no coincidences in life."

As they headed toward Alejandro and Francisco, Kyra watched with pleasant delight as Alejandro's eyes lit up when they fell upon Gabby. He moved quickly toward her, caught her in a hug, and placed a passionate kiss on her lips. They were obviously very much in love. When they reluctantly parted, Gabby introduced him to Kyra, and he responded by hugging Kyra in greeting and gave her a kiss on each cheek.

"Kyra, I'd like to introduce my very best friend, Francisco. He's originally from Madrid. Francisco, this is Kyra from the U.S."

Kyra couldn't help but notice how very handsome both men were, which fit her first impression of the men of Spain in general—physically attractive and charming. Alejandro was of average height, but standing next to Gabby, he looked perfectly matched, almost like her mirror image. He had thick dark wavy hair and a similar dazzling smile, which he did not spare when he looked at Gabby.

Francisco, by comparison, was much taller, with beautiful deep-set dark eyes that almost seemed to sparkle when he looked at her. Kyra was taken back by the charm he exuded.

Kyra's companion for the evening stepped forwarded with an affectionate greeting. Her hand tingled when he brushed against it as he reached out to embrace her. She was momentarily surprised by the sensation, not having expected to feel anything. *With Nana's passing and just ending things with Steve, being attracted to a man is the furthest thing from my mind . . . but, oh my, this man is captivating*, she thought breaking into a smile despite herself.

She managed a few polite words, but found herself staring at Francisco when Alejandro asked how she was enjoying her visit to Spain so far. Gabby noticed the blank look on Kyra's face and quickly interrupted to save her friend from embarrassment. "There will be time for talk later! Let's order some wine first, *mi amor.*"

Francisco took the lead and ordered a bottle of Rioja red wine. The friends would enjoy a *copa de vino* while they were waiting to be seated.

Once the wine had been poured, Francisco turned his undivided attention to Kyra. With an intense gaze, he said, "You look very beautiful this evening—very beautiful." Kyra felt pleasantly taken aback by the double compliment and wondered if her expression gave away her surprise, but Francisco continued speaking just the same. "It's such a pleasure to meet Gabriela's friend."

Kyra blushed, turning a similar shade to the red wine she was attempting to consume and clumsily hit the glass with her hand after she placed it back on the bar. With a lightning-quick move, Francisco caught the glass midair before it had completely tipped over. His alluring smile momentarily took her breath away.

She took a deep breath and responded with embarrassment, "Oh my, Francisco, the wine must be going straight to my head this evening! Umm . . . your compliment is very sweet . . . thank you so much. I must admit you are very handsome, too."

Kyra's eyes widened. She could not believe those words had just escaped her lips. She'd never been so direct when speaking to a man, and almost blushed a second time. She quickly changed the focus by adding, "But . . . uh, I'd love to learn more about you. Tell me, what do you enjoy doing for fun when you are not working?"

Francisco laughed lightheartedly at her flirtatious comment and then filled her in on many of the pleasures he enjoyed. He went on to describe boating, scuba diving, wine tasting, soccer games, art museums, and weekend trips to simply explore the many wonderful cities in Spain. Their conversation just seemed to flow, as did the glasses of wine as they waited for their table.

Gabby leaned in close to Kyra so she wouldn't be overheard. "I think you haven't given Steve a single thought this evening. I'm so proud of you for getting your *flirt on!*"

Kyra was enjoying her renewed confidence and getting her "flirt on," as Gabby put it. "I am looking forward to dating again," she confided. "I think this is exactly what I needed to ease back into the dating scene . . . and, *oh my*, Francisco is a handsome man."

Both women broke out in laughter, causing Alejandro and Francisco to turn toward them quizzically. There was no time to explain because their table was ready.

"Saved by the waiter," Gabby joked, and the foursome headed to their table.

When they were seated, the waiter attentively took their order, and shortly afterward the food began to arrive. Kyra didn't think she could possibly eat another bite after the huge lunch. But eat more food she most certainly did, getting caught up in the amazingly scrumptious and magical experience.

The conversation flowed, and Gabby and Kyra filled the men in on how they'd first met. Kyra then spoke briefly about her work history, but also entertained her tablemates with vivid descriptions of San Francisco and the beach and Muir Woods.

A salad started off their meal—thick slices of farm-fresh tomatoes with dollops of cucumber sorbet flavored with lemon verbena on top. Next Kyra had the Blue Seafood Bouillabaisse, while Francisco enjoyed fresh Mackerel Tartar with Caviar. Gabby and Alejandro shared an order of Glazed Pork and Oyster, which came on a bed of spinach. A second dish of Celery Ravioli with Black Truffle was to "die for," as they all agreed, and it was shared among the table.

All the while the food was coming, they continued to tell stories from their past, getting to know one another. Kyra kept watching how attentive Alejandro was to Gabby and felt truly happy for her friend. She secretly allowed the loving feeling to flow through her, deciding for now she was content to just enjoy her date for the evening.

To accompany their main course, Alejandro ordered a nice pairing of the Spanish sparkling wine called *Cava*, which was served with their dinner entrées. Then, to complete their feast, Gabby ordered dessert—a refreshing palate cleanser of Rhubarb Yogurt with Lemon Cream.

When the meal was finally over, Kyra admitted, "I don't know where I've managed to put all this food tonight! I'm so appreciative of this evening out tonight with all of you. Thank you!"

"Ah, it is our pleasure, *mi dulce y bella amiga,*" Francisco said, his eyes resting on Kyra's face.

Amazed by how intuitively she seemed to recall her high school Spanish, Kyra translated his words to mean "my sweet beautiful friend." She knew her eyes were sparkling at the flirty compliment and gave Francisco an affectionate smile in return.

"Thank you, Francisco. I can see that my friend Gabby has told you I'm trying to refresh my Spanish skills," she responded, giving her girlfriend a slight kick under the table.

Gabby let out a loud *"¡Ay!"* and the friends shared a laugh.

The leisurely dinner finally ended around 11:30 pm.

Once the check was paid, Alejandro stood. "The night is not yet over, my friends!" he said. "Let's go to *Plaça de Sol* in the *Gràcia* district. It's very lively this time of night, and we'll make a stop for a nightcap. We'll follow you ladies back to your apartment, Gabby, and then we'll take one car."

Francisco stood up next, helping Kyra out of her chair. She swayed slightly and felt his firm, comforting grip on her bare elbow. She shivered.

"That sounds wonderful," she said, keeping her voice steady. "Lead the way!" With that, she laughed. She hadn't felt this free in a very long time and was simply grateful to let her guard down. *What did Gabby call that?* she tried to recall. *Oh yes, I'm feeling more like my authentic self.* She grinned at the thought, feeling the wine going to her head.

# 12

The narrow streets of Gràcia were lined with shops and outdoor cafes that were just starting to awaken at the midnight hour. Kyra observed that the area was more culturally diverse compared to the upscale avenue of Passeig de Gràcia in Eixample where Gabby lived. The crowd had an almost a Bohemian flair, with some of the locals sporting piercings, dreadlocks, and even tattoos.

As they walked into the main square, Kyra turned to Francisco, his eyes alight with the nightlife. "This is such a cool place and much less touristy, which is kind of nice. . . . Although, on second thought," she added with a sheepish grin, "I am a tourist, so I can't complain too much about them." Francisco smiled in response. His gaze was intense, and she could feel her heart pounding. "Well, thank you for bringing me here . . . with you," she added, somewhat awkwardly.

Francisco's smile widened. "Ah, the evening is still young. *¡Brillas como la luna llena!*" With that, he took Kyra's hand in his own, and she felt a tingly jolt travel up her arm. If she understood Francisco correctly, he had just said that she "radiated like the light of the moon." She was thoroughly enjoying her date with this handsome, charming man.

The couples first stopped at Elèctric Bar, a casual neighborhood bar with a young crowd. "Bohemian chic and concert hall all in one! I love it here," Kyra declared.

*"Sí, mi hermosa Kyra,"* Francisco replied, "and the live music in the back lounge is magnificent."

Kyra felt her heart shine brighter each time Francisco called her "beautiful." Her growing confidence at accepting his compliments made her feel proud of herself. Gabby gave her a knowing look, as Francisco guided her along with a strong hand resting on the small of her back.

"This is a place where the locals hang out," Gabby explained. "Alejandro and I come here often."

"It's almost like being in your best friend's living room," Kyra commented as the foursome settled into comfortable lounge chairs around a small cocktail table.

A small band played a Spanish variation of jazz music, while an attractive female singer with flowing red hair wailed soulfully in her native Spanish tongue. The waitress took their drink order, but soon the friends began to realize the music was too loud for comfortable conversation. They mostly exchanged smiles, enjoying the ambience and the lively music for a while. Kyra had finally finished her cocktail while her friends finished their second, and then they ushered her off to the next place. It was nearly 1:30 in the morning when they made their last stop at a place called L'Entresòl.

As the foursome walked inside, Gabby piped up, "You will ADORE this place! *L'Entresòl* is the trendiest bar in *Gràcia.*"

Kyra giggled at Gabby's exaggerated enunciation. *The cocktails are most certainly taking effect*, she realized, feeling a bit lightheaded too. Francisco's steadying hand was ever helpful, and she felt him guide her inside by the elbow.

Kyra soaked in the contemporary design of the crowded bar, admiring its gleaming red countertops. Bright neon lights of yellow and blue created a trendy, upbeat atmosphere. "This place is the PERFECT way to end a PERFECT evening!" she said, as the dizzying effects of the alcohol took over.

"*¡Sí, sí!* I knew you would LOVE it!" Gabby said, her words coming out louder than she probably intended.

"Girls," said Alejandro, "if I may suggest, let's have one of their '*bebidas especiales*'—the drink is made with Tanqueray Rangpur gin. It's a delicious work of art made with limes and a green tea infusion."

*"Maravilloso!"* Gabby shouted. "*Chica*, you MUST try one."

"How can I resist?" Kyra asked, waving her hand in agreement. "But . . . this is my FINAL cocktail for tonight!"

In record time, Francisco handed Kyra the interesting concoction, which she graciously accepted. He turned back to the bartender to square away the bill. As the men waited for the bartender to return, Kyra and Gabby snuck off to the restroom to freshen up their makeup. Kyra's ears were still ringing from the music. She leaned across the vanity, her words exaggerated, "Gabby, I am very EXCITED to see you so happy! It's easy to see how much Alejandro ADORES you just by the way he looks at you. And you are very lucky to have him in your life—not to mention how RIDICULOUSLY attractive he is too!"

"Ah, I can you tell you this!" Gabby responded. "No way was I expecting to meet MI AMOR . . . I mean Alejandro. He just showed up in my life! But I will let you in on a little secret . . . if you promise not to say ANYTHING to ANYONE."

"Oh, Gabby, you can trust me!" Kyra assured her friend.

Gabby went on, "Alejandro and I are talking about getting married! . . . BUT I don't want to tell *Mamá* just yet! She will pressure us for an exact date. We just have not planned things out quite that far . . . But when we do make the announcement, *Chica,* YOU are coming back to Barcelona for the wedding! How does that sound?"

"I wouldn't miss it for the WORLD!" Kyra exclaimed, stumbling a bit as she moved toward Gabby to give her a huge proper Spanish kiss on both cheeks. *Muwahhh! Muwahhh!* They giggled at their silliness as they headed back into the crowd.

When they managed to make their way back to Alejandro and Francisco, Gabby grabbed Alejandro's hand to lead the way to the dance floor, with Francisco and Kyra close at their heels.

Kyra danced with total abandonment, not caring how foolish she may have looked or acted. Glancing up at Francisco's smiling face, she thought, *Sometimes you just have to let your hair down and enjoy the moment!* In fact, they all were being silly and simply having a fun time.

"We are acting like we are still in our early twenties!" Gabby exclaimed, throwing her arms up in the air when her favorite song came on.

Alejandro leaned over and replied in Gabby's ear, but loud enough for their friends to hear, "*¡Ah mi amor!* You look like you are in your twenties and you have stolen my heart!"

Gabby grinned from ear to ear.

Meanwhile, Kyra enjoyed the way Francisco's body moved on the dance floor. She reached out and held his hand as they swayed to the music. She felt like she could dance forever. But, by the time 3:30 am rolled around, the group agreed it was time to call it a night.

On the way out, Kyra turned back to the bar and exclaimed dramatically, "*L'Entresòl* I will miss you! I had SO MUCH fun tonight!"

She was still basking in the glow of the wonderful evening when the couples were back on the sidewalk in front of Gabby's apartment building. She and Francisco looked on awkwardly as their friends shared a passionate kiss goodnight.

When Kyra turned to say goodbye to Francisco, he leaned in for a kiss. His lips were soft and the kiss was brief, but a tingling sensation raced through Kyra's body. Desperately hoping Francisco didn't see the look of shock on her face, she tried to hide her unexpected feelings.

Francisco laughed and embraced her in a friendly manner. "Kyra," he said, "this has been an amazing night. I'm happy to have had this time with you. Enjoy the rest of your trip. I hope we stay in touch."

Her face aglow, Kyra thanked him again for the wonderful evening. She then exchanged a hug with Alejandro before she and Gabby headed inside the building. As she attempted to make her way through the front door, Kyra tripped and let out a howling laugh. "Oh my!" she cried, and the others joined her in laughter too.

The women giggled from the elevator all the way to Gabby's door. Once inside the apartment, Kyra practically shouted, "I had a fabulous night! I've eaten WAY too much, drank WAY too much, and met WAY too many handsome men tonight!" Her ears were still abuzz from the evening's entertainment. She giggled. "You know, the truth is, Gabby, I haven't let my guard down like that, since . . . uh, well, never!"

Gabby slid off her shoes and plopped down on the white couch. "It was MARAVILLOSO seeing you enjoying yourself so much, *Chica*."

Kyra took off her shoes too, a little clumsily. "Yes, I did! . . . And I never dreamed I'd end up in Spain on such an amazing adventure! I love you, Gabby."

And with that, a rather inebriated Kyra stood up and waved a kiss goodnight—with a loud *muwahhh*—into the air. She quickly made her way to the study where the small bed awaited her and shimmied out of her dress. She didn't even remember falling asleep.

It was 10:10 am when Kyra looked at the clock the next morning. Her head was spinning, but the strong *café con leche* Gabby had waiting for her started to bring her senses back around. When they sat down, Gabby pointed out that, considering how late they'd been out the night before, meeting in the kitchen before noon for a morning cup of coffee was pretty impressive.

They sipped the hot liquid at the small kitchen table until Gabby finally broke the silence: "We missed morning mass at church today. But we can join my family and Alejandro tonight at evening mass—if you are up for it."

"Church?" Kyra asked, thinking back to the last time she'd been in a church, which she was guessing was over five years ago. "Sure."

A light flashed in Gabby's eyes. "First us girls will have a fun day in the city. You'll get to see some of the phenomenal architecture, and we'll have lunch somewhere charming. How does *that* sound?"

Kyra took another slow sip of her café con leche and replied, "You don't stop for a moment, do you?" Smiling, she continued, "I'd love nothing more than to see your wonderful city today—and your *loca* family tonight at church. Truth is . . . I adore your family," she said quietly, still nursing her hangover.

The friends enjoyed an unhurried morning of sipping several cups of café con leche and had a light breakfast of *bollo dulce,* sweet rolls with jam. Kyra thought she may need to slow down a bit on her food consumption, but she was hopeful that walking around the city would burn off some of the extra calories she'd consumed the day before. She told Gabby as much.

"But on second thought," she said a bit mischievously, "I've actually lost weight these past few weeks with everything that's happened, so perhaps an extra *bollo* is needed this morning." With a smile, she grabbed a second sweet roll from the dish.

Later, they dressed in comfortable clothing for the day out in the city—colorful summer skirts, tank tops, light sweaters, and low sandals for walking. It was already late June, and Gabby mentioned the temps would be around 26 degrees Celsius, which Kyra quickly translated to 79 degrees Fahrenheit. She grabbed a bottle of sunscreen for protection.

Once the friends finished getting ready for their adventure, Gabby filled Kyra in on their itinerary. "The weather is perfect for all the walking we'll be doing today! We will be heading to *Las Ramblas*, which runs through the center of Barcelona and divides two neighborhoods *El Gótic* where my parents live and *El Raval*. Anyway, *Las Ramblas* is a very dynamic series of streets and one of the most famous areas in the city. There are beautiful flower stands, cafes and shops, street performers, and artists. . . . Then we'll make our way to the Liceu Theatre, which *es muy famoso* for its world-class opera and ballet!" Gabby enunciated "very famous" in Spanish, teasing her friend to perfect her language skills. "Then we'll finish our day with a little upscale shopping in my neighborhood on *Passeig de Gràcia*. And, last but not least, we'll meet my family for evening mass."

"That sounds like a fantastic plan," Kyra said, looking forward to the new experiences. "I can't wait to see Barcelona in the daylight!"

# 13

Kyra and Gabby arrived at Las Ramblas quickly on foot, as the area was only a short twenty minutes from Gabby's apartment. They walked side by side, strolling along the streets and simply enjoying the wonderful sights and smells of the area.

Just as Gabby had described, there were quaint newspaper stands offering both local and national news, along with the latest fashion magazines and souvenirs, too. Small cafes caught their attention with the tantalizing aromas of tapas, coffee, and sweet pastries. Each offered a unique smell that wafted delicately into the air, delighting their noses as they drifted past each specialty shop.

The streets were also filled with colorful flower stands, each one loaded with freshly cut bouquets ready for purchase. Kyra's eye caught a bunch of lovely pink roses, and she stopped to smell them. She brushed a rose bud to the tip of her nose, and a young man at the stand offered Kyra a single red carnation, saying in Catalan, the local language, "*Per la senyoreta bonica.*"

"For the beautiful lady," Gabby translated, but Kyra had understood. Kyra laughed, took the carnation, and offered the young man a tip.

"You know, Gabby, I am so enjoying these men of Spain," she said, as they walked on. "It reminds me how much romance was lacking in my relationship with Steve. And, truthfully, seeing you and Alejandro together makes me realize that I want a romantic and passionate relationship, I might add . . . not a convenient relationship like the one I just had. You are *so* teaching me things, girlfriend!"

Gabby chuckled softly. "I'm always glad to be of service my beautiful friend. You will have what Alejandro and I have, for certain. You just need to be open to it."

Kyra thought about that for a moment, knowing Gabby was right.

"Hmmm, are you hungry, *Chica?* I'm ready for a snack. Let's go eat some tapas!"

*More food?* thought Kyra a little warily, as Gabby led her to one of the neighborhood tapas bars. And despite Kyra's initial protest, Gabby ordered each of them a glass of wine.

Kyra sipped slowly as she reviewed the menu. Gabby's translations helped her decide which tapas to order—a few of the more traditional items. Gabby left the task of placing the order to Kyra for practice.

Trying her best to sound confident in her pronunciation, Kyra said to the young waiter, "I'd like to order *calamares* with fresh sliced lemons. *¿Por favor?* And a plate of *aceitunas y queso*. And an order of *patatas bravas*—potatoes with that wonderful spicy tomato Brava sauce."

The waiter smiled smugly at her attempt, but soon returned with the small plates, which the friends practically inhaled.

"*¡Bueno!*" Gabby said, when the last bite of food was gone. "Are you leaving room for our lunch at two today?"

Kyra let out an amused sigh. "I think I will need to do a *whole* lot more walking before I eat any more today."

"No worries! There's plenty more walking ahead of us," Gabby assured her.

They resumed their stroll through the streets of Las Ramblas, when they stumbled upon a dazzling array of street performers, the likes of which Kyra had never seen before. Mimes with their stark white faces and bright red lips made comical exaggerated expressions as the women walked by, and talented musicians strummed their guitars for admirers. Small tips in nearby baskets were their only form of compensation for their talented entertainment.

"Oh, look at that!" Kyra said pointing toward a woman dressed in an old-fashioned flowing dress and floppy hat. The woman was holding a single long-stemmed flower in her hand. She, her clothing, and the flower were covered from head to toe in silver paint—and she stood completely still, frozen like a statue. Kyra studied the surreal vision, watching for the slightest flicker of life. "What an amazing human work of art . . . but so spooky."

Gabby leaned over to drop a coin in the woman's basket. "Yes, my friend—almost like a carnival!"

Kyra pulled her eyes away from the mesmerizing street performer. After another fifteen minutes or so, they came across a colorful fabric-covered booth, in front of which a fortune-teller sat in a small folding chair. She was a striking woman with dark, fiery eyes, dressed in a gown of purple and gold with a matching scarf wound tightly around her head. Her thick, dark hair cascaded loosely below the scarf, and she appeared to be in her late-fifties. As Kyra walked by, the woman caught her attention and waved excitedly. "*¡Mejor será que le lea el futuro!*"

She repeated the phrase several times urgently, and Gabby finally translated. "That's strange . . . She keeps saying that you *need* to have your fortune told. Of course we can keep walking if you'd like."

Normally Kyra would have walked right on by, but for some odd reason, she found herself hesitating. She met the woman's eyes directly. The fortune-teller seemed quite serious, and the tone of her voice sounded sincere. Kyra didn't really believe that the future could be foretold, but she was on vacation and her instincts urged her to listen to what the woman had to say.

"What harm could possibly come of it?" she said. "You know, Gabby, I can't say I've ever had my fortune read before. I've always just made my own decisions. It's only fifteen euros after all. Will you indulge me?"

"Yes, I'm all in. But watch your wallet. There are many pickpockets and con artists here in *Las Ramblas*. You cannot be too careful." Gabby paused for a moment, then said decidedly, "I'll translate. Let's see what good fortune she has in store for you."

Kyra and Gabby stepped inside the small booth, the air inside a bit stuffy, and sat down in the flimsy folding chairs. After closing the hanging drape to give her clients privacy, the woman took a seat directly across from them. She inhaled deeply and closed her eyes, as if in meditation. Then her eyes flashed open. She handed Kyra a worn deck of Tarot cards instructing her to shuffle them and then to cut the deck into three piles. Gabby translated this process into English so that Kyra could comply.

Once the deck was cut, the fortune-teller flipped several of the cards face up, one by one, onto the table in a cross pattern. Kyra glanced at the cards with great curiosity, wondering what they meant.

The mysterious woman studied the cards for a few moments before beginning to speak. Gabby translated: "These cards represent your past. You have had a death recently in your family. Someone you loved very much, yes? She is always with you, and she wants you to know that she never leaves you . . . She calls you *Hon-ey*." The fortune-teller had overpronounced this English word, clearly unaware of its meaning. She paused for a moment, then continued speaking, "She is saying something else in a foreign language, but I cannot understand the words. I keep hearing Anna. Perhaps you called her Anna or a name sounds like Anna."

Kyra's throat went dry. *Oh my . . . she's saying Nana!* She simply nodded at the woman, unable to speak.

"I can *feel* how much she loves you," the fortune-teller said, pointing to her heart, indicating she felt Kyra's grandmother's love for her there.

Wide-eyed in astonishment, Gabby continued translating, trying not to miss a word. The woman looked back down at the cards again and continued, "These cards represent your current situation. You are going through many changes? Yes? . . . Changes that affect *everything* in your life. It's like you are a baby, and everything old has been stripped away from you—a new beginning for you. It may not look this way to you right now, but this is very good change and will make more sense to you later."

Gabby and Kyra exchanged a startled glance. The fortune-teller looked down a third time at the cards and said, "These cards represent your future. I see you on a journey to another land—a lush green place—and a mountain of spiritual importance. The mountain is of great significance to you—a spiritual journey of sorts? Yes, I see it!"

She paused to look deeply into Kyra's tearing eyes. "Ah, but you will also be visited by a spirit too," she said. "She is around you now. It is a different female than the one who passed over recently. This female is very close to you too, and she is desperately trying to get a message through to you. Do you see her?"

Kyra shrugged her shoulders, unsure of what to make of the premonition.

The fortune-teller waved Kyra's uncertainly away with her bejeweled hand. "If not, you will soon . . . She visits you in your dreams, but you do not remember when you wake up. She says you are very tired and need to rest. Once you are rested—and more open—she will visit you again."

The fortune-teller paused again to gaze at the cards before resuming. "I see a short journey ahead of you . . . a new path in front of you. It looks misty and dream-like. I see the color pale yellow—no beige—rocks perhaps? It's a walkway—maybe pebbles? The path is winding and dark at first, but you will see the *Light* at the end of the path. A new direction for you. It is your destiny—karma, as you call it. This is very good." Several moments passed before she concluded, "That's all I can see right now." The woman went silent.

Kyra felt stunned . . . not just by the fortune-teller's messages, but by the eerie feeling that the vision she had described was familiar to her. Her neck hairs stood on end, and her mind raced in an effort to remember something that felt too vague to grasp. It was reminiscent of a dream she'd had as a child, but she struggled to recall it.

"How will I know where the mountain is located? How will I find it?" she asked, and Gabby translated.

The fortune-teller replied, "When the time is right, you will know where to go."

Kyra had a thousand more questions, but the fortune-teller didn't have any more answers to give. Despite feeling intensely curious, she finally thanked the woman for the reading and paid the fee, adding a generous tip.

As they stood up from the table, Kyra looked at Gabby's ashen face, and she knew she probably looked the same. And then she did something unexpected. She let out a loud laugh—wondering why she had tried to suppress the laugh at all. They exited the booth into the early afternoon sunlight.

"Are you alright?" Gabby asked with concern, the color returning to her face.

Kyra looked at her friend and realized for the very first time in her life, she *was* all right. She felt inspired that something good lay ahead for her. She had no idea what that good was, but she would prepare herself to receive it—and not by seeking it out, but by allowing the Universe to show her the right direction, the right path.

*Yes,* Kyra thought, *I will take time to rest.* But, more important, she decided that instead of trying to control things, she would trust and believe that the Universe would somehow guide her to go exactly where she needed to be. That was something she had never done before. Kyra understood for the first time in her life that everything would simply unfold the way it was supposed to.

So, when Gabby asked if she was alright, she had laughed, because she had always so carefully planned every detail of her life. And now—of all things—a fortune-teller in the middle of Spain had inspired her to look at her life from a different perspective—not at the CEO of a company, not a colleague, and not *The Wall Street Journal!*

She met her friend's eyes firmly and responded, "I feel great! Let's just keep walking and see where our path leads us." She gave Gabby a playful tug on her arm.

"I'm not sure what just happened," Gabby responded, "but I need a glass of *vino* to calm my nerves. They're jumping all over the place!" Then, under her breath, she added, "*¡Ay—ay—ay!*"

She grabbed Kyra's arm and led her to a place where they could get a glass of wine, which was quickly delivered . . . and quickly swallowed. After gulping down her last sip of *Rioja tinto*, Gabby said with renewed cheer, "Okay, I think I'll live. . . . But seriously now, let's go to the *Gran Teatre del Liceu*—the Liceu Theatre, as promised. You'll *love* it; it's famous for its world-class opera and ballet performances. It's nearby."

"I'm so glad your nerves are settled," Kyra said, teasing her friend and tucking away the experience with the fortune-teller in the back of her mind for now. "You know how much I love the arts, and I'm ready for whatever comes our way!"

They walked down the main street, Las Rambles, toward the theater and arrived quickly. Gabby suggested a guided tour, which was offered in English. As Kyra listened to the docent speak with much zeal, she soaked in all the interesting history. She learned that the theater had been built in the mid-1800s, but fires had twice damaged it, with the last one in 1994 almost destroying it completely. But after its reconstruction, Gran Teatre del Liceu was now one of the largest of opera houses in all of Europe.

Kyra loved the theater's horseshoe-shaped layout with five levels of seating that reached almost to the ceiling. In awe, she murmured, "I can't believe there are *fifteen thousand* season ticket holders for this theater! Barcelona does love its arts, it seems. This place is massive."

Gabby nodded in agreement. "I love the ornate design. I know I normally lean toward contemporary, but you have to admit, the color scheme fits my style—*rojo* and *blanco!*" Gabby indicated to the red theater seats and walls, which contrasted stunningly with the ivory balconies.

As Kyra admired the gilding that decorated the walls, she had a grandiose thought that she could almost hear Jules Massenet's *Cléopâtre* being performed on the huge stage. She envisioned all of the elaborate costumes for the performance and her imagination listened to the mezzo-soprano sing to perfection. It truly was a magnificent venue, and she felt honored to be there.

When the tour was complete and Kyra's head had been filled with visions of past grand performances—they headed back to Gabby's apartment. This was Kyra's second day in Barcelona, and thankfully she wasn't feeling a bit of fatigue. After the long flight and the adventures of the day before, she'd expected she'd be ready to take a break, but when Gabby suggested they go shopping, she eagerly agreed.

"How can I resist?" she said, remembering her ride from the airport to Gabby's place and passing some of the most prestigious shops in the world—Chanel, Gucci, Louis Vuitton, Valentino, Hermès, Prada and more.

After several hours, which included a break for the "big lunch" Gabby had promised, they made their tenth stop to look at the newest fashion and try on some of the clothing. "Gabby, you do have a passion for shopping," Kyra joked.

"And you are more of a spectator, *Chica!* You need to catch up with me," Gabby teased, as she modeled a couture Chanel gown in pale pink that shimmered iridescent in the soft lighting of the store.

Kyra laughed. "I am more of a spectator in support of your shopping spree! I love that dress on you."

Truth be told, Kyra preferred more comfortable clothing for outdoor activities over the high-end couture fashion. But it was entertaining to watch Gabby try on a ton of clothing in each of the shops they visited—and then to watch her purchase only a single, albeit expensive, Hermès silk scarf for work.

Kyra finally felt the two days catching up with her. "Okay, you've worn me out with this shopping extravaganza! I need a proper *siesta* if I'm going to keep up with you tonight."

"No worries. I have worn myself out, too!" Gabby exclaimed, handing the clothes she'd just tried on back to the sales associate. "You know, I didn't really need a thing, but this was fun, wasn't it?"

Kyra rolled her eyes in mock exasperation and gave her friend an affectionate kiss on the cheek. Again, they headed back to Gabby's apartment, arm in arm, to freshen up for the 6 pm services at the church in El Gótic. Alejandro would be arriving in less than forty-five minutes to pick them up.

"*Chica*, I really hope you don't mind attending evening mass with my parents," Gabby said, as they washed up in the bathroom side by side. "Alejandro and I don't actually attend church regularly, but because we have a guest in town—and you from the United States nonetheless—my parents thought it would be *maravilloso* for us to go to mass together. We can walk around for a bit afterward and get a bite to eat. Does that sound okay?"

Kyra made a motion as if it were nothing. "Your parents were so loving and hospitable yesterday, it's the least I can do. You know, I attended church regularly as a child. My father, who was Catholic, was adamant that I go every Sunday, but you remember my mother was Jewish."

"I do recall you telling me that . . . and it must have been a bit of a contentious spot in their relationship, no?" Gabby asked with compassion. "It must have been difficult for you to be in the middle."

Kyra sighed. "I think I didn't know any better. Being in the middle was my norm, I guess. Anyway, I started going to church less and less once I threw myself into my studies. Then, later, when I began working those eighty-plus hour weeks, I didn't have a lot of time for church on Sundays . . . or much of anything else. Maybe I should have gone more often."

But before Gabby could comment, Kyra went on, "I did make it a point to go to the beach almost every Sunday morning to meditate for a moment of peace sitting on the sand. It's my own special way of connecting to God, I think. I really enjoy just being in nature with the ocean waves rolling onto the shoreline and feeling the warm sunlight on my face. It makes me feel more grounded and closer to God in some ways than sitting in church. I always give thanks for everything in my life . . . and I say a prayer for everyone who I think is in need. But tonight I am grateful to go to mass with you and your parents. I may even be long overdue for a confession, too," Kyra said, adding a little levity to her admission.

"Yes, a little confession is good for the soul," Gabby responded playfully. Then she added more seriously, "I know that God has a plan for you—God has a plan for *everyone.*"

# 14

Dressed in simple sundresses but looking stunning nonetheless, Gabby and Kyra met Alejandro on the street at 5:30 pm for the short drive to El Gótic.

"We are meeting at the *Catedral de la Santa Cruz y Santa Eulàlia*, which translated into English means The Cathedral of the Holy Cross and Saint Eulàlia—but this wonderful church is more simply known as the Barcelona Cathedral," Gabby explained.

"That's easy for you to say," Kyra said, poking fun at herself.

As they drove up to the church, Kyra could see why Gabby's parents had chosen this church for the services tonight. The Gothic-style architecture was simply magnificent and stunning. Kyra had read in her guidebook that the church had been constructed mostly during the thirteenth through fifteenth centuries. But, while the church did indeed have a most ornate and formidable-looking exterior, it reminded her of a castle from a childhood fairytale.

"Oh my, you two—what an *amazing* building! I can't wait to go inside," she declared, stepping out of the car. Then, unable to resist sharing her inner thoughts, she added, "It kind of looks like a fairytale castle."

Alejandro responded with a smile, "*Sí,* Kyra. You will be impressed by the interior. The dazzling ceilings and amazing chapels are magnificent. But we'll have to wait to see if Prince Charming shows up for mass this evening."

Kyra blushed, and Gabby chuckled, as the trio walked briskly up the gray stone steps. The women found themselves facing two huge, intricately carved wooden doors, which Alejandro pulled open. Kyra was the first to pass through the threshold. She stopped for a moment to gaze up at the church's gorgeous interior, and her sudden stop caused

Gabby to bump into her back. The women shared a brief snicker, but quickly smothered any other silliness in the sanctity of their surroundings, next dipping their fingers in the holy water and making the sign of the cross.

It *was* exquisite, just as Alejandro had promised. Huge stained-glass windows reached up to the top of dramatically high ceilings. Two huge octagonal bell towers reached heights of more than 175-feet tall. A massive gilded wooden organ played intense, melodic music, while churchgoers took their seats.

They walked around the interior for a few minutes prior to the service. Kyra couldn't believe the number of ornate and gilded chapels that lined the exterior walls of the great church. Each one was dedicated to a different saint, but the inscriptions were in a language she couldn't fully translate.

Alejandro explained in a polite whisper, "The patron saint here is St. *Eulàlia*. She was martyred at age thirteen—I believe around 300 A.D."

Kyra shivered, feeling sadness that such a young girl had been tortured for her beliefs. As Alejandro continued, she allowed that sadness to fade and focused instead on the beauty of her surroundings.

"There are close to *veintiocho*—ah, I mean *twenty-eight*—individual chapels in this church." He stretched out his arm to indicate the expansiveness. "We should have time for a quick look at the Cloister, which is famous for the Well of the Geese and the thirteen geese living there that represent the age at which our saint was martyred. St. *Eulàlia*'s remains were moved to this cathedral around the fourteenth century—and more than *one thousand* years after her death." Alejandro nodded toward the front of the church. "You can see her crypt is behind the main altar, where we will be seated for the evening mass."

"You're quite knowledgeable, Alejandro," Kyra replied, keeping her voice low as well. "It must be amazing to live in a place with such a rich and interesting history."

Gabby motioned for them to follow her for a quick step outside the building and into the Cloister courtyard. Kyra's gaze traveled upward along the building, and her eyes rested on a myriad of stone gargoyles, depicting a variety of animals. Her curiosity piqued, she asked, "What's the significance of gargoyles?"

After a thoughtful pause, Alejandro replied, "I'm not sure of their full meaning, but I do know that they direct rainwater off the roof through their open mouths. Look now and you can see the water trickling down the stone wall." Alejandro pointed to one of the tiny-winged dragon-shaped gargoyles.

Kyra noticed a light rain shower had begun and watched the water gently trickling across the tongues of the gargoyles, making its way down to the stone courtyard below. She thought it was fascinating that such mischievous-looking creatures could actually serve a functional and orderly purpose.

"*Chica*, those statues gave me nightmares when I was a child! My *papá* used to tease me about them, and they give me shivers even now," Gabby added, sounding both nervous and amused.

Kyra agreed that they were indeed a spooky sight, but told her friend with assuredness, "It's always good to let go of our fears, Gabby . . . and I definitely can appreciate that lesson."

When they stepped back inside the church and entered the main sanctuary, Eduardo and Carmen joined them. Looking a bit frustrated and out of breath, Carmen gave Gabby and Kyra a quick hug and kiss on each cheek.

"*Gabriela, lo sentimos mucho*—we are sorry we are late; the service is just about to start." Carmen turned to Kyra. "*Keeyra*, it is fantastic to see you again! We will speak more after mass *esta noche*—ah, tonight! Eduardo let's be seated. *¡Siéntate!* I mean *sit!* We are late!"

The services began just as they settled in the pew. Kyra listened carefully to the priest, trying to improve her ability to understand the language. But, as the priest went on, she found herself daydreaming about attending church as a child. Back then, when her attention would drift off, her father would take her hand and say under his breath, "Kyra, are you paying attention?" She recalled looking up into her father's young face and replying, "Yes, Father! I am." She envisioned her young mother sitting on the other side of her in the pew. Though her mother had never converted to Catholicism, she attended services at church with the rest of the family. Kyra could almost hear her saying, "Kyra, it's what's in your heart that counts. God loves us all no matter what religion we follow."

Kyra recalled her grandmother telling her how difficult it was for her mother to stop attending her synagogue. Sometimes, she would hear her parents fighting about this very subject. But her mother had made the choice to stop outwardly practicing her religion when she decided to marry Kyra's father. She could almost hear her mother's voice now, clearly in her head, and a shiver raced up her spine. In that moment, she realized that she missed her parents.

Suddenly, the elderly priest's voice rose, and she was brought back to the sermon. He was speaking more passionately now as he was reaching his conclusion. Kyra wished she could better understand the words, but she enjoyed watching the priest perform the rituals of mass—including the use of incense—just as it had been done for thousands of years. The frankincense reached her nostrils, and her thoughts drifted off back in time.

*Ah, traditions*, she thought. *It's what links the past to the present.*

The word *tradition* made her think of her mother again and the many conversations they'd had on that topic—but the focus was always on Judaism. "Kyra, it's our traditions that unite us and give us a foundation for living. Don't ever forget to honor your heritage." Again, Kyra could almost hear her mother's calm voice offering this advice and felt her heart clench in longing for her presence. *If I could see you again, Mother, just one more time, I would tell you that I love you. I do know you loved me, too.*

Returning once again to the present moment, Kyra stole a glance at Alejandro and Gabby in the pew beside her. She noticed how tightly Alejandro held Gabby's hand—the gesture was so sweet and endearing to witness. She silently drank in the feeling of their love and felt gratitude knowing she'd too have that kind of relationship someday.

The service lasted for close to an hour, and after pausing for a few minutes in the vestibule so Eduardo and Carmen could greet a few friends, they headed out for a bite to eat.

Kyra stepped outside the huge ornate church door and looked up at the sky. The gentle rain had stopped, but the ground was still wet. Taking a deep breath, she inhaled the clean, fresh air. *Mmmm. Is that jasmine I smell?* She soon discovered that jasmine did indeed grow generously along the wrought-iron fences of the houses they passed along the way.

It was a most pleasant evening in El Gótic. Alejandro and Gabby held hands, as they walked with Kyra by their side. All the while, Carmen and Eduardo bantered back and forth as they strolled, breaking out into loud laughter whenever they came to an agreement.

Eduardo entertained Kyra with more stories of the *familia* history. Gabby had given Kyra the look to "watch-out" at the start of his tales, and Kyra had acknowledged her understanding with a wink. However, she was thoroughly enjoying this adventure into Gabby's family history.

After a slow-paced walk, the group made their way to Sensi Tapas. The colorful café was small, with only about thirty or so seats inside, but Kyra could not have been more pleased with the atmosphere. Eduardo ordered for the table, and soon a variety of dishes to be shared began to arrive. Feasting on amazing food seemed to the norm here, Kyra decided, and she could hardly believe the quality at such a quaint café.

She loved the Seafood *Paella*—which she learned was a rice-and-seafood dish colored bright yellow by saffron—and the Duck *Timbale* felt exquisite on her tongue. *Chorizo* in a spicy red pepper sauce added zest to their meal, while Sea Bass *ceviche* was mild and flavorful in a light citrus cilantro sauce. A grilled goat cheese salad rounded off their dinner and cleansed the palate.

Throughout the delicious meal, Kyra sipped her sangria and silently observed the two couples as they talked intensely—and non-stop. They were boisterous and laughing and even silly at times. Kyra loved the bantering and felt like she truly had become a part of the *familia* in just a few short days.

"Here, Alejandro. Try a bite of this. It's spicy like you!" said Gabby, spoon-feeding her sweetheart a bite of the chorizo.

Eduardo turned to Carmen in a resounding voice, *"Si me amas, ¡guárdame el último bocado!"* which Kyra loosely translated to "If you love me, save that last bite for me!"

At one point, it seemed to Kyra that Carmen had become rather frustrated with Eduardo, and though she could not understand all the words, she could tell that Carmen was admonishing him for something. Eduardo looked his wife in the eye and simply replied, "*¡Mi amor, aún te veo como esa jovencita con la que me casé, con chispas en los ojos!*"

Gabby leaned over to Kyra and translated under her breath: "My *papá* just said, 'My sweetheart, you still look like the young girl I married with those sparks in your eyes!'" Gabby let out a chuckle and gave her father an affectionate look.

Carmen's features softened, and she blushed, totally forgetting her frustration and replied, "*¡Ah, mi dulce, Eduardo!*"

This, Kyra could easily translate: "Ah, my sweet, Eduardo!"

*How amazing,* thought Kyra, *that they are still very much in love after more than forty years of marriage.* It was such a different experience to see a family so affectionate with each other—laughing, hugging, kissing. *And so loud*! Kyra gave herself an ironic smile. This was not the type of family she grew up in, but it did make her think about how different her life would be in the future.

After dinner, Gabby suggested they walk to another venue for a nightcap—a bar called Karma in Plaza Real. As Kyra walked up to the bar and saw the name, she leaned toward Gabby. "It looks like lightning does strike twice, Gabby! I was told I have good karma by the fortune-teller earlier today, and now were at a bar called Karma."

"*Chica*, you were simply meant to come to here to Spain, and yes, good karma is our destiny through our positive actions—so you better get hopping! Besides, I couldn't be happier you are here." Gabby gave Kyra a kiss on the cheek with a loud *muwahhh*.

Once inside, they descended a dark stairwell to an underground room where the music was loud but the atmosphere was inviting. Kyra felt like she was in a subway tunnel, albeit a trendy one. Bright lights arched across the tunnel-shaped underground room, giving the interior a chic discothèque feel.

Despite their age, Carmen and Eduardo seemed perfectly comfortable in the club-like environment. In English for Kyra's benefit, Carmen said, "Ah, Eduardo, we will see if you can still dance!"

"*¿En serio?*" he responded with a deep laugh. And with that, the pair headed off to the dance floor.

"The club is fairly quiet right now, Kyra," Alejandro commented, "but it will be jumping in a few hours."

Gabby quickly added, "Don't worry. We are not going to wait for that to happen!"

Kyra was relieved to know it would not be another late night. "How do you Spaniards party so late in the evening?" she asked with good humor.

"We do know how to throw a party here in Spain," Alejandro replied lightheartedly, "but we pick and choose our nights."

The trio danced together, bumping into Carmen and Eduardo, who were doing crazy dance moves. *I hope I'm still dancing like that when I'm their age!* Kyra thought and laughed openly. She was once again thoroughly enjoying the dance floor and being in the present moment. By midnight, though, Carmen and Eduardo were ready to go, and after some hearty and heartfelt goodnights, they insisted on taking a taxi home. Gabby translated how Carmen put it: "We've busted too many moves!"

Kyra, Gabby, and Alejandro walked back to Alejandro's car parked near the church, and in a short time they were back on Passeig de Gràcia. Alejandro accompanied the women inside the apartment building, but gently grabbed Gabby in his arms. The pair shared a passionate kiss in the foyer before he left.

Kyra tried to conceal the awkwardness she felt, realizing that her visit was likely interrupting their lives. Alejandro waved goodbye and the women stepped inside the elevator. Perhaps reading her thoughts, Gabby said, "No worries, *Chica!* Alejandro and I see each other all the time. Right now, it's all about us and our girl time! But I can't pass up a great goodnight kiss."

Kyra appreciated the kind assurance, but still felt a bit like a third wheel. "Oh, Gabby, I hope I'm not disrupting your life. I hope you don't mind if I live vicariously through the two of you for a while," she said sheepishly but with deep admiration for her friend's passionate relationship. "Your relationship does inspire me."

The elevator doors opened on Gabby's floor. Before she stepped off, Gabby turned to Kyra and said, "Ah, it will happen for you when you least expect it."

Somehow Kyra knew her friend's words were true.

Tired from the busy day and the fun evening out on the town, Gabby and Kyra still managed to exchange an energetic *¡Buenas noches!* before they turned in. Kyra was pleased that Gabby had arranged to take the next two days off from work so that they could continue to explore Barcelona together.

*How lucky I am to have such an amazing friend,* Kyra thought, as her head hit the pillow. She was out in moments.

The following morning, Kyra and Gabby ventured out to their first destination, Parc Güell located in the Gràcia district of Barcelona on Carmel Hill. The park covered several acres, and the weather was picture perfect for the two hours of walking and exploring they had planned. Kyra had read in her guidebook that none other than the famous architect Antoni Gaudí had designed the park.

"I love the photos that I've seen of Gaudí's work, and this park is simply amazing! It reminds me of Disney World," Kyra said when they arrived.

Gabby could not contain her own enthusiasm for one of her favorite sites in Barcelona. "*¡Sí! ¡Sí!* It's a sprawling maze of mosaic collages—from crazy mushroom-shaped chimneys to that brightly colored *dragón!*"

Kyra looked around and thought of a visit she'd made with her mother to Disney World in Florida when she was about eight. They had snuck off to the park just after school had let out for the summer. Her father didn't go with them because he was too busy working. Although she had really wanted her father along on their trip, they'd still had such a wonderful time. She remembered the roller coasters, and all the performers dressed up as Disney characters. She took pictures with Mickey and Minnie Mouse, Donald Duck, and Goofy. Her mother's drinking had not yet interfered with her life, and she was still joyful at that time—and even full of laughter.

Kyra could hear her mother's words even now: "Let's go on the merry-go-round and enjoy the magic ride. You are a very lucky little girl, my sweetheart. I never got to go on rides when I was your age."

Kyra felt her heart twinge. It was only later in life when her mother began to drink to numb her loneliness that her ability to express her feelings toward Kyra had also become numbed. Kyra was lost in these thoughts when Gabby grabbed her hand and spun her around.

"Look, *Chica!*" her friend said elated, as they walked forward on the pathway into the park.

Kyra moved quickly to keep up with Gabby, loving every moment of her initial impressions of Parc Güell. Her excitement grew when she could easily see that nature was well represented in the architecture with snails, flowers, leaves, and tree trunks all nestled in the mosaic tile work—and even in the architectural design. Kyra loved the huge mosaic sea serpent that formed a long bench in the main terrace area, allowing weary visitors a beautiful respite to enjoy the view from the hilltop.

The park's Casa Museu Gaudí, or the Gaudí House Museum, was their next stop. This building housed many of Gaudi's unique pieces of furniture and sketches, which Kyra took her time admiring.

"Gabby, you know I love art in every possible form. What an incredible place this is! I can't believe this was created over a hundred years ago either. It still looks so modern and fresh."

"Ah, yes. But wait 'til you see what's next for us at this park!"

Gabby then led her to Sala Hipóstila, which looked to Kyra like a surreal *Alice in Wonderland*. But instead of towering mushrooms, the whimsical stone temple had tall stone columns resembling a forest of trees. Kyra thought for sure she had fallen through the rabbit hole. A smiling mosaic-tiled lizard, draped across an immensely long staircase, guarded the entrance to the almost heathen-looking building.

Gabby explained, "This building was originally constructed as a marketplace, but it looks like something out of a Lewis Carroll novel."

Kyra was not surprised that her friend had drawn the same conclusion. "It certainly is enchanting—with a strange bewitching charm," she agreed, admiring the strange stone-like forest created by the columns.

They then walked back to the main pathway, which wound around the perimeter of the park and worked their way back toward the entrance of the park. The sun glistened brightly through the tree branches, and the park was filled with visitors taking in the splendor of the unique setting. Kyra's mind became playful as they walked along the pathway, and she could almost imagine fairies and other mythical creatures hiding in the grassy gardens.

"It *does* seem magical here," said Kyra softly to Gabby, beginning to remember pieces of her long-forgotten childhood dream. *I seem to recall there were fairies and other magical creatures—was there a Unicorn?* She couldn't quite remember what her imagination had inspired so long ago when she still took time to dream.

Gabby paused and turned to her friend with an innocent look. "Ah, magic is what dreams are made of!" Gabby laughed and darted ahead on their pathway almost in a childlike fashion, beckoning Kyra to follow her.

Kyra was taken aback by her friend's comment. Again, it was almost as if Gabby had read her mind. Dismissing the thought that her friend had intuitive abilities, she returned her attention to catching up with her. She edged up to Gabby, slightly out of breath. "These walking trails are gorgeous—very scenic and certainly more artsy than the ones at Muir Woods, but just as tranquil . . . And you're right. It does remind me of a childhood dream." Kyra spoke these words cautiously, trying hard to recall the details of the dream. Frustrated, she changed her thought. "What's next?" She knew full well that Gabby had a lot more in store for them.

"Our next stop today will be the amazing *La Sagrada Família,* but you can call it the Church of the Sacred Family. It's back in *Eixample* close to my apartment, and another fabulous masterpiece by your favorite—Gaudí, of course! Ah, but, this massive Art Nouveau church was never finished. And *this* will blow your mind. . . . It's still under construction after more than a hundred years and only about one-half complete! How *loco* is that?" Gabby said, sounding surprised herself, even after all these years.

What was really crazy, Kyra decided, was the whirlwind adventure she was on, and before long, she found herself walking up to the front entrance of the church. The dramatic exterior of the building left her in a state of wonder. It was hard to tell it was a church at all, and this building definitely looked like a castle, but from Disney World—and nothing at all like she expected.

"I was thinking earlier today of Disney World. I visited there when I was as a child with my mother and we saw Cinderella's castle . . . and this church reminds me of it. Maybe Alejandro's comment last night about meeting Prince Charming has made an impression on me . . . How silly am I?" Kyra giggled.

"Sometimes it's good to let your imagination run wild. Let's be totally silly, and even childlike with our thoughts—Wait 'til you see the inside!" Gabby said, taking Kyra's hand to lead the way.

As they walked through the massive wooden front doors of La Sagrada Família, the interior of the church proved to be intricately designed in a way that Kyra was becoming accustomed to in Spain, but still surprised her. She could hardly believe how incredibly tall the church towers were, and she tossed her head back to look up at the ceiling. It almost resembled a kaleidoscope with its intricacy of design and surreal bright colors. Gabby explained that only eight of the eighteen intended towers had been built to date. Each tower was to represent each of the Twelve Apostles, the Virgin Mary, the four Evangelists, and of course Jesus Christ. The spires, as they were also called, were close to 600 feet in height.

"Ah, but in addition to the eight spires that are built, the church interior forms a Latin cross shape with its naves. How cool is that?" Gabby eagerly continued.

Kyra glanced back down to look around the interior of the church and absorb the breathtaking elegance of the striking architecture. "It is incredibly beautiful here." The beauty—here and in the other places she'd visited—seemed to be sinking into her very soul, stirring her emotions and expanding her heart. The history was certainly interesting, of course, but she could feel something deeper taking place within her.

Gabby further explained in respectful hushed tones, "The other cool thing is there is so much symbolism here, too. Let me tell you what I know about the three façades, one of which is still the process of being built. Yes?"

Kyra nodded in affirmation and listened intently, amazed by how much Gabby knew. Clearly this was a building Gabby adored and felt passion for.

"The Nativity façade directly ahead of us celebrates the birth of Jesus. It's also called the façade of Life and Joy—two things closest to my heart. It's divided into three porticos representing Hope, Faith, and Charity. *¡Mira!* See the Tree of Life extending up above the top of the door? That's some of the symbolism I was telling to you about . . . Pretty awesome, huh?"

"Awesome and amazing . . ." Kyra said her voice trailing off, as she gazed in wonder at the architectural design. She knew there was not another church like it in the world.

They continued exploring, stopping next at the Glory Façade—the largest and most stunning façade in the building, but still under construction as Gabby had mentioned.

Trying to keep her enthusiasm in check, Gabby whispered, but her words came out louder than intended, "And this façade represents the road to God: Death, Final Judgment and Glory, as you may remember from your childhood attending Catholic school. I like to think this also represents man's struggles . . . the road he must take, *and* his purpose in life." Gabby paused for a moment, then added, "This one may have special meaning for you."

"That's very much on my mind right now with everything that's happened recently," Kyra said, thinking of the new road that lay ahead of her and even discovering her life's true purpose.

Gabby nodded in understanding and continued her metaphysical history lesson. "There are also seven large columns in this portico dedicated to spiritual gifts, which is mentioned in Corinthians 12:8–10. My *mamá* used to remind me of that verse when I was being unruly as a child! But spiritual gifts include the gifts of miracles and healing." A tear pooled in the corner of Gabby's eye.

*Miracles and healing.* Kyra rolled the words around in her mind. She thought of her own healing process, which had just recently begun, and she felt blessed to be learning so much from her friend.

Wearing a virtuous expression, Gabby added, "The Seven Deadly Sins will be represented here, too—ah, but we don't need to cover those, now do we?"

"No, we most certainly do not!" Kyra said a bit too loudly, cupping her hand over her mouth. She then eagerly followed Gabby to the last stop of their self-guided tour: the Passion Façade.

"This façade faces the setting sun," Gabby said solemnly, "and symbolizes the death of Christ. You can see it's pretty stark and plain compared to the Nativity Façade, which is so intricate and embellished. But see the six large pillars here? They were designed to look like Sequoia tree trunks, just like your Redwood Forest back in California. You know how much Gaudí loved nature."

Kyra looked up at the large supporting columns and had an eerie feeling that she was exactly where she needed to be in that moment. Somehow it had been part of her destiny to visit this place—just as Gabby had alluded to on her first day. She felt something stirring deep within her core, and she thought longingly of her weekly visits to Muir Woods.

The synchronicities of this trip were beginning to make sense, and she was seeing more and more the amazing signs that correlated to her home. Taking one more look up at the Sequoia tree trunks, she silently affirmed, *Yes, indeed. I must be on the right path.*

# 15

"Rise and Shine, *Chica!* We have some *grandes* plans for this beautiful Tuesday." Gabby said, gently shaking Kyra awake.

"Okay, okay," Kyra said groggily.

All the physical activity was beginning to take its toll on her, and Kyra had slept soundly. But the thought of the day's upcoming adventures made her feel renewed. Today, they'd be seeing the works of one of her favorite artists, Pablo Picasso. She adored Picasso's bold use of colors, and his Cubist style ignited a spark of passion in her, inspiring her to do a painting of her own someday.

They ate a quick breakfast of café con leche and bollo dulce, and then got ready for their outing in record time. Before long, they were pulling up to Museo Picasso to park the car.

"You know, Picasso was born here in Spain," Gabby told her proudly as they entered the building.

Kyra nodded appreciatively, taking in the enormity of the museum. With several thousand pieces of art, mainly from Picasso's early years, they could only enjoy a small portion of the artwork that the museum could display. Kyra was drawn to *The Pigeons*, which had been completed in 1957. She approached the painting to examine the brushstrokes up close, trying to memorize each dab of paint.

After a few moments, Gabby laughed. "*Chica*, if you look any closer at that painting, they might arrest you!"

Kyra looked sheepishly at the nearby security guard, who gave her a thin smile.

"Ah, Gabby, I'm just drinking it all in. Did you know that I loved to paint as a child? It's just something I never found time to pursue, but I think I'd like to add that to my list of things I want to do when I return home."

Kyra stepped back from a painting and could almost hear Nana's sweet voice talking about Picasso's work as if she'd just seen her yesterday. During one of their weekly Saturday lunches, they made a visit to the Art Institute of Chicago. Nana had told her, "I love the bright colors of this one," referencing *The Red Armchair.* "That Picasso fellow really was a good painter . . . even if he wasn't from Israel!" Even now, Nana's humor made Kyra's face break into a grin. She quietly savored the memory.

"I feel so close to my grandmother here," Kyra confided as they moved on. "It's almost as if she's with me now looking at the paintings. Some of the best times I had with her in Chicago included our trips to the Art Institute."

Gabby gave her a gentle hug on her shoulder. "Ah, I know how difficult it is for you, but I love that you have such wonderful memories. . . . Come, we have much ground to cover!" she said cheerfully.

Kyra did, indeed, have wonderful memories, and she would cherish them always. This feeling filled her with tenderness, and she felt especially light as they continued their two-and-a half-hour tour of the two-story building. She could have remained in the museum the whole day, but she knew Gabby had more on the agenda.

"After our next stop, I have a surprise for you," Gabby told her, building some suspense.

Kyra's curiosity was sufficiently teased, so they drove to what Gabby explained was the smallest district in the city of Barcelona. It was located on the coastline with a lovely view of the turquoise Mediterranean Sea. Passeig Marítim proved to be an amazingly fun street with its own old-world charm, but the promenade offered many small shops and cafés along the way that attracted tourists and locals alike. The seaside marina had a calm and unhurried atmosphere, with many stately yachts and more casual sailboats wedged tightly into the small marina. Kyra was again reminded of San Francisco and the many times she had seen sailboats out on the Bay, traversing back and forth in the blustering wind. But, today, the winds were calm.

"My goodness. I do so love the ocean," Kyra said, as she and Gabby enjoyed their leisurely walk down the boardwalk, stopping occasionally to gaze out across the brilliant blue waters of the Mediterranean Sea.

Gabby smiled with enthusiasm. "I knew it would be right up your alley."

The light, salty wind gently swept Kyra's hair away from her face. "This reminds me so much of San Francisco," said Kyra, feeling a little homesick, but only for a brief moment.

"Remember that time in Boston when we went out on my friend's boat and it almost capsized?" Gabby quizzed.

Kyra's eyes widened. She remembered the day very well. At first she felt afraid when the storm hit, but then the seas calmed. The cool breeze that followed the torrential downpour was refreshing as they made their way back to shore. That day was a testament to going with the flow of the Universe and trusting that everything will be okay.

"Oh, I *remember*," Kyra confirmed, and then added with humor, "you got seasick!"

Gabby cringed, apparently recalling her embarrassment at "feeding the fish" as her friends had teased. "*Ah, si,*" she responded. "But I think the fish appreciated it!"

The women laughed as they also reminisced about other silly misadventures they'd had during their grad school days.

Once they arrived at the southern end of Passeig Marítim in Port Olímpic, Gabby suggested they stop for tapas and sangria. "I'm famished!" she said, rubbing her stomach vigorously.

"If there was an eating contest, you would win for sure," Kyra joked, motioning to Gabby's slight frame. "I can't imagine where you put all the food."

"I'm a bottomless pit!"

Once they'd finished their sangria and the plates of sautéed *bonito del norte* tuna and fresh green salad, Gabby asked, "Are you ready for the surprise?"

"Nothing about you could surprise me, but yes, please do let me in on your secret."

Gabby took Kyra's hand and led her further along the boardwalk, stopping a few minutes later in front of Casino Barcelona. "Do you feel lucky today?"

"I do," Kyra said suspiciously. "*This* is the surprise?"

"The surprise is I'm going to wager a bet against you in Black Jack." Gabby said with a confident wave.

"I will take you up on that wager," Kyra agreed, amused. Then she upped the ante: "The loser treats us both to dinner and wine this evening!"

Gabby's eyes lit up. "Deal!"

The friends walked through the shiny steel-framed glass doors into the dim interior of the casino. Small in comparison to the Las Vegas casinos Kyra had visited, the casino was lively just the same. The dark interior became brighter as the blinking lights of the slot machines lit up the area with a rainbow of flashing colors.

As they passed by the roulette tables, the tiny white ball spun wildly around, landing randomly on the winning number. Players cheered as they won or let out groans of frustration when they lost. As they moved further in, Kyra noted the serious look on the poker player's faces, who were clearly concentrating on the cards in their hands, keeping their thoughts a secret. Meanwhile, Mini Baccarat players focused more leisurely on their Punto Banco game, which Gabby explained to Kyra was a game of chance that required little skill but had very high stakes.

However, both Gabby and Kyra agreed that Black Jack was the game to play because it required some skill—and because Gabby was a bit on the competitive side. They walked around for a few minutes before settling down at the particular Black Jack table Gabby had carefully scoped out.

"This table here feels like a winner to me. Let's wager a game or two so you can buy me dinner," Gabby teased.

The dealer—a handsome man in his twenties—swiftly dealt cards to each of the players. It soon became apparent that Lady Luck or perhaps a good deal of skill was on Kyra's side after she easily won the first several games with Gabby's cards either coming in too low to beat the dealer or busting entirely.

Midway through their first few rounds, Gabby whispered in Kyra's ear, "*Chica,* you are a real card shark. You're trying to take advantage of me!"

Kyra replied innocently, "Gabby, you haven't seen anything yet." Then she went on to win the majority of the remaining hands against the house, raking in a nice sum of money. Gabby's pile of chips was dwindling rapidly.

After fifteen rounds, Kyra triumphantly proclaimed, "I have won our wager fair and square. Let's eat at Teppan-Yaki, and the sake is on you."

Gabby agreed, "*Excelente* card playing today, I must say . . . my little card shark *amiga.*"

After a tasty and slow-paced dinner of delicious tempura, sushi, rice, and several rounds of sake at the casino's Japanese grill, they decided to finish off the evening at the Eclipse Bar on the twenty-sixth floor of the nearby W Hotel.

"It's only a short walk at the end of the pier, but let's see if you can keep up with me!" Gabby said spiritedly, rushing ahead.

"I can only hope to stay up with you, dear friend," Kyra bantered.

As they walked along the boardwalk and approached the hotel, Kyra was taken aback by the enormous crescent-moon-shaped building. As it was approaching midevening, the hotel stood out dramatically against the ocean backdrop, seeming to glow just as the moon itself. Along with the moonlight reflecting brightly on the darkening waters, the whole scene had a dreamlike quality.

They took the elevator to the top floor and stepped out into the bar. From floor to ceiling, windows offered a stunning view of the city. Kyra loved the sleek layout. The blue-and-gold couches looked inviting, but she knew Gabby would pull her on to the dance floor in no time at all. Florescent pink lighting gave the club a posh, elegant feel. Kyra leaned her forehead against one of the windows and watched the city lights stretch out over the port, and even further off into the hillsides, spanning a dramatic distance from the water's edge.

"Let's dance! You need to work off that dinner," Gabby insisted, as the DJ increased the volume of the music, enticing patrons onto the dance floor.

Kyra loved the techno music and felt inspired by the view. And, once again, she simply let herself be in the moment enjoying her surroundings and not caring what anyone thought. The dancing led to innocent, but delightful, flirting with a few handsome men on the dance floor.

"This really is the most fun that I've had in a long time," Kyra commented when the music slowed for a moment. "I'm really enjoying letting my guard down. Plus, you have taught me how to flirt! Thank you for the lessons."

Gabby looked blissful, her face glowing with happiness. "*¡El gusto es mío!*" She threw her arms up in the air, and the friends continued to dance for several more hours, taking only few breaks from the dance floor to freshen up or down a glass of water.

They finally made their way home around 2 am.

"Good night, my sweet friend," Kyra said drowsily, as she headed toward the study. "Tomorrow you are back to the office grind. I hope I didn't keep you out too late."

"I may be fuzzy in the morning, but it was well worth being a proper teacher to my friend! *Buenas noches. Muwahhh!*"

They exchanged an affectionate hug goodnight and went off to their respective rooms to recuperate from the exhilarating evening. They slept soundly as if there were no tomorrow.

When Kyra woke, Gabby had already slipped out quietly for work. Her plans for the remainder of the week were to explore Barcelona on her own. *I'm looking forward to the adventure*, she told herself, *despite being alone*. Kyra smiled, stretching her arms above her head. It was Wednesday, and she would be visiting the Mercat de Sant Josep de la Boqueria—or La Boqueria, for short. Located in Las Ramblas, it was an expansive fresh market that had been closed on Sunday when she'd first visited the district with Gabby.

It hadn't taken her long to get up and out of the apartment, and when she arrived at her destination, she glanced up at the huge ornate sign hanging over the market's entrance. She chuckled, remembering

Gabby's words: "*La Boqueria* has an outstanding selection of fruits, vegetables, and seafood—some of the best in Barcelona!"

Kyra stepped inside the famous market, which was crowded with local shoppers making purchases of groceries, flowers, and even lunch. Butchers, bakers, and farmers displayed their offerings in small stands one after the other. The market overflowed with selections of fresh seafood, fruit juices, and of course wine. From the freshly baked bread to the seafood packed on ice, and from fresh fruit crepes simmering on a grill to the spicy local rice and meat dishes—the alluring aromas drifted generously through the air, and Kyra's stomach started to awaken.

Small restaurants in the expansive marketplace made it convenient for her to stop for a relaxing lunch and a glass of *Rioja tinto*—a refreshing red wine tasting of rich cherries and blackberries with a slight honey-like oaky flavor. Kyra laughed at her rumbling stomach. She had deliberately decided to wait until 2 pm to eat, but despite all the food she'd consumed in the past few days, her stomach still hadn't adjusted to the Spanish lunch schedule. She later brought her purchases back to the apartment and cooked a nice dinner that evening, surprising Gabby when she arrived home from work.

On Thursday, Kyra explored Casa Batlló and Casa Milà in the Eixample district. Both houses were architectural masterpieces designed by Antoni Gaudí, adding yet another layer to her appreciation of the Art Nouveau style.

At Casa Batlló—her first stop—Kyra noted the eerie skeletal windows and terraces. She had read in her guidebook that the house with its oddly shaped, colorful façade was thought to depict the legend of Saint George and the Dragon. The roof even resembled a dragon's scaly back. But the visual detail inside the house further stimulated her senses. To learn as much as she could, she listened to the audio tour, leading her to the Noble Floor, which had once been home to the Batlló family. The tour also guided her up to the roof where she could see the spiny chimneys up close.

The next stop, Casa Milà, was an easy five-minute walk away. Deeply contrasting with the colorful Casa Batlló, Casa Milà's exterior was white and bright—and fortress-like. Its unusual wavy stone facade and detailed sculptures made it clear it belonged to none other than Gaudí. It had been nicknamed La Pedrera, or The Quarry. Kyra discovered that this was originally a derogatory reference, as its first neighbors did not welcome the unique, if not odd-looking, house to their neighborhood. Kyra also learned an unusual fact that there wasn't one single straight line or right angle in the entire building.

She loved the idea of nonconformity, especially after all those years in the corporate world in a highly structured environment that never allowed her to think creatively. *I am definitely going to feed my creative side and take art lessons when I return home!* she thought with excitement. In fact, Kyra was looking forward to trying a number of new and different things—things that would make her feel happier and more spiritually connected when she arrived back in San Francisco. She spent a few more hours enjoying the imaginative architecture, her own creativity being sparked as she began to envision her future life.

By the time Friday morning rolled around, Kyra could not believe she had been in Barcelona for an entire week. She still didn't know when she'd be heading home, and as much as she missed San Francisco, she didn't feel in a rush to get back there.

She and Gabby met briefly in the kitchen. "See you tonight!" Gabby said with a hug. "Alejandro and I are looking forward to meeting you at the *fantástico* laser light and fountain show at the Magic Fountain of *Montjuïc.*"

"I can't wait to share it with you, too." Kyra smiled, getting excited about her upcoming day.

With a proper "*Muwahhh,*" Gabby waved a kiss goodbye and headed out.

Kyra sat at the small kitchen table, slowly sipping her café con leche and watched the steam rise out of the bright-red coffee cup. It was exactly one month since the passing of her grandmother, but the events of the past month seemed light years away this morning. She took a moment to reflect on her grandmother and finally said aloud, "Nana, I think you'd be so proud of me. I learned *so much* from you—and I was so blessed to have you in my life. I promise to start using your wisdom in every aspect of my life." Feeling a little sad, she dismissed the sensation, and took a moment to send a loving thought out to her grandmother.

After Kyra finished her coffee, she got herself ready for her day. She planned to start at Parc de la Ciutadella, one of the largest parks in the city, and then finish up at Castell de Montjuïc, a seventeenth-century castle. Just in case it was cooler inside the castle, she grabbed her white sweater. She also packed a light blanket that easily fit into her bag in case she decided to relax at the park. Later, she'd be meeting Gabby and Alejandro for the show at the Magic Fountain of Montjuïc, located in a park plaza at the base of the castle, and then they'd grab a late dinner.

Kyra arrived at the park early in the afternoon. A slightly breezy day, the temperatures would reach about 83 degrees Fahrenheit—*or 28 degrees Celsius,* she corrected herself—which was quite usual for the end of June in Barcelona.

First, she strolled around the zoo, seeing only a small portion of the 7,000-plus animals housed there, and then she made a stop at the small lake where she spread out her blanket to eat her tapas and enjoyed a refreshing bottle of spring water. She enjoyed eating her lunch on the grounds, as rowboats drifted lazily across the water. Dogs ran energetically back and forth, their tongues lapping in the breeze, and a bandstand played music off to the side, adding to the festivities of the day.

After her picnic, she stopped to admire many of the statues in the park, including an unusually large stone wooly mammoth. A group of children played underneath the huge beast, while birds chirped sweetly in the trees above her. The sight brought a slow smile to her face, reminding Kyra of childhood days when she'd taken the time to enjoy such simple things.

She left Parc de la Ciutadella early in the evening and made her way south to Castell de Montjuïc, which was known in English as Castle

Montjuïc. It was nearly an hour walk along the seaboard from the park, but a most pleasant one with a slight breeze that offered cooling relief on an otherwise sultry summer evening. The castle itself was an austere stone fortress complex resting atop a tall hillside. It had been named after Montjuïc Mountain upon which it was built, and rose up above the sea more than 550 feet.

Images of former battles, including the Spanish Civil War came to Kyra's mind, but now it was a military museum known for its panoramic views of Barcelona and the glorious Mediterranean Sea that sat directly beneath her. Kyra could not wait to reach the top to enjoy the lovely view of the sea and city. Ironically, she had also learned Montjuïc translates to "Mountain of the Jews" in medieval Catalan and may have been related to a Latin phrase meaning "Hill of Jove."

*Another strange synchronicity,* Kyra thought, as she fondly remembered all of her relatives in Israel with whom she had spent so little time, but had quickly grown to love.

After making her way to the top of the castle, Kyra could see that a traditional mote and stone wall surrounded the structure for protection. The pentagon shape, rather than the typical rectangle one might expect, surprised her. Colorful landscaping of precisely cut hedges with red and white flowers added warmth to the outside, softening the otherwise austere stone structure. She had learned from her guidebook that the castle had a long and arduous history; it had been demolished and rebuilt at the end of the eighteenth century. Most recently, it had been a military prison, but it was also a symbol of military oppression from the Franco regime during the Spanish Civil War. However, the old fortress was in a transitional phase with future plans to become an international peace center with seminars, concerts, and exhibitions.

*I like the idea of reclaiming our past and making it a positive symbol for the future,* thought Kyra, realizing that the castle was a great reminder to forgive her own past and to keep only the good things she had learned and experienced. She reflected on her parents again and how she sometimes didn't feel loved when she was a child. *Yes, I will find a way to let that go, but for now, I will continue to focus on the positive.*

After enjoying her guided tour and walk around the grounds, Kyra made her way down Montjuïc Mountain and, in about twenty minutes, arrived at Plaça de Carles Buïgas, a plaza at Montjuïc Park where Gabby and Alejandro would join her for the evening laser and fountain show starting at sundown. She found a comfortable spot at the base of the large fountain and spread out her blanket. It was now 9:15 pm, and she watched the sun set slowly in a glorious blaze of bright orange, yellow, and gold.

One by one, the stars began to appear on a velvety dark-blue backdrop of sky in the early evening twilight. *The stars are so brilliant,* she admired in awe. *They almost seem to be winking at me.* An odd feeling struck her just then. *They seem so familiar. Like something I once pictured in a dream.* She searched her memory, but soon her mind drifted off with the beauty of the evening.

About fifteen minutes later, Gabby and Alejandro approached. Gabby tapped Kyra on the shoulder. "*¡Hola, Chica!* You look like you are lost in your own world! How did you enjoy your day?" she asked, squatting low to give Kyra an affectionate hug.

Kyra squeezed her friend, glad to see her, then rose to her feet to greet Alejandro, who promptly gave Kyra a kiss on her cheek, saying in his warm raspy Spanish accent, "*¡Qué gusto verte!*" Kyra translated that to mean, *Good to see you!*

"I had such a wonderful day," she told her friends. "The park was beautiful and relaxing. I walked along the lovely seaboard to get here. I'm so glad you could join me tonight."

"Ah, it's our pleasure, and I can't wait to hear about your adventures today," replied Gabby, taking Alejandro's hand and holding it tightly.

Kyra loved watching the energy between them and again longed for the same. *That's what I want to attract.* She gave them a warm smile to acknowledge her fond sentiments. Then, picking up her blanket, she said, "The plaza has become quite crowded. Standing room only I think!"

They moved closer to the fountain's edge for a good view. Within a few moments, the fireworks began. Dramatic music played through speakers Kyra could not see, but they were somewhere overhead in the midnight blue sky. Water began shooting up from the center of the fountain in sync with the music, choreographed to perfection. A dazzling display of laser lights joined the water and music, adding brightly colored streaks of light that danced across the velvety sky.

"This show has been in production since 1929. My *mamá* brought me here many times as a child, and I have wonderful memories of this show. Not that I'm *that* old, of course," Gabby whispered.

Kyra nodded in agreement, and then turned to watch the water dance as the laser lights darted across the water and sky. "It truly is a magic fountain, Gabby, or *Font Màgica* as you would say, and perfectly named." She gave her friend a smile in agreement.

The water's movements made Kyra feel alive, and the music stirred her deeply. She felt incredibly blessed to be here in this moment and silently thanked the Universe for allowing her this special time. She tried not to cry at the beauty of it all, and took a moment to wipe her eyes so that Gabby and Alejandro would not see her emotions.

# 16

Following the magical firework display, Alejandro drove the women to a small offbeat restaurant. Kyra grinned at her friends with regard to the late hour.

*I'm usually in bed at 10:30!* she thought with some amusement. *This is so not the norm for me.* But once she stepped foot into Bodega Biarritz, the aromas instantly enticed her senses, sending her stomach into an unexpectedly loud rumble. Muffling her embarrassment, Kyra took Gabby's arm. "I can't believe I have room for more food tonight."

Gabby shot her back a playfully wicked smile.

"*Sí, sí.*" responded Alejandro, leading the way. "I'm hungry too. Let's grab a table and order a light dinner. I will treat you ladies to a glass of wine."

Shortly after the waiter had taken their order, the small but tantalizing dishes began to arrive. Gabby was the first to sample the shrimp in garlic sauce. "*¡Delicioso!*" she declared, after swallowing a large mouthful of the fresh seafood. Fresh asparagus with avocado and tomato came next. Kyra helped herself to a generous forkful, eagerly stuffing the steamed vegetables into her mouth, savoring the fresh flavors. The next plate held small *empanadas* made of tuna, spinach, and peppers in a delightful white-wine vinaigrette. As Alejandro bit into one of the pastries, he exclaimed, "*¡Excelente!*" smacking his lips. Finally, a plate of marinated Spanish olives arrived, a perfect accompaniment to their evening meal.

As Kyra sampled the dishes and enjoyed her wine, she silently observed the love between the couple again. The pair was inseparable, feeding each other bites of food and practically finishing each other's sentences. *Awww . . . they're so sweet and affectionate. My sweetheart will be just as thoughtful and loving. And I can't wait to meet him.* This daydream brought a soft smile to her face, and she cherished the warm feeling it elicited in her heart.

Toward the end of the meal, Gabby shifted the conversation to Kyra's itinerary. "I can't believe it's already time for your trip to Madrid! I will drop you off at the airport in the morning, and you will arrive around 10:45. My youngest brother, Javier, and his wife, Verónica, will pick you up. *¿Bien?* They will be happy to be show you around the city, so ask them for any help you need. . . . But watch out if they start drinking too much! They may forget how to speak English."

Kyra's eyes widened, and Gabby gave her a lighthearted look. "No, seriously," she assured her, "they are very sweet and you will *love* them." Gabby's gaze then fell on Alejandro, and she unexpectedly planted a passionate kiss on his lips. "*¡Y yo adoro mi amor loco!*" she said, which Kyra translated to "And I adore my crazy sweetheart!"

Kyra chuckled to herself. *Apparently, you have to be a little crazy to be in love . . . or just plain crazy to be part of Gabby's family.*

The next morning the girlfriends shared a long hug goodbye at the passenger drop-off area after arriving to the airport. Kyra felt her eyes tearing up. The unexpected display of emotion surprised her, and her voice cracked a bit. "I will see you again at the end of my trip for my flight back to the U.S. For now, I know Alejandro is very excited to have his *amor* back to himself."

Gabby laughed, easing her friend's apprehension. "We will *both* be excited to see you in a couple of weeks. Have a *fantástico* time." She embraced Kyra once more for reassurance, blinking back her own tears.

The friends finally waved goodbye, and Kyra walked through the sliding doors into the airport. She could hear Gabby shout to her just as the doors were sliding closed, "And don't get into any trouble I wouldn't get into! *Muwahhh!*"

With that humorous thought tucked away in her mind, Kyra soon settled into her seat. Flight 303 on Iberia Airline left just a few minutes late, around 9:00 am. When the plane reached cruising attitude, she reclined her seat and opened the Madrid travel guide she'd purchased at the airport. This was her first opportunity to plan how she would spend her five days in the city, especially after her fun, but very full days in Barcelona. The guide began by explaining that Madrid is the capital of Spain, but Kyra had already known that.

*Madrid is located in the middle of the country on the Manzanares River,* she read next. She imagined herself beside the beautiful, serene river and mentally noted that Madrid is at a much higher elevation than sea-level Barcelona. *It will still be fairly dry in June, but warmer than Barcelona,* she realized. She turned away from the guide for a moment to look out the cabin window. *I can't believe I'm flying off to a city where I barely know anyone!* She felt her heart flutter at the thought. *This will be quite an exciting journey, I'm sure of it . . .*

She began flipping through the colorful pages of the travel guide once again. Museums, castles, and plazas were prominently featured throughout and showcased the dramatic architecture. And, of course, Flamenco dancing—all of these things contributed to her growing anticipation. *So much to do and see! Yes, I might be a little nervous, but my intuition tells me I'm supposed to be here. I will have a good time.* She retrieved a small notepad from her purse and began listing all the sites she'd like to visit, taking time to fantasize about each one.

The flight was relatively short, and Kyra quickly lost track of time. She jumped with a start when she heard the captain announce they were about to land. Bringing her seat into the upright position, she placed her notes and travel guide back in her purse. Just a few minutes later, the plane touched down on the landing strip at the Madrid-Barajas Airport. Kyra glanced down at her watch. It was now10:35 am.

Excited, but still a little anxious, she took a deep breath to center her core. Then, making the sign of the cross, she added a quick prayer: *Please, God, Jesus and Angels, protect and look over me. And let this trip be for my highest and best good. Amen.*

After gathering her suitcase, Kyra walked to the passenger pickup area to wait for Javier. As she stepped outside through the sliding glass doors, the warm, dry summer air kissed her face—reminding her of a similar day in Chicago a few years earlier. It felt as if it were just yesterday that she was sitting in a park with Nana. She could almost hear her sweet voice say, “Honey, never regret any decisions you make in life. It’s what you do now that really counts.”

*Nana’s wonderful advice is exactly what I need at this moment.* Then an odd feeling overcame her. Out of nowhere, she felt a palpable warmth envelop her heart. It was the same strange, but familiar sensation she’d felt back in her condo when the crystal bear had fallen to the floor. The feeling was more intense this time and her heart momentarily ached, but strangely she felt happy at the same time.

“Nana, I wish you were here with me,” Kyra said under her breath, rolling her suitcase to the curb’s edge. *Maybe you are,* she added inwardly. The warmth continued to embrace her heart, growing even stronger. *You always did love an adventure.* The thought brought a slow, soft smile to Kyra’s lips. And while she felt some sadness, she mostly felt comfort in the gentle reminder that her grandmother was indeed always with her. *What were your last words to me? Just think of you and you’ll be with me? Ani ohev otach, Nana.*

Kyra’s thoughts shifted back to the present. Endeavoring to keep herself calm, she tried to recall how well Javier spoke English. She had met him at Carmen and Eduardo’s house her first night in Barcelona, but she couldn’t recall much of their actual conversation. So many of Gabby’s family members had been at the house that evening. She winced, remembering the overabundance of food and *vino,* as Carmen liked to call it. *I had a little too much vino that evening to recall much of anything*, she realized.

Kyra’s wandering mind came back into focus when Javier approached. “Welcome to Madrid, Kyra!” he shouted. “Verónica and I look forward to showing you around while you stay here in our beloved capital city.” He gave her a warm hug and customary kiss on the cheek.

Javier had a Spanish accent but, to Kyra’s relief, he spoke English quite well. He looked to be about thirty, and while thin in stature, he was fairly tall at nearly six feet. Kyra noted that he had inherited his attractiveness from his papá Eduardo. She instantly felt her apprehension melt away, and replied, "It's great to see you again, and thank you so much for picking me up. I'm super excited to see Madrid and really appreciate your kindness."

Tears threatened to well up in Kyra's eyes once again, catching her off guard. She hadn't expected to feel so vulnerable. *It's like I'm a teenager going on my first international trip,* she thought. She looked up at Javier with her big brown eyes, hoping her vulnerability didn't show.

Javier just smiled and gave her a moment to compose herself. "It's our pleasure, Kyra," he said, shifting the mood. "I can't recall if I had mentioned to you that I studied abroad in the U.S. and spent a year in New York City. I really enjoyed my time there, but I never visited your beautiful city of San Francisco. I would *love* to do so someday."

Kyra swallowed a lump in her throat and replied, "Well, if you ever do decide to visit San Francisco, you'll have a excellent tour guide in me."

Javier nodded with gratitude and offered to wheel her suitcase to his car. They chatted as they walked. "Verónica is originally from Madrid," he explained, "and we're visiting her parents here for three weeks. We'll meet Verónica at *Puerta del Sol* in the center of the city and then go out for a bite to eat. We have a few more sites of interest in mind to show you today as well."

"That sounds wonderful," Kyra replied. "I'm still working out the details of my visit, so I'd love to hear your thoughts on the city, too."

"I'd be happy to fill you in a little bit about Madrid while we drive—but please bear with me if my English is not *perfecto.*"

Kyra laughed. "No apologies needed. I wish my Spanish were as good as your English! I should have paid much more attention in high school to my Spanish teacher. . . You are too, too kind. *Muchas gracias.*"

Javier stopped in front of a sleek black Peugeot sedan, and Kyra admired the car. He opened the passenger door in a gentlemanly fashion, and she climbed in. After loading her suitcase into the trunk, he slipped into the driver's seat.

As they headed toward Madrid, Kyra glanced out the car window and asked, "How far is *Puerta del Sol* from here?" She'd made her best effort to correctly pronounce the name.

Javier responded with lightness in his voice, "The plaza is roughly eighteen kilometers or so from the airport, I believe. It's in the center of the city. We should arrive in about thirty minutes. But traffic will become heavier and heavier as we drive to Madrid.

Just as Kyra had hoped he would, Javier began to explain some of the nuisances of the city. "*Puerta del Sol* translates into English as 'Gate of the Sun.' It's one of the busiest plazas in Madrid and a most beautiful area of the city." Javier's eyes sparkled as he continued to speak proudly of the city, and Kyra listened intently.

As the car drove further toward their destination, they passed both quaint and statuesque buildings. *This is so beautiful*, Kyra thought. *I feel so blessed to be here . . . it almost feels like I'm meant to be here.* Kyra didn't know where the feeling came from, but she felt strangely drawn to the city. It was unlike anything she had ever experienced before.

Javier chatted away, telling her that he and Verónica had been married for less than a year—and that Mamá was anxiously awaiting the news that the couple would soon be starting a family. With a smile, Kyra thought back to the family dinner when Carmen had brought up the same subject with Gabby. She recalled Gabby's frustrated response to her mother's chiding.

Javier clarified, "Verónica and I do want children, but we plan to wait a couple of years. We are still young, and I'm settling into my new job in Barcelona. Of course, *Mamá* has no patience, but she loves us very much."

"Your *mamá* seems very enthusiastic about marriage and grandchildren . . . much to Gabby's dismay as well," Kyra joked, her grin widening.

Javier broke out into a laugh. "Yes, yes! Well uh, let me get back to telling you more about our wonderful city."

He went on to talk about the slight rivalry between Madrid and Barcelona. As he explained, Madrid's culture leaned more toward the traditional, which contrasted with the unique Catalan influence in Barcelona. "There are fewer tourists in Madrid—and perhaps more authentic Spanish food. Both cities, however, *es muy hermosa* . . . ah, quite beautiful. Madrid is actually the third largest city in Europe behind London and

Berlin. And I'm proud to say it is known for some of the world's best art museums, including *Museo del Prado*, which we will visit later today if you are interested." He glanced over at Kyra.

She nodded. "I love art, so yes, I'm *very* interested."

Javier flashed a charming smile and added, "Madrid is equally known for its many beautiful plazas, including *Plaza de Cibeles* and the Cibeles Fountain. The Goddess Cibeles represents the Roman Goddess of nature and fertility. . . Ha! *Mamá* would enjoy that, of course! Seriously, though, Verónica and I look forward to showing you around our city and answering any questions you have."

Kyra recognized the wholehearted sincerity of his words, and she thanked him for being such a wonderful extension of her relationship with Gabby. "My grandparents visited Spain many years ago when they were traveling across Europe," she shared with her new friend. "They sent me the most beautiful dress with pink, red, and white flowers from Madrid for my eighth birthday. In the birthday card, they told me how much they were enjoying their visit here. I think I was destined to come here."

Kyra kept to herself that she would have much preferred for her grandparents to have attended her birthday party instead of being away on vacation. She let go of the sad feeling and focused her thoughts back on the beauty surrounding her. *I am blessed to here today—and I want to stay as positively focused as I can,* she reminded herself.

Kyra turned her attention back to admiring the contrasting combination of historic and modern architecture. Her eyes happily drank in every detail of the city's beauty, which was even more breathtaking than the photos in her travel guide had hinted at. There were, of course, the medieval-looking Gothic churches similar to those in Barcelona, but many more of the Neoclassical-style buildings with the strong Roman influence. She found the simplicity of the white neoclassical buildings heavenly. "I love the Italian influence," she said aloud.

"Then this will be a very inspiring trip for you—on many levels," Javier replied. Kyra could not have agreed with him more.

Once they arrived at Puerta del Sol—the Gate of the Sun—she

discovered that it was just as impressive as Javier had described. Semicircular in shape, the crowded plaza was surrounded by white limestone and red-brick buildings. From the car window, Kyra could see pedestrians from all walks of life filing the sidewalks. *They're all enjoying this beautiful Saturday afternoon, and in a short while, I'm going to be among them.*

She noted that her morning jitters had subsided, but an eerie feeling crept over her as she looked around. *This feels so incredibly familiar . . . like I've been here before. . .* Again, she had no idea where the strange feeling was coming from, but her intention felt stronger now that she had reached her destination.

Javier made a sharp right turn and parked the car. "We will be meeting Verónica at the fountain, then walk around a bit," he explained. "We'll also visit *Plaza de Cibeles* and then have lunch at *Casa Labra*. It's a popular tavern, and I think you will like it. Their specialty is cod."

As the pair walked to the meeting place, Kyra could almost feel Javier's delight when his face lit up upon seeing his beautiful wife. Verónica immediately stood and the couple shared a soft kiss on the lips. Then she promptly turned to Kyra to give her guest a warm hug. "*Es tan lindo volver a verte!*" she added, and then translated her words into English: "It's so nice to see you again!"

Verónica was petite like Kyra, but had long, straight dark hair. Her olive complexion was flawless and her eyes sparkled as she glanced at her husband. There was no mistaking how much in love they were with each other.

"Verónica, it is such a pleasure to see you again, too, and"—Kyra boldly decided to practice her Spanish a bit—"*Estoy segura de que nos vamos a diverter mucho hoy.*" She pronounced the words carefully, but still stumbled over a few.

Verónica responded sweetly, reassuring her new friend that she'd been understood, "I look forward to a fun day with you, too."

Javier took his wife's hand in his and led the way. "Let's walk around and see the plaza for a bit. We have much to show our guest today," he said, enticing Kyra to join them.

They walked unhurriedly around the square so that Kyra could take in all the sights. At the center of the square, where they'd met up with Verónica, stood a large equestrian statue. A likeness of King Carlos III, a famous king of Spain, sat gallantly upon the bronze stallion. Kyra noticed with interest how his stern face was turned toward one of the red-brick buildings framed in stunning soft-gray limestone.

Javier noticed Kyra's quizzical look and explained, "This building is called the *Real Casa de Correos*. It's the oldest building in the plaza. Today, the building serves as the seat for the President of the Community of Madrid, who is the leader of our regional government. . . . Hmmm, maybe that's too much information, " Javier said with a laugh. "Do I sound too much like a scholar?"

"Oh, no! I actually love hearing about the history of a place," Kyra assured him.

Verónica shot Javier a look of pride. "My husband loves sharing the city's history. Ask him any question, and he will know the answer."

Kyra's searching eyes turned toward another nearby gray stone building, which she pointed out to her friends. "I read about that building," she said. "It's home to the famous clock tower that rings out on New Year's Eve. What is the tradition again?"

Javier looked up at the tower. "Yes, the tower is famous for our good-luck tradition of eating twelve grapes, one for each hour struck by the clock before midnight. . . . We do love to eat here in Spain."

"That, it would appear, you most certainly do!" Kyra agreed, her eyes twinkled with amusement.

Thirty minutes later, they left the plaza, heading southwest by foot. After turning down a few streets, Verónica spoke up, "This is the *Plaza de Cibeles*. It is even larger and more beautiful than *Puerta del Sol*. This is one of my favorites. Do you like it?"

Kyra had enjoyed the brisk ten-minute walk and now looked out over the square-shaped plaza at the mostly white neoclassical architecture. The building had that Roman but elegant look she had so admired when they first drove into the city. Grand marble sculptures were everywhere the eye could travel—and, of course, the famous fountain of Cibeles sat directly in the middle of the square. This square looked markedly different from Puerta del Sol. "Amazing!" she said. "It reminds me of both Rome and Paris."

"Ah, yes, but we get to enjoy it here in Spain," Verónica replied playfully.

As they viewed the fountain, Kyra could see the Goddess Cibeles sitting fearlessly on a chariot pulled by two large lions. "Very dramatic," she said, gazing admiringly at the impressive sculpture. Then, with a sly look, she asked, "Cibeles is the goddess of fertility, right?"

Verónica blushed. "Have you been talking to my mother-in-law?"

The three friends burst out laughing, and Kyra quickly added, "I do admire that you Spaniards are very passionate about everything you do. From the food you eat, to the words you speak . . . and even to being in love."

"I can't agree with you more," said Verónica, tightly gripping Javier's hand.

The couple shared a private moment, while Kyra gazed back up at the statue. Her mind momentarily slipped back to her grad school days when she and Gabby had taken a seminar together during summer break. *What was it called? Oh yes, "Awakening Your Inner Goddess,"* Kyra chuckled, thinking of how Gabby had always encouraged her to take those silly classes. Now, she didn't think it so silly anymore.

*We learned an important lesson during that course. She tried to remember the exact wording and then replied, "In the midst of our fears, we should find our source of power and strength."*

With that memory intact, Kyra realized that she'd indeed been searching for her source of power and strength these past several weeks. *Yes, Cibeles*, she reflected. *That's what I intend to do: Awaken my inner goddess! It is time to feel empowered again.* Kyra felt her self-confidence growing, and she intended to make a different decision in many areas of her life—including only accepting unconditional love from a romantic partner.

With the young couple's moment past, Verónica motioned for Kyra to follow her and Javier toward the Palacio de Cibeles. "It's more simply known as the Cibeles Place," she explained as they walked. "This is the largest building in the square. Look at its magnificent stature and beauty."

The huge building—a white cathedral-like structure—made for a visually stunning image. Javier mentioned that the palace now housed City Hall.

"Sweetheart," Verónica said, her soft voice unusually excited, "let's walk up to the eight-floor observatory so that Kyra can enjoy the panoramic view of the city. *¿Sí?*"

"Are you up for an eighty-eight step walk up to the observatory?" Javier asked. "It has *magníficas vistas.*" He emphasized his Spanish choice of words, teasing Kyra to learn the language.

Kyra glanced down at her flat sandals, which she'd worn precisely for this reason, and quickly replied, "You bet! I'd love to see the view . . . and this will be great exercise before what I'm guessing is going to be a huge lunch at *Casa Labra*."

Her guides smiled, mostly because they knew she was right about lunch, and they all headed inside for their tickets to the eighth-floor observatory deck. They made a stop at the sixth-floor terrace bar to wait for their appointed time. The terrace bar had its own lovely mini view of Madrid, and they settled onto a cozy lime green couch in the lounge outside. Not much later, Javier was guiding them up a long marble staircase with Verónica and Kyra following close behind.

When Kyra turned the corner and exited onto the observatory deck, she caught her breath at the striking 360-degree view of Madrid, feeling as if she were at the highest peak of a magical world. She walked to the edge of the railing and looked out across Cibeles Plaza, which now lay below her. The beautiful fountain of the Goddess stood silently, as cars moved quickly through the streets surrounding her. Buildings stretched off in to the distance—perhaps even miles away. And mountains stood even further away, dramatically dark against the crystal-clear blue sky. Kyra looked over at her new friends and hoped her smile conveyed to them how fortunate she felt to experience this heart-expanding panoramic view with them.

After admiring the view for a while, Kyra, Javier, and Verónica returned to Cibeles Plaza with three buildings left to visit. First, they stopped at the Buenavista Palace, which faced the Cibeles Palace and had a delightful French garden and famous thousand-year old tree. Built in 1777, the palace now headquartered the Spanish Army.

They next visited the Banco de España, which Javier explained was the national Bank of Spain. Last, they went across the street to the Linares Palace, a quintessential example of a neo-baroque architecture, which had a heavy Italian influence. The building was surrounding by a delicate, but sturdy, wrought-iron fence that securely enclosed tranquil gardens.

Although they were making mostly cursory stops, the gorgeous interior of Linares was well worth the one-hour tour. With great admiration, Kyra took in the elaborate ballrooms, the Hall of Mirrors, a private chapel, and a luxurious grand dining room. Coupled with an abundance of artwork and sculptures, it was clear that no expense had been spared decorating this nineteenth-century palace. Although it was a sensory overload of opulence, Kyra felt strangely drawn to the ornate décor, despite her more simplistic style of furnishings back home. She was reminded again of the strange feeling she'd had earlier in the square when she felt like she'd visited this area before.

A chill crept up her spine, and she would have pondered the feeling longer, but Javier interrupted. "Let us go enjoy our lunch at *Casa Labra* as promised. Then we'll head to the famous *Museo del Prado*; it is just a little further south and close by *Puerta de Sol*."

Verónica chimed in, "Yes, Javier, I'm so hungry after all our walking around today that my stomach is growling like the lions pulling Cibeles' Chariot!"

Kyra could not have agreed more. Surprisingly, her stomach seemed ready for lunch today, too. *Perhaps I have some Spanish blood in me after all*, she laughed to herself. Lingering a little behind Javier and Verónica as they walked hand in hand, she stole one last glance at the Goddess, remembering the vow she'd made. *Yes, Cibeles, with your guidance, my inner power and strength are awakening.*

# 17

Back in the Puerta del Sol area, the trio approached Casa Labra. According to Javier, the restaurant had been there for nearly one hundred fifty years. Tall dark wood panels gave the tavern a quaint appearance on the outside. The dark-wood theme continued inside, but large mirrors added a touch of lightness. Casual wooden chairs accompanied small dining tables, and each gray-marble tabletop wore a vibrant red tablecloth, adding brightness and color.

*It's casual, yet somewhat refined . . . and very inviting, almost like a family home,* Kyra thought as they headed toward the maître d' at the height of the lunch hour. She noticed that the patrons who crowded the restaurant all appeared to be young professionals.

As the hostess led them to a table in the corner, Javier commented, "As you can see, it's a very popular place with the locals. Let's enjoy some *vino*—or perhaps a *cerveza*—but only a glass or two . . . Gabriela mentioned you may not like it if we get too *loco*."

A soft snicker escaped Verónica's lips, and mild surprise spread across Kyra's face. She wondered what Gabby had said to Javier prior her arrival, but she kept her thoughts to herself. Javier's eyes only twinkled in response, as they took their seats.

"Ah, but let's talk about the food here," Javier said, changing the subject. "Cod is the specialty, as I mentioned earlier. I'll let you ladies look at a menu for a moment to decide what you like."

After perusing the menu for only a moment, Kyra looked up. "I do love my seafood, especially after living in San Francisco for five years. With that in mind, I think I'll have the house special—the cod croquette and a cod salad." She looked over at Verónica to hear what she'd decided upon.

"*Bacalao a la Bilbaína* for me! That's grilled cod with garlic and fried chile peppers," she explained, then added with a teasing tone, "Javier, order something with garlic, too, or you may not want to be around me later!"

Javier winked, then ordered the *Bacalao en Salsa Verde,* which he noted would have *plenty* of garlic. "We'll be quite the pair later," he said in a serious tone. His deadpan humor brought giggles to the women's lips.

Next they studied the wine list. Verónica ordered first. "*Hermanos Lurton, por favor,*" which she explained to Kyra was made from the Verdejo grape—soft and fruity in taste. Kyra chose a glass of San Carbás made from a local Chardonnay grape, which she noted was crisper with a touch of citrus. Javier ordered a simple local cerveza.

When their drinks arrived, Javier raised his beer for a toast. "*Este brindis es para ti.*" he said cheerfully. "Or, in English, 'This toast is for you.'" Then he added, "*¡Salud! ¡Salud, dinero y amor, y tiempo para disfrutar de ellos!*"

Kyra's comprehension of Spanish continued to improve, and she managed to translate his words for the most part: "Cheers! Health, money, love, and time to enjoy them!"

Kyra clinked the edge of her glass to her friends' and said, "I'll drink to that. Cheers. *¡Salud!*"

As they ate their meals, the couple had many questions for Kyra about her life in the U.S. She chose to place the focus on the time she spent in nature, describing Muir Woods and Stinson Beach, and her love of art and cultural events, rather than discuss her business life.

When they finished, Javier paid the bill, although Kyra had insisted on paying. "Today, you are our guest," he told her. "It's our treat," and then he would hear nothing more of it.

After lunch, they walked to *Museo del Prado,* which was located not too far south.

Arriving in front of the enormous white neo-classically designed building. Verónica said proudly but rather quickly, "*Museo del Prado es uno de los más grandes.*"

Kyra smiled politely. "My Spanish is getting better, but it's not that good yet."

Verónica gave her a bashful smile in return. "So sorry. It's one of the largest art museums in the world. It is also one of my favorite places to visit in all of Madrid. I was an art major in school. This building is quite lovely with a grand rotunda, and the central gallery is full of natural light, not artificial, which is best for looking at paintings and sculptures." She paused, and then continued, as if a thought had just struck her, "There are over seven thousand paintings here. But not all are on display. Because the collection is so large, two more buildings have been added to the original building. It's more than we can look at in one day, but *disfrutar!*"

This time, Kyra did not ask for a translation, as she was pretty sure she had understood, and replied, "I very much intend to *enjoy*. I absolutely adore viewing artwork." Kyra felt a sudden desire to express affection for their budding friendship and learned over to embrace her new friend. The hug felt natural and comfortable and was met enthusiastically.

As they strolled through the amazing collections, Verónica explained that the paintings and drawings were divided among multiple nationalities: Spanish, Italian, German, Flemish, French, British, and Dutch. While Kyra could appreciate the enormous variety of paintings, she admired the exquisiteness of the Impressionist masterpieces most of all.

Ironically, she realized she was equally admiring the attractive Spanish men who also walked the gallery floors. She shared a flirtatious glance with yet another attractive man, who looked her up and down as he passed by, which made her chuckle. She felt like a young girl again. Her mind briefly went to Steve, and she searched her feelings. *I really don't miss him . . . I no longer feel trapped and wounded.* She felt a surge of pride at that last thought, and then felt herself tingle. *The men here are rekindling my appetite. This change of scenery is exactly what I needed!* Turning to Verónica, she whispered, "Spain is stimulating all of my senses—from the fine art and the delightful food to the very attractive men."

Verónica gave her a playful, conspiratorial nod, and Kyra felt their friendship deepening.

They remained at the museum until closing time at 8 pm, and despite the long day, Kyra didn't feel the least bit tired.

"Are you ladies almost ready for *la cena*—the dinner meal?" Javier asked as they stepped out onto the street.

"I didn't think I could possibly be hungry after our lovely lunch at *Casa Labra*, but all the walking around the museum has made me famished!" Kyra said. "I think the Lions of Cibeles' Chariot are making my stomach growl now."

Verónica laughed. "We better find a place to eat quickly so we don't *starve* our guest." "I have a destination in mind, of course," Javier said. "But first let's go explore the lively Huertas District. I think Kyra's lions may work up even *more* of an appetite." Laughing too, Kyra agreed, and with that, they headed back to the car.

When they were once again on foot, Kyra found herself admiring the narrow but charming streets of the Huertas District. They wandered past pubs and clubs, many of which were jamming with loud music. It was Saturday night, after all, and it seemed to Kyra that everyone was out enjoying the night. They passed many restaurants with outdoor tables and big white umbrellas. The smell of freshly prepared tapas wafted through the air, reaching Kyra's nostrils and firing up her appetite.

Almost sensing her desire, Javier said, "We'll have dinner tonight at *Viva Madrid*. It's actually just off the *Plaza de Santa Ana* and very close to your hotel, Kyra—if that sounds good to you?"

Kyra nodded in eager affirmation, and they left the district behind in the direction of the new barrio. As they drove, Verónica told her that the venue they were heading to was quite popular with the locals and known for its attentive wait staff. "It's perfect for a quick bite to eat."

As they approached the restaurant, Kyra admired the beautiful hand-painted tiles extending halfway up the wall, adding bright splashes of gold, green, and blue to the gray facade. A few of the tiles spelled out *Vinos Finos* in small letters, which she knew to mean *Fine Wines*. When her eyes fell on the large tiled version of the Goddess Cibeles on her chariot, she stopped.

"The goddess of fertility seems to be everywhere in this city." Kyra said, looking over at Verónica, who nodded and blushed at the reminder.

As they walked inside, Kyra felt excited by the synchronicity of seeing the goddess twice in one day. She whispered under her breath, *Yes, Cibeles, I haven't forgotten . . . You've been helping me awaken my inner goddess—and I can't wait to see what's in store for us next!*

Once inside, Kyra took in the elegant, but relaxed, feel of the restaurant's old-word charm. A large crystal chandelier radiated sparkles of light in the otherwise dimly lit bar area, illuminating the rows of liquor bottles lining a mirrored wall behind the main bar. She gently rolled her head back to look up at the intricately carved wood ceiling. Small cherub-like creatures perched just below the ceiling on the wall above the bar. The winged angelic beings appeared to be keeping a watchful eye over the patrons.

*Perhaps they are protecting this place,* Kyra thought, recalling her childhood bible studies that cherubs are angels thought to be guardians. *Regardless,* she mused, *it's nice to believe they are here keeping us safe.*

With that thought, Kyra realized how playful she was being with herself, and how free her mind was becoming. Her eyes were indeed opening to all the possibilities being offered to her by the Universe. She felt comforted by the recurring signs she noticed nearly every place she visited—signs that reminded her there is a lot more at play in life for her to ponder and discover.

After they ordered a glass of wine at the bar, their waiter motioned for them to follow him to a small table in the back. As she walked past the other patrons, Kyra took pleasure in the same beautiful tile work reaching halfway up the walls. Large mirrored walls overlooked dark wooden tables, and simple modern chairs were covered in a gray and red suede-like fabric.

At Javier's request, the waiter brought sparkling water to the table before they ordered.

Kyra glanced around the restaurant; a group of six locals seated at a nearby table were exuberantly celebrating a friend's birthday. They appeared to be in their mid-thirties and well dressed. A young attractive man in a blue dress shirt raised his glass in a toast. "*¡Feliz cumpleaños!*" he said to one of the women seated at the table. The other four raised their glasses as well and shouted, "*¡Feliz cumpleaños!*" The woman of honor seemed to be enjoying the attention but looked embarrassed all the same.

Javier glanced over. "Ah, the *madrileños* are having fun tonight!" Kyra raised an eyebrow, and Javier explained, "*Madrileño* is a native of Madrid."

"I like that term," she said smiling. "Perhaps tonight I can be an honorary *madrileña*." "In that case, may I order you *madrileñas* some mojitos?" Javier asked. "It's the house specialty, and of course, we will share a few tapas."

"That sounds *perfecto*, *mi amor*," Verónica replied.

Javier skillfully ordered a wide variety of dishes, and soon the three friends stuffed themselves silly with far too much food.

"Ah, Javier, we have done it again!" Verónica said when she finished her last bite.

Turning to Kyra, she added, "And you've certainly tamed your lions. I am amazed by how much you can fit into your slim body, *¡Bien hecho, Kyra!* That means 'Well done!'"

"I think my eyes were bigger than my stomach," Kyra lamented, rubbing her very full belly.

Verónica looked perplexed, and Kyra smiled as she tried to explain her play on the American expression. "I mean I ate more than I should have! What was I thinking?"

Javier waved his hand in acknowledgment, but Verónica still looked perplexed. All three simultaneously burst out laughing, realizing that something had been lost in translation.

After catching his breath, Javier offered up a thought: "I have one last fun place for us to visit tonight—if you ladies are not too tired. The theater is close by and it's called *Cardamomo Tablao Flamenco*." Kyra's eyes lit up at the word "Flamenco," and Javier noticed her interest. "It's just around the corner and comes with a high recommendation from Verónica. The Flamenco dancers and the music will delight your senses."

"I would love that," Kyra replied without hesitation, not once giving a thought to the late hour.

Verónica clapped her hands in excitement. "It's a small and intimate venue, but if you love Flamenco, you will adore the dancers and music. Let's go!"

When they reached the club, Javier purchased the tickets for the 10 pm show, again insisting upon treating. "That's extremely generous of you, Javier," Kyra said. She'd thought about how often she and Steve had split costs on the things they'd done together—Javier's generosity felt out of the ordinary, but incredible just the same. She immediately dismissed any further thoughts of Steve, realizing that the law of attraction was at work. *My future partner will be generous and a true gentlemen, just like Javier,* she affirmed with confidence as they stepped inside.

The interior of the theater was dimly lit and narrow. Simple dark wood stools surrounded small tables covered with bright multicolored tablecloths. A single red carnation lay atop each table, completing the traditional, festive look. Kyra glanced around the room as they sat down; the aged appearance of the walls caught her attention. The dark red brick appeared to be crumbling in places, and old black-and-white photographs of famous people who had once visited adorned those walls.

*I was just thinking of how much I'd love to see a Flamenco show on my flight this morning, and now I'm here—yet another synchronicity,* Kyra realized, silently acknowledging the magical workings of the Universe.

Kyra and Verónica each ordered a *tinto de verano*, which Kyra learned was a type of sangria made with red wine, ice, and lemon soda. Fresh fruit garnished their glasses. Javier ordered *Estrella Galicia,* a local pale lager beer.

Just before the show began, Verónica explained, "Some of the dancers tonight will perform traditional Flamenco, but others will dance a more modern style of Flamenco, which will look very different. Both are excellent, and it will be fun show."

"I'm sure it will be wonderful," Kyra replied, her voice trailing off, as the announcer walked onstage and the crowd came to a quiet hush.

Soon the dancers appeared, one by one, and Kyra watched the passionate performances with spellbound attention. Musicians lined the side of the stage, masterfully strumming and plucking their guitars, while both men and women took turns dancing the Flamenco center stage. A singer wailed soulfully as each performer danced. Kyra wished she could fully understand the words—but she could not help but *feel* the passion and emotions stirring her soul.

The costumes were elaborate, as expected. The women wore long flowing gowns of red, black, and white. The fabric swirled around their expressive bodies, and their shoes tapped rhythmically in perfect sync with the beat. Bodies swayed and arms flowed with a dramatic flair, as the movement and the tapping escalated in intensity as each song progressed.

The men in their solid black pants and shirts with matching straw *Cordobes* hats especially caught Kyra's attention. They were powerful dancers who rivaled the women in skill. When one particular good-looking dancer took center stage, she and Verónica exchanged an appreciative glance.

Verónica leaned in. "Some of the men trained in classical ballet early in their careers, but tonight, they are very *macho* and passionate."

Kyra smiled at Verónica's choice of words. "Yes, very masculine indeed . . . and quite attractive in their costumes."

The dancer's shoes pounded the floor—but, at the same time, he was exceptionally light on his feet. His trim, athletic body moved precisely and artfully, as he clapped his strong hands, emphasizing the rhythm of the music. The sensual movements and raw emotion filled her senses, as her eyes rapidly followed his rhythmic actions.

As if reading her mind, Verónica whispered, "Flamenco is a dance of the heart, Kyra, rhythmically moving to awaken the soul."

Kyra could not have put it better herself—her senses had never felt so heightened. "I feel so alive tonight! I think Flamenco *is* awakening my soul," she replied.

The show ended about a half hour before midnight. Shortly after, Javier and Verónica dropped Kyra off at her hotel, the ME Madrid

Reina Victoria at the Plaza Santa Ana. The luxurious hotel stood at the opposite end of the square from the elegant eighteenth-century Teatro Español, also known as the Spanish Theatre, which Kyra looked forward to visiting the next day.

The hotel itself was about six stories tall with an exquisite white stone exterior; unique exterior lighting gave it a soft neon lavender glow. *It looks heavenly and almost ethereal,* Kyra thought as she glanced up at the top floor. The late-night crowd buzzed in the square, and she felt her eyes growing heavy with sleepiness. *Such a wonderful day,* she thought with a yawn, *but after all that walking and exploring, a good night's sleep is what I need.*

Javier lifted her heavy suitcase from the trunk of his Peugeot and effortlessly placed it on the curbside. Verónica had gotten out of the car, too, insisting they walk her into the hotel, but Kyra assured her that she would be just fine on her own. She looked at the couple with much gratitude in her heart and said, "I can't thank you enough for this amazing day. I will see you back at the hotel tomorrow evening for cocktails at The Roof terrace. This time it will be my treat!" She reached out and gave each a warm hug and kiss on the cheek. "*¡Buenas noches!*"

"It has been our delight to spend this day with you," Javier responded. "We look forward to seeing you tomorrow night. Sleep well. *Buenas noches.*"

Verónica waved a kiss in the air, reminding Kyra of Gabby, which brought a smile to her weary face. That smile was still on her lips as she quietly rolled her suitcase into the main lobby. The hotel's sleek modern design, contrasting sharply with the traditional exterior, immediately captivated her. Her feet padded across the soft beige marble floors, as she admired the lobby's décor. Built-in dark wood bookcases and plush red fabric chairs decorated the foyer, and a sizable beige ceramic vase holding white lilies added a graceful touch of elegance.

After checking in, Kyra took the elevator to the fifth floor. She had splurged for the Energy Room, which had some pleasant amenities over the standard rooms. As she walked in, she noticed that the lovely dark hardwood floors were very similar to the floors in her San Francisco condo. For a moment, she longed for home—but only briefly—and fully turned her attention back to her lovely surroundings.

The plush, neutral bedding on the luxurious king-size bed beckoned for her to lie down and sleep. Soft light emanated from above the bed and from the ceiling of the opposite wall giving the room a glowing effect. She looked at the built-in desk, and secretly felt glad that she had no work to do, placing her purse and room key down where she normally would have put her briefcase. Walking over to the curtains covering the balcony doors, she flung them back and looked outside the large glass doors to the private balcony. The spectacular view left her in awe as she looked out across the twinkling city lights.

"It's simply dazzling," she said aloud. The flicker of lights far off in the distance teased her imagination with their fantasy-like appearance.

She pressed her nose against the glass, the way she once had when she was a child. *When did I lose my ability to dream?* she wondered. *When I was younger, I was so open and free. I believed that anything was possible—long before I got into my corporate career.* She sighed and then slid the huge glass doors apart, stepping out onto the balcony. The rich, cool evening air filled her lungs, and she fully took in the wondrous view of the city.

Lost in the euphoria of the moment, Kyra felt her heart filling with joy. She momentarily forgot how tired she was and lingered on the balcony for a few moments of appreciation. *I have come so far this past month. I would never have taken this much time in my old life to enjoy my hotel surroundings . . . and, sadly, I would already be absorbed in emails at this point in the evening.*

Turning to go back inside, she stopped and added, *Thank you, God, for giving me this amazing time to rethink my life. It is truly is a blessing.*

Her eyes filled with tears as she stepped back through the door. She glanced at the bed and felt the need to lie down and sleep. After washing up and dressing in her nightshirt, she eagerly snuggled between the feather duvet bedding and the soft cotton sheets. The bed was so comfortable that she fell asleep almost as fast as her head hit the pillow . . . and then she began to dream.

She was sitting on a sandy shore of some unknown beach, but she could see the moonlight beaming down brightly on her pale skin. She stood up and then looked down at her bare feet; they were small and almost childlike.

Gazing out across the soft ocean waves, Kyra watched the moonlight gently reflecting off the water. The sky was filled with millions of twinkling stars, just like she remembered from her childhood. *The night looks magical . . . like a fairytale*, she mused whimsically, but she was part of it. She slowly turned her attention back to the ground and turned around. Her breath caught in her throat as she saw a breathtakingly beautiful woman standing right behind her . . .

Kyra awoke and sat straight up in bed, slowly becoming aware of her surroundings. The memories of her familiar dream did not fade away, but she struggled to remember it clearly. She *had* dreamed of this woman often as a child.

*Who is she?* Kyra wondered. She searched her memories but finally realized she did not know. She felt that the woman was familiar—very familiar—as if . . . well, as if she had *always* known her.

# 18

Kyra looked over at the clock. It was 8:08 am. A few more minutes passed as she collected her thoughts. Then she drifted out of bed and brewed a small pot of coffee. When the coffee was ready, she filled a white coffee mug to the brim and held the hot beverage in both hands, sipping gently. As she breathed in the strong aroma, she savored the experience and thought, *I don't know what this day will hold for me, but I'm eager to see what unfolds. It's time to start dreaming again . . .*

The shower experience in the spa-like bathroom of the Energy Room made for an incredible start to what would be an amazing day. Kyra dressed in a light blue linen skirt with a white silk tank top, and topped off her outfit with a thin black-and-white striped sweater to cover her arms in the midday sun as she walked to and from her destinations. She wore comfortable, but fashionable gold metallic Prada sandals, and her bright-red toenails added a nice splash of color to her summer outfit. She made sure to place a good pair of sunglasses in her purse.

*I feel great today!* she thought, as she looked at her glowing reflection in the full-length mirror. This Sunday morning she would be exploring Madrid on her own. The weather promised to be deliciously warm, but the air-conditioned buildings she'd visit would offer a welcome respite throughout the day.

Kyra looked down at her handwritten itinerary. "I'm so well organized—old habits die hard," she laughed aloud, thinking back to her corporate days of planning every detail of her workday. She squinted at the paper, which listed five places to see. *No, I will not be in corporate mode with my agenda,* she decided with a pleased smile. *This is going to be a leisurely day.*

Following a double espresso and fruit for breakfast at the hotel restaurant, Kyra walked, with a bounce in her step, to the east end of the Santa Ana Plaza toward Teatro Español. A light morning breeze swept through her hair, making it feel a few degrees cooler. She felt proud for venturing out on her own and did not regret the time alone to explore the city of Madrid.

As she neared the Teatro Español, she felt irresistibly drawn to the nineteenth-century neoclassic-style building. *This feels even stronger than my previous attractions to the area,* she thought curiously. Brushing off the odd sensation, she glanced up at the elegant two-story cream-colored building. Tall white Roman columns gave the building a regal presence, and old-fashioned cast-iron lampposts on the sidewalk reminded her of an era long gone. Thick wrought-iron railings on the second-floor balconies complemented the overall look, softening the aging, but still stunning, Teatro Español.

As she took a step forward, a peculiar feeling came over her, causing her to stop midstride. Her head spun, and a prickly sensation on her arms made her hairs stand on end. Taking a gasp of air, she squeezed her eyes shut to regain her composure. But when she reopened them, she still could not get her bearings. Women dressed in elegant, flowing gowns passed by, each accessorized with a decorative umbrella delicately held in their pale white hands. Kyra blinked. These women hadn't been there before. Men, too, had suddenly appeared, it seemed, dressed in black-and-white suits.

*Large top hats make them look almost dandy*, Kyra thought. . . . *Dandy? When have I ever used that word?*

She watched in perplexed amazement as the nineteenth-century-style ladies, each accompanied by her gentleman, strolled leisurely into the theater. Kyra instinctively felt as if she were somewhere else in time, although that made absolutely no sense.

With a sudden jolt, her previous surroundings returned. She glanced around the plaza in disbelief, which was now as it had been moments before. Inhaling deeply, she fumbled for the bottle of water in her purse. She took a huge swig of the cool liquid, trying to calm her nerves.

*What just happened? It seemed so faint . . . like my imagination . . . but so real at the same time. A memory, perhaps?* she wondered. She shook her head to rid herself of any such thoughts. *That doesn't make any sense at all.* Deep down, Kyra knew that she'd somehow had a real, if not surreal, experience, but her logical mind refused to let her believe it.

*It must have been my imagination,* she sternly tried to convince herself. She placed the water bottle back in her bag and started forward. When she stepped to go inside, she felt lightheaded and a tingling sensation rushed up her spine to her neck.

Once inside, Kyra embraced the cool air before standing in line to sign up for the one-hour tour. She took a moment to collect herself. Her intuition seemed to assure her that she was safe and the momentary flashback was over. She paid for her ticket and took a brochure over to a seat in the main lobby to learn more of the history of Teatro Español. Shifting her thoughts away from her strange experience, she began to read, which calmed her further.

The land upon which the building sat had originally been an open-air theater in medieval times where famous classical literature was performed. The theater claimed four hundred years of uninterrupted stage performances since the seventeenth century, which Kyra greatly admired. Appreciating the theater's long history, she fondly reminisced back to her high school days when she'd read the works of William Shakespeare. The early modern English style of Shakespeare's writing had never quite resonated with her, but she especially enjoyed the live outdoor performance of *Romeo and Juliet* she had seen at the Shakespeare in The Park series. She relished her memories of those warm summer nights in Chicago, watching many shows in the Shakespeare series under the twinkling stars. She felt thankful that being in this place could rekindle those feelings.

*I was so fortunate to be able to go those performances—first with my parents when I was very young and later with my friends. And how inspirational they were!* Kyra recalled that she could actually feel the passion emanating from the actors as they played their roles upon the stage. *Now I sit here today, still so very fortunate, about to enjoy a tour of this amazing theater.*

Kyra glanced up from her brochure just as the guide announced that the tour was ready to begin. First the small group visited both the grand main auditorium, as well as a second smaller hall that was used for more intimate performances. The main auditorium seated eight hundred people, and its ceilings and walls were ornately accented with gilt. Dark crushed red velvet and gold fabric added color and intensity to the room. By contrast, the smaller hall was much simpler in design with only one hundred or so seats, which completely surrounded the main stage in the center of the room.

*How impressive to have such a long history of theater on these grounds,* thought Kyra as she exited the small theater. *So very unlike the U.S. where most venues are less than fifty years old.*

With the tour at the Teatro Español behind her and the alarming flashback firmly out of her head, Kyra looked at the directions she'd jotted down on her itinerary. Her next destination, the Palacio Real de Madrid—known in English as the Royal Palace of Madrid—was a short walking distance away. The huge palace, located on Bailén Street, was one of the largest palaces in all of Europe. Kyra had diligently researched the palace earlier and discovered that it had been built nearly three hundred years earlier and had been loosely modeled after Versailles near Paris. *Of all my destinations today, the idea of seeing the palace gets me excited the most!*

She walked energetically to the south side of the building and arrived at the main entrance, Plaza de la Armería. The enormous stone plaza was located directly in front of the palace, and a massive wrought-iron fence surrounded the perimeter, adding to the stately tone of the entryway. Kyra walked through the main gateway. As she continued toward the front door, she observed that the baroque-style building was made mostly of limestone and granite. *Majestic* and *massive* were the words that came to mind. And as far as the inside was concerned, Kyra could hardly believe there were 2,800 rooms in all. She knew her time was limited and was a bit disheartened to think she'd only see about thirty rooms once inside.

When the tour began, Kyra learned that the palace was no longer the residence of the King and Queen of Spain; it was now used mostly for state ceremonies and special events. The Royal Couple resided in a more modest palace called Palacio de la Zarzuela on the outskirts of Madrid. As the tour commenced, the lavish decoration and rich materials—a sumptuous blend of Spanish marble, stucco, mahogany doors and windows, and fabulous works of art—amazed her. Kyra thought of Verónica and her similar love of art. *I'm sure Verónica would have made an amazing tour guide had she joined me today. But I have no regrets venturing out on my own. This is wonderful!*

Feeling her confidence increase, Kyra visited a few of the rooms, and then found herself being led to the *Salón del Trono*, the Throne Room. She'd come across photos of it in her research, which had certainly piqued her curiosity and heightened her anticipation, but now she felt pulled to it as if by a powerful magnet. She anxiously stepped into the grand room.

Crimson velvet, frescoed ceilings, and opulent full-length mirrors covered the walls, and a large red silk area rug covered much of the floor. The gilded furniture, monstrous chandeliers, candelabras, and intricate wall tapestries made for a splendid, if not over-the-top, display. The throne chairs where the King and Queen had once sat were also upholstered in crimson velvet with elaborate gold trim. As Kyra walked nearer, her eyes fell on the four awesome, life-sized bronze lion statues fiercely guarding the chairs, seemingly protecting the kingdom from harm.

But what happened next, Kyra was not at all prepared for. As she gazed at the statues, her vision began to blur. The room began to spin, and she closed her eyes to regain her composure—just as she had earlier outside the Teatro Español. When she opened her eyes, she found herself kneeling before the throne.

A young king and queen were perched atop the plush throne chairs. Glancing down at herself, she realized she was dressed in simple pants and a shirt. She instinctively knew she was a servant. When she glanced her hands, she had the startling realization that she was not a woman at all, but a young man. And, in her hands, she held a large, heavy package—a gift she was presenting on behalf of a visiting nobleman.

The stately nobleman stood directly beside her. Though he spoke in fluent Spanish, she understood his words perfectly. He knelt, too, and said, "Esteemed King and Queen of Spain. On behalf of my family, I wish to offer this small gift as a token of our gratitude to the kingdom." He signaled to Kyra to place the package in front of the king and queen.

With another jolt, Kyra was again well behind the visitors' boundaries and staring at the empty thrones. Disoriented, she felt sweat on her brow, and her mouth was dry. *Is it possible that I just experienced a past life as a servant in the kingdom? Or did I just imagine it?* Caught between admitting she'd experienced another flashback and trying to blame it on an overactive imagination, her mind raced for answers. She'd never had such an experience before. *Why now,* she wondered, *in Madrid of all places—and twice in one day!* Kyra felt a rush of adrenaline, but the answers did not come. She had no idea where the truth lay, so she took a few deep, collective breaths. To further complicate her thought process, she realized with some alarm that this second flashback—if it was indeed a flashback—was much stronger than the first.

Trying to remain calm, she immediately turned to her intuition to sense the room around her. Much to her surprise, it felt calm and safe—not at all what she was expecting. She could discern that no harm would come her way and the momentary experience had once again passed. Relieved, she let out a huge sigh. Deep in the core of her being, she believed this was a sign that she was destined to be in Spain, here and now. *But why?* she wondered.

Hoping the answers would come, Kyra decided to forgo the remainder of her tour and walked out of the throne room, then outside the palace, and back into Plaza de la Armería where she welcomed the warmth of the sunlight on her face. She squinted in the brightness as her eyes adjusted to the light and placed a hand on her brow to look out across the plaza. All seemed perfect and calm.

She took another few minutes before deciding to continue on to the next place on her agenda. *I can't let this affect me,* she firmly told herself. *It will all make sense someday—just not today. Besides, I'm looking forward to seeing the cathedral.*

Putting on her sunglasses, she headed toward the Catedral de Santa María la Real de la Almudena—more simply known as the Almudena

Cathedral—which was also located on the grounds of the palace. Kyra kept her composure while she recalled the details of the structure. The opulent Baroque-style building was less dramatic than the Royal Palace, but still quite beautiful. The monumental central dome immediately caught her eye and, from what she had read, was almost sixty-five-feet wide.

Feeling calmer, she gazed at the building. *The lovely deep gray of the dome reminds me of the deepest slate gray of the sky at twilight . . . just before the sky turns midnight blue and the stars twinkle brilliantly.* She had no idea why this image suddenly appeared in her mind, but it was a comforting thought and reminded her again of the many sunsets she had witnessed on the California beaches.

Kyra stopped and snapped a few photos before walking through the intricately sculpted bronze front doors depicting the Crucifixion of Christ. She ran her hand delicately along the door in admiration. Once inside, she was taken aback by the church's bright, modern interior. Embellished with elegant touches of gold and brightly colored stained-glass windows, the otherwise white walls offered a gorgeous sight to behold. The main altar lay atop a broad, flowing staircase leading up to a second level. Sunlight streamed through the multicolored stained-glass windows, filling the church with a rainbow of light—which in turn filled Kyra's being with joy.

As she began to walk through the cathedral, she looked up at the ceiling of the central dome—and what she saw brought her to an immediate, awestruck halt. There, above her head, was an amazing crystal sphere laced with gold filigree with four gold crosses surrounding it.

Kyra wondered if the four crosses represented the four directions. Her gaze rested on the deep sapphire blue upon which the crystal sphere and the four crosses were overlaid. To her amazement, gold stars filled the sapphire blue of the celestial dome, an almost perfect replica of the vision she had experienced in her mind's eye just outside the cathedral. She held her gaze upon the breathtaking image and imagined the dark blue sky and twinkling stars at night. *How incredibly strange! My intuition is heightened here . . . and it's growing stronger.* With that thought, she realized she was willing to embrace this innate gift, rather than trying to fight it as she had sometimes done in the past. She beamed in admiration as she took in the ceiling's wondrous light and beauty, imagining it looked just like heaven. *The light is so clear and bright here—it seems to pierce my very soul.* She felt like a child again lost in a dream.

Kyra spent another twenty minutes inside before she stepped back outside into the bright sunlight. It was close to 2:30 pm when her stomach acknowledged the time. *I'm ready for lunch!* she laughed. *When in Spain, eat when the Spaniards do.*

Kyra strolled to Plaza de Oriente, a rectangular park comprised of three different gardens that stood on the east side of the palace. She decided to purchase lunch at one of the nearby cafés and enjoy it on the grounds. Though she had more on her to-do list, taking a moment to chill after her unnerving experiences seemed appropriate and much needed.

With a small bottle of wine and a few tapas in hand, she made her way to the Central Gardens, which housed magnificent cypress and magnolia trees alongside thoughtfully laid out flowerbeds of bright red and pure white blooms. A set of life-sized limestone statues—the Gothic Kings—bordered the main sidewalks inside the garden. There were forty-four statues in all, and Kyra drifted past them, feeling almost as if she were walking in the garden of kings.

Still toting her lunch, she visited the Cabo Noval and Lepanto Gardens, both very lush with carefully trimmed box hedges and large cedar trees. As she walked past an elderly couple wandering the gardens, Kyra's stomach unexpectedly let out a loud grumble—and likely the loudest one she had experienced to date. The couple looked startled, and Kyra, who was also astonished, turned a bright shade of red.

In a delightful British accent, the man said, "Young lady, you'd better eat something soon. That sounded like a royal twenty-one-gun salute!"

His wife chuckled and added, "Just ignore him, my dear. My husband has a wicked sense of humor."

With a sheepish grin, Kyra replied, "I do seem to have developed *quite* the appetite since I've been in Spain. Thank goodness I just bought my lunch. Uh . . . enjoy your visit!"

Nodding good day to the amused couple, Kyra quickly continued along the path, trying to keep her dignity intact. *I have heightened all of my senses . . . including my desire for food—oh my goodness!* She laughed, very much looking forward to sitting down to dine and rest a bit before venturing off to her next destination.

Kyra's last garden to visit, the Sabatini Gardens, lay on the north side of the palace. The gorgeous neoclassical-style gardens were named for Francesco Sabatini, the Italian architect who had designed the royal stables that had previously occupied the site. She eyed the manicured hedges laid out in beautiful geometrical designs bordering lovely walking paths. In the center of the gardens rested a large, rectangular reflecting pond surrounded by four fountains. *A perfect spot for lunch*, she decided with delight.

When Kyra sat down, she realized just how tired she was and kicked off her sandals. Placing her bare feet in the grass beside her small picnic lunch, she tossed her head back and exhaled, *Ahhhh . . . how delicious it feels to have my feet touching the warm, soft grass.*

Opening her bag of tapas, she arranged the small dishes on a large napkin. There was a scrumptious selection of meatballs in a red sauce, fried squid, roasted new potatoes with mojo sauce, fresh mushrooms in olive oil, and a small slice of a local creamy cheese with olives. She could still hear the café owner giving her advice—thankfully in English—on which foods to choose: "*Señorita*, please try this one!" and "This *vino* would be perfect to accompany your meal."

Next she opened the bottle of wine, poured herself a generous glass, and carefully lifted the glass to her nose, inhaling the rich bouquet of the red wine. The *Marques de Riscal Rioja Reserva* boasted an aromatic blend of cherries, oak, and spice, and was well priced at only nine U.S. dollars.

Between sips of wine, she slowly at her tapas and savored each bite. The warm afternoon and the wine relaxed her immensely. Once satisfied by the delicious food and drink, she folded up her napkin and moved close to the large reflecting pond. The golden sunlight danced as it reflected on her face, and Kyra gazed down at her reflection in the pond. Her face looked so much more relaxed than it had been before her journey began. Her serious demeanor had given way to a more pleasant, smiling manner befitting a woman who craved much more passion and balance in her life.

*What a dramatic change I've experienced this past month,* she reflected. *I am no longer a successful corporate executive. I no longer have a handsome "part-time" boyfriend . . . and I no longer have my wonderful Nana in my life.*

Kyra felt a wave of sadness wash over her at the thought of her beloved grandmother, but she also felt a deep sense of gratitude for Nana's unconditional love. Her grandmother had never judged her once and had always been there for her when she needed her most. *That's something Steve was never able to do for me,* she thought. *But I'm open now for something much deeper in a relationship . . . and in a career, too. When my travels are over, I will have many new opportunities to choose from.*

Kyra glanced again into the pond at her reflection and saw a truly beautiful woman gazing back at her from the water. This woman was smiling, but more important, she was indeed becoming more empowered and purposeful in her life.

"I am an amazing woman on an amazing journey," she said aloud, not caring who might hear her, "and I am going to take this time to figure out *how* I want my life to be. I don't know where this journey will lead me, but I ask God to point me in the right direction so I can live an extraordinary and meaningful life."

Kyra felt tears of happiness pooling in her eyes. She realized how much she had been craving a very different life from the one she had in San Francisco, and she was asking God to put her on the right path—toward her real purpose in life. The choice was hers to make and she had control over her life. *It's called free will,* she reminded herself, remembering how the concept had been explained during one of her old Reiki classes back in her grad school days.

Her mind shifted, and she thought again of the fiery-eyed fortune-teller in Barcelona. A chill ran down her spine, and she trembled for a moment. What had the woman said? That she would travel to another foreign country and find a mountain of spiritual importance? That it would be a new path, and she would see the Light.

"I may not know now where I'm going," Kyra said, as she thought of Gabby's words to her when she first arrived in Barcelona, "But, yes, *¡El destino tiene una manera de llegar cuando menos te lo esperas!* Destiny does have a way of arriving when you least expect it!"

After enjoying an hour or so in the Sabatini Gardens, Kyra packed up the remains of her lunch to take back to the hotel. She thought a relaxing nap before mass that evening at St. Jerome Royal Church would be a welcome respite.

Back in her hotel room, she gratefully crawled atop the comfortable down-filled bedding. Kyra laughed when the name of her room came to mind: the Energy Room. *How appropriate,* she thought. Surely being back in the room would reenergize her, but it also reminded her of her Reiki classes and the energy healing she had been inspired to do so long ago. Right now, with her energy level low, she immediately drifted off into a deep sleep.

She began to dream and found herself standing in the middle of a great forest. While she didn't know where the forest was, she felt such peace to be there among the trees as the sunlight sparkled through their sinewy branches. The branches swayed in the gentle wind, and she giggled like a child at how they danced . . .

Kyra was awakened by the alarm at 5:45 pm, feeling reinvigorated and in a happy mood. As planned, she had thirty minutes to freshen up and walk out the door to make it in time for the evening mass at the famous St. Jerome Royal Church.

# 19

San Jerónimo el Real was located on Moreto Street just West of the hotel. The fifteen- minute walk took her close to the Prado Museum, which she had visited the day before with her friends. It was a warm summer evening, but Kyra brought her sweater with her just in case the air-conditioned church was chilly. After heading up Calle del Prado, she turned onto Calle Felipe IV, and made a couple more turns before arriving at the church around 6:30 pm.

Prior to her visit, Kyra had read that the church had moved to its current location in 1503, more than 500 years ago. St. Jerome had originally been a monastery, but it had undergone many restorations throughout the centuries. The building was an eclectic mixture of architectural styles—mostly neo-Gothic with some Renaissance influences. As Kyra approached the ancient structure, she studied the elegant gray-beige stone façade, which had been constructed during the Middle Ages. The church was now used as a beautiful setting for many high-society weddings in Madrid. She imagined the long flowing white gowns of the brides who had walked up the ancient gray stone steps—each eager to step inside to greet their beloved for their wedding ceremony.

*How ironic that I've never even imagined my own wedding!* Kyra thought with a hint of disappointment. *I've spent way too much time concentrating on my career.* Pausing, she took a moment to daydream about the details of her future wedding and thought back to her childhood. *Didn't I dare to dream back then that I'd be in an elaborate white gown with a pink rose bouquet? And my future dark-haired husband would be waiting for me at the altar?. . . Ah, my childhood dreams seem so long forgotten now.*

She came out of her daydream with a tingle of anticipation, then focused her attention again on the church itself. *I am excited to see the treasures that lay inside*, she thought, *even if my dark-haired fiancé isn't in there waiting for me.* Smiling, she headed up the gray stone steps. She had learned that the *Museo del Prado* was now using the church as an extension of its museum and that there were many unique works of art on display throughout the building.

Kyra walked through the ancient wooden front doors and dipped her fingers in the holy water near the entrance, making the sign of the cross. The bright evening sunlight cascaded through the magnificent stained-glass windows, casting colorful prisms of light in all directions. Sunset would not occur until around 9:45 pm, so the light would remain strong and vibrant throughout the duration of the mass. The window's geometric panes of colored glass formed the images of many saints, including San Jerónimo, or Saint Gerome, for whom the Church was named. The Crucifixion of Christ and the Holy Trinity were also depicted, and the strong sunlight made the figures come alive. Kyra stopped and looked at the Crucifixion for a moment, holding back tears. She simply bowed her head, making the sign of the cross, and said a prayer of gratitude before she moved on.

The contrast of the ornate gold altar against the bright white walls of the main sanctuary caught her attention, and she respectfully moved around the church, admiring every detail. With a few more minutes remaining before mass started, she continued to explore. The paintings were as magnificent as she had expected they would be, including the painting over the main altar, "*La última comunión de San Jeronimo de Teje*"—The last communion of Saint Gerome of Teje—by Jose de Méndez.

Just before the hour-long mass began, she took her seat. *How many years had it been since I'd gone to church regularly?* she wondered. *And now, here I am, attending a* second *mass in less than two weeks.* She realized in that moment she was hungering for a closer relationship with God. *I am seeking answers in my life . . . and I've been inspired to attend mass as an important step in that journey. What was it Gabby said, there are no coincidences?*

Although the mass was once again delivered in Spanish, Kyra participated as much as possible, taking what she could from the passionate sincerity in the priest's voice. The service was emotionally inspiring and exactly what she'd hoped for.

When she left the church that evening, Kyra felt much lighter and more joyful. The sun was still strong, so she slipped on her sunglasses. She became lost in her inner reflections on her journey thus far, which made the walk back to the hotel pass quickly.

Once back in her room, she applied bright-red lipstick and brushed her hair before dressing for evening drinks with Javier and Verónica. She chose a simple Christian Dior V-neck sleeveless black dress, a silver necklace with dangling hearts, and black Valentino high-heel sandals with silver studs around the ankle straps. Glancing at herself in the mirror, she felt luminescent and so much more tranquil than she had been in many years.

When she stepped into the elevator at 9:30 pm to head up to the rooftop bar, Kyra radiated calm energy. A mother and her young son were already standing inside the elevator as she stepped inside, bringing a grin to her lips. "*Buenas noches,*" she said in a friendly tone, using her best Spanish accent.

The young boy, who looked to be around seven years old, rushed to hide behind his mamá and stared wide-eyed at Kyra. The mother laughed and said, "*¡Sí, Nicolás, la mujer es muy hermosa y con tu comportamiento tonto le haces un cumplido!*"

Kyra translated in her head what the woman had said: "Yes, Nicolás, the woman is very beautiful and you pay her a compliment with your foolish behavior!" Kyra felt elated by the boy's admiration. His innocence was priceless, and she was feeling confident and at ease.

The elevator went up a floor, and the mother and son stepped off, bidding Kyra a *buenas noches*. When the door next opened, Kyra stepped out into the hotel's bar, called simply "The Roof." The chic bar stood wide open to the sky above. A faux hardwood and cream-colored stone floor in the main area gave the space an elegant, contemporary feel. Dark brown couches and sleek high-top tables stood out boldly against the white backdrop of the hotel itself. But the most spectacular aspect of The Roof that Kyra noticed was its amazing panoramic view of the city.

The sun was just beginning to set and the bright orange sky was glorious, turning from blue to yellow and bright pink before fading to a dark shade of blue, and finally completely black.

The stars twinkled brightly above her head. Soft purple light glowed around her feet and reflected off the white sculptures, giving each a pale lavender hue. The lighting made the bar seem almost celestial, and the effect brought her mind back to a childhood memory. *What was I doing? Oh yes! I was running on a wooded path in a nearby park, and the sun was just in the midst of setting . . .*

Even as a child, the glorious colors had made her think of heaven. She could see herself in her mind's eye, her long blond hair streaming behind her as she ran along the wooded pathway. She recalled this moment with amazing detail. *I came to a stop, and I could feel my heart pounding as I tried to catch my breath. And then I saw the most awesome sight: Thousands of lightning bugs, twinkling brightly. They danced all around me with their tiny blinking lights. I twirled in their circle of light with my arms up in the air, feeling the bugs gently touching my skin.*

Kyra beamed as she relived the moment from so long ago. Feeling such happiness at the simplest pleasures in life and enjoying God's nature had always been incredible gifts. Her mind slowly drifted back to her current surroundings. She took a breath of the fresh, clean evening air, and a light breeze blew across the deck. Leaning over the railing, she lost herself in the summer breeze.

"You look very far away in your thoughts, my friend!" Verónica said, as she and Javier approached. "I am so sorry we were running late. Do forgive us! *¿Por favor?*"

Kyra turned toward her friends and flashed them an affectionate smile. "It's so good to see you! No worries . . . I was just enjoying the magnificent sunset and the beautiful view of the city from up here. I have a couch reserved for us. Let's sit and have a glass of *vino* to celebrate my second day in Madrid."

The waiter seated them at the center of the bar area, and they relaxed into the comfortable cushions. "Tonight," said Kyra, "I want to treat you for showing me such a lovely time yesterday."

"Javier and I are most *encantado*—delighted—to be able to spend more time with you, Kyra," Verónica told her. "We enjoyed your company very much yesterday. You have such a sweet way about you." Kyra appreciated the compliment, and Verónica continued, "It's very generous of you to treat us tonight."

"Yes," Javier added, "thank you, *mi querida amiga*. I am reluctant to accept your gracious offer, as we would be most pleased to treat you tonight. After all these years, we are happy to finally meet my sister's friend of whom she has always spoken so . . . affectionately."

Kyra waved the idea away with a playful gesture. "Tonight is most definitely my treat, and I would not have it any other way."

With that the waiter returned for their wine order, and Kyra took the reins. "We'd love a bottle of sparkling wine . . . *Cava,* I should say. I'd like to order the *Agusti Torello Mata Kripta Gran Reserva Cava. ¿Por favor?*"

The waiter replied partially in English, "A very excellent choice, *señorita*. I will bring your wine in a moment, and then take your order if *usted está lista*—ah, when you are ready. *Gracias*."

The waiter returned promptly with the pricey bottle of Cava. He set up a silver ice bucket beside the couch and uncorked the bottle. The *pop* elicited a startled "Ah!" from Verónica, which made Kyra laugh.

Friends and laughter made for a perfect way to end her lovely—and quite interesting— day in Madrid. The waiter poured three glasses, then handed the women their glasses and passed the remaining one to Javier.

Raising his glass, Javier said, "You are much too generous with this fine selection of *Cava. Un brindis por la salud y por los buenos amigos*—a toast to good health and good friends!"

The glasses clinked loudly, and each took a sip of the fine-tasting wine. They chatted for a bit, discussing the adventures Kyra had had that day. She told them of the sites she'd visited, but she kept the more unusual occurrences to herself; she wasn't quite sure what Javier and Verónica would make of her "flashbacks." In fact, she wasn't even quite sure what she made of them yet and was still processing her experiences.

Crystal water glasses and beautiful silverware were placed at their table. They perused the menu, which included some internationally inspired tapas with unusual flavor combinations, which gave the menu extra flair. Kyra ordered a variety of dishes, wanting to make sure that Javier and Verónica would not leave hungry under her watch.

As they enjoyed their meal, the bar filled up rapidly and, within an hour, The Roof became crowded and lively. The carefree activity stirred a feeling of pleasure in Kyra, and she bounced a little in her seat.

Verónica refilled Kyra's glass and the bubbles fizzed. "You are bubbly, just like our delicious wine!"

"I am feeling much more bubbly than when I first arrived in Spain . . . and the time I'm spending with you has enhanced my good cheer. Thank you." With that, Kyra raised her glass. "Cheers to my new friends!" The three glasses clinked.

By the time they had eaten nearly every morsel served, the music in the background grew louder, transforming their surroundings into a chic party scene. Taking that as a cue, Kyra asked the waiter to charge the bill to her room. Javier good-naturedly insisted on paying, but finally, Verónica admonished her husband, "Kyra is a successful, modern woman, and we should simply say *muchas gracias!*"

Javier conceded, but then quickly added, "Then I will treat us to a nightcap!"

Kyra only laughed as she followed the couple to the bar. She glanced around the now lively rooftop and her eyes fell on many handsome, nicely dressed men. Several were accompanied by their elegantly dressed dates, but many also appeared to be single. *My passion is stirring,* Kyra thought, surprising herself a bit as she took in the tempting sights. *Hmmm . . . or perhaps I'm a bit tipsy.*

Javier squeezed into to a narrow spot at the bar and turned to the women. "What may I get you?"

Verónica responded quickly, "*¡Mi Amor, por favor sorpréndeme!*" She turned to Kyra and translated, "I told him to surprise me!"

"*Por favor sorpréndeme,*" Kyra repeated enthusiastically.

After a few minutes, Javier had three artfully prepared mojitos in hand. He gingerly passed one to each of the women, and then they once again clinked their drinks in a toast. As they enjoyed the smooth crisp concoction with sprigs of fresh mint, they talked more about Madrid and the amazing sites to see. Soon, their glasses were near empty.

Kyra was feeling effects of the mojito, especially after several glasses of *Cava,* and to her surprise, she stumbled in her high heels. A handsome man in his late twenties caught Kyra in his arms before she completely lost her balance. His eyes met Kyra's as he helped steady her. *"¡Buenas noches, señorita! ¡Es usted muy hermosa, ha caído una estrella fugaz del cielo! Permítame presentarme, soy Juan Pablo."*

Kyra blushed, as she only understood the first part—"Good evening, young lady!"—and the last part where he'd said his name was Juan Pablo.

Javier stepped forward. "The gentleman is saying good evening to you, Kyra. He said you are very beautiful, so he could not help but catch a star falling from the heavens."

Kyra blushed a second time and stood straighter, steadying her feet. Javier looked at the man and extended his hand to introduce himself. "I'm Javier, and this is my wife, Verónica, and of course this is our friend Kyra, who is visiting from San Francisco, California. Do you speak English?"

The man shook Javier's hand firmly and said in English, "Yes, I do speak English. I am very pleased to make your acquaintance, Javier, Verónica . . . and Kyra."

Kyra blushed a third time. "Juan Pablo, it's very nice to meet you, too," she said, offering him a hand to shake. "Thank you for being a gentleman—and keeping me from falling on my face! I am celebrating my second day in Madrid with my two dear friends here, and the drinks have me at a bit of a disadvantage in these heels."

Javier quickly asked Juan Pablo whether he was from Madrid or just visiting the city, what he did for a living, and most important, if he was single or married. Kyra almost blushed a fourth time when it became obvious that Javier had assumed the role of her big brother—protecting her from any ill intentions.

Juan Pablo was polished, charming, and sophisticated, having come from a wealthy Spanish family. And he worked at a large bank in wealth management making a very good living, from what Kyra could ascertain.

He was indeed single, but it turned out that he was seven years younger than Kyra—not quite what she had expected.

Kyra melted though when he spoke, and she felt like a giddy schoolgirl. *What's going on with me?*

"I'm living in Madrid now," Juan Pablo told them, "but I moved here about three years ago from Barcelona after finishing graduate school."

Javier began to explain how Kyra has known his older sister Gabriela since their grad school days and then came close to volunteering their year of graduation, which would have given away her age. Kyra staunchly kicked her new "protective brother" in the leg to interrupt his train of thought. Javier's eyes popped, and he swiftly corrected himself, "I mean that Verónica and I met Kyra through my slightly older sister, Gabriela. We are showing her around Madrid during her visit. We are in town from Barcelona, visiting my in-laws for a few weeks."

Juan Pablo nodded, but his eyes were on Kyra, his attraction for her apparent and she felt it too. *He's seven years younger than me? He seems so mature . . . and attractive.*

As the conversation continued, it appeared that everything Juan Pablo said was directed at Kyra. Eventually, Javier politely interjected, "Juan Pablo, it has been very nice meeting you this evening. We should plan to meet up again before Kyra leaves Madrid. Let us know if you available for dinner one evening this week?"

Juan Pablo replied enthusiastically, "Dinner would be very nice! I would enjoy seeing Kyra again . . . as well as you and your lovely wife, of course." He handed his business card to each of them.

Kyra felt pleased that Javier had taken the lead to offer up dinner and was looking forward to spending more time with her new friends. *Not to mention getting to know Juan Pablo better! Oh my . . .* She smiled at the thought.

After they said their goodbyes, Javier escorted the women to the elevator. Kyra rode down to the first floor with her guests to see them to the front door of the hotel. "Thank you, Javier, for the mojito . . . And for being my big brother when it seemed I needed one."

Javier gave her a serious look. "A friend of my sister is *my* sister," he said. "Sleep well this evening, and we will see you again for dinner this week."

Kyra enjoyed how his brotherly affection made her feel. "Thank you both for joining me tonight . . . Let me give you a proper hug." Kyra embraced Javier, and then turned to Verónica. "I look forward to our next adventure together. If I'm Javier's sister, then you are my beautiful sister-in-law." Kyra gave her a Gabby-style kiss on each cheek. *Muwahhh!*

As the couple retrieved their car from the valet, Kyra headed back to her room, basking in the feelings of brotherly and sisterly love, which she had never experienced before. *Uhm . . . I think I could get used to having a large and crazy family!* she mused, turning out the light.

# 20

At 8:30 the next morning, Kyra's head was still spinning. "*Ugh*," she groaned. "What was I thinking, mixing wine and rum?" She pulled the pillow over her face and lounged in bed for another half-hour before getting up to shower.

She set the water temp to a very hot setting and let the steam heat up the stall while she downed a large glass of water from the bathroom faucet. Then she gingerly stepped into the steaming shower stall.

Hot water ran over her face, streaming down her loose blond hair, and her nose filled with the heavy, moist steam. As she lathered with the spa soap, the smell of fresh citrus and vanilla mixed with the steam, filling the room with the heavenly scent. She closed her eyes, imagining that she was washing away the grogginess of the night before and tried to focus her mind clearly on the upcoming day. *Luckily, I have a leisurely day planned: a wonderful visit to Casa de Campo! The walking will do me good to enliven my senses—and get my blood pumping.*

She recalled that the immense park, which was situated just west of downtown Madrid, had once been a royal hunting estate in the late sixteenth century. Now it was home to an amusement park with twelve adrenaline-producing roller coasters, as well as a world-class zoo with more than 2,000 animals. Today, however, Kyra would forgo both of those, opting instead to visit the lake inside the park. *I want to savor the peace and quiet of the majestic woods surrounding the lake,* she thought as she lathered her hair, *and to see the wildlife. It always makes me feel like a child again when I reconnect with nature.*

However, before venturing to the park, she had one stop to make at Despertares Espirituales or 'Spiritual Awakenings', a New Age bookstore she had located nearby. She planned to purchase a few Reiki manuals there, as the park would make for a tranquil setting to relax and read. Since Reiki was a technique for relaxation and healing, Kyra felt the benefits for her alone would be immeasurable. And if she could find time to use Reiki to help others, too, that would be amazing, as it could make for a more meaningful existence beyond just finding a new corporate job.

*With all the events that have unfolded over the past month, I'm in need of something more fulfilling in my life,* Kyra thought as she finished her shower. *Crazy as it may seem, I feel somehow "guided"—if that's the right word—to reconnect with Reiki. . . . And I still need to make a decision on Gabby's offer to join her in England for the Reiki Master training class. It's less than two weeks away!*

Kyra felt grateful for Gabby's offer, realizing it did seem like an opportune time to take the class. *Divine timing actually,* she clarified, once again noticing the synchronicities in the Universe and how one thing led to another in a perfect orderly fashion.

Kyra dressed in a comfortable dark blue denim skirt and a crisp white cotton shirt. She chose simple silver and turquoise jewelry, and flat silver sandals that were perfect for walking long distances. She headed downstairs for a late breakfast and, upon finishing her café con leche and fruit bowl, walked out to the front of the hotel and asked for a taxicab.

The taxi would serve as the ideal transportation for a quick trip to the bookstore and, after dropping her purchases back off at the hotel room, she would then walk to Casa de Campo, which was about an hour away. She was certain she'd enjoy the exercise of a long walk, not to mention the opportunity to work off all the food she'd been eating.

After about a ten-minute wait, a taxi pulled up in front of the hotel. The bellman stepped forward and opened the car door. She slid into the backseat and looked at the driver. He was a middle-aged man, perhaps in his late fifties, with slightly graying hair and sideburns. A little on the burly side, he looked as if he'd enjoyed many generous meals. But Kyra immediately was drawn to his pleasant, friendly face.

The driver politely asked, "*¿Dónde la puedo llevar hoy, señorita?*" repeating again slowly in English to make sure she understood, "Where can I take you today, miss?"

Kyra thought for a moment before replying, speaking carefully in her best Spanish, *"No tengo ni idea de a dónde voy, pero hoy puede llevarme a una librería,"* which meant, "I have no idea where I am going, but today you can take me to a bookstore."

The driver smiled curiously, and she handed him a piece of paper with the name and address of the bookstore written on it. "*Sí, sí señorita,*" he replied cordially. He drove off quickly, heading east.

*The store is aptly named,* Kyra thought as the cab sped onward, *and it's the only store of its kind in the entire area.* She had already called ahead and spoken to the clerk to ensure the Reiki manuals she wanted to purchase were in stock. Surprisingly, they had all three manuals available: Reiki Level 1, 2, and the Advanced Reiki Training. The clerk had been kind enough to hold them for her.

"We do carry some English books here," the clerk had said, "but the Reiki manuals you are purchasing were supposed to be in Spanish, of course. *Tiene mucha suerte señorita*—you are very lucky—as the English ones were shipped to us by mistake! Ah, but two days later you are requesting them, so *no hay errores*—there are no mistakes."

Kyra agreed with the clerk's assessment of her good fortune and was grateful that the Universe was indeed conspiring to help her along her path.

Within ten minutes, the driver arrived at the bookstore on Génova Street. As she handed him the fare and tip, she said slowly, "*¡Gracias por su paciencia al dejarme practicar mi español! Usted ha sido más amable,*" hoping she had correctly said, "Thank you for letting me practice my Spanish! You have been most kind."

The driver nodded in understanding. "*Señorita, ha sido un placer ayudar a una joven y bella dama. Espero que no se quede perdida por mucho tiempo, pero por ahora disfrute de su viaje a mi amada España.*"

Kyra laughed as she was pretty certain he had said, "Miss, it has been my pleasure to help such a beautiful young lady. I hope you do not stay lost for long, but for now, enjoy your trip to my beloved Spain."

Trying not to chuckle, Kyra thanked the driver again as she exited the taxi and found herself in front of the Spiritual Awakenings bookstore.

The storefront was rather small, but the sign was painted a dark navy blue with gold stars encircling the name of the store.

*It's just like the dark blue ceiling and gold stars inside the Almudena Cathedral. Even more synchronicities!* Kyra thought with delight.

A chime above the front door rang merrily, announcing her entry as she crossed through the doorway. The store's walls were packed with all sorts of books on various spiritual topics, including meditation, abundance manifestation, connecting with the angels, and, of course, various healing modalities.

A Spanish woman in her late twenties stood behind the counter. Her dark hair, streaked intermittently with bright red, hung in two long braids. She was dressed in a loosely fitting tie-dye shirt, a jean skirt, and flat pink shoes. As the young clerk was finishing up with another customer, Kyra walked around the store and perused the bookshelves. She came across a small section of books in English and silently counted her blessing that the Reiki manuals had indeed been divinely sent to the store on her behalf.

The young clerk finished ringing up another customer's purchase and then approached Kyra. "*¿Puedo ayudarle con algo hoy, señorita?*" she said, which Kyra knew meant, "Can I help you with something today, miss?"

"*Hola, mi nombre es Kyra,*" Kyra replied. Then she switched to English. "I called you about some Reiki manuals you are holding for me, the ones printed in English?"

"*¡Ah, sí, sí, eres Kyra!*" the clerk replied energetically. "You are the woman who manifested the manuals in English."

Rather pleased, Kyra replied, "Yes, indeed I did."

The clerk hurried behind the cash register to retrieve the books, placing them on the countertop for Kyra to review. Kyra gazed at the purple manuals with their white bindings, thinking back fondly to her grad school days when she first took the Reiki classes with Gabby.

*How young we were back then,* Kyra thought. *And how cool we looked in our frayed denim jeans, flip-flops, and colorful t-shirts. And Gabby was going to save the world with her training! But she took the consulting job in*

*Boston, and I joined my first major corporation in Chicago. Oh my gosh, that was such a long time ago.*

She remembered now how much the classes had resonated with her. And now, thirteen years later, she was purchasing the same manuals again, with the possibility of undergoing the Reiki Master training in England.

Kyra looked at the clerk. "These are exactly the same manuals I first used when I took the Reiki training classes more than a decade ago. I've been thinking of freshening up my skills again."

To the clerk's delight, Kyra purchased the books. As the young woman handed the bag to her, a sudden look of insight flashed over her face. "*Mi hermano*—uh, I mean my brother—is a Reiki Master teacher and lives only a couple of miles from here. He is doing the Level 1 training class tomorrow at his home. You could attend if you are interested and practice with the other students. Sometimes people do that when it's been a while since they took the original classes. Do you want me to give you his phone number so you can call him?"

Kyra looked at the clerk almost in disbelief. How lucky could she possibly be? If the clerk's brother did have room for her to attend his class, that would be perfect for practice before making a final decision about the course in England. "Yes," Kyra said, wide-eyed. "I'd love to see if your brother has room for me." Then a sudden realization gave her pause. "I'm guessing the class will be taught in Spanish? My ability to comprehend Spanish is improving—and I'm getting bolder in speaking it—but I may not be able to keep up with the students if it is taught entirely in Spanish."

"My brother speaks English very well," the clerk replied, "so you can ask him if he can translate for you, and whether that would be okay with the rest of the classmates."

"That's fair enough. I will give him a call."

The clerk wrote down her brother's phone number, and Kyra stepped outside to make the call. A man with a very deep voice answered. "*Hola, habla Miguel.*"

Kyra was amused, as his voice was not what she had been expecting from a spiritual Reiki Master. He did, however, seem to have a genuinely pleasant demeanor. Kyra explained the reason for the call and her need for English translations. He immediately responded that he would be happy to have her join the class, as he had three students attending, and a fourth would be "*perfecto*," as he put it. The class would meet at 10:00 the next morning.

Following the call, Kyra popped her head inside the bookstore to let the clerk know that she'd made the arrangements. The clerk seemed quite pleased. Next she went back to the hotel to drop off the books, but placed the Reiki Level 1 manual in her oversized purse. She then set out for Casa de Campo.

It was a gloriously sunny day, so Kyra put on her sunglasses as she strolled down the sidewalk. She was very much looking forward to the three-mile walk to the park and, more important, spending time reading her newfound treasure. Imagining how her life would go forward from here, Kyra became lost in her thoughts. After twenty minutes or so, she realized she had taken a wrong turn. The street sign read Calle Toledo, not Calle Segovia—not at all where she was supposed to be.

"I must be walking in the general right direction," she said, annoyed with herself. "Oh, boy, let's see if I can figure this out." After making a few more turns, Kyra was heading west—the correct direction—but she found herself at the intersection of Bailén and the Carrera de San Francisco. Throwing her hands up in frustration, she said loudly, "I can't believe I'm lost!" A woman walking her dog passed by and gave her a quizzical look. "Okay. It may be time to stop and get directions," Kyra said to herself more quietly this time. "And why couldn't I have a better sense of direction?"

She looked around and saw that she was standing perhaps a hundred yards from a large church with gray stone archways and a simple brown brick exterior. Part of the church was painted bright yellow, and that section reached up to a huge gray dome. The architectural style was definitely neoclassical, but the structure was unique. *It has a warm and inviting feel to it. Hopefully someone there can help me,* she thought, deciding that's where she would go for help.

As she approached the gate, she spotted an unusually attractive man standing outside the front entrance. She instantly felt drawn to him—in a forceful way—unlike any other she had experienced before in her entire life. She stared at the man for a moment, taking in his features. Without a doubt, he was the most attractive man she had ever laid eyes upon . . . but much to her surprise the man standing in front of her was a priest.

As she walked closer, she felt as if a huge magnet were drawing her toward him, and she could not take her eyes off of him. And somehow, in the core of her being, she felt a strange familiarity. *It's like I know him,* she thought. *Have we met before?*

Kyra dismissed the thought as impossible, but her attraction toward this man was undeniable. As she stepped closer and was perhaps fifty feet away, the priest turned and walked inside the church; he had not noticed her approaching.

The sign outside the church read "*Basilica de San Francisco el Grande,*" which she easily translated into the Great Church of San Francisco—just like her hometown. She recognized the name as she had considered visiting the church, but had not yet taken the time to fit it into her itinerary. Now, today, she had ended up here just the same.

She came to an abrupt standstill. *What is the likelihood of this coincidence? Surely there must be a reason for my being led here today and seeing this man, but why?* She could not imagine what that reason might be, especially given that he was a man of God, but she took a deep breath to calm her nerves—and decided to go inside to meet the priest.

# 21

Taking a deep breath, Kyra steadied herself and tried to concentrate on the church's history, hoping it would ease her nerves. She recalled that it housed one of the largest central domes of any church in Spain, which was one of the reasons she had wanted to visit it in the first place. It also had been built on a site of a Franciscan convent that had been founded by St. Francis of Assisi himself in the early thirteenth century, hence its name and connection to her hometown.

Kyra thought back to her days in Catholic school. The nuns had taught her that St. Francis was the patron saint of animals and ecology, two important aspects of her life she'd come to adore. Even now, after all these years, she could still hear the words of the nun reprimanding her for not paying attention. "Kyra, my child," she had said, "St. Francis of Assisi had but one simple rule, and that rule is to follow the teachings of our Lord Jesus Christ and to walk in his footsteps." She still cringed at her lack of attention. And, as if to answer no one there, she put her hand on her heart and replied, *But, yes, Father, I do walk in your footsteps.*

When Kyra entered the church, she dipped her fingertips into the holy water and made the sign of the cross. She glanced around and saw the priest off to her left. He was talking with an elderly woman, holding her hand and offering her advice.

He was a tall man—almost six feet, if Kyra were to guess—with full dark wavy hair and a flawless olive complexion that stood out beautifully above his white collar and long dark robe. Her nerves confirmed her earlier thought; he was undeniably the most handsome man she had ever seen.

Then she noticed his eyes. They were dark, and he had long, full eyelashes, but what she noticed the most was how his eyes sparkled when he spoke to the woman. He looked warm and sincere—and very caring.

*He almost seems to . . . glow with light,* she realized, unable to quite figure out what she was seeing.

She searched her memory, and her mind raced back to a metaphysical class she had taken many years ago with Gabby. *Am I seeing his aura—his energy field?* she wondered. She recalled that a highly sensitive person could sometimes detect a person's aura. This was also the same energy field that Reiki practitioners focused on to help promote healing. Kyra's ability to detect it now intrigued her, and she decided to accept the gift rather than to question it.

She stood off to the side for several minutes until the priest finished speaking with the woman. Kyra could barely hear the woman's words, but she wore a look of appreciation and shook the priest's hand before walking away. Then the priest looked directly over at Kyra, who stood now only twenty feet from him.

For a moment, she froze. He seemed a bit puzzled, and then walked over, extending his hand to greet her. *"Señorita,"* he said, *"parece un poco perdida. ¿Puedo ayudarle con algo hoy? Mi nombre es Padre Sánchez."* Kyra's mind raced to translate his words: "Miss, you seem a bit lost. Can I help you with something today? My name is Father Sánchez."

Kyra's mouth felt dry, and her throat was tight so she stumbled over her words. "Forgive me, Father Sánchez, as I only speak a little Spanish, but perhaps I understand the language better than I speak it. I am a bit lost; I was trying to walk to *Casa de Campo*, and I seemed to have taken a several wrong turns. I apologize . . . I did not mean to waste your time today with silly directions."

Father Sánchez smiled. "*Señorita*," he replied, "I do speak English fairly well, as I spent time studying abroad in the U.S. Are you from the United States? I would be happy to give you directions. Perhaps it's much better to only need directions than to be spiritually lost, I should think." He laughed softly as he spoke, trying to put Kyra at ease. Kyra's face flushed with embarrassment. Father Sánchez seemed to notice her disorientation and asked, "Can I offer you a glass of water after your long walk here? I will also draw you a quick map on a piece of paper. Follow me this way, and I will give you both."

He motioned for Kyra to follow him. They walked down a long hallway, past one of the chapels. Upon reaching his office, Father Sánchez gave her a glass of water and asked her to sit down for a moment as he drew out a map of the area.

"You are not too far off on your way to *Casa de Campo*. It is perhaps *veinte minutos*—twenty minutes—from here," he corrected himself. "You made a slightly wrong turn south, which is how you ended up here."

Kyra gulped down the water and replied, "Thank you for your kindness. Perhaps the summer heat has gotten to me a bit today. I do apologize again . . . I don't feel quite like myself today. My name is Kyra, and I am visiting your beautiful city of Madrid for a few days. My grandmother passed away over a month ago, and I'm taking a little time to reflect on some things in my life—my path in life."

The priest nodded, an expression of compassion crossing his handsome features.

"I . . . I would like to ask you a question, if I may? I'm very curious. But, *why* did you become a priest?" Kyra could not believe the words she had just spoken, but she waited a second and hastily added, "I am seeking answers today, Father Sánchez, and I would appreciate the chance to understand why you would choose the path of a priest . . . of course, if you don't mind my asking."

The priest didn't flinch. He looked down for a moment, and then looked Kyra directly in the eyes. "I have been asked this question many times before, Kyra. And there were some unique circumstances that led me on the path of being a servant to God and my life purpose. We may have some things in common, but let me start at the beginning so you can understand my choice."

Kyra nodded, and Father Sánchez continued, "As a young child in Madrid, I had quite a normal upbringing. My father is a very successful attorney. He was well known in the city for his litigation practice. However, when I was thirteen years old, my older brother, Carlos, was killed in an automobile accident. He was with a friend, and the friend's mother was driving, but fortunately, both their lives were spared."

Father Sánchez paused for a moment before he continued, "It was a very difficult time for my family, as you can imagine. I also have a younger brother, Julio, and we both struggled with the question of *why* God had taken Carlos away at the age of fifteen.

"I actually never thought to become a priest, but one day I was praying in church seeking answers, and suddenly it came to me out of nowhere. I thought I could feel my brother's presence with me, and I could almost hear his voice say to me, '*Vive la vida para la que has nacido y serás feliz,*' which means, 'Follow the life you were born to lead and you will be happy.' I was struck by the simplicity of the words . . . and I knew, in that moment, exactly what I was supposed to do with my life.

"I left the church and went home immediately to tell my father that I wanted to become a priest. At first he questioned my decision, but he and my mother both became supportive. I was only thirteen at the time, but I never wavered from it. I did eventually go to seminary school and graduated with a Masters of Divinity. I was fortunate to spend two years abroad, studying in the U.S. as well. Once I was ordained, I came to the *Basilica de San Francisco el Grande,* where I have been ever since. Jesus sacrificed his life for us, Kyra, and my brother's death served a purpose, too. My brother's words to me that day in church were so true. I have been happier than I ever could have imagined by following the path that God chose for me."

Kyra looked at the priest's radiant face and found herself holding back tears. *There are some similarities in our stories,* she thought. *I've lost the most important person in my life, too—my sweet Nana. I have no doubt now why I was supposed to meet this man today.*

She looked at his face again. Father Sánchez radiated happiness, pure love, and joy—the light she had seen when she first walked up to him. And his was the love and joy that came from helping people every day and being a servant to God. The priest had made his own sacrifice, too, Kyra realized, forsaking carnal pleasure for something that brought him even greater joy. *Yes,* she thought, *I'm seeing his radiance of divine love.*

And then suddenly, she felt ashamed. *Was it lust I felt when I first saw him?* She silently chastised herself, and suddenly her mind flew back to her relationship with Steve. Had she really ever loved Steve or was she taken in by his attractiveness? *He is a very handsome man . . . but never once said he loved me! He is shallow and superficial—and not capable of being in love with anyone but himself.*

She looked at Father Sánchez and suddenly realized that what she was attracted to was his loving and genuine kindness. She felt as if a weight had been lifted off of her shoulders. She now knew deep in her heart she wanted a *real* relationship—true, unconditional love—with the right man. *I want the man I marry to be kind and loving—someone I can count on, someone who will always be there for me.*

*Going forward, I will say "no" to those men who do not fit my new criteria for a deeply committed relationship,* she silently vowed. *I will look deeper at a man's actions, and not just at his words . . . or his looks. I intend to attract what I truly desire—authentic unconditional love.*

As she looked at Father Sánchez, she found that she could barely speak. He quietly handed her a tissue so she could wipe away the tears that had filled her eyes. After a long pause, she said, "Father Sánchez . . . I am at a loss for words. You were right earlier—I have been lost . . . and I have been trying to find myself. I think I must have been led here today to meet you so I could learn your story and understand the decisions you made. I . . . I cannot thank you enough for your kind, compassionate guidance; I am forever grateful to you."

And with that, Kyra began to weep. She dabbed her eyes with a tissue and focused her mind on what she wanted to do.

*I need to make peace with my past and release it. More important, I need to make heartfelt decisions going forward. I've been determined to find the answers I've been seeking, and today was one step in the right direction on that journey—even if I got here in an unconventional way.*

Father Sánchez leaned forward, handing Kyra another tissue, and allowed her a few minutes to reflect on their conversation. Once Kyra had finished her second glass of water, she boldly made a request. "Father Sánchez, if you have time today, I would like to go to confession. I have not been in a very long time, and I think it would be great to let go of my past and ask for forgiveness."

"Yes, of course," Father Sánchez replied. "We can go to the

confessional now and ask God for his grace and forgiveness for your sins."

As Kyra walked alongside Father Sánchez to the confessional at the back of the church, the words of St. Francis of Assisi she had once memorized as a child sprang into her mind.

*Lord, make me an instrument of Thy peace;*
*Where there is hatred, let me sow love;*
*Where there is injury, pardon;*
*Where there is error, truth;*
*Where there is doubt, faith;*
*Where there is despair, hope;*
*Where there is darkness, light;*
*And where there is sadness, joy.*
*O Divine Master, Grant that I may not so much seek*
*To be consoled as to console;*
*To be understood as to understand;*
*To be loved as to love.*
*For it is in giving that we receive;*
*It is in pardoning that we are pardoned;*
*And it is in dying that we are born to eternal life.*

Kyra and Father Sánchez entered the confessional, and Kyra knelt. The panel slid open, and Kyra saw Father Sánchez make the sign of the cross.

"May God be with you to make a worthy confession," he said, "in the name of the Father, and of the Son, and of the Holy Spirit. Amen."

Kyra waited a moment, made the sign of the cross, and then responded, "In the name of the Father, and of the Son, and of the Holy Spirit, amen. Bless me, Father, for I have sinned. It has been . . . more than ten years since my last confession. I have taken the name of the Lord in vain; I have given my soul to a corporation that neither appreciated nor valued my work; I was in a relationship with a man who did not love me." She paused a moment, and then went on, "And I have lusted after a man I could never have, nor do I deserve." She hesitated again. "I am sorry for these sins and all of the sins of my life. I ask God for his forgiveness." Kyra then bowed her head, waiting for Father Sánchez to respond.

Father Sánchez was silent for a moment. "Kyra," he said at last, "for your penance, I ask you to reflect on the goodness of God in your life, and to repeat the Lord's Prayer one time for each of your sins, and to say the Act of Contrition."

Kyra was quiet for several minutes, trying hard to remember the correct format, before she anxiously replied in her own words, "Dearest God . . . I am sorry with all of my heart for having offended thee, who is all good and deserving of all my love." Kyra gulped in a breath of air and nervously continued, "I resolve with your grace to do penance and amend my life, and to avoid future temptation that will lead me into sin. I want to make *good* decisions about my life going forward so I can be of help to others. Amen."

The last came out in nearly a whisper. Father Sánchez waited several minutes while Kyra's head remained bowed in prayer, and then responded, "God, the Father of mercies, through the death and resurrection of his Son, has reconciled the world to himself and sent the Holy Spirit among us for the forgiveness of sins; through the ministry of the Church may God give you pardon and peace. And I absolve you from all of your sins in the name of the Father, and of the Son, and of the Holy Spirit. Amen."

For a moment, both were silent.

"Kyra," Father Sánchez said, "you are forgiven for your sins. When you return home to San Francisco, follow your heart, and God will lead you in the right direction. Go in peace."

Kyra kept her head bowed for a moment before making the sign of the cross. "Thanks be to God," she said. "Father Sánchez, you have been most kind to me today, and I cannot express how much your kindness has meant. I will think over our conversation today. Peace be with you, too."

As Kyra exited through the front door, she turned around to look back at the inside of the church once more. Her face broke into a blissful smile, and a divine feeling of peace and freedom swept over her. She walked down the church steps with her hand-drawn map in hand, knowing she would likely never see Father Sánchez again.

She stepped onto the sidewalk, and for an instant, her mind flashed back to the older woman she had met at the airport on her way to Barcelona. The fondness she had felt for the couple came rushing back. *What was her name?* Kyra wondered. *She was celebrating her second wedding anniversary with Albert. She was giggling like a schoolgirl—even though they were probably in their seventies! What did she say?* Kyra thought a moment, and then burst into a huge grin. *Love can come to you anytime.* Delighted by the memory, she looked up at the sky and declared, "Yes, love will come to me!"

Her energy renewed, she headed north at a brisk pace toward her next destination, the expansive park known as Casa de Campo.

# 22

Kyra glanced down at her watch; it was close to 1 pm. She estimated that she still had a twenty-minute walk ahead of her. Deciding not to rush under the hot sun, she slowed her pace to a lighthearted stroll, her Reiki manual still tucked neatly into her purse and the priest's map held firmly in her hand. As she enjoyed the comforting warmth of the day, she reflected more on her conversation with Father Sánchez, feeling blessed to have received his guidance and help. *Our unexpected meeting was divinely meant to be. I feel so much freer . . . like I'm ready for anything! Confession truly is good for the soul.*

Nearing the park, she spotted a small café tucked away on a side street, where she stopped to purchase a picnic lunch.

When the young clerk asked if she'd like a bottle of wine, she politely declined. "I'm doing some reading this afternoon and I want my mind to be focused," she explained. She also wanted to be clear-headed for her class in the morning.

With lunch in hand, Kyra reached the park entrance and paused for a moment to gaze across its expansive greenery. She had read that morning that Casa de Campo—or in English, "Country House Park"—was five times the size of New York City's Central Park. But unlike New York, much of the wildlife roamed freely in the wooded areas. It seemed like ages had passed since she had last been to Muir Woods, and she dearly longed to keep her connection with nature daily, if possible.

*I can't seem to get enough of the tranquility the forest offers,* she realized as she stepped foot inside the park. *I have been so blessed to see so many wonderful parks on this trip. Nature always grounds me and brings me the connection to God that I'm seeking—not to mention the joy of being outdoors in his beautiful world.*

The roar of the city traffic quickly faded away as Kyra ventured forward. Although it was nearly 90°F, the spectacular trees would offer her shade while she read. She focused on the tall trees surrounding her and absorbed the beauty of the sunlit canopy. Many of the trees bore huge green leaves with thick, dark scaly bark, and all towered far above her head.

*So these are the Holm Oaks,* she thought.

Also known as Holly Oaks, these trees—Kyra recalled from her reading—were unique to the Mediterranean region. She was taken aback by how much they reminded her of Muir Woods . . . and home. She felt her heart fill with joy as she took in the beauty of the woods.

Chestnut trees dotted the landscape as well, some soaring majestically to nearly one hundred feet tall. She gazed affectionately at the leafy giants and instantly thought of her mother. She had so loved eating roasted chestnuts in the wintertime when her mother would toast them in the fireplace. This was a special treat they often enjoyed together when her father was away on business during the season. They'd eat them hot, right out of the fire. Kyra could sense her mother's presence around her now—and, for a brief moment, felt the sensation that she had touched her hand.

*Oh, Mother—I wish you were here!* she said silently. *But I'm so grateful for that pleasant memory.* For the first time in a long while, the memory of her mother had brought feelings of fondness rather than pain, pleasantly surprising her. *This is the second time I've thought of you on this trip while visiting a park. I guess not all our time together was bad, was it?*

A faint voice in her mind whispered, *Sweetheart, I miss you.*

Not certain if the voice was really her mother's, but feeling comforted by her thoughts, Kyra spoke aloud, hoping her mother could hear her. "I miss you, too . . . And how nice, Mother, would it have been to enjoy some of that cold Chicago air today." Her thoughts shifted back to the summer heat, which was beginning to make her perspire.

As she continued along the pathway, Kyra gratefully inhaled the sweet pine fragrance of the forest. The soft smell refreshed her, bringing her back to her childhood dream. The trees and sunlight had a magical quality that whisked her thoughts away from the past several days of jam-packed sightseeing. Though she was looking forward to seeing the peaceful waters of the Manzanares River on the edge of the park, today she only planned to visit the lake closest to the entrance. She had chosen her destination carefully; with over 4,000 acres, the entire park couldn't be traversed in one visit.

After walking a bit further, Kyra came upon the serene lake, which stood at the edge of a pathway overlooking the thick green woods. She spread out her picnic blanket, unpacked her food, and placed her Reiki manual on the soft red plaid fabric. She had chosen a shady area under some of the Holm Oaks, but the hot summer sun still shone brightly just off to the side of her picnic site.

Kyra lifted her head and looked around at the forest. Birds flew overhead chirping sweetly, while squirrels scampered about playing in a nearby tree. A small gray rabbit darted past, looking at Kyra for a moment as it made its way into the brush beneath the trees. Kyra's heart skipped a beat while she watched the beautiful creatures of the forest go about their day.

*I am so blessed to share this experience with my small forest companions, just like in my dream,* she thought gratified by the much-needed peaceful shift away from the city. She drank in her surroundings, filling her heart with even more joy.

Kyra ate slowly and gazed out across the lake, watching the sunlight sparkle like small crystals on the water's surface. An occasional light breeze made small ripples on the lake, and the light sparkled even more brilliantly when the small waves drifted quickly across the lake's surface. The water and the forest kept reminding her of her recurring childhood dream, which was becoming clearer to her now. She wondered *why* she had the recurring dream in the first place. But more importantly *what* could it possibly mean, and *why* would it be coming back to her now? Struggling to understand it all, pieces of the dream played in the back of her mind.

Kyra was lost in the memory when a huge peacock boldly approached her, distracting her from her thoughts. The regal bird was splendid with his iridescent bright green and blue feathers. He turned and looked Kyra squarely in the eye as he came close. Suddenly, the bird stopped, cocked his bright blue head to the side, and spread his oval-flecked feathers proudly, as if to announce he was waiting for her to respond.

Kyra laughed. "My noble friend," she said, "I think you are most likely interested in sharing my tapas rather than making my acquaintance."

The bird continued to stare.

"No," Kyra said after a moment. "I'm not going to feed you, my new friend. Plus I'm not exactly sure what a peacock is supposed to eat!" She laughed again. "And, I don't want us to become *too* friendly and then have to end our friendship if you become too assertive."

The bird waited patiently for several minutes more, but walked away when Kyra failed to offer him her food. As the peacock departed, Kyra's intuition sparked again. *What does a peacock symbolize?* She had studied animal totems back in her grad school days and remembered that the Native Americans and Shamans often thought that animals appeared as a symbol for a special message.

Kyra quickly grabbed her cell phone and opened her Internet browser. After several minutes of trying, she finally got a signal and a few websites appeared. As she read the information, she realized that the peacock's appearance could not have been a coincidence. "Peacocks symbolize rebirth, awakening, immortality, glory, and royalty," she read excitedly. "Oh, I do get it! That seems just perfect. Or maybe I should say *perfecto?*" She giggled. "This seems to sum up my trip to Spain thus far. Thank you, Universe, for placing this peacock on my path today. I think I am finally beginning to recognize the signs." And with that, Kyra understood, without a glimmer of a doubt, that all the signs appearing to her since her arrival in Spain were indeed special messages meant just for her.

With her mind more open to embracing new ideas, Kyra cleaned up the remains of her lunch and then stretched out on her side to concentrate on reviewing her Reiki manual. There were four Reiki levels in all: Level 1, Level 2, Advanced Reiki Training, and Master Teacher. Kyra had finished the first three levels and now only lacked the Master

Teacher certification to complete her training. But she still needed to refresh her memory on the basics.

She opened the thick purple manual and skimmed through the pages. The information still felt familiar, even after all these years, which eased her mind. First she read about the definition of Reiki, a practice originated in Japan and whose name was comprised of two Japanese words—*Rei* and *Ki*. *Rei* means "spiritually guided" or "spiritual consciousness," and *Ki*—which was similar to the Chinese word *Chi*—means "vital life force energy."

"This life force energy was thought to be present in all living things. *Reiki* therefore translated to "spiritually guided life energy," Kyra read aloud. She recalled that the practice was based on the idea that when your *Ki* or *Chi* was low, you became more vulnerable to illness. And by balancing or increasing your *Ki*, you helped your body heal.

Kyra remembered that giving a Reiki treatment was relatively simple and somewhat similar to giving a person a massage. The recipient would typically either lie on a massage table or sit in a chair. The Reiki practitioner would use a very light touch, and perhaps even no touch at all, sometimes elevating their hands slightly above the person's body.

When she had first begun her study of Reiki, Kyra had thought it seemed somewhat absurd, but had been surprised when Gabby explained her interest in learning the technique. She could still hear her friend's response, which touched her heart to this day: "I lost my grandfather to cancer," Gabby had said, "and we used Reiki as a complementary treatment to ease the effects of nausea from the chemotherapy."

Gabby had gone on to further explain that Reiki was also used to promote relaxation, increase optimism, and create a better sense of well-being in the client, allowing them to heal faster. "It's great for making you feel better when you are stressed, or for releasing an emotional wound, or even as a complementary treatment to help heal ailments in your body," she had said. "In the United States alone, there are over four *million* Reiki Practitioners, *Chica!* And that number is growing each year."

Kyra had always admired, too, that many Reiki practitioners volunteered their time for organizations like hospice and other cancer programs at hospitals. Still others volunteered at Reiki circles, which are groups of those trained in Reiki who meet to practice their skills giving a free mini-session to volunteers, each lasting about ten to fifteen minutes. Kyra was even more amazed to learn there were many Reiki practitioners and Master Reiki Teachers who worked full time, charging for their services, which typically was an hour-long session.

*The most interesting thing I learned in my training class,* she thought, *is that Reiki is actually nondenominational. It is not affiliated with any one specific religion. But it's necessary for a Reiki practitioner to believe in God, and that belief can come from whichever religion is best suited to that person.*

Kyra spent the next two and a half hours reading the Level 1 training course manual. She reviewed everything, from the history of Reiki—including its inception in the early 1920s in Japan by its founder, Dr. Usui—to the various hand positions used in a Reiki treatment, to receiving the actual Reiki attunement. The Reiki attunement was unique and thought to help the practitioner better receive and direct the life energy to help others heal.

Kyra had received one attunement for each of the three levels of Reiki she had previously taken. Once an attunement was administered, one never needed to repeat it to practice Reiki. But there was also a "healing attunement," which was slightly different and given to anyone in need of healing or detoxing and cleansing.

On the phone, Miguel had offered Kyra the healing attunement as part of her refresher course since she didn't needed to repeat her original attunement. This had sounded appealing to Kyra after all her indulgences in Spanish wine and cocktails. She was pleased that Miguel had made the offer and was eagerly looking forward to reacquainting herself with the ancient healing practice.

Deciding to take a short break from her studies, Kyra put her book down and gazed out across the lake again. Now there were rowboats slowly drifting past her. Many were filled with parents and small children, likely enjoying their summer holiday vacation. She could hear laughter from one of the rowboats and waved to a couple of the children who caught her eye. The two young boys grinned playfully back and waved simultaneously as they passed her by.

Kyra's mind jolted when she suddenly realized how much she wanted to have her own children someday. Her heart pierced as she longed for her children—which startled her a bit. *Where did that thought come from?* she wondered. *I'm not even married . . . but I definitely think I want children in my life someday. And, strangely, I feel that there may be two in store for me!*

Kyra had never even thought of having children previously, given her former crazy schedule—not to mention her relationship with Steve—but now she was imagining *two* children. And, for a moment, the thought of twins popped into her mind.

*Twins?* she thought with surprise, but then she remembered that twins did run on her father's side, so it was a possibility. *I'm definitely committed to be much more careful about my work-life balance going forward—so I'll have room for both a loving relationship and my two children.*

Kyra felt her heart swell as it had become so much clearer to her that, while she did indeed love working, she never wanted to go back into another career where the work totally consumed her. *I'll never forget how the stress affected my father . . . and how much my mother and I missed having him home. There is so much more I plan to do at this point with my life,* she reaffirmed.

Kyra returned to her reading, feeling as if the park had become her own little slice of heaven. She finished the manual and glanced down at her watch. She was surprised to see it was 4:44 pm—another strange occurrence of triple numbers, she thought. Realizing the time had flown by, she quickly packed up her book and tossed the remaining picnic items in a nearby trashcan. Next she walked to the Metro station, which was conveniently located close to the entrance of the park. After a full day of walking in the summer heat, Kyra gladly boarded the subway and settled into a window seat. A young man soon took the seat next to her.

"This train is very clean and efficient," she said, making small talk, wondering if he even spoke English. "This is my first time in Madrid," she added.

The young man accepted her invitation to chat and began to offer his best advice on where to visit. He spoke in somewhat broken English. " . . . definitely visit the *Basilica de San Francisco el Grande* in Madrid. It will not look *atractivo* on the outside, but it can be a—*Cómo se dice?*—a very spiritually profound building on the inside."

*¡Ay—ay—ay!* Kyra thought, surprise washing across her face. *What are the odds he would mention Father Sánchez's church?* She laughed. "I just visited that church today—and quite by accident, I must say! And, yes, it was a most uplifting experience—as you suggest."

The man smiled. "*Sí, sí, señorita*, you must have been destined to go there."

Kyra met his eyes directly, a return smile on her lips. "I could not agree with you more."

The train arrived a brief twenty minutes or so later at the stop near her hotel, at just a little before six in the evening.

Once back in her hotel room, Kyra set her manual down on the desk and freshened up a bit in the bathroom, adding just a small dab of makeup. She brushed her hair in the mirror and pulled it back into a simple ponytail. She next slipped into a pair of dark navy silk slacks and topped off her outfit with a sleeveless pale-yellow sweater.

*Maybe I'll wear my light brown leather high-heeled sandals,* she thought as she looked at herself in the mirror. *At least this pair is fairly comfortable to walk in despite their height!* She chuckled to herself; while she loved her more comfortable sneakers, her nighttime fashion choices sometimes left blisters on her feet.

Kyra had no particular plans for the evening other than going back to The Roof for a light dinner. She then planned to return to her room for a good night's sleep before her Reiki class in the morning. Just as she was getting ready to leave, her cell phone rang. Kyra grabbed the phone off the desk, instantly recognizing the caller. Thrilled, her face brightened when she answered.

"Gabby, *mi querida amiga*—or should I say 'my dear girlfriend'—how are you and Alejandro doing?"

"The boy and I are doing *magnífico!*" Gabby replied in her bubbly voice. "The question is, how are *you* doing in Madrid? I see your Spanish is improving!"

"Oh, Gabby," Kyra replied, "you would not believe the wonderful time I've had here so far! Javier and Verónica are so gracious—and we all get along so well. It's like I've gained a new brother and sister. Not to mention, they are so adorable together. It's obvious that they are part of your family—so thoughtful and generous."

"Ah, that's so sweet of you. I know Verónica *es muy encantada* with you and feels the same way. And Javier . . . well, he's asking why it took so long to meet you!"

Kyra breathed, feeling tears of affection welling in her eyes. "Let's promise we will never lose touch again. Okay?" Catching herself, she changed the subject. "So much has happened here in the past few days—actually some unusual things I need to fill you in on since our strange meeting with the fortune-teller in *Las Ramblas*. But I'll tell you all about it when I see you back in Barcelona. There's too much to talk about this evening, and I can definitely say that I truly feel I was meant to come here to Spain. It's opening my mind to *everything* I need to do differently."

"Ah, *Chica*," Gabby replied with a chuckle, "destiny has found you after all. I will be super excited to see you back in Barcelona before you leave for home! Plus, you will have to let me know if you will join me for the Reiki training in England, but no pressure. Tonight I was calling to confirm the next leg of your trip to *Sevilla* and *Málaga.* I know you have two more days in Madrid, but I was able to reach my cousin, Raquel, who's on summer break from college. She would be thrilled to show you around the Southern part of Spain—the *Andalucía* region, as we like to call it. She lives with my aunt and uncle in *Sevilla*—exactly where you will be landing. And you might even get to see the Strait of Gibraltar, if you are lucky! But you and I will have to keep Morocco in mind for the next time you come to visit. It's a short distance from the southernmost tip of Spain, and I would love to go with you."

Excited to the point of breathlessness, Gabby took a deep inhale before she continued. "Take Raquel's phone number, and call her to finalize meeting up. She has some fantastic things planned for you, so pack comfortable walking shoes and get ready for a spectacular time. By the way, Raquel lives up to *mi familia's muy loca* reputation! So be careful, and don't get into too much trouble."

"I'm counting on your family to be *muy loca* at this point . . . and I wouldn't have it any other way," Kyra teased.

With their conversation complete, Kyra crossed the room to stare out the window. Never in her entire life had she ever imagined she would take off so much time from work, much less experience all the wondrous things that had happened since her grandmother's passing. As she looked outside, she thought of how deeply she longed to speak with Nana one last time.

*The fortune-teller gave me hope that might be possible somehow,* Kyra reflected. She knew she had felt Nana's presence around her many times since her passing. Sometimes, the sensation had come subtly, like in the sudden, faint smell of her perfume. Other times, she had thought she had seen Nana walk by, only to realize it was someone else. But she realized the feeling seemed to be getting stronger, as if she could hear Nana speaking to her—especially when she took a moment to think about her. And when she could feel Nana sending her love, it pierced her heart, making her feel happy and sad all at the same time.

Kyra glanced back at the notepad on the desk where she had written down Raquel's phone number. She decided to call her after a bite to eat, although it was only 8:15 pm and still early for dinner in Spain.

The amazing view from The Rooftop was breathtakingly beautiful, just as it had been the previous evening. She ordered a light dinner, choosing sparkling water over wine to stay clearheaded. As she ate, she admired the contours of the buildings and the evening skyline.

After the satisfying meal, she returned to her room, left Raquel a detailed message, and then set her alarm for early the next morning.

*I can't believe I'm going to a Reiki refresher course tomorrow in Spain—of all places!* she thought as she climbed into bed. *If I'd asked myself five weeks ago what I would be doing the next day, I would have said, "Going to work, of course! What else would I do?"* Kyra pressed her head into the soft down pillow. *That scenario seems like a lifetime ago . . .*

She fell into a deep sleep and didn't wake till her alarm sounded.

# 23

As Kyra prepared for the day ahead, she began to feel a subtle sense of nervousness creep over her. She sternly reminded herself to be more self-confident. *I can't go to class if my mind isn't focused.* While it had been years since she'd practiced Reiki, the other students would only just be learning. She had no reason to be apprehensive.

In the shower, she let the soapy water flow over her, imagining her fears washing down the drain. *Focus on the positive and the fear won't get the best of me,* she told herself. *I'm going to do great today! I can do this.*

After toweling dry, she took a moment to try to meditate and ground herself, something she had not attempted in a very long time. Standing in the bathroom, she firmly planted her feet on the tile. Next she closed her eyes and visualized deep tree roots extending down from her feet into the earth five stories below her.

*I am surrounded by white light,* she said silently, *and the white light is sealing me in love. I am connecting to Mother Earth, and deep within the center of the Earth, there is a beautiful crystal of white light. I now connect to that pure energy, and I am drawing that wonderful energy back up, up, up through the ground and slowly into my body. I am grounding and connecting myself to the earth. I am sealed in love and light.*

Though standing outside in a grassy area would have been more ideal, Kyra still felt calmer and more centered following the fifteen-minute meditation. *Ah, that's exactly what I needed to do,* she thought, realizing she should try to meditate every morning to get her day focused in the right direction.

She next rummaged through her suitcase and opted for a casual pair of blue jeans, low-heeled silver sandals, and a plain white tank top. Accessorizing with simple turquoise jewelry, Kyra recalled that the

Native Americans had long valued this stone for its positive healing energy. She had read about the energy associated with many different crystals and stones—but had always been strongly drawn to turquoise. *Today, I will set the intention to use the healing energy of these stones for my class. How appropriate!*

She lovingly fastened the necklace around her throat and laughed as she surveyed her outfit in the bathroom mirror.

A few minutes later, Kyra sauntered into the hotel restaurant. She wanted a full stomach this morning to make sure she kept her nerves under control. The waiter approached with notepad in hand, and Kyra glanced up. "I'd like a *café con leche* and a bowl of fruit with yogurt. Oh, if you could add an assortment of breads to my order, I'd be most appreciative. *Muchas gracias.*"

The waiter nodded and hurried away.

Once served, Kyra sipped her coffee and nibbled a delicious sweet muffin called a *magdalena,* which had a slight lemony favor and was topped with toasted nuts. She recalled having such a muffin with Gabby in Barcelona, and she smiled fondly at the memory. *How proud Gabby would be of me right now.*

After breakfast, Kyra promptly caught a taxi. Miguel's home was only a few miles away from the Spiritual Awakenings bookstore and the driver arrived at the destination fairly quickly. When she exited the cab, she asked the driver to pick her up at 5 pm in her best Spanish: "*¿Puede volver a recogerme a las 5 pm?*"

"*Sí, sí, señorita,*" the young driver agreed.

"*Gracias,*" she said, adding a generous tip to his fare. She also exchanged phone numbers just in case.

As the taxicab drove off behind her, Kyra found herself facing a small two-story apartment building. Built of beige concrete, it looked to be a bit older than some of the other buildings she had seen along her route, but bright pink Bougainvillea climbed up the exterior walls, adding much-needed charm to the otherwise austere exterior.

Kyra greeted an elderly woman walking down the stairs with a friendly "*Buenos días.*" When she reached the front door of Miguel's apartment, she paused for a moment to gather her courage before ringing the doorbell.

After a moment, Miguel opened the door. "*¡Bienvenida, Kyra!*" he said enthusiastically, his voice again deep and pleasant.

"*Gracias, Miguel.*" Kyra replied with a grin, feeling instantly welcome as she stepped inside. His home was simply furnished, and she could see that two of the other students had already arrived and were seated on the sofa.

"We are waiting on one last student," Miguel explained, "and then we will begin."

Miguel introduced Kyra to Antonio and María Carmen. He spoke briefly in Spanish, explaining to the couple that Kyra did not speak Spanish fluently and that he would be translating the day's teaching into English as well. "Antonio and María Carmen are married and taking the class together today," he told Kyra. "They speak a little English."

Kyra noted that Antonio and María Carmen were likely in their late forties and appeared to be professionals; they were nicely dressed and wore expensive watches. She felt immediately drawn to their warm, pleasant expressions. "*Mucho gusto,*" they each said, stepping forward to give Kyra a hug.

"I'm very happy to meet you both, too," she replied, grateful for her classmates' kindness. They began chatting passionately with her, and she was able to loosely translate that they were excited to be there. Kyra agreed wholeheartedly, her fears easing.

After another ten minutes or so, the fourth and last student arrived, a young woman in her early twenties with a petite build. She wore a flowing, colorful, Bohemian-style skirt and a sparkly pink tank top. *She almost looks like a fairy,* Kyra mused, feeling strangely drawn to her.

Miguel introduced the newcomer to the group. "*¡Hola a todos—esta es Daniela!*"

Daniela greeted the group with a friendly "*¡Hola!*" and said she was glad to meet everyone, too.

After taking a seat on the sofa and getting everyone settled, Miguel started teaching the fundamentals of Reiki. He first offered an overview of the course, including the definition of Reiki, the four different levels, why the attunements were necessary, and why Reiki was different from other types of energy healing. He went on to cover the history of Reiki. Then came a discussion of the Reiki attunement and what would happen during that process.

This was already familiar to Kyra, which further alleviated her concerns about what to expect. Miguel continued speaking in Spanish, and Kyra translated as best she could: "Once you receive an attunement for a Reiki Level, you never need to have it done again. But today, Kyra is taking a refresher course, so she will receive a complementary healing attunement instead, which will help cleanse and purify her. Kyra is looking forward to this special kind of attunement, as she feels it would be perfect timing with her refresher course. This is something you will learn how to do later in the more advanced class."

"Thanks so much, Miguel," Kyra replied. "It's just what I need."

Following a short break for refreshments, the students began preparations for their attunement process. Each student was asked to sit in a chair with his or her eyes closed. Miguel placed sandalwood oil on the palms of their hands and soles of their feet to aid in grounding and centering. Kyra found the scent pleasing and relaxing.

Next he conducted a brief meditation. Once they were completely relaxed, Miguel went to each student individually and performed the attunement process. When Miguel reached Kyra's chair, he performed a similar attunement, but with the intention of releasing any toxins in her body, as well as healing any physical, mental, or emotional concerns.

As Miguel raised his hands over the top of her head, above the area known as the crown chakra, Kyra felt an odd, indescribable sensation. It was as if her energy had been instantly drawn *up* into the atmosphere. Her mind's eye was suddenly enveloped in a swirl of many colors—mostly purple and green.

When Miguel placed his hands at the base of her head, Kyra felt white light race out of her body, sending her consciousness up into the universe toward another bright white light off in the distance. Even as her mind's eye absorbed these images, Kyra felt herself merging with the bright Source Light, and the most amazing warmth emanated all around her.

*It feels like pure love*, she thought, and a swell of joy and love surged all around her.

Then, suddenly, Kyra felt her consciousness being quickly transported downward and back into her body as Miguel finished her healing attunement. She felt heavier and heavier as she descended down, but the feeling of joy remained.

Once the group attunements were completed, each student was asked to open their eyes and share their experiences with the other students. Miguel helped Kyra by translating for the others to make sure she understood. Kyra was the first to speak up; she described her experience as best she could. As it turned out, her experience was quite different from those of the others.

Antonio had seen no particular colors or white light, but he had felt as though his deceased grandfather were with him. It was a subtle feeling, he explained, but he also thought he heard his grandfather speak to him. María Carmen had felt more emotions than colors, and connected with the feeling of joy that Kyra had experienced, too. Daniela, on the other hand, had found herself in a magical green garden, flying through the air alongside butterflies and tiny white birds. Kyra laughed inwardly. *She is a fairy!*

After they had all shared with the group, Miguel prepared everyone for a "practice" Reiki session, which would give the three first-time students their inaugural opportunity to use their Reiki skills. Miguel set up a massage table in the middle of the room and demonstrated the proper hand positions, explaining that, once they became more comfortable, they could intuitively move their hands to wherever they felt guided on the person's body. "Trusting your intuition is key," said Miguel.

"That's a good reminder," Kyra chimed in, "on many different levels."

Miguel nodded in agreement. Alternating between Spanish and English, Miguel said, "We need someone on the table to receive while the new Reiki practitioners gain some experience. Who would like to go first?"

The other students hesitated, so Kyra raised her hand. "I'm happy to be first," she said, "if that's okay with everyone?"

"That's fine with me," María Carmen replied in Spanish, "as long as you don't expect too much."

Seeming to sense María Carmen's apprehension, Miguel quickly reassured, "No harm can come from Reiki, and it will naturally flow to wherever it needs to go in the body. You can't make a mistake. Our intentions are sealed in love."

María Carmen exhaled a sigh of relief, and Kyra lay down on the table, making herself comfortable. The others took their positions around her, with one student at her head, one at each of her sides, and Miguel at her feet.

Kyra closed her eyes and relaxed, her head cradled by the soft pillow. Warmth spread throughout her body as each student worked on her, and she sensed their confidence building throughout the practice session. Even though her eyes were closed, Kyra knew exactly where Miguel stood, even when the students quietly rotated positions. He had a much stronger Reiki flow than the students, and it left her with an amazing feeling of relaxation and love.

After finishing the session, Antonio traded places with Kyra. Much to Kyra's surprise, she felt much more comfortable giving a session than she had expected. Her confidence clearly was growing. She experienced a strong tingling and warmth in her hands as she held them above Antonio's body, gently touching his arm and shoulders with her fingers. *Nothing has changed in thirteen years!* she thought with pleasant surprise.

They continued the process until each student had enjoyed a turn at both giving and receiving. When Miguel asked them to share what they'd experienced, Kyra again spoke up first in English, and then translating her words into Spanish best as she could. "When I was giving Antonio the Reiki treatment, I felt as if there was discomfort in his knee area." Kyra pointed to Antonio's knees to ensure he understood. Then she pointed to her stomach and rubbed it in a circular motion. "I also kept feeling as if your stomach or digestion might be a little out of whack."

Antonio's eyes widened. "*Sí, sí!*" he replied. Kyra couldn't quite follow the string of Spanish words he spoke next, so Miguel translated: "Antonio says you are correct. He does have very bad knees; it runs in his family. He also says his stomach has been giving him trouble for a week—he thinks he may have unfortunately eaten some bad food."

Antonio let out a surprised laugh and shared in Spanish that Kyra's intuition was completely accurate.

"I'm a little surprised myself," Kyra replied, pleased she had understood his last statement. "Hopefully this is a good indication that I *should* be doing Reiki more often. I have enjoyed giving each of you a session today, and it was so wonderful to receive one myself, too. I feel so uplifted."

Miguel helped translate Kyra's English for the others, and then did the same when Daniela spoke softly to Kyra: "Nothing is left to chance, Kyra. We were meant to meet you here today. This has been a wonderful experience for all of us."

The sharing continued until it was time to enjoy the lunch Miguel had prepared for them ahead of time. He made sure each had plenty of water along with the light fare.

As they were just about finished eating, Miguel announced with a playful grin, "We will finish out our day with all of you giving *me* a practice session. I will be a very glad recipient and enjoy the relaxation of Reiki for myself. This will also be a good confidence builder for my wonderful new Reiki practitioners, but this is not meant to be a test of your skills; please just enjoy yourself."

María Carmen fidgeted nervously, so Miguel reassured her, first in Spanish, and then in English for Kyra's benefit: "Be *confident,* and remember, Reiki cannot cause harm—you will do excellent!"

Miguel eagerly lay down on the table. Kyra felt blessed to share this experience with her newfound friends—especially given she was in a foreign country and a long way from home. After forty-five minutes, an alarm chimed softly on Miguel's phone, and the students closed the session by sealing the Reiki treatment in love and light. They silently asked for God's blessings and for any additional healing Miguel needed, as they had been taught to do.

When the session was over, Miguel slowly rose from the massage table and poured himself a large glass of water. As he drank, his gaze went from one student to the next, his face beaming. "*¡Muchas gracias!*" he said when he'd emptied the glass. "I am so excited to have had such excellent students today. Keep practicing and your confidence will grow. You all did great!

Miguel then asked the students if the class had met their expectations and to share their most significant personal experience of the day.

Daniela, the most energetic among them, practically sang her response, "*¡Gracias, Miguel, por tus maravillosas instrucciones hoy!*" She went on to describe how her confidence in her abilities felt stronger and she would do weekly practices with her new friends . . . if they were amenable. Antonio and María Carmen readily agreed. Kyra, of course, wouldn't be able to join them, although she did express a deep desire to remain in touch with her new friends.

This time Kyra spoke last, and Miguel translated for the others. She felt the warmth of pure joy spreading through her as she gave her sentiments. "Oh, Miguel, today's class truly exceeded my expectations! But the most profound experience I had was being able to share this class with all of you. I am truly blessed to have been guided here today. Thank you!"

Daniela leapt up from her chair to hug Kyra, and the two women shared a long embrace. Then everyone began exchanging hugs—and phone numbers.

Miguel closed the training with a guided meditation and grounding exercise to make sure they were all well connected to Mother Earth and that no one left lightheaded. As the grounding session progressed, Kyra again felt herself becoming heavier and heavier. As she had experienced that morning, she visualized deep tree roots extending from the soles of her feet, connecting her back to the earthly plane. She opened her eyes, fully present and joyful.

"Be sure to increase your intake of water," Miguel suggested, "and take sea salt baths as needed to further cleanse and detoxify. Also, get extra sleep, and avoid alcohol, if possible, for the next twenty-one days.

It will take a full three weeks for the attunement process to adjust to your body."

Kyra recalled that the attunement was thought to clear blocks from each of the seven chakras, with the energy cycling through each chakra three times, hence the need for twenty-one days of cleansing. During this process, it was believed that the body adjusted to a higher vibrational level.

Since she was nearing the end of her travels in Spain, Kyra had been thinking of drinking less alcohol anyway. Plus, being clearheaded for the remainder of the trip sounded appealing. *There are fewer negative feelings to chase away, and I feel awesome*, she happily concluded. Indeed, she felt much more relaxed and uplifted than when her trip began.

Before she left, Miguel pulled her aside, and said, "Remember, Kyra, never be afraid to do what your heart tells you is good."

She assured her teacher she would continue to do just that and cheerfully descended the stairs to wait for her taxi.

# 24

Kyra skipped lightheartedly back to her room, feeling both elated and a bit tired. She realized that her body might be adjusting to the healing attunement or perhaps it was just the excitement of the day. “A nap is definitely in order if I want to feel energized this evening,” she said.

Snuggling into the soft bedding, her head sank deep into the pillow, and she fell asleep instantly. Before an hour had passed, she awoke feeling refreshed and remarkably alert. Spying her favorite perfume on the bathroom vanity, she dabbed a bit on her wrists. *It’s nice to enjoy the scent simply for myself.*

Next she eagerly drank a bottle of water, finishing it just as a call came in from Gabby’s cousin. Once the formalities were out of the way, Raquel gushed, “We’ll get along *maravillosamente* from what Gabriela tells me about you! I’m excited to pick you up at the airport on Thursday, and we’ll head out from there. . . . Oh! I have many fun things planned for our three days in *Sevilla* and *Málaga, amiga.*”

“We will have a blast!” Kyra replied, her excitement building. “Destiny has put us on a parallel path, and I can’t wait to see you.”

Following the call, Kyra grabbed another bottle of water and ran through their conversation in her mind. Though it had been brief, Kyra had felt an instant connection with another one of Gabby’s family members. *I can’t believe how open and giving this family is toward me—a perfect stranger,* she said to herself, and then chuckled. *Okay . . . maybe I’m not so perfect . . . But this is the type of family I intend to have in the future . . . No offense, Mother and Father.*

Kyra hoped that somehow her parents knew how much she appreciated them, but she now recognized that she wanted to surround herself with loving and thoughtful people. *I will consciously focus on attracting like-minded people from now on.*

Although Kyra was accustomed to having dinner alone on her many business trips, tonight she looked forward to having a great meal on her own. *And tomorrow night, I'll once again be with friends for dinner.* She giggled as she thought about those plans, which included Juan Pablo. *A perfect way to end my time in Madrid—dinner with my wonderful new friends and an attractive man.*

This evening, Kyra planned to stroll around Plaza Mayor, which was a short distance from the hotel, and then take a walk to the nearby Barrio de La Latina to find a small restaurant for dinner. She chose a dark navy sleeveless summer dress, gold jewelry, and flat gold sandals, which were elegant, comfortable, and ideal for lots of walking.

It was nearing 8 pm but the sun would not set until 9:45. The first day of July had proven to be a hot one thus far. Kyra grabbed her directions to Plaza Mayor, and when she emerged from the elevator, she reminded herself to pay careful attention to where she was going. *I don't want to get lost again—and wind up meeting another handsome priest at a church!* She chuckled as she started on her way.

She headed south and then turned west toward Plaza Mayor. Even though it was early in the evening, the plaza was already bustling with locals and tourist alike. Kyra welcomed the idea of blending in with the folks who crowded the sidewalks.

Three-story residential buildings surrounded the rectangular plaza. A large bronze sculpture of King Felipe III, sitting gallantly upon a horse, dominated the center of the plaza. Kyra had read that the sculpture had originally been commissioned in the early seventeenth century for use in the Casa de Campo, but had been moved to Plaza Mayor in the mid-1800s.

*Some of these buildings were built as far back as the late 1500s,* Kyra thought, looking around in wonder. *How amazing is that? It's so hard to imagine living back in Spain at that time.*

Instantly, the memory of her flashbacks at the Royal Palace of Madrid leapt into her mind. "I had better change my thoughts!" she said aloud. She wanted to avoid jinxing her evening with another flashback episode. A young man walking past her gave her a funny look, clearly wondering *who* she was speaking to. Kyra shrugged at him and smiled, trying not to appear too crazy.

Her stroll brought her closer to one of the large residential buildings with balconies overlooking the Plaza. Several locals—or *madrileños*, as Javier liked calling them—were enjoying the evening out on their balconies. One attractive young man waved to Kyra as she wandered past, as if inviting her to join him. "*¡Una copa de vino!*" he called, offering her a glass of wine, but Kyra shook her head.

*What was Gabby's advice to me?* she questioned, looking up at the man. *Ah, yes. "Be careful, Chica, and don't get into too much trouble!"* She decided she'd take Gabby up on that advice. "No, no," she replied with a pleasant smile, and kept walking.

As she continued on, she studied several of the well-known buildings in the plaza, including Casa de la Panadería—House of the Bakery—on the north side. It was the one of the more notable buildings in the square and stood four stories high. Kyra recognized a Spanish Coat of Arms at the top of the building.

*That's from the reign of King Carlos II,* she recalled. The building had originally been designed to house the Baker's Guild. Today, it served as the Madrid Tourism Center. The building had closed at 8 pm, much to Kyra's disappointment. She would have liked to have gone on a tour.

The plaza had no shortage of restaurants and cafés, and the sumptuous aromas that poured boldly into the air began to stimulate Kyra's appetite for an early dinner. All of the restaurants were crowded with patrons enjoying wine, beer, and tapas, but she decided to wait for dinner and head over to the La Latina area, trusting Verónica's earlier recommendation.

Javier had also pointed out that La Latina was the one of the oldest districts in Madrid, and Kyra did not want to miss seeing it. Soon she departed the Plaza Mayor and headed slightly south, then west for several blocks, making several turns down some side streets before she arrived at Calle Cava Baja in La Latina.

Cava Baja was the most popular street in the La Latina district and was lined with bars and restaurants. It was indeed crowded with madrileños walking up and down the narrow street just as she had expected. The neighborhood was comprised of many four-story buildings in soft pastel colors. *Ah, it's has a unique old-world charm,* Kyra thought, falling instantly in love with the area. Wrought-iron balconies like those she had seen at Plaza Mayor overlooked the streets, and sidewalk cafes added ambience to the colorful district.

She wandered down the busy main street until she came upon a restaurant called Casa Lucio, which Verónica had said was famous for its celebrity visits in the past. Kyra was now quite hungry, and she hurried through the dark wooden doors, immediately noticing that the restaurant was jam-packed with people. It was standing-room only at this point, despite the early hour. Kyra looked around, trying to decide what to do. *The atmosphere of the restaurant is festive*, which she loved, but the busyness made her worry. *It's so crowded . . . maybe this is a mistake.*

Kyra tried to maneuver her way through the crowd to get in line for the waiting list. As she walked forward, she bumped into a man trying to navigate through the sea of people. A bit flustered, she hurried to apologize. *"Oh, lo siento . . .*uh, *por favor, perdóname,"* which she hoped translated to, "Oh, I'm so sorry . . . please pardon me."

*"No hay problema,"* the man replied, but his wife gave Kyra a rather annoyed up-and-down glance and grabbed her husband's hand.

"We have over an hour wait this evening," the hostess told Kyra when she finally reached the front desk, "even at our bar. Should I put you on our list?"

Kyra assured the hostess that a seat at the bar was just fine, but her face must have betrayed her disappointment. Noticing her frustration, three people at a table near the front waved for her to join them.

"Come, please sit with us!" said one of them, a handsome, blond-haired gentleman. "Join us for a drink while you wait for your friends."

"How did you know I speak English?" Kyra asked, her face breaking into a surprised smile. "And yes, I'd love to join you for a drink. I'm actually on my own tonight."

"Join us for dinner, too, then," said another of the three. The handsome man grinned, rising to his feet to greet her. He was of average height and looked to be in his mid-thirties, light blond hair and fair-skinned—and American, judging by his accent. "I'm here on an extended trip with my company. I'm from *Noo Yawk* actually. I miss the Big Apple. But to answer your question, you look a bit more American with your blond hair, and I could hear you speaking English."

Kyra laughed. *His accent is adorable*, she thought. As she stepped closer to the table, he introduced himself properly. "My name is John," he said, "and these are my coworkers, David and Susana. They are natives of Madrid, and we all work at the same company. Their English is very good. You should definitely join us, and I shall enjoy the company of a fellow American tonight—and a very pretty American, I might add!"

His distinctive New York accent and flirtatious tone caught Kyra's ears again, making her smile. She looked him directly in the eyes and replied, "Thanks, John. It's very nice to meet you, and David, and Susana, too."

She extended her hand to warmly greet John's coworkers, and then seated herself next to John, who continued the conversation by asking Kyra why she was in Spain and how long she planned to visit. She told them she was taking some time for herself and explained why.

"I am so sorry about the loss of your *abuela*—Nana did you call her?" Susana said. "I am happy you have come to beautiful Madrid to find peace."

Kyra thanked the woman for her kind words and soon found herself describing her life back in San Francisco. This, of course, included such details as her eighty-plus-hour workweeks at Vortex.

David interrupted firmly but with good humor, "You Americans work much too hard and need to learn to *celebrar la vida*—'celebrate life'—as we say here in Spain."

"I think I have learned the hard way that you are absolutely right," Kyra replied. "Meeting you all is a great confirmation of what I need to do when home—and that's to never let my life get so out of balance again."

When the waiter took Kyra's drink order, John expressed surprise that she had opted for a sparkling water with lime and would not be joining them for "a real drink," as he had put it. But Kyra had stood firm in her decision, and explained, "I'm doing a little detox right now. It's just a personal choice and something I want to do for myself."

"Well, Kyra," John replied, "we will not *force* you to have a glass of wine with us, but you do not know what you are missing. The wine selection here at *Casa Lucio* is excellent!"

"I can totally appreciate that," she replied cheerfully, as the waiter placed the nonalcoholic drink before her, "but right now this is important to me. I will toast you with my *sparkling* water—and my *sparkling* personality. We will enjoy the evening just the same. To balance!" she said, and with that, they all raised their glasses in a toast.

John gave Kyra a nod of understanding as he sipped his wine.

A few minutes later, the waiter returned for their order.

"Can I suggest several dishes to share? I know the menu quite well," John offered, and they all agreed. "*Won-da-ful.*" he replied, his strong New York accent causing Kyra to grin again. He placed the order in both Spanish and English to ensure that Kyra understood. "We'd like the *churrasco,* or grilled beef. An order of the *cocido* too—which is an amazing chickpea-based stew, Kyra—some *croquetas,* or fish croquets, *ensalada*—we must have our veggies!—and *Casa Lucio's* very famous *huevos estrellados.*"

"That's a unique dish of eggs served over french fries," David clarified.

"They all sound delicious!" Kyra agreed, as her new friends continued chatting to become better acquainted.

After the dishes were served, David turned to Kyra before she took her first bite and said, "I've been told even the King of Spain comes here for the *huevos estrellados* dish—so please, do enjoy."

Susana helped herself to a gooey fry. "These are my favorite!" she noted. "The trip is worth it just for this dish alone."

As they ate, John kept the dinner conversation lively with his flowing

"*Noo Yawk*" accent, and it quickly became apparent that he loved to talk. Kyra also enjoyed his charming pronunciation of certain words: "coffee" became "cawfee," "order" became "ordah," and "New York" became "Noo Yawk." She delighted in sound of his distinctive accent, guessing he was perhaps from Brooklyn.

The conversation had a central theme of how much John adored New York and how much he missed his hometown. *Ah, so very true of a native New Yorker,* she thought fondly. *They are very proud of their city.* John entertained her with his wit and his take on politics, not to mention his knowledge of art, which impressed her.

They finished their meal with a cup of "cawfee." Kyra glanced down at her watch and realized was almost 11 pm. "I must say that I've *truly* enjoyed our time together," she offered, "and I most certainly appreciate being able to join you tonight. That was most kind—I would have waited forever to be seated." Kyra eyes turned toward John as she continued. "But even more important, I would not have had so much fun on my own. This really was a special treat, but I must call it an evening. I know I'll be back to Spain sometime soon, so maybe I will see all of you again."

"It's been our *plesha* to have you as our *dinna* companion. We will definitely stay in *tauch!*" John said with a wide grin.

Kyra's smile broadened. "The pleasure has been all mine," she replied.

"You will be enchanted by *Sevilla* and *Málaga,*" Susana said affectionately. "They are two of my favorite places to visit for a leisurely weekend."

David added, "As we say in Spanish, you are *muy agradable*—very delightful—and we are so glad you made *our* evening more fun. Let's do stay in touch."

Kyra stood up and John gave her a warm hug goodbye.

"It's been wonderful to have a very attractive American join us tonight," he said close to her ear in a flirtatious tone. "I will let you know when I'm back in the States. You are welcome to visit me anytime in *Noo Yawk.*"

Kyra smiled and waved goodbye to her new friends. Stepping to the curbside, she hailed a taxi and one pulled up in a matter of seconds. *Ah, God is helping me now even in the smallest things!* she thought happily.

Settling into the backseat, a yawn passed over her lips. *It's tempting to stay out late, but a good night's sleep is best given my full day of Reiki training,* she resolved. Already, she felt very proud of herself for making decisions that aligned with her new spiritual and physical goals. *Yes, I'm on a very good track and the Universe seems to be seems to be in agreement with me.*

The alarm buzzed loudly at 8:00 am, and Kyra woke abruptly. She sat up in bed, feeling groggy, and recalled the dream she had been having. She had been on a mountaintop in a strange lush, green land. *A jungle, maybe . . . or somewhere tropical?* she thought. The mountain was covered in a thick blanket of mist. It seemed like morning, but Kyra couldn't quite recognize where she was standing.

She had looked to her left and saw a large Asian temple about fifty feet from where she stood. It was bright red and gold and adorned with intricate woodcarvings—but what surprised her most was the strange man standing near her.

She had turned around to look behind her and was met by a man with Asian features. He appeared to be in his fifties with hair slightly graying at the temples. He was dressed in simple black silk pants and a robe. The man motioned for her to follow him with a wave of his arm—and that's when the alarm clock had sounded.

Kyra felt goose bumps on her arms. *My dreams are becoming much more vivid and memorable since I started on this journey . . . I felt like I was really was standing there!* She mentally filed away all the details of the dream, at least hoping that the meaning of the dream would make more sense to her soon. *If the alarm had not gone off, would I have discovered where the man had intended me to go?*

Unsure of the answer, she stepped into the shower and felt her body rejuvenating with the flow of the water. Shaking off the eerie dream, she noticed how light and relaxed she felt after her Reiki attunement.

Following her shower, Kyra drank a large bottle of water and then got dressed, opting for flat, dressy silver sandals, a gauzy lavender skirt, and a white sleeveless top that was perfect for the heat of the day. She headed to the hotel restaurant and ordered just one café con leche and a serving of sliced fruit. She planned to eat light today so she'd have plenty of room for dinner that evening with her friends.

As the waiter brought her cup of coffee, she was reminded of the itinerary she had made for the day. She had planned to visit another famous plaza and a well-known art museum while still allowing plenty of time to get showered and dressed for her evening out.

*Ah, it's my last day in Madrid,* she realized with a hint of sadness, wishing she could stay longer. *I don't want to miss a thing! But I'm so looking forward to seeing Juan Pablo tonight—despite not having any expectations.*

# 25

Kyra's first destination that day was to be Plaza de España, which was about twenty minutes northwest from her hotel. The bellman waved her goodbye and she smiled in return, as she breezed through the front door of the hotel. She reviewed her handwritten directions noting the plaza was located at the end of Calle Gran Via, which was one of the busiest streets in Madrid. *Ah, but it's such a gorgeous warm July morning and I know the walk will be perfect. But, more importantly, I can't wait to see what the Universe has planned for me!*

Donning her sunglasses, she briskly strolled down the sidewalk and arrived at Plaza de España in what seemed like no time at all. Kyra immediately noticed all the soaring office buildings, but the surrounding trees and shrubs softened the urban feel of the area. *This is very different from the other plazas I've visited. I love the blend of city and nature. It reminds me a bit of home.* She turned her head back toward the ground and noticed, of all things, a beautiful stone monument commemorating the Spanish novelist Miguel de Cervantes. A bronze sculpture stood nearby depicting the heroic character of Don Quixote, Cervantes's most famous literary work.

Kyra's lips curled up in fondness as she surveyed the statue. She'd read the novel in a high school literature class and was amused that Don Quixote loses his sanity and dons a knight's suit—only a mere century or two after knights ceased to wear such armor. In the story, he sets forth with a simple farmer turned squire, Sancho Panza, to reignite chivalry in the world. The people they encounter are convinced Don Quixote is crazy, watching him trying to slay windmills he believes are malicious giants.

*Yes, he definitely seeks out adventures in a very unconventional, if not eccentric, way. . .* This last thought gave Kyra pause, and she almost burst out laughing. *And how appropriate for me to bump into this statue today,* she thought, *considering the strange adventures I've been on since leaving San Francisco! I am—without a doubt—learning to look at my world differently, but I'm certain that I'm not crazy.*

As she looked around the square, Kyra glanced back up at a large skyscraper that overlooked the plaza. She shielded her eyes with her hand despite the shade afforded by her sunglasses. She instantly recognized it as the Torre de Madrid, amusing herself by thinking of its name in Spanish. With its nearly forty floors, she never imagined how tall it would actually look in person. Turning her gaze downward again toward the plaza, she spied an empty bench in a shaded area near the Tower. *A perfect spot to brush up my Reiki training manual for Level 2,* she thought, hurrying forward to claim her spot before anyone else could take it.

Just then a squirrel scampered toward Kyra, begging her to play. But she just smiled at the creature, and shook her head no. "Not now my friend," she said, "I have work to do!" She shifted her attention back to the task at hand and spent the next two hours reading her book. When she reached the end, she flipped the purple manual closed and slipped it deep into her purse, ready for a break after all her time spent studying. *I can never have enough art in my life—and, for now, I'm taking advantage of my time off here to enjoy it.*

Kyra had already visited the Museo de Prado, which was well known for its European art, so today she decided to visit the Thyssen-Bornemisza Museum. This museum was famous for its collection that included the early work of Impressionist painter Rembrandt, fine pieces of the cubism style of Picasso, and even some of the more abstract and modern works of Kandinsky. Kyra was most looking forward, however, to viewing the works of Van Gogh, Degas, and Cézanne—some of her favorite artists. *This will be my inspiration for those painting classes I will be taking when I return home!* she thought without hesitation.

As Kyra rounded a corner, her eyes captured the exterior of the three-story museum, filling her with anticipation. She already knew that the museum, which had been built in the early 1800s, had once been a mansion. It was named after a famous Baron named Heinrich Thyssen-Bornemisza, and his son, Hans Heinrich. The father and son had originally purchased the mansion to house their private collection of art. Eventually, they made their collection available to the public, and in 1992, it became the museum. *How wonderful to share such a fabulous collection so everyone can enjoy it!* she reflected with appreciation, taking in the gentle reminder about sharing in general.

The museum proved to be even better than Kyra had expected. She thoroughly delighted in all of her favorite artists, once again memorizing each brushstroke just as she had done at the Picasso Museum with Gabby—but purposely keeping her observations much more subtle this time. She smiled as she passed by a serious-looking guard, whose face lit up in wonder that she might be flirting with him.

It was late afternoon when Kyra arrived back at the hotel, but she still had plenty of time before her 9 o'clock dinner date. Despite the busyness of the day, she did not need a nap. In fact, she felt incredibly energized—even more so than she had that morning. *I wonder if the Reiki healing session is doing its magic and increased my energy level.* She wasn't sure, but she definitely had energy to burn, so she changed into her workout clothing and headed to the Club Metropolitan Palacio next door.

As she ran on the treadmill, Kyra made a mental note to add daily exercise to her ever-growing list of positive changes she wanted to make in her life. *I will make more time to get back into good physical shape when I get home. All the walking here has made me feel great!*

Kyra's list of work-life balance activities was growing quickly: healthy relationships, proper diet, painting, Reiki, and amped-up physical activity. She was very much looking forward to eventually returning home . . . but first, she had dinner plans tonight with her wonderful friends *and* Juan Pablo.

Kyra wanted to look especially fantastic, so she chose a simple but elegant white silk dress, paired with gold jewelry, and high-heeled gold sandals. She felt unfazed now by the idea of eating at such a late hour. *I'm looking forward to getting my flirt on!* she chuckled, reminding herself of Gabby's encouragement to do so.

Javier and Verónica picked her up promptly at 8:45 pm.

"You will love both places we are visiting tonight!" Verónica said as soon as Kyra got in the car. "The DRY Cosmopolitan Bar at the *Gran Meliá Fénix* Hotel is very chic and popular with our *madrileños.* It has an incredible selection of cocktails. Then we'll head to *La Gabinoteca*, which is just a little bit further north. The food there is excellent! You must try their signature *El Potito* dish—egg, potato, and truffles in a jar."

"Egg, potato, and truffles? Hmmm. That's an interesting combination," Kyra said cautiously. "I'll be curious to taste that." Verónica made an *mmmm* sound, and Kyra laughed. "I'm curious about Juan Pablo, too. But this time I will have my wits about me."

"I will *still* offer my assistance if you need me," Javier joked.

The car rounded the corner of Calle de Hermosilla and pulled into the driveway of the Gran Meliá Fénix Hotel to valet park the car. Stepping out of the car, Kyra stared in wonder at the grandiose hotel. It reminded her of its sister property, the hotel where she was staying, with its similar white exterior. The soft evening light shining on the building radiated an understated elegance.

As the three friends entered the hotel lobby, Kyra found herself caught off guard by the amazing decor. Brilliant white walls topped with elaborate crown molding blended seamlessly with the polished white and beige marble flooring. Bright couches of plush red fabric and lounges in muted, traditional fabrics contrasted elegantly with the white walls. Each chair housed its own complementary pillow in purple, green, and neon blue.

"I expected sophistication and luxuriousness, but this is sensory overload. It's incredible!" she declared.

"*Sí, sí!*" Verónica agreed. "But wait until you see the rest of the hotel."

Kyra tilted her head back to look up at the lobby ceiling. "Oh my," she gasped. "It's just stunning." A huge half-dome with an elaborate crystal chandelier dominated the center of the ceiling, but what really caught Kyra's attention was the dark blue stained glass that circled the dome, giving it the appearance of the sky at twilight—the moment just after the sun had set but before the stars were fully out. A deep, visceral sense of familiarity crept over her.

*I see the night sky with the stars twinkling everywhere I go . . . just like in my dream.*

"I wanted to make sure you didn't miss this," Verónica said, interrupting her thoughts. "I know *que te encantó*—how much you loved—the stained-glass windows in the churches you've seen on this trip."

Kyra felt her heart fill with wonder at all the synchronicities she'd been experiencing, and she silently gave thanks once again for all of her amazing experiences. One place connected to the next, and they all were connecting with opening her heart. "I do love it, *very* much. It couldn't be more perfect."

Verónica reached forward to give Kyra a warm hug before they moved on.

The DRY Cosmopolitan Bar encompassed the entire first floor of the hotel. They chose a table inside to avoid the evening heat, although the patio had looked inviting.

"Your signature DRY Martini with three olives, please," Javier requested when the waiter asked for their drink order. "My wife will have a rum mojito. And what will you be drinking this evening, Kyra?"

Kyra had already scanned the menu and replied, "I'd like your fresh fruit orange martini, but please make it with dash of champagne instead of vodka." After a light cocktail, she planned to switch to sparkling water.

Just then, Juan Pablo arrived, and Kyra stood to greet him. "Ah, my beautiful falling star!" he exclaimed, warmly kissing her on each cheek. His hand brushed hers, and the touch sent chills up her spine. She kept her expression neutral, but the reaction had startled her. *Oh yes,* she thought firmly. *I'm only having one drink this evening for sure! That man is most charming.*

Juan Pablo turned to Javier, and the pair shared a firm handshake. "And, Javier, it is very nice to see you again, my friend. Ah, and I see your wife, Verónica, is even more lovely this evening than the last."

Verónica's face flushed with mild embarrassment, and Javier replied on both their behalves, "It is our pleasure you could join us tonight before Kyra leaves for *Sevilla.*"

The waiter, who had moved a polite distance away, took a few steps forward to add the new guest's drink order to the rest: a blackberry lemon gin and tonic.

The four companions settled into the luxurious, wood-paneled atmosphere of the bar. Kyra thought her friends and Juan Pablo would enjoy hearing about the Reiki class, but Juan Pablo quickly took over the conversation, discussing first his passion for traveling. After several minutes of talking, he finally asked, "What are your favorite places to visit, Kyra?"

"I'm sad to say my eighty-hour workweeks at my old job didn't leave me much time for vacations," she replied. "Even when I did take a vacation, I was still answering emails and on conference calls. But I'm truly taking time off for the first time in my life now. I think I'm making up for all of that lost vacation time by traveling to Israel and Spain. I can't wait to see where life takes me next."

"Well, let me tell you about the wonderful places I've been that you should visit," he replied.

Kyra listened intently as he regaled them, almost nonstop, with stories of how he had spent his time in France, Morocco, Belgium, Germany, Greece, England, Ireland, Italy, and even Africa over the previous five years. The thought of seeing so many places thrilled Kyra.

"I am inspired," Kyra interjected, and although she had intended to say a bit more, Juan Pablo cut her off.

Her mind wandered for a moment as he rambled on about his travels, and she began to think back to the dream she had had that morning. *Where was I standing? On a mountaintop in Asia somewhere? Which country?* She could easily picture in her mind's eye the man with Asian features who had waved for her to join him. A chill suddenly raced down her spine. "Oh! I know!"

For a moment, she did not realize she had exclaimed aloud. Startled, Juan Pablo paused, but he quickly resumed talking about his adventures. Kyra returned to the conversation at the table, feeling a little embarrassed but smiling despite herself. Javier was in the process of paying the bar bill; he had insisted on treating everyone, just as he always did.

"You are so sweet and generous," Kyra said, thanking him, and Juan Pablo echoed her gratitude. Verónica leaned in and gave her husband a soft kiss on the lips. "*¡Muchas gracias, mi amor!*"

Kyra spied Javier and Verónica holding hands beneath the table, and once again thought about her future life. *Ah, to be in love like that.* She glanced over at her dinner companion, wondering if she could ever feel that way about him. *Hmmm* . . . she thought, unsure of the answer.

The next stop was La Gabinoteca, which was only a few minutes away and just slightly north of the Gran Meliá Fénix Hotel. Kyra rode with her friends, and they met up with Juan Pablo outside the restaurant. Once inside, Kyra noted the two-level layout.

"Wow. I've never seen anything like that," Kyra said surprised at the sight of a suspension staircase leading up to the second level.

"It does look like it's floating in air," Javier agreed, then added quietly for Kyra's ears, "but we won't drink too much wine before we ascend; we wouldn't want you to fall into another man's arms."

Kyra laughed good-naturedly, but inwardly she thought that her last fall didn't turn out too badly. Her eyes settled on Juan Pablo's handsome face, and she felt a flash of desire rush through her body. This quickly passed, however, when she recalled his somewhat self-centered monologue over drinks at the hotel.

Once they were ready to be seated, the group ascended the unique staircase to the second level. "I love the way the light ash of the walls match the wooden staircase railing," she commented to Verónica. "And the built-in wine rack housed in the railing is so clever. You certainly don't disappoint. This place is awesome!"

"It almost makes you want to select a bottle of *vino* as you walk up the stairs," responded Verónica, carefully taking the steps in her high heels. "But let's look at where we're going, not at the wine."

The walls of the top floor were predominantly light ash, but accented with a few black rectangular walls in some of the niches. Bold, modern artwork added splashes of bright color, livening up the decor.

Once the foursome was seated, Javier took the lead and ordered drinks. Kyra decided on sparkling water to start with, which Juan Pablo immediately commented on. "*Ah*, do not worry about drinking too much," he said. "I will catch you if you fall again."

Kyra laughed, but replied firmly, "*Gracias,* I most certainly appreciate your offer, but tonight I plan to drink only sparkling water; I have an early flight in the morning. I shall be just as entertaining though. I promise."

"You can sip on my drink if you change your mind, *mi hermosa amiga*," her date declared gallantly.

*My beautiful darling?* Kyra repeated to herself with a hint of amusement. *He is quite good at flirting!*

Javier prepared to order a large selection of dishes for the table, but first made sure that everyone agreed with the choices. "May I suggest one of the house specialties, fried artichokes? Ah, and let's have a *Pascualete* pumpkin puff for appetizers. *¿Sí?*"

"*Ah, mi amor*," Verónica chimed in, "we must have the *El Potito*. It's the egg, potato, and truffles in a jar."

"We also should try their scallops grilled with peppers," Juan Pablo commented.

Javier continued, "And the duck tacos . . . and why don't we try the grilled steak mixed with fresh herbs? We won't go hungry tonight!"

"My mouth is already watering," Kyra added, as they finalized their selection.

Once the dishes were served and they'd begun to eat, Kyra observed that Juan Pablo had dominated the conversation once again. He discussed how successful he had become at the young age of twenty-eight, how he had come from a wealthy family that had allowed him to experience only the best things in life, how much he *loved* to travel, and so on. Much of it was a repeat of the earlier conversation.

Javier and Verónica listened graciously, and Kyra nodded to appear interested when appropriate, but her mind began to wander off again. She realized that, perhaps, the initial chemistry she'd felt with Juan Pablo might have worn off a bit.

She looked at his face while he was taking. *He is an attractive man, no doubt about that . . . but more self-absorbed than I would want in a future mate.* Her mind flashed back to her relationship with Steve, and she remembered how very self-absorbed he had been. *Hmmm . . . Juan Pablo may fit Steve's type a little too closely.* While Juan Pablo was excellent at speaking about himself, he most noticeably didn't ask Kyra any questions to get to know her. *Well, I'm enjoying my evening just the same, and it's nice to be out with my friends.*

Juan Pablo interrupted Kyra's thoughts with a question. Kyra looked startled and asked, "Oh, I'm so sorry. Can you repeat that please?"

He asked her again for her opinion on his choice of clothing for the evening. She politely responded, but made a mental note that, in the future, she would concentrate on attracting a man who would be more genuine in his attempts to get to know her likes and dislikes. *And someone I have more in common with,* she added, *instead of just someone who is so darn handsome!*

At last, after the dinner plates were clear, the waiter brought out a dish called *Juan Palomo* with which the couples could build their own desserts. Kyra delighted in the experience of everyone sharing in the making and eating of the brownie covered with chocolate sauce, whipped cream, and rosemary sorbet.

Once the artful dessert had been consumed, Kyra said, "Oh my, that was excellent and fun! I've had just a lovely evening, everyone . . . and Juan Pablo, I can't thank you enough for joining us tonight for drinks and dinner. You've made my trip to Madrid even more special."

"Yes, Juan Pablo," Verónica spoke up, "it has been a pleasure to have dinner tonight with you."

"It has most definitely been my pleasure to share this evening with two such beautiful women. And, Javier, I've enjoyed speaking with you as well. I look forward to seeing you all again. *¿Dentro de poco? ¿Sí?*"

Javier thanked Juan Pablo and promptly asked the waiter to bring their bill. Once the bill was paid—and Javier again generously insisted that he treat everyone to dinner—the two couples left the restaurant. Juan Pablo walked alongside Kyra as they made their way to the valet to retrieve their cars. He slowed down, trailing a little behind Javier and

Verónica, giving them some space, and then turned to Kyra. He stopped her for a moment with a strong hand on her bare shoulder, and said, *"Buenas noches . . . mi encantadora Kyra."* Before Kyra fully realized what was happening, he pressed his lips to hers.

In surprise, Kyra briefly kissed him back. She gently pulled away and then gave him an affectionate, but awkward, hug.

Javier looked back and gave Kyra a brotherly look that begged, "Are you okay?"

Kyra winked, letting Javier know she was indeed just fine, and they waited for the valet to bring the cars. Juan Pablo chatted with Kyra for a few moments more before saying a final goodbye, as she slipped into the car.

"I wasn't sure if I had to rescue you or not," Javier commented seriously.

Kyra replied with a chuckle, "Juan Pablo behaved like a perfect gentleman, but I do appreciate your looking out for me." She sighed, but not out of regret. "Juan Pablo and I will likely never see each other again. And to tell you the truth I'll be looking for someone more down to earth than him. Still, this was an entertaining evening."

"I think you need to find your *own* Javier," Verónica replied with a giggle. "Someone who is sweet and thoughtful."

"I can't agree with you more," Kyra replied immediately. "Let's hope that I do indeed find someone as special as your husband."

Javier looked a bit embarrassed and hurried to change the subject. "I'm glad you had fun tonight, but tell me about your plans in *Sevilla* with my cousin, Raquel."

Kyra obliged, barely able to keep the excitement out of her voice.

Once they arrived back at the hotel, she enveloped Javier and Verónica in an affectionate goodbye hug, thanking them profusely for the wonderful kindness and generosity they had shown her during her stay in Madrid. When she reached the door of the hotel, she turned back toward the couple one last time.

"I can't wait to see you again when I return to Spain!" she said sincerely. She raised a hand and threw them a Gabby-style kiss. *Muwahhh!*

A short while later, as she lay down in her soft bed, she counted her blessings to have met such wonderful people thus far on her trip. Gabby's family had proven to be just as kind-hearted, loving, and accepting as her dear friend. And now, she would be meeting yet another of Gabby's family tomorrow.

Her head was clear, and so many wonderful thoughts raced through her mind. Despite her eagerness for what tomorrow would bring and the adventures that lay ahead, Kyra quickly fell asleep and began to dream. She once again found herself standing on a mountaintop and staring into the face of the man dressed in black silk pants and a robe.

# 26

Loud buzzing jolted Kyra awake at 5:30 am, and she slapped the alarm clock, immediately quieting the noise. Sitting straight up in bed, she took a moment to regain her senses, trying hard not to think about the early morning hour.

As she rubbed the sleep from her eyes, she recalled that she'd been having the same dream again—and the Asian man had just beckoned her to follow him. This time, however, she stared him squarely in the face and asked, "*Who are you?*"

He only smiled in response and reached out to gently take her by the arm.

When Kyra looked down at her feet, she noticed they were stepping onto a cobblestone pathway. Side by side, she and the man followed the path . . . until, unexpectedly, Kyra found herself in a beautiful Asian village. She looked around again, discovering that she was now inside a small hospital. Within moments, she was kneeling beside a bed, using her hands to perform a Reiki session on an elderly woman.

That's when the alarm had gone off, disrupting her dream.

*How strange to have dreamed of the same man two nights in a row!* Kyra thought. *He looks so familiar, as if I should know who he is.* Her intuition suddenly flashed. She felt certain she *did* know the man, as if his name were on the tip of her tongue, but her mind struggled to make sense of it all.

"And why am I in a hospital giving Reiki to an elderly woman?" she asked herself aloud.

While she couldn't answer that question, she was excited to now know the answer to a different one: the location of the mountain in her dream. *I can thank Juan Pablo for that!* She chuckled, recalling last night's dinner at La Gabinoteca with her friends. During one of her date's long monologs about himself, the answer had come to her while lost in a daydream. She'd even blurted, "Oh, I know!" but her interjection into the conversation had barely fazed Juan Pablo. Kyra grinned at the memory as she lay back down on her pillow. She reached her arms above her head and stretched out fully.

Although the mountain's whereabouts had sprung into her mind, it still didn't make any logical sense. The intuitive hunch had just somehow *flowed* into her thoughts as if she had read the answer on a piece of paper. Even stranger was the coincidence that the fortune-teller in Barcelona had told her she'd visit a mountain of spiritual importance—and the mountain in Asia seem to fit such a description perfectly.

She said a silent prayer: *God, if it is your intention for me to go to Asia, please let me see the path there. But, most importantly, let me understand why I should go. I ask you to send me a clear sign or message so I know what I'm supposed to do. Amen.* Kyra made the sign of the cross, trusting she would be led in the right direction.

Excited about her upcoming day and with little time to spare, she sprang out of bed and took a hot shower. After dressing and packing her suitcase, she made her way to the hotel lobby to grab a quick breakfast. She had less than twenty minutes before her taxi would arrive to take her to the airport for her flight to Sevilla.

She gave the waiter her order, then added, "*Por favor, que sea rápido*—I'm in a bit of a rush this morning. *Muchas gracias!*" When the food came, she ate hastily and left cash for her bill. Just as she stepped outside to begin the next leg of her journey, the taxi rolled up to the curb.

Kyra slid inside. "*Buenos días,*" she said to the driver. "*Aeropuerto de Barajas, por favor.*" She had rehearsed her pronunciation earlier, so the words rolled easily off her tongue. She felt proud how far her Spanish speaking skills had come and spoke confidently.

The driver grinned, clearly appreciating her efforts, then drove off rapidly in the direction of the airport to the northeast.

Kyra settled comfortably into her seat and stared out the window mesmerized by the scenery. With a smile on her lips, she silently said goodbye to the amazing city of Madrid. She could hardly believe she was off to another exciting part of Spain.

The taxi arrived at the Madrid-Barajas Airport close to 7:00 am, and Kyra made her way through security with ease due to the early morning hour. When she arrived at her gate a few minutes later, she discovered that her flight was already in the midst of boarding—an unexpected miscalculation on her part. Rushing up to door, she nervously handed the agent her boarding pass for flight 3777, then hurried to find her seat. Her adrenaline was flowing at the realization that she'd be landing in Sevilla in just over an hour after takeoff.

Securely strapped into her seat, she took a deep breath, and soon the Boeing 717 climbed sharply up into the sky. As the plane reached cruising altitude, the pilot leveled off its ascent and announced they were in for a smooth flight with beautiful, clear weather ahead.

*Mmmm, clear weather ahead—maybe that's a metaphor for this part of my trip.* She closed her eyes to focus her thoughts positively, but her mild apprehension over meeting Raquel still managed to seep through. Despite the warm phone conversation they'd had, she began to worry if she'd even recognize Raquel from the photo she had texted. More importantly, she wondered what Raquel would think of her. *I hope we have enough to talk about.*

Kyra replayed in her mind what she knew about Raquel, which, as it turned out was very little. She was twenty years of age and a statuesque girl—just an inch shy of six feet. To her amusement, Kyra calculated that Raquel was a *full* eight inches taller than she, and of course, there was the fifteen-year age difference.

*Yes, we will make quite the pair!* She let out a laugh.

Despite their differences, she had really liked Raquel on the phone, and she had such a warm demeanor in the photo she'd sent by text. During their conversation, she also came across as fairly direct, but still sincere and sweet—all qualities Kyra deeply admired.

*We will have an amazing time together, and I will not let my unfounded fears get the best of me!* she decided, flipping open her laptop to watch a movie she had loaded earlier. It was aptly titled *Life Is Beautiful* by

Roberto Benigni. Though she would not be able to watch the entire film, she looked forward to enjoying the first half.

Kyra felt her heart melt as she became lost in the storyline. Before she knew it, it was time to hit the pause button and safely stow her laptop in preparation for landing. The captain soon announced their on-time arrival.

Kyra made her way to the luggage carousel without delay and wheeled her suitcase to the outside curb to wait for Raquel. The instructions she'd been given were to look for a "vintage white Volkswagen Beetle," which Kyra could somewhat picture in her mind. While she had always had an appreciation for well-kept classic cars, she momentarily wondered if her bulky suitcase would fit inside the small trunk.

As if to answer her question, a Volkswagen Beetle pulled up alongside the curb, and a tall, slender girl jumped out of the car. Raquel was dressed in a casual pair of faded jeans, a loose-fitting yellow halter-top, and dark brown flip-flops. Kyra instantly recognized her from the photo, but she was even prettier in person. Her chestnut brown eyes lit up as she approached.

"*¡Hola!* And welcome to *Sevilla.*" Raquel called out in a velvety Spanish accent. "It's so exciting to finally meet you, *mi amiga.* My cousin Gabriela speaks of you like a sister!"

Raquel gave Kyra an affectionate hug and proper *muwahhh* on each cheek before Kyra could even answer. She waved her hands energetically as she spoke—immediately striking a tender cord in Kyra's heart. *So like my dear friend Gabby,* she thought.

Following the lighthearted embrace, Kyra reciprocated "*Hola,* Raquel! It's great to finally meet you, too . . . and—" Her eyes were drawn toward the Beetle, but she quickly looked back at Raquel, trying to hide her surprise. "*Uh,* Gabby has told me all about you as well."

Although Raquel did indeed look exactly like her photo, and perhaps even prettier in person, the "vintage white Volkswagen Beetle" was not at all what Kyra had pictured in her mind. Instead of a well-cared-for older model car, the exterior was rusting and covered in colorful but fading flower stickers. *Oh, my,* she thought, trying to hide her surprise. *It's a throwback to the nineteen seventies!*

"May I put your suitcase into the trunk?" Raquel asked politely, extending her hand to help.

"Let me help you," Kyra replied. "It's quite a bit heavier than it looks . . . I hope it fits."

Both women winced as they jointly lifted the suitcase into the front trunk of the car, which miraculously accommodated the luggage. Kyra let out an audible sigh of relief when it eased into the small compartment. "*Whew*, we're in luck! Thanks so much."

*"De nada."* Raquel responded, as Kyra made her way to the passenger door. "Here, let me open the door for you. It sometimes sticks."

Kyra swallowed her pride, trying to maintain her positive focus. *I will keep a cheerful face,* she thought as she slipped into the snug passenger seat. Her hand brushed across the seat cover made of wooden beads, which made the car feel even more like a throwback to the seventies. But despite her initial concern, the engine seemed healthy, making its famous hummingbird sound as they sped away.

With a glance around the interior of the car, Kyra noticed that it looked super clean. *Well, that's something to admire . . . even if we look like a pair of hippy chicks from a bygone era!* She let a smile spread across her face.

Raquel shifted the clutch, speaking as she put the Beetle into gear. "I know that Gabriela—ah, Gabby—told you my parents live in *Sevilla,* but I thought first we can go to your hotel and drop off your suitcase?" she asked. "We'll get better gas mileage since it's a little heavy for my trunk."

Kyra cringed, but swiftly recovered. "Yes, that's fine of course. Thank you."

Raquel nodded in appreciation and downshifted the clutch.

"By the way," Kyra added, "I'm so touched by your parents' offer for me to stay at their house since they're away for the summer. But, as I mentioned before, I'm staying at the hotel tonight as a special treat to myself. I hope you understand."

"Whatever works for you, works for me," Raquel replied cheerfully. "Let's head to the *Cathedral de Sevilla* after we unload your suitcase. I know it's on your list of sites to visit. Then we'll have lunch at a local favorite called *Modesto*. Does that sound good, *amiga?*"

Kyra looked at into Raquel's deep-set, animated eyes and instantly felt her excitement. "I can't wait to experience the *Andalucía* region with you. We will definitely have a blast together, girlfriend!"

"*¡Excelente!*" Raquel said, throwing her left arm up in the air and making a victory sign.

Kyra flinched, hoping her new friend was paying attention to the roadway. The Beetle made a slight right turn, and to Kyra's relief, Raquel's long arm landed safely back on the steering wheel. She noted that the engine let out a relieved sounding *hummm* as if it agreed.

"Ah . . . I have spent much time studying the history of my hometown, so I have lots to tell you about our wonderful city of *Sevilla*. Gabby mentioned you are very excited to see it."

Kyra nodded enthusiastically, and Raquel continued, beaming as she described her hometown. "Our *bella* city is over two thousand years old and believed to have been settled in Roman times—perhaps by Hercules himself!" She giggled. "But regardless of legends, the Moors, who are Muslims, captured *Sevilla* in the early eighth century. Our beloved King Ferdinand III reclaimed *Sevilla* in the mid-thirteenth century, making it Christian again. I'm telling you this because you'll see a lot of Moorish influence in our buildings, which is something very special to this part of our country."

"I did take a peek at some of the Moorish architecture in my travel guide," Kyra replied. "It's incredibly beautiful—*and romantic*, I must say," she added teasingly.

"*Sí.* It's a very romantic place . . . uh, but it will be only us girls for this trip." Raquel glanced over with an awkward look of concern.

"Yes, Raquel, just us girls for this trip," Kyra confirmed, "but I'm definitely coming back here someday—and with someone special."

The pair continued chatting, and Kyra once again noticed with amazement the synchronicities of the Universe. She was thrilled to discover that she and Raquel shared many common interests—and despite her initial concerns, she felt as if she had always known Raquel. She no longer questioned the strange sensation of familiarity and enjoyed their back-and-forth bantering.

As they drew closer to the center of the city, Kyra marveled at the inviting squares, picturesque neighborhoods, and impressive historical buildings. While there was a mix of Gothic and nineteenth-century neoclassical elegance sprinkled throughout the city, just like she had seen in other parts of Spain, she could easily detect the exotic Moorish influence that Raquel had so thoughtfully pointed out.

Most buildings were three to four stories tall, and many were painted in vibrant colors, which differed dramatically from the other regions of Spain. Even the neoclassical buildings were brightly colored, a design choice that contrasted sharply with the more traditional stonework framing their structures.

Kyra's eyes drank in the bright pinkish-orange and coral colors, which alternated nicely with warm golden-yellow hues. More traditional bright white or brick buildings added to the mix. Rich tile work was evident all over the city and, to her astonishment, in every imaginable color. Distinctive carved wooden archways on the exteriors of some buildings gave the city an unusual North African infusion. The buildings were bright, colorful, and some even looked surreal. *Almost like a Vincent van Gogh painting*, Kyra thought whimsically.

"*Sevilla* appears to have a quaint yet colorful look, more so than Barcelona or Madrid. It feels like I've entered a whole different country," Kyra said in awe of the surrounding beauty.

"It's like no other place on earth!" Raquel agreed, the pride evident in her voice. "Of course, my travels have not taken me to a lot of places yet, but I know my city is very unique in Europe."

As they drew closer to the center, Kyra glanced out across the narrow, cobblestone streets, which were dotted with horse-drawn carriages. They gave the city a delightful turn-of-the-century character, and she watched admiringly as a couple, hand in hand, climbed into one of the carriages for a ride. *How adorable and sweet they look,* she mused. Her mind drifted to imaginings of her future sweetheart and herself taking a carriage ride together, which filled her heart with joy and wonder.

When Raquel made a turn into the Meliá Sevilla Hotel valet area, Kyra was shaken out of her romantic daydream. Moments later, she stepped out into the fresh air, followed by Raquel, who twisted the Beetle's stubborn latch to open the trunk.

The valet attendant greeted them, raising his eyebrows sharply as he surveyed the rusting car. Nevertheless, he extended his arm and offered in a stern voice, *"Señorita, ¿puedo ayudarle?"* He added in English, "May I assist?"

At Kyra's nod, he hoisted the suitcase out of the trunk and placed it on the sidewalk.

"*Gracias, señor.* We are only going inside for a moment," she explained, "so I can check in early. No need to valet the car right now. We'll be right back."

The valet nodded and slid into the front seat. He promptly pulled the car off to the side as the women walked through the glass and steel doorway.

Raquel entered first and Kyra followed, lugging her suitcase behind her. Both women were immediately captivated by the ultramodern interior of the lobby. Stark white walls made a perfect backdrop for sleek, contemporary black-and-white couches. A huge black granite infinity fountain stood squarely in the center of the stunning lobby, surrounded by bold red and black sculptures. Raquel ran her fingers over the velvety texture of the couches, while Kyra headed to the reception desk.

The young woman behind the desk spoke very good English. "Yes, we are more than happy to hold your suitcase, *señorita*. Our check-in time is later this afternoon—at three pm."

"Thanks so much for your kindness," Kyra said, taking the luggage claim ticket and safely placing it inside her wallet. "I'll do a proper check-in after three."

Kyra and Raquel shot playful smiles at the doorman as they strutted past him to retrieve Raquel's car. The valet attendant haughtily raised an eyebrow again, but looked surprised when Kyra handed him 10 Euros for his service.

*Ha!* she thought, not letting the attendant's negative impression of the car get the best of her. *You can't judge a book by its cover—or, in this case, a vintage car!*

The valet attendant closed the driver's side door firmly, and Raquel immediately hit the gas pedal, shouting, "We are on our way to the *Sevilla* Cathedral. *Hold on!*"

The Beetle let out an excited-sounding *hummm*—clearly in agreement—and sped off to take the women to their next destination. Kyra settled comfortably into her seat, brushing her hand affectionately across the beaded seat cover. She was more than ready for whatever came next.

"Not only is *Sevilla* Cathedral the *third* largest church in the world, it is also *the* largest Gothic cathedral." Raquel explained. "Gabriela mentioned you loved the Gothic cathedral in Uncle Eduardo and Aunt Carmen's neighborhood, *El Gòtic*. I hope you'll be impressed when you see ours. It's very special to me and my family."

"I do *love* my cathedrals," Kyra said, peering out the window. "When I visited your aunt and uncle, I felt like I'd been transported to Gotham City . . . you know, from the *Batman* movies. You have a much more simple, yet enchanting, neighborhood here. And you're right—the Moorish influence is different and imaginative."

The women eagerly continued discussing the rich history of the cathedral, and before long, Raquel announced, "Oh! We have arrived." She slid the Beetle into a nearby narrow parking space, even outdoing Gabby's parking skills in Barcelona.

Kyra thought she heard the car make a satisfied *hummm* right before its engine shut down. It struck her as strange that she could detect an emotion from the car at all, but then again, everything on this journey had a magical element to it. She tucked the thought away for now as they walked toward the building.

Kyra was taken aback—awestruck, in fact—by its beauty. Made of a luminous white limestone, the Gothic cathedral was similar to the other buildings she'd seen elsewhere in Spain. And while the detail was exquisite and grand in stature, the building was so white that, to Kyra, it almost resembled a filigree wedding cake.

*What a silly thought for me to have,* she laughed, wondering where that idea had come from. She walked closer to the structure to get a better look. Once again, the Gothic architecture filled her heart with reminders of long-forgotten fairytales and magical princess weddings.

"I am having so much fun with these gorgeous Spanish cathedrals." She turned toward Raquel, smiling. "My silly imagination is running wild. You'll have to forgive me, but being here in Spain is reigniting my childhood love of fairytales and Prince Charming weddings."

Raquel's face lit up. "These places fire up my imagination, too! Perhaps our princes are not too far off in the future . . . although I need to finish college first," she added quite seriously.

Kyra gave her an amused look, and the pair burst into giggles as they stepped through the intricately carved stone archway and entered the massive structure. Their laughter died down when Raquel pointed to the incredibly tall ceiling. Staring overhead in amazement, Kyra came to a complete standstill.

"Oh, my," she whispered, her breath catching in her throat. The interior of the church felt surprisingly ethereal and the beauty further inspired Kyra's longing for a deeper relationship with God. She could clearly see why this cathedral was admired for its central nave reaching up an amazing 140 feet, just as Raquel had mentioned. After dipping her fingertips in the holy water and making the sign of the cross, Kyra offered up her gratitude in a short prayer: *Thank you, Father . . . for all your continued blessings.*

Kyra glanced back across the crowded room, and as she stepped forward to walk alongside Raquel, she stopped short in her tracks, nearly stumbling over her feet. She was surprised to catch the eyes of a smiling woman as she passed by—a woman whom she would have sworn was Nana!

Kyra knew this could not be possible and watched as the woman disappeared back into the crowd moments later. Her heart raced, and her mind came upon a similar experience she'd had of seeing her father walking across the second-story balcony in their home in Chicago soon after he had passed away.

Kyra caught up to Raquel and hurriedly apologized. "I just need to catch my breath for a second." Attempting to compose herself, she swallowed hard and explained further, "Spain and these cathedrals are making me feel somehow closer to God . . . and my grandmother who passed away recently. Does that make sense? I so dearly miss her . . . I think the beauty overwhelms me at times . . ." Her voice trailed off as she tried to remain calm. A tear welled in her eye.

"*Awww* . . . I am so sorry for your loss, *amiga*," Raquel said, then paused to give Kyra a private moment. "But I'm so happy you are getting something special out of your visit here." Keeping her voice upbeat, she added, "I knew you'd be impressed! Come. *¡Sígueme!*" She took Kyra's arm in hers and led her further inside.

The two walked arm in arm, and Kyra squeezed Raquel's hand, feeling their new bond deepening. Raquel spoke in soft tones, offering her guest a history of the church. Kyra listened attentively.

The interior was elegant, but more restrained in decoration than Kyra had expected. The Gothic influence was apparent, with gold gilt on most of the wood and gorgeous stained-glass windows numbering more than seventy-five, from what Raquel described. But, despite the grandeur of the interior, the cathedral was well balanced with soft elegance and simplicity, perhaps due to its sheer size and volume.

Raquel whispered, "I think there are *ochenta*—uh, I mean, eighty or so chapels inside here. We can stop and see as many as you'd like. . . . Oh, but the *most* exciting part is that this is also the final resting place of Christopher Columbus! We are very proud that he is buried here in *Sevilla*. Look, we are coming up on his tomb now."

A laugh escaped Kyra's lips, causing Raquel to pause. "Oh, my sincerest apologies." Kyra eyes twinkled as she explained, "I'm reminded of your uncle Eduardo's love of the family history. He spoke quite fondly of Mr. Columbus—and King Ferdinand and Queen Isabella—and how your family is descended from royalty."

Raquel's face paled. "Ah, you *have* been talking to my uncle Eduardo!" Her voice softened, almost to an inaudible murmur, and she grabbed Kyra's arm. "Every family must have its historian . . . even if he is *un poco loco y se toma unas cuantas de libertades con nuestra historia*."

Kyra smiled, understanding that Raquel had said her uncle was perhaps just a little crazy, taking liberty with the family history. *Aw, yes, the family resemblance is priceless.* She chuckled.

The women stepped up to the huge tomb, and Kyra stood directly in front, gazing up at the stately fifteen-foot-tall structure. The statues of four noblemen, each perhaps eight feet tall, stood silently, carved in stone. Heavy wooden posts rested squarely on their shoulders, holding up the tomb bearing the remains of Christopher Columbus.

"Each man represents one of the four kingdoms of Spain at the time Columbus was laid to rest here," Raquel told her. "That was about five centuries ago—a *short* period of time here in Spain."

"I'm always amazed by the rich history here—all kidding aside." Kyra reached out to give Raquel a quick shoulder hug. Then she quietly snapped a photo of the tomb and placed her camera back in her purse.

Raquel motioned for them to move on, diverting Kyra's attention away from the tomb. "Let's look at this amazing stained-glass window depicting the Virgin Mary—now that you have the *full* history of our famous Mr. Columbus!"

The women shared a quick laugh over the subtle joke and went on to spend the next couple of hours absorbing the beauty of the heavenly stained-glass windows and visiting several chapels within the cathedral.

As the lunch hour drew close, Raquel's stomach grumbled, and she rubbed it vigorously. "*¡Ay—ay—ay! Mi estómago está gruñendo como un león.* Let's go to lunch. All this walking has made me famished."

"Ah, yes, the lions are back," Kyra said, glad for once it was not her stomach making the announcement.

Raquel raised her dark eyebrows, indicating she did not understand.

Kyra playfully added, "I'll explain later, but growling stomachs seem to run in your family."

When the women stepped outside, Kyra noticed how much warmer the Andalucía region felt compared to Madrid. The month of July was just unfolding, and the strong Mediterranean sun bore down fiercely on their skin. They walked briskly to the Beetle, and Raquel flipped on the air conditioning to full blast as they drove away.

"*Modesto* is one of my *mamá* and *papá's* favorite restaurants here in

*Sevilla*. I wish they were not away on vacation because they would've loved to join us today. Anyway, I do think you will really like the food. It is simply *incredible!*" Raquel dramatically kissed the tips of her fingers with a loud smacking sound to illustrate just how delicious the food would be.

"Thanks so much for taking me to a family favorite—and lunch today will be my treat to you," offered Kyra.

"My *mamá* gave me her credit card and insisted I treat you," Raquel replied with an impish look. "But thank you. It is sweet of you to offer."

As Raquel drove on, Kyra became lost in all the details of the local neighborhood, admiring the bright orange tile roofs, which accented the colorful buildings, perfectly complementing the Mediterranean backdrop. Simple, lush green courtyards were attached to many of the small houses and storefronts. Pots of bright red geraniums added splashes of color to the otherwise plain white exterior of a building they passed, delighting Kyra's sense of style. The neighborhood was refreshing and invigorating—each structure looked to be lovingly manicured and well cared for.

After finding a suitable parking space, the women approached the restaurant housed in a lovely, off-white, three-story building. There was no mistaking the traditional neoclassical architectural style. Kyra appreciated the welcoming ambience of the restaurant's patio area with its oversized umbrellas since shade was a necessity on this hot summer day.

"Inside or outside?" Raquel asked.

"I'm sure it's quite lovely inside," Kyra replied with slight hesitation, "but despite the heat, I'd love to dine outside. We can sit under one of the umbrellas and get some cold drinks with lots of *hielo*—ice—of course. Okay?"

Raquel agreed, and the hostess led them to an outdoor table. After Kyra ordered her usual *agua con gas*, the waiter turned to Raquel, who asked for *vino tinto*—a glass of the house red wine—choosing a more traditional beverage for her afternoon lunch in Spain.

"*Modesto* is known for its authentic *Andaluz* dishes," Raquel began. "I wanted to make sure you get to taste some of our unique southern Spanish food." Kyra smiled in appreciation as Raquel continued, "They're most famous for a dish called *Marqués de Villalúa*, which, in English, is clams with prawns and wild mushrooms—My *papá* loves that dish the best! Another great specialty is *Foie de oca con mermelada de naranja sevillana y pastel de patatas.* It is *delicioso,"* Raquel added, rubbing her stomach. "I guess that's a mouthful since I know you are still learning Spanish. It's goose liver with orange marmalade and potato pie."

"Say no more! They both sound interesting," Kyra replied, though she had no idea what to expect. "Order whatever you'd like and we'll share several dishes."

After the beverages were served and lunch was ordered, the women continued chatting. Still surprised at how comfortable she felt with Raquel, Kyra spoke openly. "You remind me so much of your cousin Gabby," she said with affection. "It must be the family resemblance, so to speak. Don't take this the wrong way, but you are so mature and very well spoken for your age."

Raquel blushed. "*¡Qué amable eres!* I can only hope to turn out as awesome as Gabriela."

Appreciating the sentiment that she was "very kind," Kyra gave Raquel a reassuring smile. "But I'd love to know more about you," she added. "What are you studying in college? What are your favorite things to do for fun?"

Raquel's face became serious and her eyes softened. "I'm actually going to University of Barcelona to become a teacher. I know it doesn't pay as much as some careers, but for me, it's more about helping children. I really enjoy helping little ones discover that they really do love to learn—and to encourage them to think more creatively by teaching them about our past."

Kyra could now see why she connected so well with Raquel—they both shared a strong desire to be of service to others.

"I plan to become a history teacher!" Raquel continued. "Perhaps you've noticed how much I've enjoyed telling you about the history of *Sevilla* . . . oh, but of course talking about *historia* does run a bit in our *familia*"—she emphasized the Spanish words for comedic effect—"as you may have gathered from Uncle Eduardo." Raquel giggled.

Kyra shot her a look of pride. "I so admire that you've chosen a profession that will help shape the minds of children! That's a special gift—one that should never be underestimated." She reflected for a moment before adding, "To be honest, as I look back on the last thirteen years of my life, I realize I wasn't very happy in my successful corporate career. I based my career decisions on my parents' idea of what success looks like—to make lots of money. Now I can see, all these years later, that I should have defined success *very* differently." She gestured to Raquel, her face breaking into a grin. "Perhaps just the way you are doing now."

"That is so funny!" Raquel blurted, then softened her tone. "I mean, I've been struggling with my decision because so many people in my family are *so* successful. But I was defining that by how much money they make. You just helped me realize that I would be very successful by helping children through teaching them!" Her enthusiasm rang clear in her voice. "That is where my heart really lies—it's what I am passionate about." She reached across the table and clasped Kyra's hand. "I am so enjoying our conversation, *amiga. Gracias.*"

Kyra's heart melted at the thought that she could have such an amazing connection with a twenty-year-old college student—and in the south of Spain, of all places. Her eyes filled with tears at the reminder that the Universe is truly perfect and that the right people do come forth into our lives at any given moment to give us exactly what we need. *If you are open to meeting them,* she added to herself.

Kyra thought back to her initial judgment of the "vintage white Volkswagen Beetle," and her initial reaction that the car wasn't good enough for her. She gazed across the table at Raquel's sweet face and further reflected on her desire to curtail her love of luxury for more authentic things in her life.

"Oh my gosh," Kyra said aloud, startling herself. "I am definitely learning so much about myself on this trip. I should be thanking *you*, Raquel!"

# 27

The waiter arrived with tantalizing dishes of *Marqués de Villalúa* and *Foie de oca con mermelada de naranja sevillana y pastel de patatas.* No sooner had he stepped away than Raquel scooped up a generous spoonful of the clams with prawns. She murmured *mmm* as she savored the delicate flavor of the mushrooms.

Kyra followed her lead with a bold forkful of the goose liver with orange marmalade and potato pie. Without expectation, she placed the bite of pie delicately into her mouth. Pleasantly surprised, she sighed an enthusiastic *ahhh,* enjoying the taste of the unusual dish, the flavors melting on her tongue.

"You are right . . . I *do* love the food here in southern Spain." she said, patting her lips with her napkin.

With her mouth otherwise occupied, Raquel could only nod in appreciation. The pair ate enthusiastically until they'd each savored their last bites. As the waiter cleared away the empty dishes, Kyra resumed their earlier conversation. "Tell me about your hobbies and what you like to do for fun."

Raquel's expression revealed her passion even before the words came out of her mouth. "I have lots of interests. In some ways, I'm a *chica poco femenina*—I think you call it a 'tomboy' in America. I love the outdoors, especially exploring and spending time in nature. But, at the same time, I like cultural things too like museums and *exposiciones*—I mean, exhibits, of course. That's probably the history teacher in me."

"We seem to have so much more in common than you'd think," Kyra responded, a bit surprised.

"Ah, yes! But I have a spiritual side, too, and that's something Gabriela and I have talked about often," Raquel said, pointing one slim finger toward heaven. "I attend Catholic Church regularly—my parents are very strict about that—but I love exploring ways I can make my life . . . better, I guess? My cousin and I have often talked about Reiki and how she became interested in it after our grandpapa became ill with cancer. I've never taken any classes, but I want to do so after graduation. I think it would be another way of helping people."

"Oh, gosh, Raquel, that's *amazing* that you're interested in Reiki, too! I just took a refresher class in Madrid two days ago. Gabby and I took levels one, two, and the Advanced Reiki Training classes when we were in grad school together in Boston. But once I started working crazy hours, I never did anything with the training. Reflecting back, it would have been so beneficial for me to use Reiki to manage my work stress better. Plus, it would have given me an outlet for something more spiritual too."

Raquel gave her a serious nod of understanding and Kyra continued, "I'm seriously considering taking the Reiki Master Training in England with Gabby in less than two weeks. It's so funny you'd bring that up right now, especially since I've been debating on whether to pursue it. How perfect is the Universe to bring it to my attention again?"

Raquel looked surprised and replied, "I guess I'm amazed too, *amiga,* that *you* are interested in Reiki and spiritual topics. I wasn't expecting that just by looking at you."

Kyra appreciated Raquel's frank honesty and burst into a grin. "You are refreshing, Raquel, and I so adore your honesty."

The waiter interrupted to ask if they would like anything else. When the women shook their heads no, he placed the bill on the table. Raquel offered her parents' credit card, but Kyra waved it away, insisting again that it would be her treat.

Their bill paid, the pair walked energetically back to the lovely vintage white Volkswagen Beetle. Slipping on her sunglasses, Kyra settled in the passenger seat, now admiring the beauty of the car and her new friend. Raquel hit the gas pedal hard, and in response, the car let out an affectionate *hummm*, whisking the women off toward the hotel.

Just as they arrived, Kyra glanced down at her cell phone and noticed a voice message. "Ha! It looks like I have a voice message from Gabby." It appeared to be another coincidence since they'd just been discussing her, but Kyra knew better. She looked forward to catching up with Gabby later on.

As Kyra stepped out of the car and thanked her new friend for an awesome day, Raquel reminded her about dinner that evening. "See you again around 8:00 pm this evening. *¿Vale?*"

"I'm truly looking forward to it, Raquel! I'm sure we could talk for hours."

The valet smiled as he closed the passenger door, and Kyra slipped him a generous tip. She waved goodbye as Raquel and the Beetle drove away. The car let out a cheerful-sounding *hummm,* and oddly she thought it was saying, "'See you later!'"

"I think I've grown to *really* like that car," Kyra said affectionately, before stepping inside the Meliá Sevilla hotel to check in and retrieve her suitcase. She took the elevator to the fourth floor and slid the key card into the lock.

Once inside, Kyra noted that the room perfectly matched her impression of the lobby. The walls were soft, neutral beige, and the bright white sheets on the queen bed looked crisp and fresh. A crimson desk chair, which sat beneath a clear glass desk opposite the bed, added a wonderful splash of vibrancy to the room.

"*Ahhh,*" she said, propping her suitcase up next to the bed, and her eyes fell on the large sliding glass doors across the room.

Pulling the thick curtains fully open, she glanced outside and let her hand gently rest on the edge of the glass for a moment. When she stepped outside, a turtle dove gently landed on the balcony, almost close enough to touch. Stunned that the bird would venture so close, she remained perfectly still and stared back at the small creature.

The dove boldly stared Kyra in the eye and made a loud *coo* as if to say hello. Its piercing black eyes studied her with curiosity, but its demeanor radiated sweetness and calm. This brought to mind her otherworldly sighting of Nana earlier in the day—if it really was her grandmother's spirit she had seen—and she wondered if this could be a sign. *Nana always loved doves,* she thought fondly. Moments later, the bird fluttered away.

*How funny you would choose to visit me here, my little friend. Nana always reminded me that doves are a sign of peace and love—and just what I needed today.* She remembered in the bible that Noah had sent out a dove after the flood to determine if it was safe to leave the Ark. "Perhaps this is a spiritual symbol for me that the worst is over and it's safe for me to venture forth into the world . . . and be at peace." Kyra felt relieved as she spoke the words. "Well, at least that's the way I'd like to interpret it."

After taking the remainder of the afternoon to review her Reiki manuals and refresh herself with a shower, Kyra slipped on a pair of white jeans, adding high-heeled cork sandals and a simple sleeveless navy top. She accessorized with her turquoise jewelry to create a casual but polished look.

Applying the finishing touches to her lipstick in the mirror, she thought again about the age difference between her and Raquel. *What really matters is who a person is inside—outer appearances don't matter in the least bit. Age is just a number!* Deciding to let her insecurities go, she took a step back, proud of her reflection. Her thoughts shifted when she suddenly remembered the voicemail from Gabby, and she retrieved her cell phone from her purse.

An animated voice gushed loudly out of the speaker. "Hey, *Chica*, my ears were burning! I'm just checking in to see how things are going in *Sevilla*. Call me when you can."

A tingling sensation raced up Kyra's spine. The voicemail had been received a little after 3 pm—precisely when she had been at lunch at Modesto with Raquel. How in the world had Gabby known she'd been talking about her?

She dialed Gabby's number, and her friend answered. "*¡Hola!* So, have you been enjoying your adventures in *Andalucía?* Raquel's a pretty *sensacional* tour guide, wouldn't you say?"

"I'm having a blast! Raquel is such a sweetheart, and yes, she's an *excelente* tour guide," Kyra agreed wholeheartedly. "The fact that she's a history major with plans to become a schoolteacher is perfect for my time here. Plus we have so much in common, including Reiki and other spiritual topics—but you probably already knew that! . . . Oh, were you being serious when you said your ears were burning?"

Gabby chuckled. "I've always been fairly intuitive. I had a funny feeling you were talking about me . . . so I called you. Was I right?"

"Oh, my gosh, yes! But we were talking about you in a most favorable light, I might add—right around the time you left the voice message. It sent a chill up my spine."

Gabby responded, "My grandmama always told me to follow my intuition. In fact, she used to say *'Confía en tu corazón y tu voz interior, y vivirás una vida excepcional.'* It means, 'Trust your heart and your inner voice, and you will live an exceptional life.' I always loved her advice."

Kyra felt her heart tug with thoughts of her own grandmother's wonderful advice over the years; she was certain Nana would have said something very similar.

"But, if that isn't enough," Gabby added, laughing, "you can always take Oprah's advice, 'Follow your instincts. That's where true wisdom manifests itself.'"

Kyra giggled. "I couldn't agree with you more. I am definitely learning to trust my instincts more and more. This has been an incredible journey, and I have *you* to thank for inviting me to Spain. *¡Gracias!*"

Kyra's sentiments were not lost on Gabby. "Thank *you* for taking a risk and coming here. Love you. *Ciao.*"

Feeling happy to have reconnected with Gabby, Kyra ventured down to the hotel lobby. In a few minutes, a text message came through on her phone from Raquel: *I'm on my way. Excited about tonight!*

Kyra stepped outside to wait for her arrival, and within minutes, Raquel pulled up in the Beetle. This time, the valet smiled appreciatively as he glanced across at the car, jiggling the car door handle to make it open. Kyra waved hello to her friend as she climbed inside.

"*Hola, amiga.* Long time no see." Raquel chuckled. "Just a little American humor." She adjusted the air-conditioning vents toward Kyra to make sure she was comfortable.

"Yes, it's good to see you . . . and your car, Raquel. I feel like I've made *two* new friends." Kyra laughed.

The car appeared to agree, letting out a pleased *hummm*, and all three sped off toward El Rinconcillo. Raquel mentioned that El Rinconcillo was one of Sevilla's oldest restaurants at 350 years, with an *atmósfera muy fina.*

The bar area was crowded when they arrived; patrons were standing shoulder to shoulder, enjoying their favorite beverages while chatting with friends and new acquaintances. Large whole hams hung in a row from the ceiling, which gave the bar an authentic pub-like feel. The backsplash and the walls were adorned with colorful Moorish tile work featuring intricate woven designs in every imaginable color. The Andalucía influence captivated Kyra's eye, as she adored the local ambience.

Raquel ordered her favorite dish, *espinacas con garbanzos,* or spinach with chickpeas, a house specialty, and Kyra decided on the *jamón ibérico,* or Iberian cured ham, which would be sliced from whole hams she had seen upon entering. They both decided to add a simple *ensalada*, or green salad, to their order to satisfy their cravings for fresh vegetables.

Again, the conversation flowed easily as it had at lunch, and they discussed numerous topics of interest with passion. Kyra was amazed by how wide Raquel's interests ranged—from art and sports to history and metaphysics, including sacred geometry. She listened intently as Raquel explained that the concept of sacred geometry was based on Plato's idea that geometric patterns occurred naturally in nearly every living thing on earth.

"So the spiral in my inner ear would be exactly proportionate to the spiral—say, in a seashell? Geometrically, it's exactly the same and divinely orchestrated," Kyra offered to make sure she understood.

"*¡Claro!*" Raquel confirmed.

Such deep topics were not at all what Kyra had expected, especially from someone so young, but she was thoroughly enjoying them. Throughout the meal, she admired her friend's vivid facial expressions and gestures, which made for a fun and delightful evening. When the Beetle finally dropped her back off at the hotel, Kyra had a huge grin across her face.

"I will see you in the morning for our final day in *Sevilla,*" Raquel exclaimed when Kyra exited the car, "and then we will head out late afternoon for *Málaga.* I can't wait to show you more of *Andalucía. ¡Buenas noches!*" Raquel waved a sassy goodbye to the valet, and then threw Kyra a Gabby-style *muwahhh.*

"*Buenas noches,* and I will see you in the morning!" Kyra said adding a *muwahhh* of her own. As the Beetle drove off, Kyra strolled into the hotel, feeling quite content with the day's adventure and captivated by her new friend's lively, passionate spirit. *Ah, yes, my dear friend, Gabby, I think you are here in some ways.*

# 28

Kyra slept soundly—even overslept because she had accidentally turned off her alarm instead of hitting the snooze button. Grabbing the clock, she realized it was nearly 8 am. She hurried out of bed to get ready for what promised to be a fun-filled day with Raquel. She sprinted into the hotel restaurant with her suitcase in tow and ordered a cappuccino and bowl of fruit.

Raquel pulled up less than a half an hour later, honking the horn just as Kyra swept through the hotel doors. The valet readily offered to help load the suitcase into the trunk, smiling at Kyra's generous tip. "Enjoy your vacation!" he offered in his best English. Both women gave him a friendly wave goodbye.

"I am so excited about heading to *Málaga* this evening," Raquel said, "but first we will enjoy your last day in *Sevilla. ¡Lo vamos a pasar muy bien!*" She hit the gas and the Beetle purred a contented-sounding *hummm* as they hurried off.

"Tomorrow will be an amazing day in *Málaga*," Kyra agreed. "I can hardly wait to see the *Andalucía* coastline and the sparkling waters of the Mediterranean Sea again. But, right now, I'm excited to see your famous *Real Alcázar de Sevilla,*" she said, making sure her pronunciation was authentic. "Or the Royal Palace, as I like to say. I know we'll have an adventure!"

As Kyra spoke, her intuition flashed again, giving her the same eerie feeling she had experienced in Madrid. *I am not going to let my nerves get the best of me*, she thought, determined that the flashbacks she experienced in Madrid would not happen again. She had no idea what lay ahead for her the first night in the picturesque town of Málaga, but she sensed something incredible was on the horizon.

After arriving at the Real Alcázar de Sevilla, the women paid their tour fees and the attendant behind the counter kindly informed them that the tour would last almost two hours.

To Kyra's astonishment, the palace was actually made up of several distinctively different buildings, each a miniature palace in its own right. The original building was a Moorish fort, built in the eleventh century, and featured a combination of both Moorish and Christian architectural styles. This made the palace distinctively unique and unlike any other in the world.

Just as the tour started, Raquel's exuberance got the better of her and she blurted, "This is one the oldest palaces in Europe still occupied by a royal couple!"

The tour guide gave her a stern look for interrupting his introductory monologue, and Raquel covered her mouth with her hand to stifle a giggle. Kyra attempted to keep her composure, but a soft laugh escaped her lips just the same.

They began in the Patio del León, or Courtyard of the Lion, just past the main entrance. Kyra listened carefully as the tour guide explained that the name came from the nineteenth-century tile work depicting a crowned lion holding a cross atop the main gate known as Puerta del León, which they'd just passed through.

Next they walked through the Palacio Mudéjar, or Palace of King Don Pedro I, with its exquisite workmanship, an incredible fusion of Muslim and Iberian styles. In the middle stood the Patio de Las Doncellas, or the Courtyard of the Maidens. Ornate Moorish archways surrounded an elegant reflecting pool, and long corridors on either side offered shade as the tour group passed by.

Kyra could easily imagine kings and queens of bygone eras strolling past the pool, contemplating their next strategic battle or perhaps preparing for a royal celebration. When the tour guide explained that the courtyard was named after a legend that the Moors demanded a hundred virgins a year as a payment from the Christian king and queen to keep peace, Raquel let out a snicker, which prompted another stern look from the guide.

"No one knows if it's true, but a funny legend, *¿Sí?*" Raquel whispered to Kyra when the tour guide turned his back.

"That makes being Jewish much more appealing," Kyra whispered back, trying to keep a smile from breaking through.

The tour guide turned around to glance at the women, and Raquel bit her lip to keep from laughing.

The tour took them through many different buildings, including the original palace to the west called Al-Muwarak, which housed a magnificent Moorish-style interior, and the Salón de Embajadores, or Hall of Ambassadors, with a dramatic, honeycomb-domed ceiling dripping with gold, red, and blue tiles. Both made for a visually stunning sight.

The Renaissance Palace included the House of Trade, where Christopher Columbus had signed his contract with Queen Isabella. Kyra nudged Raquel, reminding her of their earlier discussion, but Raquel promptly pursed her lips to avoid discussion of that topic again. The tour guide pointed out the many Italian features of the palace, including marble columns, and noted that Columbus was originally from Italy.

Kyra especially enjoyed the Gothic Palace, which consisted of several large rooms with even more of the stunning tile work she had now come to expect in Sevilla. This building, she learned, contained several magnificent friezes, or murals on large wall panels, many of which were decorated with the shapes of animals, including snakes, birds, and lions, of course.

"Wow! This palace is indescribable," Kyra declared. "I've never seen anything like it. The colors are so rich and vibrant, and the design in the tapestries, tile work, and friezes are so . . . *imaginative.*"

"*¡Sí, sí!*" Raquel agreed, taking Kyra's arm as they stepped outside the palace. "But you must see the gardens. They will take your breath away."

Having finished the tour, the women drifted leisurely through the outside area enjoying the bright sunny day. Kyra noticed that some of the lush gardens were protected by high stonewalls, while others were more expansive and open. The deeply weathered cobblestone walkways, dark and uneven, reminded her of just how ancient the palace grounds really were. Running her hand across several of the stone fountains, she once again felt an eerie sensation. "Have I been here before?" she murmured to herself.

Without an answer, she brushed off the peculiar sensation and followed Raquel around the peaceful grounds, noting the lush palm trees, colorful water fountains, manicured hedges—and, to Kyra's delight, even a few peacocks. She laughed as the birds strutted by and recalled her humorous visit with the peacock at Casa de Campo in Madrid.

*Ah, my royal friends, you visit me twice now in Spain! But I now know the Universe intends for me to see you as a sign—a sign that symbolizes rebirth, awakening, glory, and royalty. Thank you!*

Feeling quite content with all the beauty they had witnessed, the women headed back to the Beetle and hopped inside.

"*Amiga*, let us grab a quick bite to eat at *Bodega Santa Cruz*," Raquel suggested. "This time it will be my treat—well, my parents' treat." A wide grin spread across her face.

Kyra willingly agreed. "That sounds *perfecto*—I'm always willing to accommodate eating out here in Spain."

As they neared the restaurant, Raquel offered some trivia: "*Bodega Santa Cruz* is located in the old Jewish Quarter of *Sevilla*, not too far from the Cathedral of *Sevilla*, where we visited yesterday. You remember I told you that King Ferdinand III took *Sevilla* back from Muslim rule and it became Christian again? Well, he moved the Jewish population into this neighborhood and gave the Jews a choice: convert to Christianity or be expelled from Spain. Many of them left, but those who stayed finally were able to keep their Jewish faith—and the proclamation wasn't actually formally revoked until the *nineteen sixties!*"

Kyra's heart momentarily ached as she thought of her Jewish side of the family and all they'd been through to find safety and religious freedom both in Israel and the United States.

"The neighborhood is now a popular tourist area," Raquel continued, "but it's a maze of narrow streets. There are many cool shops here and interesting plazas to visit too . . . Look, we've arrived!"

With the Beetle snugly in a parking spot, the women walked up to Bodega Santa Cruz. High-top tables on the sidewalk in front were already filled with the *regulares*, or regular customers, as Raquel pointed out. The restaurant had a unique bright yellow brick exterior and two large stone columns on either side of the doorway, which they passed through as they stepped inside.

"This place is super crowded," Kyra observed, "so I'm guessing the food must be great here."

Raquel nodded affirmatively and waved her hand, catching the attention of the bartender. She ordered a *tinto de verano*, which was a local specialty of red wine and lemonade, and Kyra decided on a simpler *agua con gas* with lots of ice.

The women reviewed the menu on the chalkboard and ordered several *Montaditos*, or small open-faced sandwiches. Once the waiter placed the dishes on the table, they ate at a leisurely pace, thoroughly enjoying their lunch break and each other's company. After they were pleasantly full, they returned to the car and embarked on their two-hour road trip to the city of Málaga.

As Raquel drove, Kyra felt immensely happy to see more of the gorgeous Andalucía countryside from her snug position. The roads were well laid out, and traveling in the Beetle made the trip fun. The Beetle let out a perplexed-sounding *hummm* or two, perhaps struggling under the weight of her suitcase. The strange human-like responses were not lost on Kyra's ear—and her childlike imagination ran wild: *Does this car really have feelings?!* Nevertheless, she noted that the car overall seemed to be in good cheer, as all three made their way across the Spanish countryside.

Kyra enjoyed the view from her window, admiring the rich farmland, as she and Raquel continued to chat. When they passed *almendros*, Raquel explained that the almond trees bloomed delicate white flowers in the early springtime. "However, in July," she added, "the soft, fuzzy fruit ripens in the hot summer sun, and the hulls split open, revealing the wonderful sweet almonds inside. *¡Deliciosas!*"

"Ah . . . I love almonds. They're one of my favorites—chestnuts, too," Kyra added. Her heart brightened at the subtle reminder of her mother and roasting chestnuts with her in winters past.

When Kyra's eyes danced across the thousands of olive trees that dotted the hillsides, she pleasantly recalled the countless varieties of olives she had eaten during her trip so far. *Yummm*, she thought, and rubbed her belly, ready to eat some more. Then a completely different tree captured her attention—orange trees. She cracked the window and deeply inhaled the sweet fragrance of orange blossom, savoring the scent. But soon her attention was captured by hill after hill of tantalizing vineyards. She could see the grapes swelling in the summer heat on the lush, dark vines. Both of these were fond reminders of her home back in California.

Raquel pointed out her favorite trees—the avocado—saying that some were close to fifty feet tall. Kyra noted that the heavy branches dripping with the dark, alligator-skinned fruit, looked ripe for picking. The car unexpectedly swerved, and an odd thought occurred to Kyra: *Is the Beetle tempting Raquel to pull over to pick avocados?!*

Raquel corrected the turn, and then threw her hands up in the air. She too looked perplexed by the car's sudden shift in direction.

With all the glorious countryside to relish along the way, the drive went by unexpectedly fast. Soon they were approaching the picturesque city of Málaga, which lay majestically on the glorious turquoise coastline of the Mediterranean Sea.

As they approached the city limits, Raquel explained, "The mountains off in the distance are called *Sierra Nevada*, which actually means snowy mountains in Spanish. Aren't they *fantástico?*"

Kyra admired the cool beauty of the snowcapped peaks that lay far off in the distance. "They are quite beautiful and we have our own Sierra Nevada Mountains in California too," she replied, letting herself enjoy the loveliness of the moment. "Between that, the vineyards, the orange trees, and everything else—I'm so amazed by the synchronicities between this place and California! A few months ago, I never imagined I'd be taking this trip—but here I am. The reminders of my beautiful home are amazing."

"Everything happens for a reason," Raquel replied in a soothing voice. "Gabriela always tells me that."

*Yes, indeed it does*, thought Kyra. She could almost hear Gabby's bubbly voice reminding her of the same.

Fully embracing all the coincidences and her deep feeling that she was traveling a path for her highest good, Kyra finally caught a glimpse of the sparkling city of Málaga directly ahead of them.

The Beetle soon zipped through the center of the city and then down to the gorgeous coastline. Raquel had suggested that, instead of booking a hotel ahead of time, they just "wing it." Now, Kyra laughed nervously as they searched for a hotel on the main street closest to the water.

"You know, Raquel, I've never just winged *anything* in my life. I always plan everything out ahead of time." She reflected and then added, "But I'd like to make that a part of my past. In the future, I want a balance of planning ahead, but also allowing things to manifest . . . I so appreciate your idea to just look for a hotel that grabs us."

"Sometimes the best things in life are a *sorpresa*—or a surprise! But we don't want to end up in a *dump*, as you say in America," she said with humor. "That one over there looks good!" Raquel swerved again, pointing out the AC Hotel Málaga Palacio.

"The name is cool—almost like our very own palace. And it's located right across from the Port of *Málaga*." Kyra glanced quickly toward the roof as they passed it by. "Oh, there's a rooftop swimming pool too! I'm wagering it has a spectacular view of the sea. This looks *perfecto, amiga*."

They made a quick U-turn and pulled into the valet parking area. The valet attendant unloaded Kyra's suitcase, and Raquel grabbed her modest backpack—which, to Kyra's surprise, apparently contained everything she needed.

"Do you have any available rooms for tonight?" Raquel asked the clerk at the front desk. Kyra held her breath, thinking they should have left the suitcase in the trunk until they found out.

The young woman behind the desk tapped her fingers across her keyboard before answering, "Oh!" she said excitedly. "Usually we are completely booked this time of year, *señoritas*, but it looks like we just had a cancelation about an hour ago for a Junior Suite. It has two twin beds. You are most lucky!"

Relief swept across Kyra's face. She was grateful once again for the reminder that if she trusted in the Universe, it would indeed provide perfectly for her. *All I need is a leap of faith*, she silently confirmed as they walked toward the elevator.

The women proceeded to the seventh floor and checked into room 777. Kyra did a double take as she slid the card key into the door. "*Hmmm*, I was on flight 3777 to *Sevilla* and now we're in room 777. I keep seeing triplicate numbers everywhere I go! They must have some special meaning."

Raquel winked as she placed her small backpack on one of the twin beds. "Well, *amiga*. If there's a special message for you, I'm sure you will find it—even if you have to Google the answer," she said mischievously. "Until then, let's go up to the rooftop restaurant for a glass of *vino!*"

After spending a few minutes unpacking, Kyra followed Raquel up to the rooftop. The swimming pool looked cool and inviting, and the women grabbed a table near a glass wall that overlooked the turquoise waters of the sea. The tranquil harbor, sprinkled with boats, lay directly beneath them. Mesmerized by the view, the women ordered drinks, and Kyra's eyes lovingly absorbed the serenity of the water.

After they had toasted each other, Kyra asked somewhat tentatively, "Would you be open to a quiet day tomorrow? Maybe lunch close to the harbor and some swimming at the beach?"

"I've loved showing you *Andalucía*, but a quiet day of swimming in our warm sea sounds perfect! A day of rest it is," her friend agreed.

The women enjoyed their drinks and watched the glorious sun sinking slowly into the calming crystal-blue waters. And after a quiet dinner at the hotel restaurant, they slipped off to their room and settled in for a good night's rest.

Kyra tossed a bit before falling asleep. The last thought she remembered was hearing Raquel let out a soft snore—and before she knew it—she was standing at the edge of a forest.

# 29

Kyra woke up in the middle of the night, unsure why she'd so abruptly come out of her dream. She lay still in her bed, the details vividly replaying in her mind almost like a film on a movie screen. She'd been standing on a vast, sandy shoreline, staring out across the ocean. The serene, beautiful beach stretched on forever, and she'd glanced up at the rising full moon. Its glowing light reflected brightly across the ocean, dancing upon the tips of rippling waves. The light disappeared as each wave crashed gently upon the shoreline.

*That dream is familiar*, Kyra thought. *I had it often when I was a child, but . . . Wait, I can remember almost all of it now!* She recalled her small hand reaching up to the darkening skyline because she had wanted to touch a star. The stars looked like a million twinkling diamonds against the black velvety backdrop. She could still feel how incredibly happy she was to be in that special place, and her heart felt like it would burst with joy. *It was such a perfect moment in time . . . standing there felt exciting and magical.*

Kyra recalled playing in the warm, salty water. With childlike curiosity, she had stooped down to pick up a seashell, examining it carefully in the radiant moonlight. Suddenly her intuition ignited with a strange feeling that she was not alone, and she'd quickly spun around. Startled, she saw someone standing there—a strikingly beautiful woman. They began to have a conversation, and the woman had taken her hand . . . and that's when the dream had ended and Kyra woke up.

As she lay in bed trying to recall the details of her conversation with the woman, Kyra tried to turn over onto her side—but instantly realized she could not move. To her shock, she was completely paralyzed! Her body felt frozen, but her mind was fully conscious. With sheer determination, she tried to open her mouth to make a sound—but her body simply would not respond. She couldn't even wiggle a single finger.

*How strange!* she thought with alarm. *What is wrong with me?*

Trying not to panic, Kyra rapidly searched her memory for any answer that might shed some light on her situation. She recalled experiencing something similar as a teenager and she'd briefly researched it, not daring to tell her parents about the strange occurrence. It was called sleep paralysis and only a temporary condition.

*It feels as if you're awake, but you can't move. It's fairly common, and it isn't dangerous,* she assured herself. *But still a little scary. . .*

Her sense of the room around her was clear, if not heightened, and she tried patiently to get her body to respond. Curious about the time, Kyra made a strenuous effort to glance over at the clock on the nightstand. Though her head refused to turn, she suddenly felt herself floating up out of her body and hovering just above it. Her physical body had not moved, but she could now see the clock. It read 3:33 am.

In her floating conscious state, Kyra looked over at Raquel in the next bed. Her friend was fast asleep, totally unaware of her bizarre experience. Raquel was making funny snoring noises—taking in an occasional loud gulp of air through her mouth, and then making a snorting sound when she exhaled.

*Snoring must run in the family!* Kyra thought, remembering that Gabby too made the same noises when she slept. She chuckled—lending a moment of levity to her situation. The humor soon faded, though, when she began to wonder again what was happening to her.

*An out-of-body experience, perhaps?* She had read about the phenomenon, which was called OBE for short, but she'd never expected to actually experience it. Her consciousness scanned the room from its vantage point—and then she looked down at the foot of her bed, completely taken aback by what she saw.

A strikingly beautiful woman around the age of thirty was standing there—and looking back at Kyra. But what surprised her most was that the woman did not appear to be fully embodied, but instead more of a silhouette, floating about three feet above the bed. Her color was pale, almost silver, and she seemed to be *glowing*, her face brightly shining as she smiled.

Kyra tried to remain calm as she looked closer at the woman. *She's translucent and radiating light!* She noticed that the woman was wearing an ancient-looking gown and had long flowing hair that cascaded down her bare shoulders. But what struck Kyra as most strange was the sensation that the woman seemed *familiar*—like Kyra had always known her—and her mind suddenly shot back to her childhood dream once again.

*It is you! I recognize you! The fortune-teller said we would meet when the time was right, but I didn't realize it would be you.*

The woman smiled back, and her eyes filled with love as she stared at Kyra. At first Kyra wanted to be afraid, but her intuition rapidly took over to assess the situation. Kyra looked the woman squarely in the face and tried to sense if her intentions were good. To her surprise, she immediately felt an overwhelming feeling of calm, and a strong sensation of love began to envelop her being. She could clearly detect that this woman was indeed safe and that everything was very good. There were no negative intentions, no fear, nothing to be afraid of—just an immense feeling of love that continued to grow.

*Why are we meeting now?* Kyra asked with her mind. She had never experienced an ability to communicate like this before, but it felt quite natural to her all the same.

The woman gazed kindly at Kyra, and then answered her in a soft, calming voice. She could see that the woman's mouth was not moving, but somehow she could still hear her words, just as if she were actually speaking.

*My name is Arianna. Please do not be afraid. Are you comfortable, dear one, with my being here?*

*Yes, I'm just fine . . . uhm, thank you for asking,* Kyra answered hesitantly. *But why are you here?*

Arianna looked at Kyra with adoration in her eyes. *To answer your question, let me begin by explaining that we have known each other for a very long time—eons I should say. I'm visiting you today, dear one, because it is finally time to for us to meet in this lifetime. You are ready now. You have done so much work on yourself this past month and you are now in a space where you are much more relaxed and open. I am so very proud of you.*

Kyra's thoughts flashed back to the fortune-teller, and an energizing thrill raced through her mind as she recalled their conversation. *Yes, I was told I would meet you when I was ready. The fortune-teller in Barcelona made that very clear. She said you visited me often in my dreams.*

The woman nodded. *I know you are wondering how we know each other.*

Kyra felt herself nod, though her body made no physical movement. *Yes, I'd very much appreciate your telling me that. I do want to understand.*

Appearing to reflect first upon her answer, Arianna replied, *Kyra, we have met many times before, in many different lifetimes. I am a part of your soul family, and we have always been together. We have traveled through eternity together . . . time does not really exist the way you think it does.* Arianna paused, letting this sink in.

*I do feel like I've always known you . . . but what do you mean that I'm ready now. What am I ready for?* Kyra asked.

Arianna wore a tender smile and answered slowly. *In this lifetime, I am your spirit guide, dear one, and I am here to assist you on your journey. I am visiting you at this exact moment in your life to help you because you are finally ready. I am here to help you through the transition you are now experiencing.*

*Transition?* Kyra echoed, not fully understanding.

*Yes, transition, Kyra. Spirit has been assisting you to make changes in your life so you can fully embrace your life's true purpose. These changes are necessary and will lead you to a life that is better suited for you. There are no coincidences—ever—and all the events in your life have been with purpose and meaning. With your permission—free will, as you call it—we will help you live the life you were meant to live. A life full of happiness with extraordinary blessings, but more importantly, a life in which you also help other people.*

*I see,* Kyra replied. *I would love that very much! Can you tell me more?*

Arianna readily complied, as she had much to share. *You have a special purpose in this lifetime, and I will explain everything to you fully. But first, let us review your life so you can understand the choices that you've made so far, and why you are where you are now.*

*Thank you, Arianna. I will listen carefully,* Kyra promised.

Arianna began with Kyra's birth and the parents she had chosen prior to incarnating on the planet at this time. She explained that everything had been carefully orchestrated ahead of time, and it was a part of God's divine plan. Kyra had learned much from her parents and from her young friends, but sometimes, as Arianna pointed out, *You experienced the negative aspects of life to fully appreciate and value all the positive ones.*

Arianna carefully explained how Kyra's parents had influenced her choices and her feelings about herself. She then discussed how her teenage friends and even society had also affected her values. Kyra had learned to focus on more external things, such as her appearance and building a career, instead of balancing that with internal feelings of love and true connection to those around her. But, more importantly, Arianna discussed how Kyra sometimes let fear influence her decisions and led her to settle for less than she truly deserved.

Kyra reflected back, agreeing that many of her choices, which she had made of her own free will, had indeed been learning opportunities and a chance to grow. For an instant, she felt an overwhelming wave of sorrow as she listened, but she chose instead to embrace her sadness—and feel only love for all the people she had encountered who had helped her grow. *I was a student of sorts, and now I can appreciate all of my teachers. They were only doing what they were supposed to do. I understand, Arianna. Please go on.*

*In Spirit, there is no judgment,* Arianna continued. *Only one thing really exists, and that is love—God's love.*

Kyra felt her heart intensify with joy. *Yes, I see that now. Thank you! I will make my decisions in the future based on what my heart tells me is good—and not let the opinions of others or my own fear determine my worth or focus. I remember Uncle Saul and Father Sánchez saying the same thing to me—to follow my heart. And of course, dear sweet Nana's advice, too . . . I miss her so much.* Kyra let a wave of sadness pass through her before she continued, *Despite Nana's being gone, I still feel very connected to her—like she is always with me. I will focus my feelings on love, not sadness. I know I can feel Nana thinking of me at times, and she sends me her love often, when I allow it.*

Arianna smiled softly. *Yes, dear one, there is no separation in Spirit. Your grandmother is very happy, and she is always with you, even when you can't see her.*

Kyra felt relief to have her experiences validated and felt immensely grateful that Arianna had shared this with her. *There is so much more I want to learn*, she said, changing the subject, wanting to get all her questions in before their time together ended. *May I ask what my purpose is in this life?*

*Your purpose is that of the Light, dear one*, Arianna replied. Her smile lingered on her lips. *Do you remember your childhood dream of the forest, and how you followed the path that took you to the shore of the great ocean? I was always there with you in your dream, waiting for you. But now you are ready to embrace your life's true purpose, and that is the path of a Lightworker.*

Kyra's mind raced back to her metaphysical classes with Gabby, when they had discussed the term. *I've heard that word before, but it's been such a long time. Please help me understand. What is a Lightworker?*

Arianna replied in her soothing voice, *A Lightworker is someone who helps others to seek out and embrace spiritual enlightenment.*

Excited, Kyra asked her next question: *And what do you mean by spiritual enlightenment—especially as it pertains to a Lightworker?*

Arianna did not hesitate with her response: *Enlightenment is simply the state of having knowledge, awareness, and wisdom. But spiritual enlightenment—the kind of enlightenment you're meant to help others remember—takes this one step further. It means to become more knowledgeable about your spiritual self and to gain an understanding of your connection to others and God through your thoughts and actions. Lightworkers, like yourself, help others to regain the knowledge of who they really are: Divine beings of Light.*

Kyra tried to nod her head, but couldn't—still caught somewhere between the physical and nonphysical. Arianna understood her acknowledgment and continued, *Some will call this God. Others may refer to it as Source Energy, and still others may call it Universal Consciousness, but it is really all the same. God, as you call him, also sent his son, Jesus, to bring the Christ consciousness into the world. Jesus reminded us of how important it is to love each other. You recall his words in the Book of John: "Love one another. As I have loved you, so you must love one another."* Arianna paused, allowing Kyra to fully absorb her words.

*Lightworkers, dear one, also have a special purpose: to help humankind heal from the effects of fear-based thoughts and decisions, and to instead make decisions from a place of love.*

Kyra fought back tears, and when she felt ready, Arianna continued, *A Lightworker helps others to choose a life of love, not hate; to experience joy, not fear; to embrace peace, not war; and to be kind, not selfish. Often they have special gifts from Spirit such as heightened intuition or healing abilities.*

Kyra felt her heart swell; her emotions seemed intensified in her out-of-body state. *I do love helping people in a positive way. I realize, too, that I haven't always taken the time to do that. Nana taught me the importance of helping others, and I was reminded of this again at her funeral in Israel, when so many people spoke of her acts of kindness . . . I'm also finding my intuition is becoming much more heightened, and I've rekindled my interest in Reiki.*

Arianna assured her that she knew these things. *There's more, dear one. Lightworkers often help others to heal their lives through counseling, teaching, writing, and working in the healing arts. Some Lightworkers volunteer their time to help preserve the precious Earth and to safeguard our animal companions through their efforts. Even our plants and oceans need nourishment and protection from the actions of humankind. We are all one in God's eyes, Kyra. We do not walk this Earth alone.*

Kyra thought back to her special time in nature and how much she had come to realize she wanted to be of service to others and even help preserve the wonderful Earth that God had given humanity. Arianna's words rang true to her heart. *I have always adored my time in nature. It brings me such joy to see the forest creatures . . . and the ocean truly feeds my soul. I would love to do more to help protect our wonderful Earth and our animal friends. I've been craving a much deeper meaning for my life on so many levels, Arianna. Please tell me: how do I fit into this?* Kyra anxiously awaited her guide's response.

*Your purpose, dear one, is to help others through your healing and intuitive gifts. It will bring you happiness beyond your imagination. Do you realize you have intuitive gifts from Spirit? Think back in your life when you simply sensed the correct decision to make—hunches or intuition, as you call it. Did you make a good decision?*

Kyra felt her mind jump. *Yes! When I was a child, I always knew if something was good or bad, whether it was a person, situation, or even an event that was about to happen. I could . . . feel it, I think that's the right word. I sensed what was the right thing to do, even when it didn't always make logical sense.* Kyra paused. *But I didn't embrace this again until later in my career. I used my intuition to sense the right decision, even when the data didn't fully support it. Sometimes the decisions I made were risky, but I was always right when I followed my gut feelings.*

Arianna nodded. *Yes, dear child. Listen to your heart, not just your head, and you will always make the best decision. You will also be given the opportunity to increase your intuitive skills once you return home. When the time is right, you will find a teacher who will mentor you. You are drawn to the healing arts, yes?*

*Yes! I have been reminded how much I loved Reiki—healing energy work—back in my grad school days. I just took a refresher course in Madrid, and my friend Gabby invited me to go to England to complete the Master level training. I was thinking the timing was right to do this now.*

*Yes, dear one,* Arianna replied. *Everything has perfectly synchronized to this exact moment so that you can pursue these interests now.*

Another question came to Kyra's mind: *I've been having a new dream, and I'm standing somewhere in Asia. In the dream, I meet a man who is beckoning me to follow him. Am I supposed to visit this country?*

Arianna paused . . . *Look into your heart, and you will find the answer.*

Kyra hesitated, but suddenly the answer shot into her mind and became crystal clear. *I do know who the man is and why I'm supposed to go there! It makes perfect sense to me. Thank you so much for all of your help, Arianna!*

Arianna beamed a sort of nonphysical warmth that felt pleasant and comforting. She slowly began to rise, giving Kyra the feeling she was leaving. *I love you, dear Kyra,* Arianna said in parting. *I always have and always will. I will be here for you—even when you cannot see me. Continue to work on your healing and intuitive skills, and you will be able to connect with me again soon.*

*I will. I promise!* Kyra assured her guide.

As Arianna continued to rise, she left Kyra with one last thought: *So that you do not wake up thinking this was all a dream, I have a secret to share—one that will come to light very soon. Your dear friend Gabby—who is also part of your soul family—is with child. She will have twins, and they will be an important part of your life very soon.*

At this news, Kyra felt incredible joy.

*Remember, dear Kyra, I am always with you.* With that, Arianna faded away.

Kyra consciously looked at the clock; it was now 4:44 am. Over an hour had passed since she had first starting speaking with Arianna. She felt herself drifting gently down toward her bed again and back into her physical body. Once she could feel the weight of her physical body around her, she struggled to gain control of her limbs. At last, with much effort, she moved her mouth slightly, and then one of her fingers, and finally wiggled her toes.

A few minutes later, the effects of the sleep paralysis had completely worn off, and Kyra glanced over at Raquel. She was sleeping soundly—and still taking in an occasional loud gulp of air through her mouth followed by a snort when she exhaled. *After all that, she's still snoring!* Kyra laughed inwardly.

She sat up in bed and gazed around the room. It was dark, but she felt calm, and an immense sense of joy enveloped her being. It felt as if only love existed. Her mind carefully reviewed the details of the conversation, making mental notes so she would remember it all. *Could this have all been a dream?* she wondered, but then she thought of Arianna's parting words. *I need to think over—very carefully—what to say to Gabby. Do I tell her she's pregnant with twins? Hopefully I'll know the right thing to do when the time comes.*

Feeling drowsy but amazingly blissful, Kyra laid her head back down on the pillow and gently drifted off to peaceful slumber.

# 30

The alarm sounded at 8 am. Kyra tapped the button softly and sat up in bed. Stretching her arms up above her head, she noticed she did not feel any grogginess. *I feel amazingly light—like a feather! I've never felt so rested in my entire life!*

The feeling was unlike anything she had ever experienced. *It's like every stress point in my body had been released, and I'm incredibly relaxed.* But that didn't even begin to describe how fabulous she felt. Kyra lingered for a moment, enjoying the warm sensation that surrounded her, filling her aura with a delicious sense of joy. She then quietly slid out of bed, so as not to awaken Raquel, who she thought looked completely adorable all snuggled up under the covers. She also found it amusing that Raquel had slept right through the alarm—just like her dear cousin Gabby would have done.

Kyra tiptoed to the bathroom and quietly freshened up for a relaxing day at the beach. Splashing cool water on her face, she broke into a huge smile. *I am so excited to see what the future holds*, she thought as she brushed her teeth with vigor. She slipped on a comfortable swimsuit, faded jean shorts, and a bright orange t-shirt for extra sun protection.

She thought again of Gabby as she brushed her hair, and the wonderful secret Arianna had shared with her. *What, if anything, should I say to her?* she wondered. *Maybe I should have asked Arianna for guidance. I don't want to make a mistake.* Deciding that the right answer would come to her, she pulled her hair back into a ponytail just like she always did at Stinson Beach in California.

*Ah, I do miss home*, she realized with nostalgia, *but this has been the adventure of a lifetime. So much has happened since Nana passed away—and while I miss her, only positive things have come to me and will continue to come to me. I'm sure of that now.*

Taking a private moment to meditate, she sent Nana a sweet, loving thought, deliberately deciding not to feel any sadness. Focusing on the feelings of love, she felt a sudden twinge, warm and familiar, in her heart center. Without any doubt, she knew *who* was sending her love and smiled.

"Thank you for always being with me, Nana, just like you promised," Kyra said, placing her hand on her heart. "*Ani ohev otach*—I love you too."

She slipped back into the bedroom and gave Raquel a soft shake to wake her up. Her friend's *arghh* in response elicited a chuckle from Kyra.

"So sorry, *amiga.* I'm always a bit groggy in the mornings. How did you sleep last night? *¿Bien?* Ah, I mean did you sleep well?"

"Yes! Quite well," Kyra responded. "I can't tell you what a glorious night it was. I feel great today!"

Raquel looked at Kyra, a bit perplexed, wondering what, if anything, she may have missed. "Ah, well . . . excellent! My *mamá* has said that I sometimes snore, so I'm very glad I didn't wake you up."

Kyra's heart filled with affection. "No, Raquel—you were perfect last night. You slept like an *angel.*" She laughed. "But let's get this day rolling. I'm ready to see what's in store for us."

Raquel quickly slipped into the bathroom to put on her beachwear and freshen up. The friends then took the elevator down to the first floor and ate a light breakfast at the hotel restaurant. It was a gorgeously warm morning, and the sun shone brightly through the huge window next to their table.

"We usually have beautiful weather this time of year," Raquel commented, her eyes brightening. "My *mamá* always tells me, *Esperan lo mejor y seguramente vendrá*. That means, 'Expect the best and it will surely come.'"

That sounded to Kyra like something Nana would have said, and a pleasant expression crossed her features. She could not have agreed more.

They scarfed down a light breakfast, and then practically skipped outside and across the street, making their way to the splendid harbor.

Raquel walked briskly, trying to keep up with Kyra's energetic pace. "I'm not sure what's come over you since last night, but *me gusta!* Perhaps some of that will rub off on me."

"I hope it does! Maybe I'll let you in on my secret later," Kyra replied as they passed a few yachts and fishing boats docked in the harbor. She pondered whether she was ready to disclose her mystical experiences to Rachel but decided to change the subject for now. "I loved the fabulous views we had last night from the hotel swimming pool, especially at sunset, but today it's even nicer up close." She spun around and pointed toward the sea. "I'm ready to get settled at the beach and do some swimming! It will be like a spa day with the warm temperatures."

Raquel waved her slender arm, leading the way, and the pair proceeded north from the harbor on a street called Paseo España. '*Spanish Walk,*' Kyra repeated to herself, easily translating the street sign. *And most appropriate!* She reflected on her journey across Spain and everything that had transpired.

The women arrived a few minutes later at a scenic beach called Playa de la Malagueta.

The beach looked picture-perfect, covered with soft beige sand that appeared mostly untouched. The day was early, so tourists and locals were just starting to arrive. The beautiful soft sand contrasted dramatically against the crystal aqua water of the lovely Mediterranean Sea. Kyra could not have been more pleased when she glanced toward the skyline and saw the stunning Sierra Nevada Mountains off in the distance. They rose majestically up from the horizon, their dark browns and greens a bold contrast against the pale blue sky. Amazingly snow was still barely visible on their highest peaks. Her heart skipped a beat, mesmerized by their beauty.

"This is all so amazing. I must say, *Andalucía* is simply gorgeous and just what I needed."

"The pleasure is all mine!" Raquel exclaimed. "Let's grab some beach chairs with umbrellas and *beat the crowd*, as you say in America. I've learned *that* phrase from watching your movies."

"Beating the crowd sounds like a great idea." replied Kyra, looking over to her right. "That looks like a good spot over there."

Raquel agreed and laid their towels on the bright blue-and-white-striped chair cushions. After paying a rental fee for the umbrella chairs, the friends settled in.

Kyra pulled the last Reiki manual out of her purse and held the book affectionately. "This is the third book in the series of classes that Gabby and I took back in grad school," she explained. "It's called *Advanced Reiki Training*, or ART for short. As I mentioned yesterday, I'm still deciding whether to join Gabby in England for the Master training, but time to decide is growing short. The final ceremony will be in Stonehenge—if you can imagine that!"

Raquel looked over at the manual. "I'd like to take that class myself someday. You have inspired me to do it *sooner rather than later*—another great American phrase."

"I think I may be inspiring myself," Kyra agreed, feeling more confident. "I'm so glad we met each other."

"You know, *amiga*, I believe we were destined to meet—perhaps to help each other take our next steps." Raquel shifted in her chair to fully face Kyra. "Or, if nothing else, to have fun together in southern Spain!"

"Ha! You make me laugh, Raquel. And I love that you call me *amiga!* You are my dear *friend*, too—and so much like Gabby." Kyra playfully tossed a handful of sand at Raquel's feet as she stood up. "Alright, who's jumping in the water first?"

Raquel sprung up and the pair raced to the water, splashing when they reached the height of the waves. Raquel's long legs carried her there more quickly, and she shot an arm up in mock triumph. The pair spent the next several hours alternating between sunbathing and swimming in the balmy waters. Later, when their lions began to growl, they eagerly left their towels on the beach to grab some appetizers at one of the *chiringuitos,* or tiki-style beach bars.

They let their flip-flops dangle almost off their feet while their legs hung lazily down the sides of the tall barstools. Chatting about nothing in particular, they sipped on fruit drinks decorated with mini umbrellas and slices of fresh strawberries and ordered their lunch. Kyra jokingly called their food "beach tapas" and Raquel agreed that she liked the new term "*playa de tapas.*" Afterward, they returned to the beach for more sunbathing. Though Kyra had used plenty of sunscreen, she knew her skin was pleasantly sun-kissed, and all the sun and salt water had made her look forward to a nap before their evening activities.

For dinner, they chose a simple restaurant, just ten minutes from the hotel, called Tapeo de Cervantes. They sauntered leisurely enjoying the evening, and by the time they were seated, Kyra was feeling incredibly relaxed and comfortable. She decided to share a bit about what she'd experienced with Raquel, but not every detail.

"I think you could call them spiritual experiences," she went on. "And then last night, I had an incredible experience. Perhaps it was a dream, but it seemed so real. The most amazing part is how *light* I've felt all day today! I can't even put it into words, but I think I'm just now getting myself grounded again. Anyway, I know this may sound a bit strange to you." Kyra waited for her friend's response.

"I've had crazy dreams, too," Raquel replied, not for a moment disbelieving anything Kyra had told her. "Sometimes I feel like I'm flying! I seem to wake up before I realize where I am. Maybe someday, I'll remember them better and figure it all out."

A vision flashed into Kyra's mind as Raquel continued to speak, and she saw her friend at an awards dinner. Kyra seemed to be observing the event rather than being there physically, but she could hear and see everything. Raquel appeared to be about ten years older, perhaps around the age of thirty. Her face had matured, and she was wearing a navy suit with high heels. She looked much more business-like and serious than she currently appeared.

The speaker at the awards dinner stood at the microphone and handed Raquel an award. She stepped forward to accept it and make a speech. Kyra could see how very poised she was, and that the award had something to do with children and humanitarian work. Kyra glanced back at the stage directly behind Raquel and could see the word "UNICEF." In another second, Kyra flashed back to their conversation, momentarily lost when she realized Raquel was asking her a question.

"I'm so sorry, I didn't hear your question. Sometimes, lately, I feel like I'm somewhere else—and it just happened again." Kyra took a deep breath before continuing, "To be honest with you—and please don't think I'm crazy—I think I just saw you about ten years into the future. You were receiving an award . . . maybe for some work you had done for UNICEF." Kyra waited for Raquel's response, unsure how her friend would respond.

A puzzled look crossed Raquel's features as she processed the information, but then her eyes grew wide. "*¡Ay, Dios mío!* I have always loved UNICEF and its mission to help children. They provide food, education, child development, and even protection services—if you didn't know that." Her face grew luminous as she spoke. "I would *love* to be a volunteer for them. You've inspired me to find time after I graduate to check them out! Thank you for sharing your vision with me . . . and for being so brave about your experiences."

Relieved, Kyra smiled. "I can't wait to hear what awesome work you do."

"*Ah, sí,*" Raquel said with gratitude. "I will let you know in ten years or so what happens."

Kyra felt thrilled to share such a strong connection with someone in such a short time. They continued to talk about all things metaphysical as well as their future goals. Before long, the waiter began serving plate after plate of food, and they enjoyed a pleasing selection of local dishes. After stuffing themselves silly with the tasty feast, Raquel whipped out her parents' credit card.

Kyra graciously accepted her offer to pay. "Please thank your parents for their generosity. I look forward to meeting them someday. There is something about your family—all of you—that makes me feel like I'm part of something very special."

"'*Mi familia es tu familia,*' my *Mamá* always says! And just so you know," she added with a snicker, "my parents aren't as *loco* as Gabriela's are."

Laughter danced across Kyra's lips. "The Universe could not have sent me a better travel companion for my stay in *Andalucía* than you," she said sincerely.

# 31

When Raquel dropped Kyra off at the airport the next day an hour before her flight to Barcelona, the Beetle let out a sad but heartfelt *hummm*, acknowledging that their time together had come to an end. The sultry, crisp Mediterranean air caressed Kyra's face as she stepped outside and hoisted her suitcase out of the trunk. She gave the car an affectionate pat goodbye.

"Raquel, I am so going to miss you—your car—and *Andalucía*, too," Kyra said, choking up. "I've sincerely appreciated your companionship and kindness. I'm so blessed to have made a new friend . . . I look forward to staying in touch." With that, she stepped forward and gave Raquel a warm hug.

Not normally at a loss for words, Raquel paused for a moment, lost in the embrace. "Awww, *amiga*. I will miss you, too . . . We have so much in common! My first impression of you when we met was that we were from two different worlds."

Kyra burst out laughing at Raquel's refreshing honesty. Truth be told, her first impression of Raquel didn't do her justice either—or her awesome car!

"I hope you can make it to my award ceremony—in ten years," Raquel added, smiling and blinking back her own tears.

With a parting smile, Kyra waved goodbye to Raquel and the beautiful vintage white Volkswagen Beetle, which lovingly let out its final *hummm* in farewell as they both drove away.

After checking her luggage and making her way through security, Kyra arrived at the Iberia Airline gate terminal to wait for boarding. She left Gabby a quick but heartfelt voicemail, telling her how excited she was to see her again in just a few hours—and how her time with Raquel had been beyond amazing.

Next she dialed an international number to an old colleague from Vortex. "Angela, this is Kyra. I booked my flights last night, and I will arrive a little after eight am on Tuesday morning. I am *so* looking forward to seeing you. Thanks so much for agreeing to pick me up at the airport—and on such short notice! This will be an exciting next leg of my journey."

When Kyra ended the call, she reflected on everything she needed to tell Gabby, including her newest travel plans. She had made them on the spur of the moment the evening before, but she had absolutely no doubt that it was the next right step.

After boarding, Kyra settled in and rapidly began reviewing a new travel guide she'd purchased for her next adventure, which she'd embark upon the following day. She wanted to visit some very specific places and fervently studied the city maps. *Gosh,* she thought, *I have so much research to do before Angela picks me up!*

She studied her guide, trying to make sure everything would go as smoothly as possible, especially given her short five-day stay and then her departure to England for a one-week visit. That thought reminded Kyra again of Gabby. *Gabby will be ecstatic that I'm joining her for the Reiki Master Training in England! We'll be roommates again, just like back in grad school.*

Kyra paused, seriously debating whether she should disclose her conversation with Arianna who had foretold that Gabby was pregnant. She struggled with what to do, especially since Gabby was not yet married to Alejandro. *What if the information is wrong?* she worried. Suddenly, an unusual feeling of calmness surrounded her, and she heard a faint whisper, *God answers those who listen, Kyra. Pray for the answer and you'll know what to do.*

After taking a moment to meditate on these words and feeling more at peace, she concentrated on her travel guide. *Six weeks ago, I couldn't have imagined my life would be heading off on such a completely different path than the one I'd been on.*

Once the flight reached its destination, Kyra gathered her bag and headed toward the passenger pick-up area. She hurried outside to the curb anxious to see Gabby, who pulled up a few minutes later in her red-and-white-striped BMW MINI Cooper.

Her friend immediately jumped out and hugged her. "Welcome back to Barcelona, *Chica!* I'm eager to hear all about your crazy adventures. But first, and most *importante*, are you hungry? It's two thirty, and I'm starving!" Her smile was brilliant and her bright red lipstick glistened in the sunlight.

Kyra laughed as she hoisted the suitcase into the trunk, telling Gabby she could handle it on her own. "I most certainly am hungry! We do have a lot to talk about."

Gabby flashed her another smile. "I chose a very casual place for lunch today. It's Sunday, after all, and the restaurants will be super busy. The service at *La Flauta es muy rápido*—and I'd love to eat as soon as possible."

Kyra chuckled. "*La Flauta* sounds awesome, and it's so good to hear your appetite hasn't waned any."

"It's super close by and near my apartment in *Eixample*," Gabby said, catching her breath. "Whew! I'm not sure if it's the summer heat, but I've been extra hungry the last few days. I think I've also been a tiny bit under the weather, too—maybe a bug or something."

Kyra's eyes grew wide. *Can she really be pregnant?* She still wasn't sure how she would handle the information she'd been given, so she decided to hold the thought for now.

La Flauta was quite packed at the peak of lunch hour, but Gabby apparently knew the headwaiter, winking at him when they entered. The tall young man winked back and waved his hand, acknowledging that he had a table ready.

"I feel like royalty," Kyra teased. "You must come here often to get seated so quickly."

"I know the owners of this restaurant, so I gave them a call ahead of time," Gabby said happily. "We'll be seated immediately, so let's order quickly. I'm famished!"

The menu was simple, and true to form, Gabby ordered a variety of tapas to share. When the waiter asked for their beverage order, Kyra ordered her usual *agua con gas*. To her surprise, Gabby ordered the same.

Giving it some thought, Kyra finally got up her nerve and asked, "Is everything okay? You didn't order your usual *vino*."

"I'm fine." Gabby replied instantly. "I'm just a tiny bit under the weather, but nothing keeps me down for long. I'll be back to a hundred percent *pronto*, I promise."

In a soft voice so no one would overhear, Kyra asked, "Have you thought about taking a pregnancy test? . . . *Uh*, just in case?"

Gabby seemed surprised. "Ha! There's no way I'm pregnant." She paused for a moment as if reconsidering. "But, yes, I'll make a trip to the drugstore if I don't feel better in a week or so. You are a dear friend and I appreciate your sweet concern."

Satisfied that she'd planted a good idea in Gabby's head, Kyra changed the topic. "I must tell you how much I enjoyed my trip to Madrid! Javier and Verónica were so gracious in showing me all around. I feel like I've known them my entire life." Her face glowed as she thought of the amazing bond she had formed with the couple.

"*Awww* . . . They said the same about you," Gabby replied, "like they had gained a new sister. *¡Mi familia te adora!*"

Kyra blushed and pressed a hand to her heart. "That's so sweet. I *adored* being with them too, and we had so much fun together. Oh, but my time with Raquel in *Andalucía* was also amazing. She is such a doll . . . and reminded me so much of you! Despite our age difference, I felt like we really connected. It turns out we have so much in common—more than I ever would have guessed by just looking at her." Kyra reflected on her statement and added, "Thank goodness she didn't judge me, and we really opened up to each other."

"I'm thrilled you love my *familia*. They are such a special part of my life, and I am so blessed to have a large family—plenty to share with you!" Gabby chuckled as she continued, "Even if they are a bit crazy at times, I love them just the same." She raised her hand to indicate a change of subject. "But tell me more! What was so important that you wanted to share with me earlier?"

Kyra let out a nervous giggle. "I've had so many wonderful . . . and *strange* experiences in both Madrid and Andalucía! When I tell you about them, I hope you won't think I'm *loca.*"

"*Mi familia*—now that's the definition of crazy! Nothing you say will surprise me. I promise," Gabby said with a comforting laugh, which eased Kyra's fears.

"Oh, gosh. I don't even know where to begin, but here goes . . ." Kyra took a deep breath. "When I was in Madrid, I experienced two *flashbacks*, I guess you could call them. The first one happened in the front of the *Teatro Español*—the Spanish theater in Madrid. I had an overwhelming feeling I had been there before. Then my head started spinning, and I closed my eyes. When I finally opened them again, I swear I'd been transported back to the eighteen hundreds! The people around me were dressed in old-fashioned clothing, and then, within a minute or so, I was back in the present moment."

Kyra paused a moment, watching Gabby's eyes grow wide with astonishment. Then she continued, "The second time was at the Royal Palace in Madrid. This episode was even *stronger* than the first. I was standing in the throne room when suddenly I felt like I was in an even earlier time period—as a young boy, no less! I was kneeling in front of the King and Queen of Spain. I was a servant accompanying my master, a nobleman. I was so shocked . . . but, even stranger, I *totally* understood the language they were speaking, which of course was Spanish! Within a minute or two, I was back in the visitor's area of the throne room with the other tourists. I know this all sounds too incredible to be real, Gabby . . ." Kyra's voice finally trailed off.

"Of course I totally believe you! *A veces el mundo está loco.*" Gabby replied.

Kyra nodded, *The world is crazy*, she agreed.

Gabby went on, "I think I've heard of this type of thing before . . . but didn't you say there's *more* that happened?"

Kyra laughed. "Well, there was Juan Pablo. I met him when I was out with Javier and Verónica one evening. At first I thought he was very attractive, but perhaps a little too young for me." Kyra grinned but dismissed the thought with a wave. "Truthfully, I quickly realized he was pretty shallow and that made him much less attractive . . . a good lesson for me."

"Don't be too hard on yourself. He was not your destiny." Gabby reassured her.

"It was fun and did help build my confidence, but yes, he was not my destiny. Oh, but wait 'til I tell you about the priest!" Kyra teased, fully capturing her friend's attention. "I got lost one day, and I stumbled upon a church in Madrid where I ended up asking a very handsome priest for help. When I first laid eyes on him, I swore he was the most attractive man I had ever seen. The connection was so strong, it felt like I had known him in another lifetime," Kyra's voice trailed off again.

"Go on," Gabby urged, clearly enjoying her friend's rundown of her adventures. "I'm all ears!"

"I wondered for a moment if we were destined to be together, but that didn't make any sense because he's a man of God. I mustered up my courage and asked for directions. After speaking with him, I realized he was an amazingly kind and selfless person. He was so helpful to me, and as it turned out, we shared similar experiences in that the death of a loved one changed our lives forever. In his case, he lost his younger brother who inspired him to become a priest."

Gabby sat on the edge of her seat as Kyra continued, "I may have been attracted to his energy—his aura—and his kind and loving demeanor. I was so impressed with his desire to help people through his love of God and his position with the clergy. It turns out we *were* destined to meet . . . so that I could see his amazing work in helping others." Kyra took another deep breath.

"I'm very proud of you, *Chica*," Gabby responded with empathy and understanding. "You've come so far."

"I hope you know how much I appreciate your support," Kyra thanked her, "but I'm not done rambling just yet."

Gabby reached across the table to give Kyra's hand a squeeze. "That's okay, I'm not done listening yet."

Kyra laughed, becoming more animated in her story telling. "While in Madrid, I also went to a bookstore and found the exact same Reiki manuals we used back in grad school—in *English*, no less—which was a miracle in and of itself! But even stranger is that the store clerk's brother is a Reiki Master, who was offering the Reiki Level 1 Class the *very next* day. I couldn't believe my luck and took it as a refresher course! Plus, I met the most wonderful people in the class."

Gabby's eyes lit up. "Yes, the Universe *is* conspiring to help you—most definitely." She grinned from ear to ear. "*El destino tiene una manera de llegar cuando menos te lo esperas.* Or should I say, destiny *has* found you."

"Yes, perhaps it has indeed. I also had a *third* strange intuitive flash in *Málaga*. But brace yourself for this one. . . ." Kyra paused, collecting herself. "I was talking to Raquel and all of a sudden I could *see* her somewhere in the future." Kyra described the entire vision to Gabby, and as she concluded, she felt a tear pooling in her eye.

Astounded, Gabby responded, "Your gift has expanded dramatically. I can't wait to see if Raquel becomes a volunteer for UNICEF!"

"Oh, but I've saved the strangest experience for last—which happened at the hotel in *Málaga*." Kyra felt her skin tingle as she thought back on her experience.

Gabby leaned forward, almost falling off her seat.

"When I was a child, I had a recurring dream, which I had forgotten until recently. In the six weeks since my grandmother passed and I began this journey, I've been remembering bits and pieces of it. Finally, the dream came back to me fully one night in *Málaga*. At the very end of it—the most important part—I'm standing by the ocean on a long sandy beach."

Gabby looked intense, but Kyra kept speaking without missing a beat. "Remember, as a young child, I had never actually seen the ocean. But, in my dream, I'm a child, of course, standing on the shoreline at nighttime. The moon is full and the light is reflecting across the ocean waves. I'm playing at the edge of the water, and suddenly, I sense that I'm not alone. I turn around and see a woman standing next to me. She's dressed in an ancient-looking gown and we have a conversation, which I couldn't remember until now—"

Gabby started to speak, but Kyra put her hand up, asking her to wait.

"I woke in the middle of the night at the hotel in *Málaga* and the same woman visited me again. She was hovering at the foot of my bed, and said she was part of my soul family. She also said she was my *spirit guide* and visiting me because I was finally ready. She revealed to me my life purpose, which included Reiki and helping others. She even told me about a future event to make sure I wouldn't later think it was all a dream."

Gabby's head bobbed, begging Kyra to continue, and she complied: "Raquel didn't seem to notice anything out of the ordinary—in fact, she slept straight through till morning. She snores just like you."

Gabby rolled her eyes, pretending she had no idea what Kyra was talking about.

"The next day when I woke up, I felt . . . well, *amazing* is the only word to describe it! I felt like I'd had ten massages, and my body felt so relaxed and I was light as a feather! Oh, but do you remember when the fortune-teller predicted I'd go to another foreign country that was lush and green with a mountain of spiritual importance? Well, I started having a *new* recurring dream in Madrid, and in this dream, I was standing in that foreign land. A man in his fifties was motioning for me to follow him somewhere. At first, I couldn't figure out where I was standing or who the man was. But suddenly it hit me like a bolt of lightning—the man is Dr. Mikao Usui, the founder of Reiki."

Gabby gasped, her expression both shocked and delighted. "That's amazing!"

"I wanted to tell you all this, because, yes, I'm definitely joining you in England for the Reiki Master Training class! I contacted the Reiki Institute and, to my surprise, they had a last-minute cancelation to accommodate me. They'll even put us together in the same room. I'll arrive late Saturday night for the five-day training course. That's a week from today! How's *that* for synchronicity?"

"I'm *soooo* thrilled! We will have a blast—just like back in grad school. If you were Alejandro, I'd kiss you," Gabby said giddily. "Oh, I just might just do that anyway." She leaned across the table and gave Kyra a big kiss on the cheek.

"I'm excited too, but I have one more thing to share with you." Kyra clasped Gabby's hand with a knowing look on her face. "Remember the lush green land with the mountain of spiritual importance?"

Gabby nodded in anticipation.

"It finally struck me *where* I'm supposed to go and *why*. You won't believe this, Gabby." Kyra paused, looking her friend directly in the eyes. "In the morning, I have a whole different trip planned. I'll meet you in England a week from today, but tomorrow I'm off to Japan!"

# Part 4

# Journey to Japan

# 32

Kyra breathed a grateful sigh of relief when her flight to Kansai International Airport took off without delay. It would be a long journey indeed, with her first flight leaving Barcelona and landing in Paris in just under two hours. Now her connecting flight to Osaka would take eleven-plus hours.

Kyra calculated the total travel time, including her layover, to be more than fifteen hours. "*Whew!*" she exclaimed silently, recalling how frequently she had flown to Asia for work. *That feels like a lifetime ago. I'm so excited to be taking this trip just for me!*

She thought about her arrival the next day and meeting up with her friend and former colleague, Angela. The women had initially struck up a friendship because they had been among the few females in the executive ranks at Vortex. This had given them a unique bonding opportunity, despite their vastly different cultural backgrounds. That being said, Kyra recognized how little she knew about Angela outside of work. *How ironic that destiny has brought us together now,* she mused.

A Senior Vice President at Vortex, Angela had a role similar to Kyra's former position at the company, but she headed up the entire Asia Pacific region. She was now living in Kyoto, which was more than an hour's drive from the airport. If Kyra remembered correctly, Angela was around forty-three years old or about eight years her senior.

Kyra thought back fondly to their first meeting. Angela had worn a conservative gray suit, and her medium-length, silky black hair perfectly framed her dark, almond-shaped eyes. When she'd stepped forward and extended her arm for a handshake, Kyra noticed she was slender in build, and stood about five-foot-four—just slightly taller than she.

Energetic and witty, Angela was from Tokyo originally. As they gradually got to know each other, Kyra learned that her family had immigrated to the United States when Angela was a child. So, while Angela was now quite American in her mannerisms and outlook, she also spoke fluent Japanese. This had made her the ideal candidate for promotion to the general manager role heading up Vortex's Asia Pacific region, which required her relocation back to Japan.

The women had been meeting up over the years during Kyra's quarterly trips to Asia for supplier meetings. Their friendship and respect had deepened over long hours spent working together, but they'd never really discussed much beyond business and simple pleasantries. *Ah, but that was our old corporate life!* Kyra decided, eager for new possibilities. *This is a fresh chapter—and a chance to deepen my friendship with Angela.*

In fact, Angela had completely surprised Kyra by offering up her home in Kyoto when she'd simply asked for a hotel recommendation. Given her impromptu planning, Kyra felt tremendously grateful for the unexpected kindness. Indeed, she felt blessed by the opportunity to see Angela again, especially since they were no longer colleagues.

*I'm excited to get to know her better,* Kyra said, smiling to herself. *I've always admired her street smarts and work ethic—not to mention her direct and no-nonsense style.* This last thought made her chuckle. She wondered what her friend would be like in a purely social setting.

Kyra spent the next several hours of flight time mapping out the places she planned to visit. Her short stay of four days required careful planning to accomplish her goals, but she knew that Angela would have some recommendations too.

*How lucky for me that Angela's taking tomorrow off so we can spend the day together,* she thought, as she finished flipping through the last few pages of her guidebook. Then her brow furrowed. Given Angela's jam-packed work schedule, taking a day off on such short notice was virtually impossible—which made Kyra worry if everything at Vortex was okay for her friend.

A flash of intuition suddenly flowed into her mind. Despite how frequently Kyra had come to experience this type of sensation lately, it still sent chills along her arms. She rubbed her skin to warm herself.

*It feels like Angela is unsettled or contemplating something new in her life.* Trying to sense a little deeper, she took a breath, but the exact details of Angela's circumstances weren't clear. *My intuition seems to be telling me that everything is fine overall . . . I guess I'll just trust the Universe and see what unfolds.* When the curious feeling subsided, Kyra took a sleep aide and drifted off to sleep for her overnight flight.

The Boeing 777 touched down uneventfully the next morning at 8:10 am local time. After passing through customs, Kyra breathed a huge sigh of relief when she saw her black bag with the purple ribbon tied on the handle waiting for her on the luggage carousel.

"I am truly blessed *you* were not lost during any of my travels!" Kyra said softly to her suitcase. "Thank you, Angels—for all of your help."

She wheeled her bag quickly away and stepped outside to wait for Angela—finding herself embraced by the heat of the morning. Glancing at the weather app on her phone, she was surprised it was already 77 degrees Fahrenheit. It was early July, and Kyra had forgotten how pronounced the summer heat would feel later in the afternoon, reaching temperatures of over 90 degrees. Perspiration began to drip down the back of her neck as she waited, feeling the full-on humidity. She wiped her brow with a tissue, determined to adapt to the sultry temperatures prevalent in Japan this time of year.

Angela pulled up several minutes later in her lotus-gray Audi sedan. The car appeared to fit her friend perfectly; it was sleek, metallic, and clearly matched Angela's no-nonsense style. Despite the vehicle's cool-looking exterior, it radiated a calm beauty beneath the surface. Kyra stepped forward as her former colleague got out of the car, and extended her arm for a friendly handshake.

"Kyra, it's so very nice to see you again, and welcome to Japan!" Angela said, as a smile spread across her lips. "Come, let's get your suitcase into my trunk."

"It's really terrific to see you again too, Angela," Kyra replied, wheeling her suitcase to the back of the car. The two women hoisted the bag into the roomy trunk.

Angela took a moment to catch her breath after the heavy lifting. "I'd love to hear all about your travels since leaving Vortex. I'm still shocked that they eliminated your position . . . it's just so ridiculous and unfair."

"I think I'm over my shock—but I'm feeling confident that only good will come from all this." Kyra slid into the passenger seat and added, "But more importantly, I'm looking forward to spending time here in Japan—and with you!"

During the nearly one-hour drive north to Kyoto from the airport, the women chatted openly, first briefly updating each other on their personal lives and then discussing Vortex and current happenings at the company. After listening politely to Angela, Kyra deliberately changed the subject from Vortex to focus on more positive things. "I know we're not stopping in Osaka today because it's south of the airport, but can you tell me a bit about Osaka and Kyoto? I'm trying to get a handle on the subtle differences between the cities since I've never been to either before."

"Oh most definitely," Angela replied, happy to accommodate her friend's request. "I know you've spent considerable time in Tokyo for business—which is, of course, the capital of Japan—but Osaka and Kyoto *are* distinctly different. Osaka is perhaps viewed as a more modern city." She paused and looked over at Kyra with a slight grin, softening her more formal demeanor. "And you'll find this humorous—Osaka is known for *kuidaore,* which in Japanese roughly means 'eat 'til you drop.' Here in Osaka, we seem to be obsessed with food."

An unexpected giggle burst from Kyra's lips. "I can certainly appreciate that one. In Spain, I definitely ate 'til I've dropped! Those Spaniards have a passion for their food too."

Angela smothered a laugh, beginning to let her guard down. "Ah, you must be a *foodie!* I look forward to hearing about your adventures in Spain—including the amazing food."

Kyra indicated that she would gladly comply.

"Excellent, but first let me finish telling you about Kyoto," Angela continued. "It's about half the size of Osaka, but a nice mixture of both modern and traditional Japan. I guess you could say Osaka is thought of as more *urban*, while Kyoto is more *refined*. That's actually why I choose to live there, but I do spend a lot of time in Tokyo for work, not to mention all my heavy traveling across the region…"

Angela's voice died away, and she looked at Kyra, who sympathized with her stressful work schedule. "I understand where you're coming from," Kyra assured her.

"Yes, but I'm truly pleased you wanted to visit Kyoto specifically," Angela added. "It was spared a lot of the devastation of World War II, and there are some really cool historical sites to see." Her enthusiasm seemed to grow with her smile. "I'm looking forward to showing you our city."

Kyra returned the smile. "Thank you so much for your generosity. I really owe you for this."

"You don't owe me anything. It's my pleasure! I do have some fun places planned for us today—we'll cover the major highlights of the city. I thought we'd visit the famous temple *Kinkaku-ji*." Angela pronounced the name slowly so Kyra could practice saying it.

"In English, it's known as the Golden Pavilion," she explained. "*Kinkaku-ji* is covered in fourteen-karat gold leaf—and it's a sight to behold! We'll also see *Ginkaku-ji*, the Silver Pavilion, which, by the way, has *no* silver on it at all. I'll explain that later. But, first, we'll stop by the *Fushimi Inari-taisha*, which is a shrine complex not to be missed. It honors the *Inari Ōkami*, the fox spirit, who is the patron of rice, fertility, and prosperity in business. It'll be a fabulous place for you to see as well."

Excited for the adventures to come, Kyra kept her full attention on Angela's descriptions. She wasn't sure how rice, fertility, and prosperity all fit together, but it sounded like a triple blessing.

"Last but not least…" Angela paused for effect. "Later this afternoon, we'll stop for some refreshment at a Japanese teahouse, and afterward, I have an outstanding dinner planned."

"That's a lot to take in, but it all sounds incredible." Kyra laughed. "And, as for an outstanding dinner, I have no doubt it will be! You do know how much I love my food."

Angela's thin eyebrows rose playfully. "I know you've planned your itinerary for the next two days, but on your last day here if you'd like to spend more time in Kyoto—or if you're interested in visiting Osaka—let me know, and I'll make some recommendations."

"Thank you," Kyra replied. "Let's talk about that more over dinner. Again, I so appreciate your taking today off on such short notice—by the way, *how* did you pull that off?"

"As you know, my schedule is typically booked a month in advance." Angela laughed at the absurdity. "I told my boss I had a family emergency and completely cleared my calendar today. I rarely take my vacation time, so I thought, *What the heck?* I told my secretary to just do it." Angela sounded like a mischievous child skipping out of school for the day.

"You go, girl!" Kyra encouraged. Back in her corporate days, she would never have had the nerve to make such a decision.

"To tell you the truth, I've been secretly wishing I could play hooky from work, so you couldn't have contacted me at a better time." A pensive expression crossed Angela's features. "I enjoy what I do for a living, of course, but I'm realizing, as I get older, there's so much more to life than just working all the time. . . ."

Kyra recalled her flash of intuition on the plane. She could clearly sense that Angela's life was indeed unsettled. In the back of her mind, she wondered, what Angela was planning to do.

The women stopped first at the Fushimi Inari-taisha, which was the southernmost destination they planned to visit that day.

"As I mentioned earlier, Kyra, this is the most famous shrine dedicated to *Inari Ōkami*. It's also one of our busiest Shinto shrines here in Kyoto. We're seeing it first to avoid the crowd later in the day."

They parked the car and walked toward the entrance. Once again, Kyra felt sweat rolling down the back of her neck, but she stepped forward lightheartedly, not letting the weather dampen her enthusiasm.

"As you can see," Angela began as they walked along the trail, "we're approaching the main gate near the entrance of the shrine. It was built back in the late fourteen hundreds, but some of the original structures go back to as early as *eight hundred A.D.* Isn't that fascinating?"

"I've been truly humbled by all the ancient architecture I've seen since starting my journey, first in Israel, then in Spain . . . and now here." Kyra blinked back an unexpected tear. She felt incredibly appreciative of every step along her path and looked forward to what the day would hold. "I finally know how important it is to take the time to appreciate how something old can still be so beautiful *and* meaningful. . . . It's rather like our best relationships, too."

In her mind, Kyra replayed Nana's advice on this topic: "Sweetie, in life, our most important relationships withstand the test of time. They're like King David's tomb on Mount Zion. Now *that's* been around since ninth century CE!" Kyra's heart warmed, feeling like Nana's presence had pierced the veil, and her grandmother was actually whispering to her now, so clear was her voice.

Angela interrupted her thoughts with her own reflection: "My grandmother had a wonderful family saying about the beauty of relationships that endure the test of time. She said, 'The noblest of oak tree starts from a single acorn. As it ages, it reaches its branches up toward the heavens. It chooses to grow, even during the worst of storms—but it's not until the tree becomes old that its full beauty is revealed.'"

Kyra was taken aback by the synchronicity of their thoughts. "That's amazing, Angela—and so strange. I was just thinking about my grandmother and how she told me something incredibly similar. I guess we have a wise grandmother in common, too."

"I think we have both weathered a few storms in our lives." Angela's eyes lit up. "But now it's time for us to thrive! I've been giving that a good deal of thought."

The women now stood in front the giant rōmon, or tower gate, the massive red-and-white painted wooden portal that lay just on the outskirts of the main shrine. Kyra stepped forward and felt as if she had been transported into yet another strange but wonderful world. *I've fallen through the rabbit hole twice!* She laughed, recalling when she and Gabby had compared *Parc Güell* to *Alice in Wonderland.*

But, today, instead of a whimsical stone temple and a mosaic-tiled lizard, the first marvel that captured Kyra's attention was a set of bronze foxes guarding the entrance of the main gate. One fox had a key in its mouth, and both were more stylized than realistic.

"The *kitsune*, or foxes, protect the entrance to our temples Kyra," Angela explained. "The foxes are thought to have magical qualities that increase with age or wisdom."

"I can *feel* the magic," Kyra replied, "and it so reminds me of a childhood dream I had with enchanted creatures like these foxes." Kyra could clearly picture the forest animals and the mystic feeling of being in the dreamscape. She took a moment to let the happy feeling permeate her aura, and then signaled to Angela to lead them further along their magical adventure.

The women explored a series of buildings on the property, each of which made Kyra's heart jump. They tried not to walk too fast to fully appreciate each site. Angela offered descriptions of the Gai-haiden, or outer hall of worship; the Nai-haiden, or inner hall of worship; and finally the honden, or main sanctuary.

As Kyra stood in front of the main sanctuary, she noticed it was the same bright red and white as the giant rōmon style gate they had seen when they'd first entered. It had an elongated black sloping roof, and the exterior of the building bore an intricate design of gold filigree. Kyra's eyes danced over the elegant, graceful facade.

She especially enjoyed seeing the interior of the main sanctuary, as well as the many statues and fountains on the grounds. She could imagine long-ago Japanese noblemen gracefully strolling the grounds, lost in quiet meditation. A peaceful feeling settled deep in her core, and she felt completely at ease alongside Angela, thoroughly appreciating this guided experience. Soon, they began to draw near the far end of the lush grounds.

"Now we're going to see the inner shrine called *Okumiya*," Angela informed her. "It's reachable by a pathway called *Senbon-Torii,* which means *one thousand gates*, and they are all bright red. The gates are so close together that they create a remarkable optical illusion of being in a red tunnel."

"That's fascinating . . . and what are these markings on each of the gates?" Kyra asked, studying the first gate as they approached it.

"That's a great question." Angela chuckled. "As I mentioned before, *Inari Ōkami* is actually the patron of business, prosperity, and success in Japan. And you will appreciate this." She paused to build suspense. "Each *torii*—or gate, in English—was donated by a Japanese business sponsor. The price of a donated gate can range from two hundred thousand Yen to *over one million Yen*—and there may be more than *ten thousand* gates here. Yup, we invented sponsorship of our shrines here in Japan long before Westerners ever dreamed of it." A resounding laugh escaped Angela's lips, but she quickly regained her composure, as quiet respect was the norm for walking about the grounds.

"You crack me up!" Kyra responded in a respectful whisper that was loud enough for her friend to hear.

Feeling lighthearted, the pair continued their ascent through the nearly one thousand bright red gates on the pathway leading up to the hiking trails.

"It's like walking through a giant kaleidoscope—it's unlike anything I've ever experienced," Kyra remarked, as they reached the halfway point. But, an unexpected feeling of disorientation overcame her, and she admitted this to her companion. "It's almost giving me vertigo. Kyra came to a full stop and caught her breath.

"Are you okay?" Angela asked with concern.

"I'm fine," Kyra replied shakily. "I need a moment to adjust to the elevation, I think. Right now, though, I'm just enjoying the view."

Sensing her friend's anxiety, Angela came to a stop and looked up at the sky wistfully. "I find that nature is my . . . well, *sanctuary,* I suppose," she said softly. "It helps me release stress and gets me grounded when I'm not at work. I come here often for meditation and spiritual connection—a moment of sanity in my insane schedule."

Angela fell silent then, and Kyra suspected she was contemplating her life again. She looked at her former colleague and intuitively felt her deep longing for something more meaningful in her life. The feeling was a familiar one, and she took a breath to center herself. "I always feel closer to God when I've spent time in nature, too. That's exactly what I do in California, but at Muir Woods and the beach too."

"How amazing we have that in common too," Angela responded. "We have a beautiful proverb here in Japan: 'The winds may fell the massive oak, but bamboo bent, even to the ground, will spring upright after the passage of the storm.'" Angela glanced at Kyra, misty-eyed. "You know, Kyra, I think I needed to be reminded of that today."

Just as Kyra was about to respond, a sleek red fox ran out onto the path and stopped in front of them before darting off back into the shelter of the woods. Startled, Kyra caught her breath, but she noticed with surprise that Angela was smiling at the tiny creature's brief visit.

"I seem to be attracting wildlife wherever I go lately," Kyra commented quite seriously. "Many different animals have been crossing my path, and it makes me wonder if the fox has a message for me. That may sound a bit strange to you . . ." Kyra's voice lowered, wondering what her friend's response would be.

A sly look crossed Angela's face, catching Kyra off-guard. "We regard foxes as messengers of *Inari* here in Japan, and actually, I've come to appreciate our more ancient traditions from my grandmother's stories. Or perhaps it's my own way seeking of wisdom as I grow older—not that I'm that old, mind you!" She laughed.

"Neither of us is old," Kyra agreed. "And the best is yet to come."

Angela turned and pointed to a fox statue on the ground nearby. "Have you noticed that many of the fox statues are holding a key or a jewel in their mouths? The reason I smiled when the fox ran out in front of us is because the jewel, Kyra, is a symbol of wish fulfillment. Make a wish, and perhaps it will come true."

Kyra closed her eyes and silently made a wish. When she opened them again, she said playfully, "I just put in a very attractive, tall order, so let's see what the Universe grants me."

Angela giggled. "I look forward to hearing how your wish is fulfilled, my dear Kyra. You've inspired me to make a wish too." And with that, Angela closed her eyes and silently offered the Universe a different wish—one that was near and dear to her own heart.

# 33

A lovely walk on the hiking trails with stops at smaller shrines along the way concluded their visit to the Fushimi Inari-taisha. The lush, green grounds were in full summer bloom, with an assortment of white chrysanthemums, bright yellow roses, and blue hydrangea mixed into the greenery. Splendidly tall trees offered a canopy of shade when the women needed a break from the sweltering heat, and sunlight filtered through the leaves, sending sparkles of light across their path when their branches swayed.

Kyra's heart filled with joy when she finally glimpsed a breathtaking view of the city of Kyoto. They had just stopped on Mount Inari, having reached their turnaround point, and the city rested serenely beneath them.

"I adore the Japanese affinity for nature. I think I may have been Japanese in another lifetime." Kyra joked, but silently wondered if it might be true.

"Yes, this is a most enchanting place," Angela acknowledged, glancing lovingly at the forest surrounding them. "It feeds my soul. I never grow tired of visiting this place."

Kyra felt awed by the new dimension added to their friendship through the sharing of their spiritual connection to nature. She knew without a doubt that she and Angela were meant to connect right now and share this special experience together.

After finishing their walk, they headed to the Kinkaku-ji, or Golden Pavilion. Angela filled Kyra in on the uniqueness of this temple as they drove toward their destination. "You already know the *Fushimi Inari-taisha* is a Shinto shrine, but the Golden Pavilion is actually a Zen Buddhist temple. It's really spectacular with the top two floors completely covered in *fourteen-karat gold leaf!* It was owned by one of our shōguns—who was a military leader here in Japan." She raised her voice slightly, communicating her excitement. "The shōgun who owned this house donated it in the early fourteen hundreds to become a Zen Buddhist temple or a place of worship. Unfortunately, the original structure was destroyed several times by fire, but the building we'll see today was rebuilt in the nineteen fifties. I think you will enjoy it just the same."

Kyra wasn't sure another temple could top the last one, but to her astonishment, it most certainly did. As they approached the Golden Pavilion, she saw a refined, but richly decorated exterior, covered in sparkling fourteen-karat gold just as Angela had described. The sunlight radiated off the top two floors, giving it an ethereal not-of-this-world mystique. The temple sat directly across from them, beyond a large, pale green pond that reflected a soft mirror image of the shimmering structure. The pastel blue summer sky above was also reflected in the water, infusing the scenery with the peaceful feeling of a Monet-inspired painting.

As they ventured nearer, Angela explained that although they could not actually enter the Golden Pavilion, they could somewhat view the interior by looking through the first-floor windows from across the pond.

Kyra squinted and spied what she thought was a large Buddha statue through one of the windows—and would have sworn that the Buddha had also caught a glimpse of her! *Is he smiling back at me?* she wondered, noting a peculiar but joyous sensation in her heart. Her imagination felt untethered and playful—an awareness that had started during her journey through Spain. She was enjoying her view of the Universe in this more childlike way, and she chuckled to herself. *Buddha looks very happy today.* She did a double take, though, when she thought the Buddha winked back at her!

Angela didn't seem to notice anything, and instead offered some noteworthy details of the interior as they gazed across the water. "Each floor is decorated in a different architectural style." She gestured toward the temple. "The first floor is done in the *shinden-zukuri* style, or palace style, which was common in the mansions built for our nobility. It's an open space that uses lots of natural wood pillars and white plaster. The second floor is built in the *buke-zukuri* style for our military noblemen, and is simpler with lots of sliding wood doors. The third floor is done in a traditional *zen* style and has a more spiritual feel to it. And, finally, the roof is capped with a golden phoenix! See it up there?" Angela pointed to the top of the temple.

Kyra shielded her eyes and peered upward. A magnificent golden phoenix was indeed perched on the roof, and its finely etched feathers glistened in the bright sunlight. "The phoenix is a mythical bird, right? At least I don't think it ever really existed."

"Yes, you're right," Angela said, her voice sentimental. "My grandmother used to tell me stories about the phoenix when I was a child. In Japan, the phoenix is a symbol of the Imperial House or the Japanese monarchy. It represents the power sent from the heavens to the emperor." Her voice shifted to a more teasing tone. "You probably already know the legend of the phoenix. . . When the bird dies, it bursts into flames, but springs anew from the ashes. It's *reborn.*"

"I *love* that legend," Kyra said. "In fact, it's the perfect metaphor for me right now. I feel like I'm entering a new phase of my life with a major transformation underway—just like the phoenix."

"It seems we both are in the midst of major transformations," Angela replied, her voice a little pensive, "but mine has yet to unfold."

For a brief moment, Angela's reflection brought Kyra back to a difficult time in her life when, as a child, she had longed for her parents' love. A pang of hurt washed across her heart as she remembered her own transformation and journey of healing. Letting the feeling pass, she sent her parents a silent message: *I hope you are being born anew in heaven, Mother and Father—just like the phoenix—and that you are happy now.*

A lighthearted feeling of warmth, similar to the experience she had whenever she thought of Nana, instantly engulfed Kyra's heart. It felt like a confirmation from the beyond that her parents were sending their love in response to her sentiments.

Feeling renewed and hopeful, Kyra walked with Angela back to the car and next ventured to Ginkaku-ji, the Silver Pavilion, which stood on the east side of the city at the base of the Higashiyama Mountains.

Angela quickened her pace, clearly enjoying the task of sharing her beloved homeland with Kyra.

"The Silver Pavilion was also donated by a famous shōgun," Angela began, "so it could be turned into a Zen Buddhist temple, too. But, like I mentioned earlier, while the Golden Pavilion is covered in gold leaf, the Silver Pavilion doesn't have a spot of silver on it!" Angela gave Kyra a sidelong glance. "Are you wondering why?"

"I adore gold, but silver is my true love," Kyra said deadpan. "So you certainly have my attention."

"It's good to know I have your attention, my *onna shōgun*—I just called you a female shōgun in Japanese." Angela laughed and repeated the term slowly so Kyra could learn the pronunciation. "Our legend says the temple was supposed to be covered in silver, but the shōgun never got around to finishing it. Another legend says that the moonlight at nighttime reflected silver off the once-dark-lacquer exterior, making it look silvery. I'll let you choose which story you like best."

Kyra recalled the silver moonlight in her childhood dream, feeling as if she'd momentarily stepped into a fantasy. She envisioned herself standing on the shoreline, watching the beautiful, silvery light reflecting off the crashing ocean waves. She began playing in the water and knew that Arianna would be arriving soon.

Coming back to the present moment, she spoke softly, still lost in her thoughts: "I love the idea of the moonlight reflecting off the building, giving it a silvery appearance . . . *very* mysterious and maybe even a little eerie."

"Eerie indeed," Angela replied. "Are you alright? You look like you just saw a ghost."

Intrigued by her friend's seemingly intuitive observation, Kyra replied, "I was just remembering a childhood dream. It was also full of silvery moonlight . . . and a very special woman visited me there." She cast a nervous glance at Angela. "Perhaps I'll fill you in on the details of it later, if you'd like."

"I'd like that very much," Angela agreed, and then she fell silent. Kyra sensed by the far-off look on her friend's face that she too was revisiting her own forgotten childhood dreams.

The grounds were deeply wooded and covered in delicate soft moss. Angela led Kyra to the Kannon-den, or Kannon Hall, the temple's main building. It stood two stories high, and its exterior was covered in dark wood, but as Angela had previously mentioned, much of the lacquer that had once adorned the building had long ago worn off. The matching dark wood roof sloped gently upward in the traditional, elongated Japanese style, giving the building a time-honored but mystical look. Large windows with white shades softened the somewhat foreboding appearance, and a calm sea-foam green pond lay serenely in front of the building. After a brief tranquil visit, the women headed to the nearby Tōgu-dō building.

Respectful of the other visitors, Angela whispered, "This building is famous for its study room covered in *tatami,* floor mats made of rice straw. It's thought to be the earliest known example of the *shoin-zukuri* architectural style used for our shōguns. *Tatami* are very traditional, but they are still in use in many of the homes and restaurants throughout Japan."

Kyra stepped closer to Angela to make a subtle reply. "I admire the simplicity of the style. I'm definitely feeling very Zen today." She laughed softly, seeing the simple beauty that existed in everything and realizing how much she longed to spend time meditating.

The women continued their walk around the grounds and came upon a unique sand garden called the *Ginshadan*, or sea of silver sand, as Angela pointed out. Kyra was fascinated by the simple elegance of the carefully raked lines in the sand, which gave the garden a rich and textured design. The sand drew her thoughts back to her many peaceful visits to Stinson Beach.

*A sand garden would be a serene addition to my future new home with my sweetheart,* Kyra contemplated, *and a perfect place for daily meditation.* She snapped a few quick photographs to capture the scene and to file away later for future manifesting.

The women finished their visit with a stroll through the moss garden, which accommodated several ponds, many of which housed islands with small wooden bridges. A pathway worked its way up a gently sloping hill, offering a nice elevated, expansive view of the peaceful grounds.

"I'm so thankful for our visit here today," Kyra commented. "It's really inspired me, and I feel confident that I was meant to come here to Japan. I can't wait to discover how the next three days are going to unfold."

"I can't wait for you to tell me about the remainder of your plans," Angela replied, eager to hear more. "Let's head to the tea ceremony and you can fill me in there. Okay?"

With a nod of her head, Kyra agreed and the pair strolled energetically toward their next destination. The cozy teahouse, Hana-An, was just off a busy street in the district known as Gion, the area famous for its *geisha*—traditional Japanese women trained to act as hostesses and entertain men with song, dance, and conversation. Angela mentioned this teahouse was geared a bit more toward tourists since the entire ceremony would take about an hour to perform. The more traditional tea ceremonies, she explained, could take up to four hours of time, which did not fit their schedule.

The place was indeed tranquil, but Kyra began to sense that they had stepped back into a totally different era. And much to her delight, it was a time in which things were not rushed and traditions were cherished. They were seated on traditional tatami mats on the floor, and quietly waited for the ceremony to begin. Kyra spoke softly, trying to fill Angela in on her plans, but she quickly realized it was more about the experience of tranquility than the ability to have a conversation in the teahouse.

After a few minutes, the Tea Master slowly approached the mats at which Kyra, Angela, and a few other guests were seated. Kyra could not help but be captivated by her intricate pastel-pink kimono decorated with rose-colored flowers. Shimmering silver strands flowed through the fabric's design, reflecting the light and giving the gown an unparalleled exquisiteness. Her thick, shiny black hair was pulled back into an elaborate bun, and accentuated with pink flowers that cascaded softly down one side of her head. The flowers reminded Kyra of a fragrant waterfall and the entire ensemble was striking down the last detail. Glancing toward the floor, Kyra saw that the woman's feet were covered in traditional white socks separated at the big toe as she gingerly stepped forward to front of the room.

"The socks are called *tabi*," Angela whispered.

To Kyra's relief, the woman spoke English very well with only a slight accent. "Welcome to *Hana-An*. My name is *Mitsuko*. I am pleased that you could visit us here today. I hope you will find your experience to be peaceful and enlightening. I am more than happy to answer any questions you may have." She bowed her head for a moment, waiting for a response, then continued, "If you would like, I will explain the origins of tea in Japan first, and then we begin your tea ceremony today at *Hana-An*."

Mitsuko respectfully bowed her head again. A few murmurs of affirmation were made by the guests before she continued. "Green tea originated in China around the twenty-seventh century B.C., but the first seeds were brought to Japan during the Heian period in the early ninth century A.D.—or about thirty-six hundred years later. The first formal tea ceremony was believed to have originated during the eighth century from a Chinese Buddhist priest who wrote a book on the proper method of preparing tea. The book is called *Cha Kyou* in Japanese and *Ch'a Ching* in Chinese, which in English may have a very different meaning."

The joke was not lost on Kyra, who giggled softly and responded almost on cue, "Yes, Mitsuko, in English, *cha-ching* refers to the sound of making money. We associate it with the closing of a cash register after depositing money into it."

With that, all the patrons shared a laugh, and Mitsuko smiled in acknowledgment. "Thank you for sharing your very correct answer," she said to Kyra, and then continued in a more serious tone, "Back to our lesson on tea. Originally, the tea grown in Japan was consumed only by noblemen and priests as a type of medicine. But, eventually, green tea went through a transformation from being used only as a medicine to being consumed as a beverage among the very wealthy. Many years later—in the year eleven eighty-seven, to be exact—*Myoan Eisai*, a famous Japanese Buddhist priest, traveled to China and upon his return, began using tea for religious purposes. He was also believed to be the first person to teach the grinding of tealeaves before adding hot water."

Mitsuko paused and daintily stepped across the room and picked up a tray displaying some of the utensils. "During the same period," she continued, "Emperor *Kisou* in China referred to using a bamboo whisk to stir the tea after hot water was poured over it, in his book *Taikan Saron*, which translates into English as *A General View of Tea*. You will see in our preparation of the tea today, both of these two methods are still in use and form the basis of the tea ceremony you are sharing with us."

Mitsuko bowed her head again and waited for questions.

Angela took the opportunity to express her sentiments. "Thank you, Mitsuko, for your very thorough explanation. Kyra and I are looking forward to the tea ceremony, and we appreciate your kindness." Angela bowed her head to Mitsuko, and several of the other guests at the table offered their gratitude as well.

With the history lesson delivered, Mitsuko offered confectionary sweets or *wagashi* to each guest, which were enthusiastically consumed. Next she retrieved the tea service setup and began the ceremony. The formal, gentle flow of Mitsuko's movements fascinated Kyra, which reminded her of a t'ai chi class she had once taken. There was a certain unmistakable precision in the movements of her hands and arms, which were slow but ever so artful. It looked like a choreographed dance with each step lovingly performed. First, Mitsuko began with the proper cleaning of the tea-serving utensils, which included cleaning the bowl, tea scoop, and tea whisk.

Next Mitsuko used graceful movements to add scoops of *matcha*, or powered green tea, to the tea bowl. Then she gently ladled hot water into the bowl and used the whisk to rapidly mix the tea. She added more water until the tea was just the right consistency. Then Mitsuko handed the tea bowl to Angela, who was familiar with the proper procedure.

Angela admired the front of the bowl for a moment, bowed her head, and then turned the bowl slightly clockwise before taking a few sips. She then wiped the rim of the bowl carefully with her cloth napkin and turned to give it to Kyra, who nodded in acknowledgment, bowed her head, and repeated the process. The green tea was thick and slightly bitter tasting to Kyra, but the hot liquid warmed her throat. The sweets served earlier nicely offset the bitter flavor of the tea. Kyra next handed the bowl to the guest beside her.

Once each guest had a few sips of the tea, Mitsuko carefully cleaned the utensils and left the room. Upon returning, she prepared additional tea that was thinner in consistency and served each guest an individual bowl.

Angela whispered into Kyra's ear, "The drinking of the tea is done in silence. It's thought to help with one's spiritual satisfaction—a sort of 'meditation in motion.'"

Kyra bowed her head in acknowledgment and enjoyed the peacefulness of the moment.

After all the guests had finished their tea, Mitsuko carefully cleaned the utensils again, and then offered them to the guests for examination, as was their custom. Once finished, she collected the utensils with reverence. Each guest thanked her, as they made ready to leave the teahouse. Bows were graciously exchanged at the front door one last time.

"That was a very different experience from what I was expecting," Kyra commented, moved by the tranquility of the experience as they left Hana-An. "I've had tea in restaurants on many occasions here in Japan, but this was so much more formal—like a Zen-inspired tea meditation! Very nice to watch and experience."

Angela looked pleased. "I think the art of ceremony is very much missing in modern life. That's why I'm so glad we were able to enjoy Mitsuko's slow and loving preparation of the tea. It is almost a type of meditation or art in motion, depending on how you look at it. *Slow* is sometimes better than *fast*—unlike the culture they foster at Vortex."

Kyra nodded and felt glad to be free of her old company's regimented thinking. She had come to appreciate her friend's wisdom and made a wish that Angela would find a path that was right for her.

After the tea ceremony, the women drove to Angela's home in the Gion district, which was a short distance from the Hana-An. On the way, Angela explained that she had rented a modest two-story house, and like other similar houses in Japan, "It contains no wasted space."

When they stepped inside the main living room, Kyra could see that it was indeed tiny, but nicely furnished with modern, dark wood furniture and a large flat-screen TV on the main wall. Angela's home office computer sat on a small stand directly next to the TV, and a simple gold-toned couch offered guests a place to sit.

"Let me show you the kitchen. It's very charming," Angela said, pulling Kyra's suitcase aside so there was room to pass. Directly to the left of the living room sat an equally tiny but efficient kitchen with stainless-steel appliances, including a refrigerator and stove, but no dishwasher as there wasn't enough room.

"The homes here are smaller than what we're used to in the United States," Angela observed, affectionately running her hand across the gray granite countertop, "but this location is ideal, and I really enjoy the simplicity and the efficient use of space. Let me take you to your bedroom on the second floor."

"Thanks, Angela," Kyra replied warmly. "It's very tranquil here and I love the ambience; your home is just heavenly."

Kyra followed her hostess up the narrow staircase, carefully lugging her heavy suitcase one step at a time. She recalled Raquel's simple backpack for their overnight stay in Málaga and rolled her eyes. Once she reached the top, Kyra heaved a sigh of relief.

The two bedrooms took up the entire second floor. Both were artfully painted in subtle shades of tan complemented by light bamboo hardwood flooring. Angela's bedroom window faced east, and a quiet stream flowed outside, just beneath her window. The guestroom faced west and opened out onto a lovely balcony. Each bedroom housed a simple futon-style bed that could be folded up during the daytime, plus a simple chest of drawers for clothing. A large tatami mat sat squarely in the middle of each room. Kyra observed that a single upstairs bathroom, recently updated, included a modern sink, toilet, and shower stall, but no bathtub. Angela explained that the bathroom was shared between the two bedrooms and was the only one in the house.

"It's looks just perfect and beautifully updated. I like the efficiency, Angela," Kyra commented. Her eyes twinkled as she thought back to her luxurious bathroom in San Francisco—which was nearly the same size as Angela's guestroom.

After helping Kyra settle into her room, Angela swung open the sliding glass door and stepped out onto the balcony, inviting Kyra to follow. Once again, as soon as they were outside of the comfort of the air conditioning, the heat of the summer air drenched Kyra's skin. She rested her arms on the railing and looked out at neighboring houses.

Angela gazed off into the distance, too, seemingly lost in the moment. When her attention returned, she spoke with fondness. "In the springtime, the cherry blossoms are in full bloom. The view from this balcony is simply stunning." She turned toward Kyra. "I hope you will come back someday in the spring. It looks almost like a fairy-tale and is the most enchanting time to for a visit here."

"I would *truly* love that," Kyra agreed. "Kyoto is inspiring my need for simplicity and more time for quiet and meditation. Tokyo, by comparison, is so much more urban and busy, but beautiful just the same. I'm very much looking forward to seeing more."

After enjoying the view for a while longer, the women freshened up, taking turns in the bathroom to shower and change clothing. Kyra chose a simple black dress with her flat gold sandals, since they would be walking to the restaurant that evening. Angela decided on black slacks with a modern silk top in light yellow that wrapped around her waist, tying into a pretty bow at the back.

"Tonight we'll be dining at a really terrific restaurant called *Minoda.* Because I'm always entertaining clients for work, I was able to get us a reservation on short notice. I think you'll appreciate the experience of a traditional Japanese dinner—and I'd be honored to treat you this evening," she offered warmly.

"How sweet and very generous of you," Kyra said, feeling remiss for not having offered first. "I wish we'd spent more time getting to know each other more personally when we were colleagues—but I'm thankful that I'm getting this chance now to really know you."

"The pleasure is all mine . . . plus, you've really got me thinking about my own destiny. Your timing couldn't have been more perfect." Angela squeezed Kyra's hand affectionately.

Surprised, Kyra thought, *I'm so pleased to be helping Angela on her journey. Perhaps this is part of my life's purpose too—helping others discover their own personal truths, as I discover mine.*

As they strolled to the restaurant, Angela filled Kyra in on her upcoming business schedule, which made Kyra cringe; she definitely did not miss those jam-packed days.

"Even though I'll be traveling for the next three days, I'll be back home Friday evening, so we can have dinner together that night, too, if you'd like."

"I'd love that," Kyra responded without hesitation, "but dinner will be on me. I insist!"

Angela acquiesced, and then offered in a teasing tone, "Let's see how you like tonight's restaurant. It's over a hundred years old . . . and a *unique* dining experience."

Anxious to work on her accent, Kyra carefully pronounced the name of the restaurant and other Japanese terms once they neared the restaurant. "*Mi-no-da* looks fabulous from the outside—very simple and unassuming. You mentioned we'll be having a *Kyo-ryori* experience. What exactly does that that entail?"

"Ah, good question! *Kyo-ryori* means 'Kyoto cuisine,' but tonight we'll be treated to their *Huh Ryuh Kaiseki* dinner specifically. It's a mere eleven courses." Kyra's eyebrows arched involuntarily, and Angela laughed as she explained further, "Dinner will include a variety of foods, many of which are local delicacies found only here in Kyoto. We'll definitely be testing your ability to eat *true* Japanese cuisine tonight." Kyra's eyes widened, and Angela broke into a mischievous grin.

Kyra composed herself and said somewhat doubtfully, "Thanks, Angela . . . I *think*."

Both women smiled at her dubious tone, each well aware that

admitting a weakness at Vortex would have meant defeat in business. Kyra was glad, for once, that it was not a competition.

When they arrived at the restaurant, Angela spoke to the head hostess in fluent Japanese, explaining that they had a 7:30 pm dinner reservation for two. Kyra understood just a few words of the conversation since she had learned mainly key phrases for her many meetings in Tokyo. The hostess bowed her head and escorted the pair down a long, black-tiled hallway into an intimate dining room.

Beautiful, dark red tables with low-lying chairs furnished the room, and the pale beige coloring of the walls soothed Kyra's senses. Large sliding panels made of a soft cream fabric and light brown lacquered wood sat directly across from the women. The panels had been moved back to the edge of the walls, revealing a large window that overlooked a peaceful outdoor garden. Kyra was delighted with the calm ambiance of the room, which incorporated the natural beauty of the outdoors into the restaurant.

"This is very lovely indeed," she said. *"Dōmo arigatō!"* Kyra felt confident she had correctly said 'thank you very much' in Japanese.

"*Dōmo arigatō* . . . Mr. Roboto!" Angela replied with amusement, referencing the popular eighties song of the same name.

"The rock band Styx was an excellent Japanese language tutor," Kyra said seriously, and both women chuckled, looking quite pleased with themselves.

When the waitress arrived to take their order, Kyra admired her delicate pale-yellow kimono, which was decorated with bright red flowers. A flowing hair ornament adorned her head, and she too wore the traditional tabi white socks.

In Japanese, Angela politely ordered the *Huh Ryuh Kaiseki,* or eleven-course dinner for two, as well as a bottle of chilled sake, or rice wine, for them to share, plus green tea for two. The waitress returned with the sake and poured it into two traditional, white ceramic *choko* cups, each not much bigger than a shot glass.

"I've ordered *Daiginjo,*" Angela explained, "a premium grade sake for you to try."

"Thank you, Angela," Kyra replied, realizing she had not mentioned to Angela her temporary abstinence from alcohol.

Angela raised her tiny white cup and said, "Cheers! To your health, happiness, and wonderful journey, my dear friend."

Not wishing to appear rude, Kyra took a sip of the sake. The cool liquid was enticing on her tongue, and the light fragrant flavors melted in her mouth, reminding her of a soft fruity white wine. "Thank you so much. The sake is divine." She paused and set the cup down. "Just a few sips for me, though. I'm doing a bit of a detox. I hope that doesn't offend you. I do apologize."

"Oh, not at all. That means much more for me!" Angela replied in good humor.

At that moment, the waitress entered the room and gently placed two beautifully arranged trays of appetizers on the table. Kyra instantly recognized the dishes, including prawns boiled in spices, vegetables, and tofu. Angela wasting no time took her first bite, and Kyra began to tell her about her upcoming three days in Kyoto.

"I know I mentioned to you that I'm taking a little time off before I look for a new position," she began, "but what I haven't told you is that I'm on a spiritual journey of sorts . . . That may sound strange to you." Kyra waited patiently for Angela's response.

"I totally understand, Kyra," Angela replied, setting her chopsticks down to give Kyra her full attention. "I'm struggling with work right now because I'm burned out. I'm truly to a point where I'm seriously debating *what* changes I can make at this point in my life . . ." Kyra looked at her friend with a sympathetic frown, but Angela smiled and added, "But I digress. I would love to hear more about your spiritual journey. Please go on."

Taking her friend's cue, Kyra obliged. "It's been a difficult time for me, with losing my job . . . but more importantly with losing my grandmother, too. Nana was the most important person in my life, and she passed the same day I lost my job . . ." Kyra paused, feeling choked up. "The Universe kind of . . . gave me a double-whammy, so to speak, but it's helping me make important changes in my life and really evaluate my priorities."

"I'm so sorry," Angela said, keeping her voice steady. "Please know that you can call me anytime, even with the sixteen-hour time difference between here and San Francisco. I feel like we were meant to be in each other lives, and I know what it is like to lose a loved one."

"That's very sweet of you," Kyra replied. "I'd love to stay in touch." She smiled at her next thought. "Perhaps I got hit with a *triple* whammy—if you include the breakup with my boyfriend, Steve. But that was a loss that was clearly for my highest good." She allowed herself a moment to laugh. "I've come to realize how all my losses may have been huge blessings. They caused me to pause, take time off, and focus on myself for a change—my authentic self, and not the image of what I thought I was supposed to do to be happy. I've even been revisiting a lot of interests I had as a child and up through my grad school days—before my corporate career consumed all my time."

Angela's attention didn't falter as Kyra filled her in on her trip to Israel and then her adventures in Spain. She spoke energetically as she described her amazing time with Gabby and her crazy but lovable family members. "Those several weeks traveling across Spain helped me unwind . . . and find my passion for life again."

Kyra grinned as she recalled her more unusual experiences in Spain. Then she even shared with Angela some of the metaphysical occurrences she'd experienced, keeping her words simple, unsure if Angela would comprehend. Much to her astonishment, her friend didn't flinch, and seemed to be more open and knowledgeable than Kyra had been expecting.

"I've been consciously making decisions to spend more time doing things that truly makes me happy going forward," Kyra explained. "As you know, my career at Vortex was successful, but looking back . . . it really sucked the life out of me!"

Angela giggled. "I'm in my forties now, and I'm evaluating all areas of my own life—so I'm listening closely. Maybe you'll inspire me *before* the Universe decides to do an intervention."

Just then the waitress returned and quietly set down a tray with tea.

She poured Angela and Kyra a cup, and bowed her head as she placed the cups in front of them. After taking a generous sip, Kyra continued, "One area of interest that I intend to pursue is Reiki. When I was in grad school, Gabby and I took Reiki classes together. Do you know what Reiki is?"

"I do," Angela replied, surprised at her friend's question. "I actually had some Reiki sessions back when I lived in San Francisco. Now that I'm living in Japan, I'm scheduling a session every four weeks or so. Ironically, it was harder to find a practitioner here than in the U.S. I do find the sessions very relaxing, and I feel it helps manage my stress level with working so many hours." Angela paused for a moment, her expression introspective. "You know, Kyra, to be honest, I'd love do more fun things, like meditation and yoga classes. Sadly, I just haven't made the time."

Kyra could see the frustration on Angela's face and assured her friend, "It's never too late to make changes in your life. My grandmother taught me that—even after her death." Kyra smiled at the thought of Nana, making a conscious effort not to feel sad. "Anyway, when we were in grad school, Gabby and I took the first three levels of Reiki training. When I leave here on Saturday, I'm going to meet Gabby in England to do the Reiki Master-level class! I'm super excited to spend a whole week there—and our final ceremony is at Stonehenge! What do you think of that?"

Angela let out a laugh of irony. "Did you ever in a million years think the two of us would be sitting here, discussing life changes, spiritual journeys, *and* Stonehenge?"

"I never thought I'd do any of the things that I've done these past couple of months," Kyra replied, "but God is wonderful, and I feel blessed to have this special time for myself."

Angela rose a bit from her seated position to reach across the table for a hug. Kyra met her halfway, thrilled that her friend was finally letting her guard down. The women embraced affectionately for a moment, and as Angela returned to her seat, she happily said, "We were definitely meant to reconnect right here—right now."

In her best Japanese accent, Kyra cleverly replied, "Ah, yes, my *onna shōgun.*" Her pronunciation and sentiment elicited a giggle from Angela. "But that brings me back to why I'm here in Japan!" She let the suspense build, and Angela waved her hand for Kyra to continue. "I was guided to come here," Kyra explained, "so I'll be visiting a few spiritually oriented sites. Then, on Friday, I'll do more touristy stuff in Kyoto—especially since it's the *Gion Matsuri* holiday the entire month of July. I'll save Osaka for another visit, but I appreciate your suggestions."

"Awww . . . you are welcome, Kyra. As for me, I'm looking forward to our dinner on Friday and hearing even more about your journey—once it unfolds."

The waitress in the pale-yellow kimono returned to the room, bearing a dark wooden tray, and slowly proceeded to bring different dishes to the table. There was a delicious clear soup with tiny mushrooms and sprigs of green garnish, light and slightly salty to the taste.

*Sashimi*, or raw fish sliced thinly, a dish with which Kyra was very familiar, arrived soon after. She skillfully used her chopsticks to pick up each piece of fish, savoring the fresh flavors of the tuna, salmon, sea bream, and sea urchin.

Next the waitress brought several of the delicacies that Angela had alluded to earlier: one bowl contained whole baby eels that almost looked like noodles, another grilled fish heads, and the third sliced raw octopus.

Angela closely watched Kyra's face as she sampled the local cuisine. Kyra bravely sampled one of the fish heads, picking at it with her chopsticks for the meat the way Angela had done. Then, after she ate some of the octopus, Kyra tentatively picked up a baby eel between her chopsticks. "Um, you know," she said with a straight face, "I'm getting a bit stuffed. I may have to allow you to finish this fine delicacy by yourself."

The friends broke into spontaneous laughter.

"Feel free to eat as much as you would like," Angela replied. "I know you've had *unagi* before—but these baby *anago* eels are the best!" With that, she moved the dish of eel closer to her and dug in.

Once the bowls of delicacies were nearly empty, thanks mostly to Angela, the waitress brought rice and miso soup, then dessert—fresh seasonal fruit. Just a few bites satisfied the women's sweet tooth, refreshing their palates.

When Angela asked for the bill, Kyra knew the meal had come to a small fortune. She debated again on offering to pay or at least splitting the bill, but decided to graciously accept her friend's generosity. *Sometimes it's good to receive, and allow others to give generously to you. Steve taught me that lesson!* She chuckled inwardly. Besides, Kyra knew that she would have the opportunity to return the favor soon.

As the women made their way to the front of the restaurant, an older, distinguished-looking gentleman warmly greeted Angela. His confident, friendly demeanor suggested he was the restaurant owner, and they chatted in Japanese for several minutes. Kyra stood silently, patiently waiting for a lull in the conversation, and when the moment arrived, she interjected. Speaking carefully and slowly, she said, *"Kon-ya-wa Sutekina Oryouri-wo Arigatou Gozaimashita."*

Angela's eyebrow shot up in disbelief. Kyra had correctly said, "Thank you very much for the lovely meal this evening."

Clearly delighted that she spoke the language, the man responded rapidly in Japanese. A blank expression fell over Kyra's face, revealing, to her chagrin, that she barely understood a word. The owner offered her a big smile instead and then turned to Angela with a few parting words. He politely bowed his head to both women before they departed.

"Well done, Kyra!" Angela complimented her outside the restaurant. "You were right—Styx was a good tutor." She laughed. "But seriously, you impressed Mr. Minoda. He was appreciative of your effort—and I was impressed with your correct pronunciation. You go, girl!"

"All those meetings in Tokyo taught me a few key phrases," Kyra said humbly. "Obviously I can't carry on a conversation . . . but I do try!"

Angela's face beamed with amusement, and with that, they made short work of the walk home and quickly retired to their rooms for the evening.

Kyra unfolded her futon bed and found it more comfortable than she imagined it would be—firm, since it lay directly on the floor, but well cushioned and soft.

Stretching out on her side, she fell into a deep sleep—and in no time, she found herself once again dreaming of the Asian man. She now knew that he was Dr. Usui, the founder of Reiki, and they were standing on the same misty mountaintop they'd been on before in her dreamscape.

Just like in her previous dream, he was waving for her to join him. This time, though, she simply smiled at him and stepped forward.

# 34

The next morning when Kyra awoke, she rolled over on her side to glance at the clock. It read 9 am. *I can't believe I slept so late! I'm totally on vacation,* she thought with pleasure. She was still adjusting to the seven-hour time difference between Spain and Japan, but now she was feeling refreshed and ready to start her day.

Angela had left much earlier that morning for her business trip, so Kyra knew she had the house to herself. Ready for a morning shot of caffeine, she padded down the staircase and swung into the kitchen to make a cup of green tea.

Flipping the electric stovetop to its highest setting, she filled the kettle full of water. Next she measured out the tea Angela had left out on the countertop for her, placing several scoops of it into the teapot. She added the hot water a few minutes later, and then glanced at the note Angela had left, instructing her to look in the refrigerator for breakfast.

When she opened the small refrigerator, she cracked a smile. Several sticky notes saying "EAT ME" were stuck to various containers. She thought back to her reminder of Lewis Carroll's *Alice in Wonderland* from the day before at the Fushimi Inari-taisha. Shocked, she realized she had not even mentioned to Angela that the shrine had reminded her of the novel. It appeared to be another strange coincidence! First, in Spain when she and Gabby had compared Parc Güell to the novel simultaneously, now once again with Angela seeming to have read her mind too.

*I hope consuming this doesn't have the same effect on me as it did on Alice!* She giggled and placed a couple of containers on the countertop: miso soup, white rice, and a hardboiled egg. *A few inches of height might be nice, but I certainly wouldn't want to outgrow the house!*

Once the tea had been sufficiently steeped, she sipped the steaming beverage slowly, enjoying the traditional Japanese morning brew. *While in Japan . . . do as the Japanese do!* she thought playfully, remembering she had done the same while visiting Spain.

She enjoyed the traditional local breakfast that Angela had thoughtfully labeled and finished her tea before heading back upstairs for a shower. Afterward, she dug through her suitcase, and chose comfortable clothing for her day: a simple pair of dark blue jeans and a plain white cotton sleeveless shirt. She slipped on a pair of silver ballet slippers, which felt nice on her feet, and added some of her silver jewelry for fun.

After carefully studying her city map, Kyra tucked it into her purse and confidently stepped outside to begin her spiritual adventure. She headed several blocks north to the closet bus stop. At almost 11 am, she was right on time to meet her chosen mode of transportation for the day. The bus noisily pulled up, and Kyra boarded through the back door, making her way to an empty seat. Staring out the large window at the buildings and scenery, she became lost in sentimental thoughts. *The city of Kyoto is so beautiful*, she daydreamed. *I hope today goes smoothly.*

Twenty minutes later, Kyra paid the bus fare and exited through the front door. She stepped onto the sidewalk in front of a large modern white building that stood nine stories tall—a hospital. The bus gave a loud *hiss* and a groan as it quickly pulled away. A little nervous, she took a deep breath and walked toward the entrance stairs. The outside was meticulously landscaped with vibrant green trees and bushes of salmon-colored roses, giving the building more of a relaxed, country feel than the sterile clinical look she'd anticipated.

Her fears diminishing, Kyra went to the front reception desk and spoke to the male receptionist in English. She had written down some Japanese phrases, just in case. "I'm here to do volunteer work today," she explained and asked where she should go for her visits. The receptionist peered through his bright purple-framed reading glasses and politely responded in relatively good English, "You go to second floor, room two-twelve. Fill out paperwork and waiver. Coordinator will help you then."

Kyra bowed her head halfway in acknowledgment of his help and said, "*Dōmo arigatō,*" before heading to the elevator. On the second floor, Kyra made her way down a long corridor and entered the room where the volunteer program coordinator, a slim woman in her twenties, was sitting behind a large desk.

"My name is *Satomi*," the coordinator said, clearly enunciating her name. "Fill out paperwork, please, and I make copy of your certificates of Reiki training and then show you first patient today. Yes?"

Relieved, Kyra was grateful that Satomi spoke English. She had signed up for the program online and didn't know what to expect once she arrived. "Yes, thank you, Satomi. I'm looking forward to being of help today." Kyra spoke slowly to make sure Satomi understood her. "I'm so appreciative that you were able to fit me into your new volunteer Reiki program. I have my certificates right here. They were faxed to my hotel in *Málaga*, Spain, last week."

The young woman looked at Kyra and then glanced down at the certificates, but did not respond.

"I guess that's a little more detail than you may have needed," Kyra added nervously.

After carefully reviewing Kyra's Reiki certificates and signed waiver, Satomi replied, "Yes, Reiki program is brand new to hospital, and thank you for help today. I show you first patient and introduce you to parents, but they speak no English. I will speak to explain process to parents. You will have one full hour for Reiki session. Yes?"

"Yes, Satomi," Kyra replied, standing up and slightly bowing her head respectfully. "Thank you again."

Satomi escorted Kyra to the children's wing on the third floor. They entered a semiprivate room where a young Japanese girl, about five years old, lay in a hospital bed. Satomi turned to the girl's parents and spoke in Japanese, introducing Kyra and explaining the process for the Reiki session. Kyra couldn't fully understand her, but heard her name mentioned. She noted the girl's parents both looked grateful once the conversation had concluded.

Satomi next turned to Kyra and said, "They wish to offer their thank-you for your help today. Daughter has cancer, and Reiki helps nausea after chemo treatment. Please make comfortable? Daughter has Reiki before, so she understands. Any questions?"

Caught off guard, Kyra's eyes welled up briefly before she could gain her composure. She took a small, calming breath and replied, "Thank you, and please offer my gratitude to the parents as well."

Satomi and the parents quietly left the room. A stool waited nearby for Kyra. She closed the curtain around the bed to allow a little privacy. Sitting down, she looked lovingly at the child's face. Mustering up a smile, she pointed to herself and said, "My name is *Kyra*." She spoke slowly to emphasize her name.

The girl smiled back, pointed to herself, and said, "*Chiyo*."

"Nice to meet you, Chiyo. I will begin our session." Kyra bowed her head and offered a brief, silent prayer to seal their session in love and light, and then she silently asked God, Jesus, and the Angels to be an instrument of healing for Chiyo.

After the meditation was complete, Kyra carefully drew the Reiki symbols she had been given so very long ago in the air above the child. Then she gently placed her hands on Chiyo's left arm. Feeling a warm, soft sensation, Kyra closed her eyes as the healing energy flowed through her hands and into the child. Chiyo looked peaceful and fell into a slumber as the session continued.

Kyra kept an eye on the time, finishing the session in just under an hour. After offering a silent closing prayer, she quietly waited. Satomi soon reentered, along with Chiyo's parents and she stood up to greet them. Both parents shook Kyra's hand and thanked her in Japanese, saying "*Dōmo arigatō*." Kyra looked pleased and offered back, "*Dōitashimashite*," meaning *You're welcome*.

Feeling her heart tug, Kyra's intuition during the session had strongly suggested that Chiyo was a fighter—and not ready to leave this earth. She kept her emotions guarded and silently debated what to do, struggling with her courage to offer words of hope. Hesitating, she spoke to Satomi, whom she knew could translate. "Please say it was my pleasure to be of help. Chiyo is *quite* a fighter and such a strong girl. Please tell them that." She paused. "She has a sweet spirit, and I am honored that I could be here today to help her."

Satomi translated Kyra's words, and after a few additional bows of gratitude, she escorted Kyra to the next patient she would help today. They walked back down the long hallway to the elevator, and this time they made a stop on the fourth floor in a different wing. Satomi stopped outside the hospital room and detailed the patient's diagnosis to Kyra before the Reiki session would begin.

"This man has stroke and paralyzed completely," she said softly. "He cannot talk. But he has Reiki before and likes it very much. He can hear you okay and think okay—so yes to introduce you, and then you do session. Understand?"

"Thank you, Satomi. Yes, I understand."

They entered the room and approached the patient, a middle-aged man with slightly graying hair around his temples. He was of average height, but fairly overweight. His face did indeed look paralyzed; one side appeared more elongated than the other, but his eyes looked bright and alert. Satomi spoke in Japanese to the man, and once again Kyra heard her name mentioned. Then Satomi motioned for Kyra to sit down. "I be back in one hour," she said, and then she exited the room.

Kyra hesitated, unsure how she should address the man before she started the session. Following her intuition, she spoke in English, using a calm tone of voice. "Hi. My name is *Kyra*." Again, she pronounced her name carefully, hoping he could see her arm motion as she pointed to herself. "I know you can't understand English, but I wanted to thank you for allowing me to do this Reiki session today. I will begin now, and I will be very gentle."

The man's bright eyes seemed to beam an acknowledgment, and Kyra felt as if they had connected. She stood next to the hospital bed and drew her Reiki symbols in the air again, silently offering a prayer of healing before she began. Sitting down on the small wooden stool, she soon felt the warmth of Reiki flowing through her hands.

Suddenly, she felt an instinctive urge to stand up. She quietly pushed her stool aside, and gently moved around the man, concentrating on his arms, legs, feet, and shoulders, doing the best she could to reach him by leaning over the edge of the bed.

When Kyra touched the man's feet, she could almost *see* a moment of the man's life in her mind's eye. She seemed to flash back to a year earlier, and the man appeared to be healthy, but still overweight. He was in a living room and seemed to be having an argument with his daughter, but Kyra could not understand the words they spoke. She instinctively *felt* that he had not communicated with her since that time and that he longed to do so. The feeling was haunting, and the sadness sent a chill through her body.

*What should I do?* Kyra contemplated. She finished the Reiki session and then waited patiently for Satomi to return. As she entered the room, Kyra politely asked, "Satomi, may I tell you something important?"

"Yes, please." Satomi looked directly into Kyra's eyes, but followed her as she motioned for them to step out into the hallway for privacy.

"I know this may sound a bit odd," Kyra began hesitantly, "and I hope I can explain this to you properly. But I had a strong feeling that this man has a daughter, and she's very important to him. I also had a feeling he had a disagreement with her just before he became ill, and that he may not have spoken to her since then. Is it possible for you to check to see if he has a daughter and whether she's aware of his condition? I'm not sure of her name, but I thought I heard the name 'Aiko.' If it's possible to do this, I would be very grateful to you."

Satomi looked a little surprised, but responded kindly, "I not aware of daughter, but let me do checking and see what I may do? Thank you, Kyra."

Unsure of what Satomi may be thinking of her intuitive vision, Kyra appreciated her politeness nonetheless. The two women walked back to the elevator and rode it to the sixth floor of the hospital, where Kyra's last Reiki session for the day was scheduled. After exiting the elevator, Satomi led Kyra to the hospital room. They made their way to the bed where an elderly woman lay. She looked to be quite frail, her skin wrinkled and drawn.

*She seems familiar*, Kyra realized. *But how?* The answer flashed instantly into her mind: This was the woman she had dreamed of in the hospital room after Dr. Usui had motioned for Kyra to follow him! She didn't recall much else of the dream, but felt certain she was meant to be here today, helping this kind-looking woman. Kyra gazed at the woman's face. When their eyes met, Kyra noticed that she seemed to shine with sweetness.

Satomi introduced Kyra in Japanese, as before. The woman offered Kyra a bright smile when Satomi finished speaking, indicating her delight that Kyra had come to help her. Satomi turned to Kyra and explained, "Mrs. Takahashi had become . . . um, *un-hydrated,* I think is correct English word? She is very ill and been to hospital many times. The Reiki help her sleep and she find joy in it very much."

"I am very pleased to meet Mrs. Takahashi," Kyra replied, "and please tell her it is my pleasure to help her today."

Satomi did so with much reverence.

When they were alone, Kyra once again drew her Reiki symbols in the air, saying a silent prayer before she sat beside the bed.

She lightly touched Mrs. Takahashi's arm and once again felt the warmth of Reiki flowing through her hands and into the fragile woman's delicate body. Mrs. Takahashi gave Kyra a warm smile, but soon closed her eyes and drifted off to sleep. Kyra moved her stool around again, touching several different areas of Mrs. Takahashi's body. Each time she moved, she envisioned the wonderful life Mrs. Takahashi had led.

The visions were faint, as if Kyra were imagining them, but she could *picture* Mrs. Takahashi as a young woman on her wedding day. Next she saw Mrs. Takahashi with several children, and then she saw those children waving goodbye as they left for college. She caught glimpses of the children starting their careers and their own families. She could even see, in her mind's eye, Mrs. Takahashi surrounded by young grandchildren . . . and lastly, Kyra saw the death of Mr. Takahashi, her husband, many years earlier.

Mrs. Takahashi drifted in and out of sleep throughout the session. But just before the Reiki was completed, she woke up—and gently squeezed Kyra's hand in hers. Kyra's heart melted at the kind and loving spirit of the woman who lay in the bed next to her; it was beyond words, and Kyra felt as if their spirits had connected. She thought back once more to her strange dream that they would meet.

Saying a silent closing prayer for Mrs. Takahashi's healing, she added, *Thank you, God, Jesus, and Angels, for allowing me to touch these special people today and aid in their comfort and healing. I am so very appreciative of your guidance and for leading me here. Amen.*

Kyra made the sign of the cross, nearly in tears from her gratitude. She thought back to Nana's funeral in Israel, and the commemoration of all the good deeds she had done in her life. Kyra swallowed a moment of pain, released it, and deliberately chose to focus her heart on feeling love for each person she had spent time with today. She sent a little love to Nana—and to her parents, too, just for good measure.

Just as she was finishing the session, Satomi returned and walked up to the bed. Mrs. Takahashi moved suddenly, startling Kyra. She raised a frail arm and spoke as loudly as she could, just a sentence or two in Japanese. Satomi paused to listen—but a look of astonishment washed over Satomi's face, and her eyes widened for a moment. She finished her conversation with Mrs. Takahashi, who then quietly fell back asleep, and turned to Kyra. What she said took Kyra's breath away.

"Mrs. Takahashi said thank you much for Reiki today. She kept repeating the name '*Mana*' and said woman named Mana has a message for you. The message says, 'You are *very* strong healer and she with you always.'" Satomi paused and added, "The words may seem silly to you. Mrs. Takahashi is dying."

Kyra was stunned, and she gulped in an anxious breath of air. Clearly Mrs. Takahashi was saying "Nana." Kyra had received yet another message from her dear, sweet grandmother. She steadied herself before softly replying, "No, Satomi. It makes *perfect* sense to me. I am most grateful to you today . . . beyond words."

The women bowed a respectful goodbye to each other, and with that, Kyra took the elevator down to the first floor and left the hospital. She waited patiently for the city bus and quietly contemplated her day on the way back to Angela's home.

The remainder of her day was spent in quiet reflection, and she ate a light dinner, lighting a candle for ambience. Despite not being terribly hungry, she savored each bite.

*I want to ensure that I'm ready for tomorrow's adventure in Kyoto. I have no idea what will unfold, but I know the Angels will be with me!*

# 35

Kyra awoke at 7:00 am to the gentle chiming of the alarm clock. She had slept extra soundly, realizing that yesterday's Reiki sessions must have also done their magic on her as well. Stretching her arms above her head, she remembered that when a practitioner gives a Reiki treatment, they also receive Reiki themselves. "I feel awesome today—and hungry!" she said aloud.

Popping up out of bed, she went downstairs and fixed herself a steaming cup of green tea. Again, she ate a simple breakfast of miso soup, white rice, and a hardboiled egg, throwing in some leftover octopus for good measure. After showering, Kyra chose outdoor clothing for lots of walking: a pair of jean shorts, athletic shoes, and a navy T-shirt, much like what she'd wear at Stinson Beach. She brushed her teeth and pulled her hair back into a ponytail before making her way back downstairs to load up her backpack with a few bottles of water and some light snacks.

With a bounce in her step, she headed back to the bus stop where she'd been the day before. As she waited for the city bus, Kyra pondered the day's destination, her mind drifting back to the fortune-teller in Barcelona. She could still hear the woman's fiery words advising her of a journey to a lush green land and visiting a place of spiritual importance. With a prayer, Kyra affirmed, "God, please help me be on the right path today. Amen."

She inhaled the warm, sticky air to quiet her thoughts, and soon the bus pulled up to the curbside. Kyra boarded by the back door again and sat down in an empty seat. In what seemed like no time at all, she paid her fare and exited the bus.

Today, she found herself standing on the sidewalk in front of the

Demachiyanagi train station. The building was small, gray, and unassuming. Kyra might have missed it entirely, but a sign out front displayed the English name of the station beneath the *kanji*, or Japanese characters, confirming she was in the right place. While she had often traveled internationally for work, when in Tokyo and other cities, she had always taken a limo service to her destinations. Traveling like a tourist was an adventure, and Kyra looked forward to the train ride. *I hope I don't get lost!* She crossed her fingers for luck. *Well, at least not like I did in Spain.* Her features brightened as she thought back to Father Sánchez and their incredible destined encounter.

Kyra purchased a train ticket for just over 400 Yen. She then boarded the Eizan Electric Railway, carefully triple-checking the name to ensure she was on the right train. The ride would be about half an hour, and Kyra took a comfortable seat by the window to peer out at the scenery.

She studied the city of Kyoto, watching the buildings swiftly rush by and found herself wondering, *Who are the people inside?* She recalled that she had once been one of those people too, rushing through her busy day in pursuit of her corporate goals. A feeling of gratitude that she was no longer caught up in the "rat race" made her feel at peace—and that *everything* was now possible.

The scenery looked like any city, in nearly any part of the world, with many low-rise buildings and houses that all looked the same. But soon the train moved out of the city, and the scenery changed dramatically. The foliage became thick and green, and Kyra could see many different types of trees and even flowers outside her window. She had read that the most spectacular time of year here was the fall, when the leaves on the trees burst into brilliant shades of red, gold, and orange. The colors in the photographs she'd lovingly viewed had overwhelmed her—setting her senses on fire.

*Yes, I'll come back in the spring, Angela . . . but maybe in the fall, too.* She then thought about winter and how the leaves would turn brown and drop to the ground just before the freezing snow set in. Shivering at the thought, Kyra realized that the cold air conditioning on the train had brought her back into the present moment. She looked outside again and admired the colors of the summer foliage with its subdued, deeper shades of green and brown. An occasional splash of colorful wildflowers dotted the countryside. The clear, soft blue of the morning sky completed the summer palette, creating a beautiful backdrop to the beautiful Mount Kurama as the train drew closer to its destination.

Kyra exited in a rural town called Kurama, just on the outskirts of Kyoto. She followed the town's main road for about half a mile, enjoying the scenic sites along the way until she reached her first stop of the day.

"My first destination—the *Kurama Onsen!*" Kyra said, taking care to properly pronounce the name of the *ryokan*, or Japanese inn. She stretched her legs once she'd finished the walk up the winding road and stood outside the front door.

The inn was nondescript and minimal in styling, with a plain beige exterior and simple gray roof. With its unpretentious exterior, Kyra would likely have passed by if she hadn't known about the hidden gem that lay within. This particular inn was very well known for the natural, outdoor hot spring baths that gave it the name *onsen*.

Guests at the inn enjoyed full use of the facilities, but Kyra went inside and paid the day fee of 2,500 Yen. Slipping into a white towel in the changing area after showering, she gently slid into the naturally hot mineral waters, tossing her head back as the warm water enlivened her body. She was grateful to enjoy the heat of the spa despite the warmth of the summer day.

Kyra knew it wasn't so much the temperature of the spring that was important, but the minerals so readily abundant in the waters. The heat of the spring came naturally from a nearby active volcano, and there were many such springs located throughout the country.

"I can already feel the mineral water cleansing my body and doing its healing magic," Kyra said under her breath, recalling how the waters, with their rich sulfur and iron content, were believed to have therapeutic properties.

The view of the mountainside was spectacular and soothing, and the foliage surrounding the bathing area was colorful, creating an idyllic meditative environment. Crickets sang somewhere off in the distance, offering a melodic song of nature, and the morning mists swirled on the nearby hillsides, rising up only to completely disappear as the morning quietly faded into midday.

Kyra spent close to an hour soaking in the heated mineral waters, falling into a state of deep relaxation. She silently meditated, and afterward she enjoyed the sauna before finishing her visit in the indoor bathing area, which offered cooler water that helped bring her skin temperature back down to normal.

After showering again and toweling herself dry, she dressed and departed the inn, starting her journey toward her next stop of the day: Mount Kurama. Kyra had planned a hike that would take around an hour, and the exercise would be most invigorating after her day-spa experience.

Upon reaching the base of the mountain after a short walk north, Kyra peered up at the steep mountainside and adjusted her backpack. The sunlight beamed directly overhead, as it was now midday. She first made her way to Kurama Temple, where the hiking trail would take her up the mountain. The steep wooded pathway looked twisting and mysterious, but Kyra decided not to let fear get the best of her.

She took a step forward and thought again of the fortune-teller in Spain, who had described a mountain of spiritual importance located in a different country. Even now she could hear Gabby translating the woman's words: "When the time is right, you will know where to go." The words had haunted her, and she'd replayed them a hundred times in her mind, until it had struck her like a bolt of lightning. It had come to her while daydreaming during dinner with Juan Pablo. She was meant to go Japan—to Reiki's place of origin.

*Mount Kurama is a mountain of spiritual importance*, Kyra recalled clearly and it was the same place where Dr. Usui had meditated for twenty-one days, receiving the Reiki energy and his spiritual enlightenment. *I'm very much looking forward to experiencing my own time there. My journey has brought me so far.*

Kyra began her ascent on the narrow pathway leading up Mount Kurama's peak, paying careful attention to each step along the way so as not to stumble; huge tangled tree roots made walking challenging. The path seemed dark and winding at first—not a path she would have intentionally chosen to walk alone. But while the area was fairly isolated, she knew she was destined to make this journey. She inhaled deeply for courage and then offered a simple prayer: *I know I've been guided to be here. Thank you, God, for keeping me safe.*

She continued her ascent, enjoying the sight of a few of the temples she passed along the way. The sunlight filtered through beautiful green trees and the forest became brighter as she hiked her way up. The light seemed to dance across the tops of the branches that swayed gently in the light summer breeze. *You are making me miss my home and the redwood forest.* Kyra thought lovingly as she continued to climb.

She noticed how peaceful the forest felt, with its magnificent giant cedar trees stretching up into the sky. Occasional irises, lavender, and even wild sunflowers offered small bursts of white, purple, pink, and bright yellow to brighten her way. As her eyes adjusted to the light, she could see many birds, rabbits, and squirrels darting through the forest as she continued her ascent.

*It feels so joyous here . . . like I'm somehow in heaven!* Kyra thought with delight. *I now know why I had that recurring dream as a child . . . and that I was destined to meet Arianna, my spirit guide, too.* She directed a loving thought toward Arianna and reflected on their first meeting. *I can't wait to speak with you again when the time is right. Ah, but I'm so appreciate being here today, and I adore all of the wildlife I keep seeing.*

Kyra was tempted to go barefoot to enjoy even further connecting to Mother Earth, but decided to keep her athletic shoes on, just to be safe. The path was steep and her ascent unpredictable. Time just seemed to magically disappear, and Kyra knew that when the time was right, she'd find a place to meditate. *I will stop wherever I'm inspired to go*, she told herself with confidence.

After walking another half mile or so, Kyra did find the perfect spot. A beautiful waterfall about twenty feet high appeared directly in front of her, and she stopped to watch the water dance down the side of a mountain ledge, lapping rhythmically as it flowed into a large pool. The waterfall was mesmerizing, and the heat of day combined with the movement of the water caused a faint mist to rise, making the whole area feel mysterious in the shade of the trees.

Kyra's intuition sensed this place was safe and calm, so she chose a rock close to the water's edge, which was perfect for sitting on. *I will take off these silly shoes!* She laughed like a child, placing her shoes and socks on the ground near her. Dipping her feet in the water for refreshment, she gathered herself into a half-lotus pose. She took several deep, cleansing breaths and gazed out at the water's rhythmic flow. Then Kyra closed her eyes and began to pray.

She pictured herself covered in a white light of protection, and slowly relaxed each part of her body. Next she envisioned her own energy light moving down into the ground to connect with the center of Mother Earth. After anchoring herself to the Earth, Kyra brought her energy back up and into her body. She said a prayer of thanks to God and sent love to all her amazing friends, Uncle Saul, Arianna, her parents, and lastly to Nana, of course. She then silently asked the Universe, *What guidance do I need today?*

After taking a few minutes to relax and focus, she thought she heard the word "forgive." The faint voice came from within her mind, and so subtly that it did not sound like any person known to her. But, as she listened, she heard the voice more clearly. *Forgive yourself.* In Kyra's mind, she silently replied, *Yes. Please tell me how.*

After a few moments of stillness, Kyra began to feel her energy slowly being lifted up. It was as if she were floating up into the misty vapors of the waterfall until she *was* the waterfall. She then floated up into the sky, and she *was* the sky. She moved past the sky and realized she was completely surrounded by *Light.* She was no longer sitting in the dark shadows of the forest trees. She was floating up past the earth's sky until it became black as velvet, with millions of white stars twinkling all around her. And then she *was* the stars. She could see a beautiful white Light off in the distance, and she slowly glided toward that Light.

But before she reached the Light, she heard a familiar voice behind her say, "Kyra, I want to ask you to forgive me."

Kyra turned her energetic self around and saw her mother, Sarah, in front of her. She appeared to be about thirty years of age and very healthy, unlike she had been in her later years on the earth. She was bright and made of light. Kyra could feel her mother's love for her, and in her mind, she replied, "Yes, Mother. I forgive you and release the past. I love you."

Kyra then heard another familiar voice, this one a man's, and she turned her energetic self around again to see her father, Robert, standing in front of her. He looked very handsome and healthy, and also in his early thirties. His light shone even brighter than her mother's had. Her father gave Kyra a most loving look and said, "My sweetest daughter. Please forgive me for the way I treated you. I meant well."

Kyra looked her father in the eyes and gently replied, "Yes, Father. I forgive you and release the past. I love you."

And in that moment Kyra felt a huge *rush*—a release of energy unlike anything she had experienced before. It was as if a weight had been lifted from her soul, and she instantly felt immense joy and love beyond her wildest imagination. The feeling completely engulfed her, and in a flash, she was sitting on the rock in front of the waterfall again, listening to the sounds of the water gently lapping down the ledge.

Kyra hesitantly opened her eyes. A huge smile crossed her face, and she burst into a loud laugh, saying, "Yes, Mother and Father, I *do* forgive you! I am so appreciative of the time we spent together on this earth. You taught me so much," she added, feeling sentimental, "and for that I am eternally grateful. I do love you, but more importantly, I love me."

Kyra sat on the rock for a little longer, savoring the moment and the memories of her life with her parents. She made the sign of the cross and said a closing prayer, then carefully slipped her socks and shoes back on her feet. Slowly making her way back down the mountain trail, she took a little over an hour to arrive back at the train station.

After boarding the train and making her way back to Kyoto, she took the bus to a shop where she could purchase a journal. *I plan to capture all the details of my experiences thus far on this most magnificent and purifying journey,* she pledged after making her purchase.

When she arrived back at Angela's home, she curled up on her futon and spent the remainder of the evening writing.

Wanting to be completely rested up for her fourth and final day in Kyoto, she slipped off to bed early. She was rewarded with a deep, restorative slumber, sleeping like an angel that night.

# 36

Kyra awoke around 7:30 am and stretched out fully across her futon bed. She felt remarkably refreshed, much like she'd felt the morning after she had met her spirit guide Arianna in Málaga. She tried to remember her dreams, but nothing came to her. Instead, she was left with an incredible feeling of bliss that seemed to fill her aura. *Arianna*, she thought happily, *I feel like I was with you last night . . . if only in my dreams!*

Kyra jumped into the shower and then chose her clothing for the day. *A simple pair of faded blue jeans will be perfect!* she thought, rummaging through her suitcase. *And my light blue chambray sleeveless blouse . . . oh, and my gold jewelry seems to be calling me today.* Kyra didn't care how silly her thoughts sounded; she felt like a child again, a child who had been given a second chance to feel her parents' love.

Of course, she would meet Angela later that evening for dinner at the Hafuu Honten restaurant, but today, she was excited to further explore of city of Kyoto. She looked forward to the activities she had planned.

*My itinerary is so well thought out*, she laughed, grabbing her notes for the day and heading down the stairs. *Some things will never change!*

After preparing her morning green tea, whimsically attempting the same care and flourish that Mitsuko had used at the teahouse, then eating her traditional breakfast, she grabbed her purse and walked out the door around 9 am, just as her taxi rolled up. Today, the taxi took her to the Kyoto Station, which, unlike the nondescript and smaller exterior of the Demachiyanagi train station from the previous day, was very modern and futuristically styled. Its heavy steel construction and seemingly countless glass windows made it look much more "big city," reminding Kyra of Tokyo.

Despite the morning hour, the station was quite busy. People crowded the corridors, ready for their own adventures to unfold.

After paying the taxi driver and tipping him generously, Kyra entered the state-of-the-art station to purchase a train ticket. Next she made her way to the waiting area, double-checking she was boarding the correct train. She'd be heading west toward the Arashiyama district, which lay on the outskirts of city of Kyoto. The ride was quick and efficient, and in almost no time at all, Kyra exited the train at the Saga-Arashiyama station. She then walked another half mile to reach the entrance to the Tenryū-ji Temple, her first place to visit today.

Kyra had read up on the Tenryū-ji Temple the night before to fully understand the historical significance of the place she'd be visiting. She had learned the temple was registered as a United Nations World Heritage Site, and stood among the top five Zen Buddhist temples in Kyoto. She had learned that the most unique aspect of this temple was actually not the buildings themselves, but the spectacular gardens that had survived centuries of devastation and still held true to their original form.

*I'm excited to see the phenomenal outdoor gardens, despite this summer heat!* Kyra thought as she approached the temple grounds. As she drew near, she walked faster, eager for her first glimpse of the grounds. *It's so remarkable that gardens in Japan are given as much attention as the design of the temples themselves. They're practically an art form.*

She had been equally excited to read that the gardens had once been used by the Buddhist monks, who had deeply understood the importance of staying closely connected to nature for meditation too. Her heart felt elated as she reached the temple entrance.

After visiting several of the buildings on the grounds, including the Daihojo, or main hall; the Kuri, or temple kitchen; and the Hato, or the dharma hall, Kyra finally found herself standing in the middle of the grounds. She looked out over the Arashiyama Mountains, which lay just across the Ōi River, creating a dramatic backdrop for the surrounding tranquil gardens. The mountains were a dense green, and the light-blue summer sky made them appear even darker. But what truly fascinated her was the unique way the faraway mountains were cleverly incorporated *into* the design of the gardens.

Much to her amazement, the garden created the optical illusion that the mountains were just past the hills and almost right in front of her, rather than many miles away. The gentle elevation of the garden hills sloped up above her head, covering the view of the distance at which the mountains actually stood. The dense trees and bushes on the hill blended with the mountains, making them look as if she could reach over and touch them.

Kyra almost wept with gratitude for all the places she had visited thus far and how they'd inspired her in so many different, life-altering ways. *I am so grateful for my special meditation time yesterday at Mount Kurama . . . and for the chance to finally forgive my past.*

Kyra's thoughts quickly returned to her surroundings, and the ancient beauty of the garden mesmerized her once again. She could almost imagine in her mind's eyes the monks from so long ago quietly moving about the grounds until settling upon a special place to sit and meditate.

*Japan is turning out to be a most enchanting part of my journey. And, tomorrow it's time to continue forward . . . but for now, I'm right here.* Kyra knew she was gathering extraordinary memories and would carry them with her for the rest of her life. She still had so much more she planned to see, and soon she'd be off on a new adventure, but with no moment like the present, she wholly embraced it.

Kyra gave one last glance over her shoulder as she exited the North gate of the Tenryū-ji Temple and strolled to the nearby Arashiyama Bamboo Grove. Its sinewy stems towered gracefully overhead. She enjoyed the palpable sense of oneness the forest offered, which was unlike any other she had visited so far. When she left the grove, she felt completely at peace and filled with hope for a bright future of her very own design.

She returned to the Kyoto train station and hailed a taxi for her next stop of the day. "*Nishiki Ichiba made one-gai-shi-ma-su*," Kyra enunciated slowly to the driver, adding nervously in English, "Uh, please take me to *Nishiki Market?*"

The taxi driver replied with a quick but friendly nod, saying, "*Hai, Wakarimashita.*" This Kyra understood to mean, "Yes, okay."

Ten minutes later, Kyra arrived at her destination. The streets were very narrow, and the market was jam-packed with people walking up and down the five-block shopping area. She had read that the area was also called "Kyoto's Kitchen," and rightfully so, as there were more than one hundred vendors offering a huge variety of meats and produce.

Kyra reminded herself of what Angela had said on the day she arrived: *Osaka is famous for kuidaore—"eat 'til you drop,"* but for now she was excited to explore Kyoto's famous kitchen. Kyra recognized the similarities between the Nishiki Ichiba and La Boqueria, Barcelona's spectacular outdoor market. *Maybe I really am a foodie!* She'd had so many culinary adventures in Spain and now in Japan, but she was still taken aback by the variety of food on display.

Marveling at the many wooden barrels, similar to the ones she'd seen in Barcelona, Kyra soon discovered some of the more interesting, if not totally unrecognizable, fare the market offered. In addition to the usual colorful displays of produce and fresh raw seafood on ice, there were bins brimming over with everything imaginable, including pickles, noodles, tofu, sweets, and even fresh sushi to tempt her palate. The air smelled delicious, filled with savory scents ranging from that of fish being sautéed to the pungent fragrance of roasting oolong tea.

Kyra even saw novelty items, from cookware and knives to clothing and sandals. Food samples were freely offered, and Kyra delighted in tasting some of the more unique items such as the dried seafood, sweet-and-sour octopus skewers, and quail eggs. She kept her poker face, however, when she walked pass the vendors selling *narazuke*, pickled gourd; *takotamago*, quail egg embedded in octopus; and *unagi* or huge fresh water eels that had been chargrilled and sliced, ready to be taken home and eaten.

*Maybe I won't eat 'til I drop after all—at least not any of* these *items!* She giggled at her own silly wariness of the cultural differences in taste.

Stopping at one of the shops, she said to the shop owner, "Your place is wonderful."

The man, who spoke some broken English, explained that his shop had been in his family for several generations. Kyra noted that he seemed delighted to speak to "a polite Westerner." When Kyra inquired about that, she learned from him that occasionally Westerners would become frustrated by the lack of fluent English spoken at the market. They were, after all, visiting Japan, he joked with affection.

Although she had sampled many of the vendors' fares, Kyra still stopped for lunch at a nearby restaurant. "I'd like to try the *O-ko-nom-i-ya-ki?*" she said, making a concentrated effort to correctly say the name of the dish. *Okonomiyaki*, she had learned from Angela, was a traditional savory Japanese pancake cooked to order at the table. She noted the wide range of toppings that were available to her, and the dish reminded her somewhat of an American omelet.

The waiter nodded and muttered something in Japanese, which Kyra took to mean he understood her before he swiftly headed toward the kitchen.

When he returned to her table, Kyra was pleased by her choice, despite it being prepared in the kitchen. She had boldly chosen the squid and prawns with a topping of green sprouts, mushrooms, and tomatoes—just to keep things somewhat familiar. The colorful pancake turned out to be quite large, but it was so tasty that she nearly finished the whole thing.

When she left the market behind, a taxi took her to the Gion district to observe the preparations for the special *matsuri* or festival that would take place. She felt elated when she arrived and was eager to fully enjoy at least part of the preparations for the month-long festival. There would be two major float processions: one in mid-July and the other in late July. While her timing was such that she would be leaving in the morning for England, a week before the first parade, she decided not to feel sad at missing the celebration.

*There's so much more I'd love to do here . . . if only I had the time.* she thought. Rather than hurrying herself to see everything, she deliberately slowed her pace, realizing that the time she had now would be better spent appreciating the moment.

She enjoyed wandering along the streets and stopping every so often to watch the workers assembling the floats. She had learned from Angela that the parade tradition dated back to the ninth century and was one of the oldest parades still in existence. But the most unique aspect of the festival was the enormous size of the floats.

"I can't believe that some of these floats weigh up to twelve tons!" Kyra remarked to another tourist whom she'd eased up alongside to more closely see the intricacies of the work. "How cool is that?"

The red-haired man winked back an affirmation, and she felt grateful that her English had been understood.

The craftsmen were out in full force, and she found it fascinating that not a single nail was used. Instead, they painstakingly hand-tied the different parts of the floats together with rope and other natural, lightweight materials.

*I love that this was originally a ceremony to ward off evil spirits—well at least those that caused epidemics,* thought Kyra, appreciating how her special visit to Japan had helped her let go of her own "evil spirits," so to speak. *Yes, our intentions are like magnets, and we attract what we focus on. Having a positive intention attracts the good stuff—and, in this case, it's also so much fun!*

Later that afternoon, Kyra made her way back to Angela's place, enjoying the light exercise, and then took time to freshen up before meeting her friend at the restaurant around 7:30 pm. Angela had written down the address of Hafuu Honten and had given Kyra instructions to take a taxi since it was only a short ride.

Kyra stepped through the entrance right on time, but Angela, so far, had not yet arrived. While she waited, she took a moment to admire the mixture of traditional and contemporary styling in the restaurant. The rich gold tone of the walls and the modern furniture were complemented with bright splashes of artwork adorning the walls. Enticing smells tempted her nose, and Kyra tried hard to keep her stomach from grumbling.

When Angela came flying through the front door, arriving quite late, she stopped to catch her breath. Kyra gave her a comforting look, but Angela apologized profusely, explaining that her flight had landed more than thirty minutes late. She then spoke at length in Japanese to the maître d', whom she apparently knew quite well. The man replied cordially, and while Kyra did not understand much of their conversation, her ears perked up when she thought she heard the maître d' call Angela *"Chika,"* which Kyra found confusing.

"I've had the most spectacular time here in Kyoto," Kyra said as soon as they were seated. "I'll tell you all about it in a moment, but first may I ask you a question?" At Angela's nod, she went on. "You know that I understand little Japanese, but did I just hear the maître d' call you *Chika?*"

"Oh, yes," Angela said with a mischievous lilt. "My Japanese name is Chika, but when we moved to the United States, my parents Americanized it so that I'd fit in better culturally. My family and close friends use my given name, but you can still call me Angela, of course."

"I think it's charming that you have *two* names to choose from," Kyra said with sincerity. "Meanwhile, my friend Gabby calls me *Chica!* It's her nickname for me." She giggled. "You two would really love each other if you met."

"I'm sure we would," Angela replied. "We already have one amazing thing in common—you!" Kyra blushed at the compliment, and then Angela changed the subject hearing Kyra's stomach rumble: "This restaurant is a bit off the beaten path, being in a residential neighborhood, but don't let that fool you. This is one of Kyoto's top restaurants."

Kyra agreed to be brave in her food choices as they perused the menu. Angela ordered a traditional dinner of tuna and Japanese mushroom tartar, oven-roasted salmon in a delightful vegetable ravigote sauce, sweet potato cream soup, Wagyu filet steak with rice, and dessert. Kyra, on the other hand, ordered a dinner combination, which consisted of lightly roasted beef, the soup of the day, grilled salted cow tongue, Wagyu sirloin steak with rice, and dessert. She threw in a side order of octopus—just to just to make sure Angela would notice.

During their beverage service and before their food arrived, Kyra talked about her heartwarming adventures in Kyoto, including her Reiki sessions at the local hospital and her meditation on Mount Kurama—and how proud she felt for letting go of her past wounds. Angela appeared moved by Kyra's tale, even more so than Kyra had expected she would be.

"You are living the life I only dream of," Angela said, the regret in her voice notable. "I've been contemplating making changes, but I just haven't had the guts to do *anything*. You are truly motivating me to spend more time doing the things I love . . . and to pursue some of my spiritual interests."

Kyra started to respond, but was interrupted by Angela's cell phone. A perplexed look crossed her friend's face when she glanced at the caller ID. "It's a U.S. number," Angela shared. "Um . . . I'm not sure who this is, but would you mind terribly if I take a moment to answer it? Just in case it's related to work—I do apologize."

Kyra nodded and replied, "Yes, of course. Take all the time you need."

Angela took the call outside. Though, she was gone for quite some time, Kyra quietly sipped her green tea and allowed her mind to freely navigate all the memories she'd collected along her journey. When Angela returned, nearly twenty minutes later, her face was ashen.

"Is everything okay?" Kyra asked hesitantly. "Can I help you with something?"

It was apparent that Angela had been crying; there were still tears in her eyes and Kyra tried not to cry with her.

"It's more than okay," Angela responded shakily. "My brother just called me . . . and we haven't spoken in fifteen years! He's still living in the U.S., of course, but he found my contact information on the Internet." Angela took a deep, unsteady breath before continuing, "To make a long story short, he just apologized to me for the disagreement we had so many years ago, and asked if we could try to start our relationship over again. I'm totally stunned . . ." Angela's voice trailed off.

Kyra immediately reached over the table and gave Angela's hand a warm squeeze, wiping a tear from her own eye. "I can't express how excited I am for you. It seems that this is a week of forgiveness for us both."

Angela wiped her eyes and gathered her composure. "I guess I'm not made of steel like I thought I was, am I, Kyra?"

"Neither of us is made of steel," Kyra replied with a reassuring smile, "because like you said at the Fushimi Inari-taisha, we bend just like the bamboo trees that spring up after the passage of the storm."

"Oh my, Kyra!" Angela suddenly blurted out. "I just remembered the wish I made when we were there after the fox crossed our path!"

Kyra waited, wide-eyed, for her friend to explain.

"I *wished* my brother would somehow come back in my life," Angela said, her voice choked with emotion. "It was his birthday a week ago."

Kyra stared at her in astonishment, feeling incredibly happy for Angela's good fortune. She then recalled the very attractive, tall order she herself had wished for in that same moment. *Oh, my gosh . . . is it possible my wish will come true too?* she wondered. God had certainly been good to her so far, and she had learned that anything was possible.

~

As the women enjoyed their dinner, they shared their innermost thoughts about life, relationships, God, and spirituality, becoming closer than either had ever imagined they could in such a short period of time. When they returned to Angela's home, they turned in for the night almost immediately.

The next morning, they awoke early, ate a hearty breakfast—and, as Kyra walked out the front door of Angela's home, she bowed her head in acknowledgment to the house for her wonderful stay there and secretly said thank you.

They jumped into Angela's Audi sedan, and headed toward the Kansai International Airport. Angela dropped Kyra off at 9:30 am, about two hours before her flight to England was scheduled to depart.

After the women had heaved Kyra's suitcase onto the sidewalk, Kyra gave Angela a long, heartfelt hug goodbye. When she pulled back, she met Angela's eyes and said, "I'm so looking forward to continuing our friendship, even after I'm back home in San Francisco. You are welcome to visit me anytime."

"Oh, Kyra." Angela paused, almost at a loss for words. "I'm very much looking forward to seeing you again. You've helped me learn so much about myself these past few days. We *were* destined to reconnect—I'm sure of it. But, more important, I realize I do need to make some major shifts in my life . . . and to think even bigger when I make a wish!"

Angela laughed with genuine joy and Kyra's intuition sparked—telling her with certainty that her friend's life would never be the same from that moment forward.

# Part 5

# Journey to England

# 37

Kyra's watch read 9:09 pm. Her flight to Bristol, England, would be arriving in fewer than fifteen minutes. Excited to see Gabby again, she could hardly sit still. Her body tingled as she anticipated sharing stories of her Japanese adventures with her friend. *But more important,* she thought, *I'm so excited to experience the Master training in Stonehenge with Gabby! I can only imagine what will transpire on our metaphysical journey together.*

She stretched her arms up and shifted her legs forward to keep her circulation flowing. Her body felt stiff, and her mind drifted back over her long, arduous travels. Her first flight from Kansai International Airport had lasted over twelve and a half hours before landing in Paris at the Charles de Gaulle Airport. After a brief layover, Kyra had boarded her next flight at the Amsterdam Airport Schiphol in the Netherlands, which lasted just over an hour.

She managed to grab a blueberry muffin and espresso before boarding her final flight, which was now heading to Bristol Airport in England. This flight was short in duration, but her travel time totaled nearly eighteen hours. She relished the idea that her journey was soon coming to an end. In fact, when she had handed the airline agent her boarding pass at the last gate, she'd blurted, "I'm almost there!" The agent had only smiled politely at her curious outburst. Kyra laughed at her silliness, chalking up her unintentional comment to fatigue.

She stretched her legs out one last time. *I can't wait for a real bed with a soft, fluffy pillow. Tonight I'll get a good night's sleep!* she promised herself.

Kyra had chosen a quaint hotel near the airport to allow her plenty of time to rest up. In the morning, she'd make the nearly one-hour drive to the Glastonbury Abbey, where the Reiki training would be held. She hoped that the eight-hour time difference would be a breeze and she'd avoid the effects of jet lag.

After a routine landing and deplaning, Kyra rapidly arrived at the baggage claim area and yanked her suitcase to the ground. The large piece of luggage made a loud *thunk* as it landed on the concrete. Kyra briskly rubbed her bicep and rolled her eyes in frustration.

A short, burly man beside her took note and let out a loud bellow. "You are much too young to break your *bum* lifting that heavy piece of luggage!" he said in a heavy British accent.

Kyra felt an embarrassed flush spread across her face and tried to retain her dignity by politely agreeing with the man. With her head held high, she wheeled her now infamous suitcase toward Passport Control to gain entry into the country. After spending more than thirty minutes in line, an agent finally stamped her passport several times and motioned for her to move on. It was nearly 10:30 pm when she stepped outside to wait for the hotel shuttle bus.

Greeted by the cool crisp evening temperatures, she finally spied the Winford Manor hotel logo on a bus and waved vigorously to catch the driver's attention. He politely loaded her suitcase, and the bus arrived at her destination a few minutes later. Kyra had hoped to catch a glimpse of the manor's seven acres of manicured grounds, but the pale evening moon was only a sliver and did not offer her enough illumination. She'd have to wait until morning to fully appreciate the Somerset countryside.

Once inside the hotel, the night clerk greeted Kyra. A man in his late fifties, he had soft graying hair at his temples and spoke in a cheerful voice. "Miss, your room is on the second floor," he said. "The *lift*, or elevator as you call it, is to your left, and we'll have a traditional English-style breakfast starting at six thirty am. If I can help, give me a shout, alright?"

"Thank you so much for your kindness, sir," she replied, warmed by his friendly mannerism. "I'll need the shuttle bus back to the airport in the morning for a nine thirty departure. I'm picking up my rental car, and then I'm driving to Glastonbury." She gave him a pleasant but sleepy smile. "I'm super excited to see your beautiful English countryside. I've heard it's just stunning."

The man nodded affirmatively. "Oh, I think you'll find it quite pretty," he said knowingly. "There's no place like it in the world." He leaned forward and handed her the room key.

In what felt like the blink of an eye, Kyra settled into her room and had fallen asleep without any further ado. When her alarm went off the next morning, she flipped over and reached out to turn it off, but her body was stiff and her brain felt foggy. She reluctantly sat up and rubbed her eyes. *Ugh . . . I feel like I've been hit by a train!* she thought, realizing that the heavy travel schedule and time change had taken its toll after all. *I think a proper cup of tea—well maybe some very strong coffee is in order!*

After a leisurely hot shower, she changed into comfortable clothing—a pair of navy slacks and a yellow cotton sleeveless blouse. She surveyed her jewelry and felt her turquoise necklace was needed today.

"I'm choosing you for your positive healing energy," she lovingly said aloud to the jewelry, not feeling at all silly. "You're perfect for my first day in Glastonbury."

She carefully draped the necklace around her neck, as she had done in Spain, and silently asked the stones to revitalize her energy level.

Confident the turquoise would do its magic, Kyra arrived in the breakfast room and spotted a community table. A young couple was already seated enjoying their meal when she approached. They appeared to be in their mid-twenties and very much in love. Sitting side by side, they laughed as they tasted each other's food and bantered back and forth finishing each other sentences.

Recognizing there was little seating available, Kyra placed her purse on the table and walked over to the breakfast buffet. A variety of appetizing items were artfully displayed on the credenza, which was covered with a crisp white tablecloth. Sterling silver serving dishes offered a sophisticated touch to the charming cottage-like feel of the room. Kyra took a plate and started by selecting a few of the more familiar food items—scrambled eggs and fruit.

"*Hmmm*, this looks a bit like the Canadian bacon I get back home," Kyra said aloud as she placed a piece of the unfamiliar meat on her plate.

"That's the *British* version of bacon," the guest in line beside her politely confirmed. She emphasized it was of much higher quality than what Kyra was used to in the U.S.

"And baked beans?" Kyra added. "I've never seen that served for breakfast before, but they do look delicious."

The woman chuckled, acknowledging the culinary differences between the two countries.

Kyra decided to forgo some of the less familiar foods, such as the fried tomatoes and *black pudding*, which she learned was a type of sausage prepared with pig's blood.

After seating herself across from the young lovebirds, a stout middle-aged waitress scurried over to ask Kyra for her choice of beverage. "We have tea or coffee—whichever you prefer." The lines on the woman's face reflected years of hard work, but her cheerful demeanor softened her otherwise weathered features. "And, if you'd like, we have omelets or *eggy bread*." Kyra quickly noted to herself that *eggy bread* was the British term for French toast.

"Oh, no thank you. The buffet is just perfect," she replied. "But I'd love a cup of coffee, if you don't mind."

"Certainly, miss," the waitress replied, darting off to the kitchen. Moments later, she returned with a large insulated coffee pot and plunked it down on the table.

Kyra filled her cup to the brim and let the hot steam fill her nose before she took a sip. *I need this full strength to get my blood pumping!* she told herself, glad she had decided to forgo any milk to drink the strong, black liquid in its purest form.

As she set her coffee cup back down, the young couple made eye contact.

The woman was slender with long, dark silky hair, and vivid blue eyes. Her stylish look and sweet mannerisms reminded Kyra of Emma back in San Francisco. "My husband and I are just leaving this morning to enjoy a *bit* of time away," she said. "Are you on *holiday* here in England, too?"

Kyra instantly recognized she was a native Brit by her accent.

"Actually I'm meeting a friend in Glastonbury for a seminar, which I'm super excited about," Kyra replied.

"Glastonbury? Oh, you will like it. It's a *smashing* town with some most unusual Wiccan and New Age shops," the young woman said with a lilt in her voice. "But of course you must visit Stonehenge, too."

"Oh, I do plan a visit to Stonehenge, of course," Kyra replied, but a puzzled expression crossed her features. "Did you say there are *Wiccan* shops in Glastonbury?"

The woman nodded, taking a sip of her tea. "You will definitely have an *interesting* trip—I'm sure of it."

With an air of merriment, the young man added, "My aunt Joanie loves to visit the Glastonbury shops, especially during the Avalon Spring Faery Fayre . . . but she is a bit *dotty*."

*What have I gotten myself into?* Kyra wondered with an inward laugh, though she secretly enjoyed the idea of a visit to the strange shops.

While she continued to enjoy her breakfast, the couple offered some other touristy advice before they headed out for the day. Charmed by their devotion, Kyra watched as they departed hand in hand and savored the last few sips of her coffee.

With her suitcase at her side, Kyra waited outside for the hotel shuttle bus to take her to the car rental area. Looking up at the sky, the weather was noticeably overcast—a thick, wet mist made for a gloomy start to the day. A chill shot through Kyra's body, but she shook it off, determined not to let the weather ruin her first day in England.

When the bus pulled up, the driver stepped out and asked courteously, "Are you getting a *car hire* at the airport, miss?"

"Yes, I am. Please take me to the *Hertz Car Hire*. Thanks." Kyra smiled, enjoying the slight variations on English words from her native homeland. *Of course they did invent the English language*, she reminded herself with a giggle.

Kyra picked up her Kia compact car, which she made sure would be outfitted with a GPS. She had listened carefully to the woman behind the counter to make sure she understood how to use the device before she'd even think about pulling out of the parking lot.

"I know everything will go quite smoothly today," Kyra assured herself, trying to quell her uneasiness. In the past, she had always taken limo service on her business trips, so driving in a foreign country was brand-new territory.

"Okay, I can do this," she said, gripping the steering wheel firmly, but her nerves got the best of her. "Not only am I'm driving on the *left* side of the road and the *opposite* side of the car—it's a stick shift too!" She flinched. "Oh, and did I mention I'm in a foreign country and I don't know where I'm going?"

Determined to overcome her fear, she shifted the car into first gear and drove forward a few feet, but the car lurched, making a loud grinding noise. Kyra realized it had been more than ten years since she had driven a manual transmission. Making a mental note to be more prepared next time, she groaned as she tried to shift the clutch. *Okay, Angels, help me get to Glastonbury safely!*

Hoping her prayer had been heard, Kyra shifted into second gear and cautiously drove the silver Kia out of the car park area. The small car lurched back and forth while she awkwardly shifted the gears. A car behind her blared its horn, and Kyra glanced down at the speedometer. She was driving a full 15 kilometers under the speed limit while she attempted to regain her skills. Struggling, she mustered up her courage and hit the gas pedal hard, managing to gain some speed.

As she drove along, the GPS offered its verbal instructions right on cue, but soon she discovered that despite the words being in "English," the voice sounded muffled and she had difficulty understanding some of the street names. Rather than risk getting lost, Kyra decided the best course of action was to pull over to look at a physical map. She shifted the car into gear and hurriedly sped off, taking a side dirt road after spotting an open field on the right-hand side. *That's a perfect place for quick stop*, she thought and pulled inside.

The car idled quietly, and after studying her map, she tried to shift the car into reverse to head back the same direction from which she'd come. And, that's when she realized the problem—the gearshift would not budge. *Argh . . . Surely I'm doing this correctly,* she thought franticly, tension filling her body. Gritting her teeth, she shouted, "I was a Senior Vice President at a Fortune 500 company. I know I will figure this out!"

Giving it another try, she threw her arms up in frustration. "I cannot shift this car into reverse!" Kyra decided that heading back to the car rental company for instructions was her only option, but *how* would she get the car there?

Scrunching up her face, she analyzed the situation and determined her next steps. She put the gearshift into neutral, making sure the parking brake was not engaged, and jumped out of the car. She planned to physically *push* the car into reverse to back it up. Once the vehicle was backed up far enough, she could make a U-turn and maneuver the car back onto the road again—this time in the right direction.

*"Ugh,"* she said with her initial hard push on the front hood of the car to get it rolling. Once the car was finally in place for driving again, she shouted an even louder victorious, "*Yippee!*"

Kyra slid back into the driver's seat proud of her accomplishment and gulped down a large swig of water for courage. She put the car into first gear, stomped her foot on the gas pedal and accelerated, leaving the small field far behind. Soon she arrived back at the airport.

After pulling into the Hertz Car Hire for the second time, she was given instructions by the rental agent on the proper way to maneuver the reverse gearshift. "You need push *down* on the stick shift when shifting it into reverse—it's a safety feature."

Rather than feeling embarrassed, Kyra responded, "Thank you so much for your help today. *Jolly good*, I must say . . . I appreciate it!" She swiftly pulled away to begin the drive to Glastonbury, thankful that her delay would have no effect on her plans.

Glancing up at the skyline once she was underway, Kyra could see it was still quite overcast. The dark clouds made the landscape look gray and gloomy. *Okay, I need to shift my energy and focus positively*, she reminded herself, *especially after this crazy morning.* Taking a cleansing breath, she said a prayer for safety, asking the angels for their protection. A few minutes later, she felt remarkably much lighter and happier. *I am feeling better,* she acknowledged. *Thank you, God, for this amazing day.*

Her excitement growing, Kyra looked up and noticed the sun peeking its way out from behind the clouds. The light grew brighter and brighter, and she watched in amazement as the steel-gray sky changed into a brilliant robin's egg blue. Soft, white billowing clouds replaced the dark gray mist, making the transformation breathtaking. The nearby fields suddenly turned an emerald green, reminding her of a favorite childhood movie, *The Wizard of Oz.* She felt truly humbled by how quickly the scenery had changed, almost as if it had reflected her own changing thoughts.

With a smile penciled across her lips, she watched small picturesque towns sweep past her. Rustic country homes and quaint, colorful shops added charm to the now bright landscape—*It does look like the Emerald City*, she said with a childlike giggle, half-expecting to encounter a good witch along the way.

She admired the thatched roofs on the smaller cottages and glimpsed the aged stone walls enclosing the dwellings. The homes appeared well cared for and nestled safely inside their low-lying walls. Farmland, both crops and pastures, added further interest to the scenery. Large black-and-white dairy cows and smaller fuzzy sheep grazed lazily in the bright green pastures.

Kyra began to hum a favorite song, feeling happy as she confidently drove to the town of Glastonbury. *The English countryside is simply stunning and quite inspiring,* she affirmed with appreciation. She felt the angels supporting her on this journey and silently thanked them.

It was nearly noon when Kyra finally arrived at the Abbey House where the Reiki Master training course was to be held. A beautiful nineteenth-century retreat house, it stood on the edge of the famous

Glastonbury Abbey grounds, which she was excited to explore this coming week.

The manager, a tall woman with short blond hair and inquisitive hazel eyes, met Kyra in the lobby and gave her a warm English greeting. "Welcome! You must be here for the Reiki Training class," she offered sweetly, extending her arm.

Kyra nodded as she and the woman exchanged a friendly handshake.

"My name is Mary. Where are you from, *luv?*"

"Hi, Mary—so very nice to meet you," Kyra replied, her face full of anticipation. "I'm Kyra from the U.S. I've been to the U.K. before on business, but never to the English countryside."

"You will have a *fab* time this week," Mary replied. "There will be twenty-six students in all—from all over."

"Yes, it is going to be a *fab* week—I can't wait to meet everyone!"

Mary motioned for Kyra to follow her. "Come this way, my dear, and I'll check you in." She walked behind the reception desk to retrieve Kyra's room key.

"It's quite lovely here," Kyra commented glancing around. "This place must have a very rich history."

"Oh, I have many interesting stories to tell you about our retreat house and the Abbey. And don't be surprised if you encounter a ghost or two," Mary said with a wink.

Kyra's face went ashen with the news that ghosts were thought to visit the premises.

"Ha! Just a little British *humour,*" Mary said jovially. "But do watch your photography here. You may see a strange ball of light in your photographs. We call them *orbs* here in England."

Kyra recalled that orbs were believed to be spirit energy that appeared in photographs as small round lights floating mid-air. "Thanks, Mary, for the heads up," Kyra replied with a hint of unease. "Hopefully it will be a quiet week for paranormal activity."

Mary smiled and handed her the room key, which she pointed out was on the second floor. While the retreat house was the newest building at the Abbey, she explained, the nineteenth-century building did not have an elevator. Much to Kyra's dismay, she had to lug her suitcase up a flight of stairs—one step at a time—just as she had done in Japan.

*Yup . . . next time I'm packing much lighter!* she vowed, letting out a sigh of relief when she finally reached the top of the landing.

She turned the key in the lock—and swept the door open—revealing a simply furnished, tiny room. There were two twin-sized beds with black wrought-iron frames that sat beside a small chest of drawers. The plain bleached walnut chest was to be shared by both guests and offered one drawer each for their clothing.

Kyra glanced around the sparse room. Trying not to cringe, she stepped toward the large window on the wall across from her. Pulling the shutters gently aside, she looked outside . . . and was *stunned* at the magnificent view her eyes beheld. A huge estate stood before her, like the page from a storybook. Thick green grass and well-manicured hedges framed the lawn, but it was the ancient ruins on the grounds that immediately captured her eye.

*This seems so familiar to me,* Kyra reflected, feeling the same strange sensation she had experience in Spain. She knew the buildings at the Abbey had an amazing and colorful history dating back to the seventh century. She recalled having read that five hundred years after they were built—or around the twelfth century—a major fire had destroyed most of the buildings. Many had been rebuilt and even newer ones had been added over the next two hundred years. The Abbey had gone on to become one of the wealthiest monasteries in England.

*Ah, but history has not been kind to you.* Kyra shuddered, recalling more of the Abbey's torrid past. In the mid-sixteenth century, the infamous King Henry VIII became angry with the Catholic Church for refusing to annul one of his marriages. In an act that would forever change the history of England, the king dissolved all monasteries in England. He placed himself as the head of the newly created Church of England—taking the authority completely away from the Pope in Italy.

"I'm so glad I wasn't here to see what followed," Kyra said aloud, remembering that the king had seized all of the Abbey's land and money. Over the next several centuries, the buildings began to crumble, falling into decay from lack of repair. Today, Kyra could see only the ruins of the once beautiful Abbey. She looked across at the soft gray, weathered stones of the buildings, many of which had fallen, leaving only partial walls behind. Roofs were completely missing, and sunlight streamed onto the grass-covered floors. Kyra's imagination ran wild as she visualized England's wealthiest lords and ladies from the past visiting there.

The velvety grass, the ethereal lighting, and the crumbling buildings made for a haunting, yet romantic, vision. She enjoyed the view with joy in her heart. *Ah, you are still beautiful in my eyes,* she thought. *Still?*

To Kyra's wonderment, she slowly began to perceive a faint memory of having once lived at the Abbey. While she couldn't envision any of the details, she felt a warm, happy sensation. She took a moment to cherish the feeling, not pushing for anything more, and closed her eyes to allow the sunlight to caress her face.

When she was ready, she turned her attention back to unpacking, but only a few items fit in her drawer. She set the suitcase off to the side and plopped herself down on one of the twin beds.

Mary had told her earlier that the room did not have a private bathroom. She'd be sharing a single bathroom down the hallway with all the second-floor guests.

*I don't really mind that too much,* she thought with a bounce on the mattress. It felt undeniably firm and she ran her hand over the simple floral bedcover. *I'll make sure I get up extra early for my morning shower*, she playfully told herself. She wanted to ensure she'd have plenty of time to do her hair and makeup in the room before leaving for breakfast. *Some things may never change*, she decided with a laugh.

Tucking away her amusing thoughts, Kyra gathered her purse and retrieved her cell phone to send a few text messages.

The first was to her dear friend back in San Francisco: "Emma, I've been so remiss for not staying in better touch. I do apologize! I'm having a fab time here in England. Can't wait to catch up with you when I return home. Talk to you next week. Luv you. K."

Next she typed a message to her soon-to-be roommate: "Gabby, I'm at the Abbey. OMG that rhymes! LOL I feel like I've stepped into

Hogwarts School of Witchcraft and Wizardry. You have some explaining to do. See you soon ☺"

Gabby had sent a text earlier letting Kyra know that she'd be arriving at the Bristol Airport around 7:00 pm local time. Alejandro had arranged for a limo to take her to the retreat house. He did not want Gabby driving in the English countryside by herself. *How sweet of Alejandro*, Kyra thought . . . *and, boy, how I wish I'd done the same! Well, life is an adventure.* She chuckled as she slipped the phone back into her purse.

With plenty of time to spare, Kyra grabbed her sweater and purse. She stepped gingerly down the flight of stairs, eager to explore the grounds. At the ground level, she took a sharp right turn toward the back of the house. As she walked past the entryway, Kyra ran her hand admiringly along the rich dark wood paneling. She imagined that she could feel its energy, as if the walls were alive with the memories of all that had transpired in this place. The lovely turn-of-the-century Tudor-style interior felt soothing and communicated a warm historical feeling. She retrieved her camera and snapped a few photos to capture the essence of the moment before stepping outside into the gardens.

*The temperatures are dramatically cooler than in Japan*, she realized with a shiver and slipped her sweater over her shoulders. The air felt crisp and inviting. She had read earlier that Glastonbury would reach only the low seventies during the day and then drop to the fifties in the evening.

Turning her attention to the grounds around her, Kyra knew the Abbey had four acres of garden area alone—but the entire site was a *whopping* thirty-six acres of fields and trees. As such, she planned to spend only a few hours exploring the grounds before returning to freshen up for dinner and then await Gabby's arrival.

A nearby patch of flowers with blooms in every imaginable color caught her eyes. Kyra noticed that each garden area was more gorgeous than the next with its extensive variety of flowers and trees. "Surely there must be fairies hidden in here," she said with childlike spirit as she continued her walk across the expansive grounds.

The sun shown brightly overhead, and Kyra felt delighted to be beneath its glow. She slipped on her sunglasses and studied her map of the Abbey, before stepping toward the medieval ruins in front of her. Across from her stood the enormous twin towers she had seen from her room, but sadly only a few partial sidewalls of the entire building remained.

*According to the map, this was once the Great Church at the Abbey*, Kyra noted. The crumbling towers were the original site of the high altar—or the chief altar upon which the Holy Sacrifice of the Mass was performed. The walls stretched up into the sky, soaring way above her head.

Kyra walked slowly through the ancient ruins, running her hand along one the crumbling walls. She felt happy and strangely sad at the same time to be there, wishing she could have seen the church in its glory days. The feeling was bittersweet, but hauntingly familiar. She was lost in her thoughts when she exited the church—and suddenly stumbled.

Coming to a complete standstill, Kyra was shocked by what she saw. A nondescript metal sign offered some unexpected information about the Abbey. *"Oh my!"* Kyra said under her breath. Her heart skipped a beat, as she took a step back to look at it a second time. The small sign read: "Site of King Arthur's tomb. In the Year 1191 the bodies of King Arthur and his Queen were said to have been found on the south side of The Lady Chapel."

The sign went on to further say, "On April 19th 1278 their remains were removed in the presence of King Edward I and Queen Eleanor to a black marble tomb on this site. This tomb survived until the dissolution of the Abbey in 1539."

Kyra knew that this was due, of course, to King Henry VIII.

*I've always been fascinated with the legendary love story of King Arthur and Queen Guinevere*, she thought dreamily. *I can't believe it's still being shared all these centuries later!* But truth be told, Kyra knew that it wasn't clear if King Arthur actually ever really existed or was just a legend. Even today, scholars still actively debated this topic, and the truth may never be known. *Even if it is just a legend*, she concluded, *it is an inspiring legend . . . And one that also tells of the Isle of Avalon, the great wizard Merlin, the Sword Excalibur, and the Holy Grail!*

A thought flashed into the forefront of her mind. *Am I standing on the old Isle of Avalon?* Intrigued by the idea, she made a mental note to ask Mary for clarification when she returned to the Abbey House. She knew from her history classes that much of the area had been marshlands centuries ago and largely covered in water, so it fit the description.

Kyra tossed her head back and closed her eyes to better use her intuition to *sense* her surroundings. In her imagination, she could see the mists of Avalon with fog swirling across the marshy land—perhaps on a cold fall day.

*The Abbey does have a mystical feel to it*, she admitted, recalling the same strange feeling she'd experienced when she'd first stood at the window in her room. She soaked in the wondrous sensation, then opened her eyes, and continued her walkabout with reverence.

After more than two hours exploring the ruins—with a few side trips to some additional flower and herb gardens—Kyra made her way back to the Abbey House. Following a light dinner in the dining hall, she stretched out on her mattress to quietly read her Reiki Master manual while she awaited Gabby's arrival.

# 38

A loud, familiar voice roused Kyra from sleep. "*Chica*, wake up! Wake up! It's too early in the evening for you to be dozing off! We have lots of catching up to do."

That was followed by a hearty shake on the shoulder that jolted Kyra fully awake. When her awareness retuned to the room, she immediately perked up. "Gabby, it's so great to see you! You look . . . well, simply *glowing*." she said, straightening up.

Gabby's demeanor seemed particularly bright, and she blushed. "Yes, *uhm* . . . It's funny you would choose those words. I do have a *tiny* bit of good news to share with you," she said in an extra bubbly voice and settled down next to Kyra on the small bed.

Kyra looked at her expectantly.

"*Bien*—You're listening. And you're sitting down—of course you are . . . you're still in bed!" Gabby waved her hands, and with a sparkle in her eye, continued, "Remember when we last saw each other in Barcelona I was bit under the weather? Well, I took your advice about visiting the doctor—*this is very confidential*—but Alejandro and I are expecting!"

"I knew it!" Kyra exclaimed, giving her friend a proper Spanish hug. "You just look so . . . *radiant*. I'm beyond happy for you both!" Shock and amazement that Arianna's words had come true danced in the back of Kyra's mind.

"Ha! It is a little unexpected," Gabby said, rubbing her tummy. "But you knew about our secret engagement. We were waiting to tell *Mamá* about our plan to be married *after* we figured out the when, where, and how a little better. She'd want an exact date, you know."

Kyra smiled, recalling with affection how Carmen had chided Gabby at the family luncheon for being her only unmarried child. "I totally understand," she replied offering a sympathetic look.

"You also recall that *Mamá* was pressuring me to start a family, because I was getting too old," Gabby said, rolling her eyes in mock exasperation. "Alejandro and I have talked it over, and we're planning our wedding date for six weeks from now."

"I am so looking forward to your wedding, Gabby! You know I wouldn't miss it for the world." Kyra felt relieved she didn't have to worry about her work schedule interfering with her ability to make future plans.

"Awesome, *Chica*. Oh . . . but I must finish my story!" Gabby inhaled deeply and continued, "You can imagine how worried I was about telling *Mamá* and *Papá* the news that I was already pregnant since they are traditional Catholics of course." She stood up to release some nervous energy. "Alejandro explained our good news, and *Papá* immediately looked him in the eye, and said in a serious tone of voice. 'Welcome to the family, Alejandro . . . but if you ever break my daughter's heart, I will break your—ah, *neck*.' Of course, you should have heard *that* in Spanish." She giggled, suggesting that she might have softened her father's choice of words. Kyra couldn't contain her laughter and motioned for her to continue.

"Alejandro shook *Papá*'s hand firmly and replied, 'Sir, I love your daughter with all of my heart. I promise to take very good care of her, but I know that I could never replace her *papá*.'"

Kyra let out a heartfelt "*Aww*," and Gabby added, "His words were so beautiful, I almost burst into tears." Her voice lowered a notch, becoming serious again. "Oh, but *Mamá* . . . now that's a different story."

Kyra sat on the edge of the bed in anticipation.

"*Mamá* was the quietest I have ever seen her in my *entire* life. She only uttered the word '*¿Qué?*' . . . which in English of course means, 'What?'"

Gabby grabbed her chest, mimicking her mother. "She grabbed her heart and *fainted* dead away—falling to the floor! I was so panicked. I thought she'd a heart attack and died!" Gabby theatrically lowered herself to the floor, as if she had fainted.

"Oh no!" Kyra interjected.

"Right?" Gabby sat up on the floor and let loose a full-fledged giggle. "Once she came to, the only words she could utter were: 'Praise our Father in Heaven! It's a miracle,' and then she made the sign of the cross. She added, 'My last baby is getting married.'"

Kyra laughed almost falling to the floor to join Gabby.

"*Mamá* was back to herself in no time. I was so relieved! *¡Ay—ay—ay!*"

Both women burst into a fit of giggles. When their laughter died down, they talked about Gabby's wedding plans and the preparations she and Alejandro would be making for the baby. Afterward, Kyra filled Gabby in on her mystical experiences in Japan, which Gabby was very open to hearing.

"I'm a firm believer that *everything* happens for a reason," Gabby reassured her. "All the signs are telling you that you're on the right path now, and amazing things are happening. God does have a plan for you. God has a plan for everyone. *Muwahhh!*" With those final words, Gabby rubbed her belly.

As the women prepared to turn in for the night, Gabby dramatically fluffed her pillow to ensure her comfort, while Kyra set the alarm for 6:00 am hoping she'd have first access to the hall bathroom. She turned off the light and fell into a gentle, deep slumber.

At 5:12 am, Kyra woke abruptly. She'd left the shutters to the window wide open, and the sun was just beginning to rise. *Ugh . . . too early!* she thought, as the bright light streamed into the room. But it wasn't the light that captured her attention—it was the entrancing *sound* she heard coming from outside.

Kyra stumbled out of bed and quietly made her way over to the window. The site she beheld completely took her breath away. A short distance away, a massive oak tree, ancient in appearance, was filled with hundreds of blackbirds sweetly singing. Their song was melodic, and their voices grew in volume with the rising sun. It appeared as if they were singing to God, welcoming in the brand-new day.

*Oh my!* Kyra's heart fluttered. *They sound like angels!*

In amazement, she stood riveted to the windowpane as she watched the choir of blackbirds fill the air with their endearing melody. Her eyes filled with tears, and she pressed her hand against her heart center. *Maybe the angels are welcoming me to this magical land of Glastonbury.*

Kyra remained at the window a few minutes longer, drinking in the sweetness of the moment, and then gently closed the shutters. She glanced over at Gabby, who let out a soft snore having slept through the whole adventure. She smiled at the fond reminder of Raquel in Andalucía. *Yes, the family resemblance is priceless.*

Returning to her bed, Kyra snuggled under the covers and closed her eyes to fall back asleep. However, the birdsong reached a pulsating crescendo—growing *louder* and *louder*—until Kyra realized she couldn't sleep. She pressed her pillow over her head, hoping to muffle their sweet song. *Even angels can be a bit too noisy sometimes!* She chuckled and drifted off into a light sleep.

When the alarm buzzed at 6:00 am, Kyra jumped up straightaway and tiptoed down the hallway to shower, easing in and out before anyone else stopped by. When she returned to the room, she woke Gabby up with a gently shake.

Gabby lazily opened her eyes. "I think I'm sleeping a bit more soundly with the baby on the way," she said with a dreamy expression. Then her eyes grew wide and she completely perked up. "And I'm starving. *¡Date prisa!* I will shower immediately and then we are off to breakfast. I could eat an entire cow!" She took off down the hallway.

The women arrived in the dining hall on the first floor promptly at 8:30 am, but the room was already full of their classmates in the midst of eating. They found a couple of seats at one of the tables and were greeted by a man in his mid-fifties with short salt-and-pepper colored hair.

"Hi, my name is Jonathan," he said in humble distinctive drawl that gave away his Texas roots. "I'm the Reiki Master Teacher who will be leading the class this week. It's very nice to meet you both. Welcome." He extended his hand to Gabby first.

In turn, each woman introduced herself to Jonathan and shook his hand. Kyra finished by saying how genuinely excited she was to be in Glastonbury and experience the area.

"It will be an exciting adventure for us all," Jonathan responded, his blue eyes twinkling. "Enjoy breakfast, and we'll talk more later." He motioned toward the buffet.

Kyra and Gabby stepped forward to survey the choice of breakfast items laid out on a traditional cherry wood table covered in a crisp linen tablecloth. The table was overflowing with fresh seasonal fruit, cereals, yogurt, scrambled eggs, hard-boiled eggs, English crumpets, toast—and of course coffee, tea and juice. Both women helped themselves and met back up at the table.

Kyra glanced over at Gabby's plate, which was noticeably piled high. "Well, Gabby, I can safely say that you are definitely eating for two with the looks of that plate," she joked, knowing her friend would enjoy the ribbing.

Gabby blushed, and then raised her chin indignantly, "*¡Sí!* I feel like I'm eating for more than two. This baby is starving."

A look of surprise washed over Kyra's face as Arianna's words sprang to mind: Gabby was expecting *twins*. Smiling, she quickly regained her poker face and took a sip of her coffee.

As the women ate, they engaged in introductions and conversation with their tablemates. A married couple sitting across the table introduced themselves. Both appeared to be in their late-fifties and had bright features accentuated by their lively eyes. Their soft Southern drawl fondly reminded Kyra of Emma. Tom and D'Lisa, as it turned out, were from Arkansas.

Another woman, Ella, had responded to Gabby's greeting with "*G'day. How ya' going?*" There was little doubt she was from "Down Under." She happily confirmed that she was indeed from Australia and the conversation between the two flowed on from there.

Kyra soon found herself chatting with Ivan from Russia, who was seated on her left. His voice was deep and serious, but his tone was kind and gentle. They discussed many topics, including politics. When their conversation concluded, he offered Kyra a hearty, *"Mir s Vami."* which he explained meant 'Peace be with you.'

Kyra thanked him for the blessing and replied, "Peace be with you, too."

"This is going to be a fascinating class, Gabby!" Kyra said, turning back to her friend. "I can't wait to meet the rest of the students and learn about them and where they come from."

"There's a whole big world out there, *Chica,* and *you* are just beginning to see it." Gabby responded, turning next to speak to Isabella, who it turned out was from Brazil.

The room buzzed as everyone got acquainted and finished up their morning meal.

When the last of the dishes had been cleared away, Jonathan stood at the front to make an announcement. "Good morning, everyone, and welcome to this wonderful place called Glastonbury!"

The students clapped and someone let out a cheer. Jonathan laughed before continuing. "We have a *very* exciting week planned for you. Let's assemble in the sitting room down the hall at 9:30 am. Please bring your training manual—and a positive smile with you—as we will begin our magical journey. I look forward to seeing each of you shortly." With that, he left the room, allowing the students time to gather their belongings.

~

The spacious sitting room had a charming, country atmosphere with soft green walls, thick wool carpeting, and tall ceilings framed in white crown molding. Bright morning light flooded the room through the floor-to-ceiling triple-paned windows, which perfectly framed the colorful outdoor gardens. Kyra breathed a happy sigh. *My inner child wants to go outside and play!* she thought, but she sat down instead on one of the leather chairs assembled in a large circle around the room.

A huge cherry wood coffee table sat squarely in the middle and was filled with polished and natural crystals of every imaginable kind. Gabby stopped to examine several of the geodes, including a sparkling amethyst.

She marveled to Kyra that it was of the deepest purple she'd ever seen, before taking a seat across the room.

Jonathan arrived on time and began their day with a quick overview of the coursework for the week ahead. "If anyone has questions as we go along, please speak up and ask. We'll also spend time outside on these extraordinary grounds for some of our sessions this week. I think you will have a truly special experience, so let's get started."

Next Jonathan gave the students an overview of his background. "I've been involved with Reiki for more than thirty years, long before it became more mainstream in the United States and elsewhere. I was seeking answers for my own healing. Through my daily meditation, I received guidance to travel to Japan to learn Reiki. I met with several masters who had directly trained with the original students of Dr. Usui, the founder."

When Jonathan finished sharing his own story, he asked the students to do the same. "Please begin by telling the group your name, your country of origin, and a brief description of what you hope to gain from the training this week."

After all twenty-six students had all complied with his request, Kyra's jaw nearly dropped open. She quickly calculated that they represented *eighteen* different countries—spanning *six* continents! From the U.S. came Tom and D'Lisa from Arkansas, Jean from New York, Elsie from Florida, Kevin from Georgia, and of course she was from California. Rafael was from Mexico, and Carolyn was from Canada, which rounded out the North America continent.

From Europe there was Nina and Alain, a delightful couple from Belgium, Dimitra and Kostas were both from Greece, Ivan from Russia, Zoé from France, Vicki and Di Di were from England, Carmelo from Italy, Heinrich or "Henry" from Germany, and lastly her dear friend Gabby from Spain.

From the Asian continent came Arjun from India, Daniel from Israel, and Nicholas from Singapore. From South Africa there was Benjamin, which checked off the African continent, and Isabella from Brazil, who represented South America. Lastly there was Ella from Australia, which is its own separate continent, and last but not least, Sophie, who came from New Zealand. Kyra scratched her head recalling that New Zealand wasn't actually a part of any continent technically, but rather was thought to be a large island. She laughed inwardly when she remembered there was some controversy on that topic.

*I'm in total awe of these amazing people from all over the globe!* Kyra thought, stunned by their diversity. She felt truly blessed by the opportunity to make many new friends over the next five days. *Yes, the Universe indeed intended for me to be here today—and I'm so glad that I decided to listen.*

With the introductions concluded, Jonathan led the group in a relaxing guided meditation—a scenic visualization up a mountainside—to help shield, protect, and ground each student. With eyes closed, Kyra visualized walking through a golden meadow and then up a mountainside, eventually coming to a stop when she encountered a large obstacle blocking her path—a massive boulder.

The students were asked to visualize the boulder crumbling, as they continued forward to reach their destination—a magical crystal palace.

*What a wonderful metaphor,* Kyra thought. *And a perfect reflection of my own journey.* An overwhelming sense of accomplishment flooded her aura. She felt proud for overcoming all of the obstacles on her own path to reach her destination. *Wherever it may take me*, she affirmed.

The day continued with a variety of class discussions and exercises, culminating with the review of the Advanced Reiki Training attunement that both Kyra and Gabby had received previously. They opted instead for a healing attunement, which both found incredibly enjoyable.

After finishing the day's lessons, the students met up in the main dining hall for dinner. Gabby led Kyra quickly to one of the long tables. The home-style dinner included generous bowls of pasta drenched in lemon-artichoke pesto, freshly baked bread called a cottage loaf, and colorful crisp vegetables sprinkled with rosemary and thyme. Every guest took as much, or as little, as they desired. Second helpings were plentiful, and while Kyra was hungry from the day's activities, she couldn't help but notice again how *famished* Gabby appeared to be. She wore an amused expression as her friend heaped piles of pasta on her plate and had two-second helpings, despite her small frame.

With a forkful of food nearly to her mouth, Gabby looked over at Kyra and noticed the wry expression on her friend's face. She burst into laughter. "As I said this morning, I know it looks like I'm eating for *three* instead of two, but I'm just soooo hungry. . . ."

"This is your time to indulge," Kyra joked.

"Yes, but don't tell Alejandro!" Gabby added and smugly slid the bite of pasta between her lips.

Kyra thought again about Arianna's words and whether Gabby was indeed eating for three. *If so, it will be another unique confirmation of my experience with Arianna.* But she already knew in her heart that her experience had been real. The fact alone that Arianna had predicted that Gabby was pregnant had astounded Kyra. She also knew deep in her core that Gabby was indeed a part of her soul family—just as Arianna had described to her. A sweet smile illuminated her face as she returned to the moment.

"Ha! My dear girlfriend—I'd enjoy nothing more than to see you eating for *three*. Someday I will do the same," Kyra said, startling herself that she had made it sound as if she too planned on having twins. *Where did that come from?* she thought suddenly. Her mind drifted back to the odd feeling she had experienced in Barcelona about the possibility of her having twins someday, but she filed the idea away when Gabby interrupted her.

"I look forward to the day when *you* are pregnant," Gabby said, pointing at Kyra.

"We will share stories, no doubt!" Kyra said in anticipation and scooped up the last bite of pasta on her plate.

After a few moments, Gabby excused herself to go check out the desserts, and Kyra turned to the couple sitting next to her—Nina and Alain from Belgium. "Hi. I'm Kyra. I haven't yet had the opportunity to meet you, but I'm very much looking forward to getting to know you both this week."

Alain spoke up first, with a slight Dutch accent, "Hi, Kyra. It's nice to meet you too. Nina and I are excited to be here. It's a very special trip for us both."

Kyra learned that Alain and Nina were in their mid-thirties and had been married for about eight years. They had two children, a boy and girl, ages seven and five. She also learned that Alain had a corporate career just like she once did and that Nina was taking time to pursue her metaphysical interests while raising two kids as a stay-at-home mom.

"It's fantastic that you both were able to take the training class together," she commented. "May I ask how you became interested in the master training?"

In a sweet, soft-spoken voice, Nina took control of the conversation, "Actually, there's a very good question, Kyra," she said, glancing over at Alain, who nodded for her to continue. "The reason we are both attending this class is because five years ago I was a diagnosed with stage-three ovarian cancer."

Kyra held back a gasp, trying to hide her surprise.

Nina calmly continued, "I know that's shocking. I had surgery of course, and we did chemotherapy, but the survival rate after five years is only about forty percent. I began to do research on alternative treatments, and Alain and I both agreed to try Reiki as a *complementary* treatment too," Nina said, making sure she used the correct English word. "I found a Reiki Master in our hometown of Brussels, and we immediately started weekly sessions. I felt so much more positive about healing myself after I started the sessions. I quickly made a decision to take level one and two classes and Alain joined me as well."

Alain's face softened, and he interjected, "To be honest, Kyra, I never had an interest in learning Reiki, but Nina means the world to me. I thought long and hard, but once I made the decision to take the classes, I began to appreciate the relaxation benefits," he said, turning more fully toward Kyra. "Of course that's on top of the healing aspect of the practice. I wanted to do whatever it took to heal my *lieverd*—that means 'darling' in Dutch." Nina gazed lovingly at her husband as he continued. "We sit here today with a 'clean bill of health,' as you say in the U.S., and continue our path as Lightworkers."

"I'm just stunned, to say the least . . . that's a miracle indeed," Kyra said, squeezing Nina's hand. "I now realize that my own path as a Lightworker is just beginning to unfold. You are *such* an inspiration to me, and I'm sure we were meant to meet." Kyra swallowed a small lump in her throat and reached out to embrace Nina; her gesture was warmly accepted.

Settling back in her seat, Nina said, "I truly enjoy helping people, Kyra—it's my passion. I'm building a Reiki business back home. It would be wonderful to stay in touch so that we can share 'best practices,' as you call it."

"That sounds perfect Nina. I'd love that!" Kyra replied, excited by the idea of building a network of Reiki practitioners. "I'm making big changes in my life when I return to California. I just left the corporate world and you've helped me see even more how much I enjoy helping others. My grandmother taught me that lesson as well, but I didn't give it much attention until after she passed away . . ." Her voice trailed off as she stared into the faces of the amazing couple. She thought of how difficult Nina's health challenge must have been on them, and she tried not to cry.

Nina looked deeply into her eyes and responded, "Don't feel sorry for me, Kyra. Looking back, I believe the cancer had a divine purpose . . . from God to put me on this new path."

Alain concurred. "Although I still work in the corporate world, Kyra, I too believe my path has forever been changed. I'm now completely embracing my spiritual side. Becoming a Reiki Master is just one more step for me, and for Nina, so we can help others heal. Everything in life has a purpose . . . this was just God's way of showing us what we were meant to do."

Kyra wholeheartedly agreed. She retrieved a piece of paper from her purse to jot down their contact information. *The Universe is simply remarkable,* she thought. *I'm so blessed to have the chance to get to know this amazing couple.*

She lovingly reflected back on her conversation with Arianna on the topic of Lightworkers. *I truly now understand, Arianna, why this path was been chosen for me—despite its not being obvious at first. Thank you so very much for all your help*. She closed her eyes, hoping that Arianna could hear her thoughts.

As Gabby devoured the last morsel of her apple tart, Kostas from Greece was standing up to make an announcement. With dinner nearly finished, everyone gave him their full attention.

"It's been great to make so many new friends on our first day!" he said enthusiastically. "Tonight I'll be exploring the grounds and everyone is welcome to join me. We'll meet on the back patio in about ten minutes and go from there. Thank you."

Gabby leaned over. "A little walk on the grounds after this huge feast may be a very good idea for this *bebé*."

*Bebés*, Kyra secretly corrected, excited at the prospect. "A group walk sounds perfect. I'd love to see more of these enchanting grounds."

With Kostas in the lead, a group of about a dozen students proceeded toward the ruins Kyra had explored the previous evening. Smaller groups soon formed, and Gabby slipped off with a new acquaintance. Kyra ended up beside Victoria—or Vicki as she preferred to be called—whom she knew from their earlier class introduction lived in London.

The Englishwoman looked to be about forty-five or so and stood about five-foot-ten. Thin like a runway model, Vicki had deep ebony skin. Her long black hair had auburn highlights, and her luminous green eyes shimmered with gold flecks when she spoke. Kyra instantly felt as if she knew this woman, and they both took an immediate liking to each other. They walked side by side like they had always been friends.

"Kyra—that's a very *lovely* name, I must say. Is this your first time to visit our *wicked Blighty?*" Vicki asked. Her voice had a mischievous lilt. "That means 'Britain' in case you didn't know."

Kyra's ears soaked in Vicki's delightful accent like a sponge. "Yes, I've been to your *wicked* country before, but mostly to London on business," Kyra replied. "This is my first trip here for pleasure and this area is truly enchanting . . . but I've had the strangest feeling like I've been here before."

"Oh, you stand upon the very grounds of Avalon—the place where King Arthur and Queen Guinevere once walked—but that was a *blimey* long time ago!" Vicki gaily laughed. "Truthfully, I've always had an affinity for this place myself. It's very near and dear to my heart. I shall be a cracking good tour guide for you here this evening at the Abbey. It would be my pleasure."

"I would be most appreciative," Kyra said, her intuition kicking in. She had a hunch that she and Vicki would become lifelong friends.

"Fantastic! Let me tell you about this incredible Abbey," Vicki said, gesturing across the grounds. "First thing to note, we are *favoured* to walk about after hours since we are guests at the Abbey House. It's a special privilege reserved only for us because the grounds are closed now to the regular tourist."

"Fantastic indeed." Kyra agreed, feeling thankful for the privilege.

"The Abbey's buildings were mostly destroyed by fire in the late twelfth century—give or take a few years—but rebuilt in the fifteen century. Then our beloved Abbey went on to become one of the richest monasteries in all of England. That is, until our famous King Henry VIII dissolved all monasteries in the sixteenth century, seizing the land and its coffers of money—that *dodgy bloke!*" She laughed again. "We're now walking through the main church, and in just a moment we'll see the splendid Lady Chapel dedicated to the Virgin Mary. . . . Ah, such a shame that it all lay in ruins now."

Kyra echoed her sentiment. She thoroughly enjoyed Vicki's colorful storytelling of the Abbey's history and couldn't wait to see what was in store for them next.

Once they reached the Lady Chapel, the women paused inside to view the semi-restored interior of the medieval building. Many of the walls had been gently cleaned to remove years of grime and restore the natural stone color. The walls stretched straight up into to the early evening sky—but the roof had long ago disintegrated. Now the sun shown brightly across the grass-covered floor, and small vines of ivy grew along some of the interior walls. Centuries of rain, snow, and sun had taken its toll on the once lavish splendor of the chapel.

Kyra closed her eyes and envisioned the chapel during the height of its glory in medieval times. She spun slowly around, and in her mind's eye, she could picture English nobility leisurely strolling across a stone floor. Accompanied by noblemen or knights, ladies were dressed in long, flowing gowns of rich jewel-tone colors. A choir sang, while worshipers made the sign of the cross before taking their seats for Sunday mass.

Kyra's daydream faded when Vicki spoke again, spinning yet another imaginative tale of the Abbey's heritage. "You know, legend says that Joseph of Arimathea—that's the Uncle of the Virgin Mary by the way—founded this Abbey in the first century. About a century later, Christian missionaries were thought to have built the first church here, right where the Lady Chapel now stands. *Wicked,* yes?"

"Not *too* wicked, I hope," Kyra quipped.

The gold flecks in Vicki green eyes sparkled as she spoke. "Let's look around a bit more, *luv*, before the sun sets. Did I mention that St. Patrick is also thought to have visited this area, and there's a chapel here dedicated to him too? You'll definitely want to visit that chapel during the daytime to fully appreciate the stained-glass windows and the lovely wall etchings inside. They're just fabulous!"

Kyra loved the idea of a daytime visit—and felt strangely drawn to the chapel, but she had no idea why. She brushed off the sensation and responded, "You're such a doll, Vicki—and your spin on history simply entertaining."

Vicki's face brightened. "Thank you," she said with a grin.

Soon the women came upon an expansive herb garden, which was surrounded by a gravel walking path. Kyra noted a variety of herbs, most of which were in full bloom. She squinted to read the small signs. Among them were lemon thyme, rosemary, French tarragon, parsley, and chamomile—many of her favorites. She stooped down to take a pinch of the rosemary, rubbing the herb on her fingertips to enjoy its distinctive fragrance.

Vicki spotted a rustic-looking wooden bench beneath a mature elm tree and motioned for Kyra to join her. The tree's gnarled branches were thick with summer leaves, offering them a shady spot for a short break.

Vicki pointed across the way. "The building over there is the site of the original kitchen for the Abbey. It's one of the oldest and best-preserved medieval kitchens found in world." Kyra admired the unusual shape of the stone exterior and the sloping roof, as Vicki continued, "There's a fantastic tour of the grounds here during the day. It includes an actor portraying a fourteenth-century monk who works in the kitchen. His sense of *humour* is quite *brilliant*, not to mention his informative presentation on how the kitchen worked and the foods consumed back then. Well worth the visit, if you can fit it into your schedule."

"That's like something out of *Monty Python and the Holy Grail*," Kyra joked, which elicited a knowing nod from Vicki.

Realizing it was getting late, the women headed back for the evening. They were chatting away when Vicki reached out to steer Kyra away from a gnarly tree root. "I'd hate for you to fall on your *bum, luv*," she said.

"I'm glad you have my *arse* covered," Kyra replied with a mock English accent.

With laughter on their lips, they walked into the retreat house and said good night to a few of the students who were still milling about inside.

When Kyra reached her room, Gabby was already fast asleep. She gave her friend a kiss on the cheek, put on her nightshirt, and slid into bed. Kyra drifted off immediately—and thought she saw, in the distance, her parents smiling at her.

# 39

Like clockwork, at 5:13 am the next morning, the choir of blackbirds woke Kyra with their lyrical morning song. This time she had remembered to close the shutters, but again their voices increased in volume as the sun continued to rise. Kyra smiled, and gently pulled the pillow over her head to muffle the sound, drifting back to sleep until the 6:00 am alarm.

The morning proceeded in much the same way as the day before with the two friends joining the other students in the main dining hall for breakfast. Kyra looked forward to the opportunity to get to know more of her classmates.

At 9:30 am, the students drifted into the peaceful green study and took their seats. Jonathan elaborated on the coursework planned for the day. "After we finish our morning meditation, we will move outside into the backyard. The weather is much too nice to sit inside today. We have chairs set up in a semicircle for us to work on our lessons, so we'll enjoy nature at the same time."

Once the guided morning meditation concluded, the group stepped outside and sat in the red fabric-covered chairs. Kyra sat beside Zoé from France, whom she had also spoken to briefly at breakfast. Rafael from Mexico, whom she had not yet met, sat down on her opposite side. He was of average height and slender build with a fair complexion. His deep-set, dark brown eyes and sweet demeanor immediately captivated Kyra.

"Hi, Rafael," she said, extending her hand. "It's nice to finally meet you. What brought you to this training class from Mexico?"

"Hello, Kyra—nice to meet you too," he replied, taking her hand in his and pulled her in for a warm embrace. Kyra felt a tingling sensation similar to what she'd experienced when she met Francisco in Barcelona, but she kept her thoughts to herself.

"I plan to become a Reiki Master Teacher and do healing work full time when I return to Mexico City. I feel very blessed to be here today. What about you?"

Kyra noticed that his English was very good and he only had a slight Spanish accent. "That's so exciting," Kyra responded, glad for her new friend. "I came to the class kind of serendipitously. . . . I guess that's a mouthful." She giggled at her choice of words. "I've recently been through some major life changes, which has me rethinking my life. Then out of the blue, my friend Gabby invited me to join her this week. I booked this course last minute and was extremely lucky to get a spot—one of the students canceled, so I was able to take her place." Kyra's eyes danced as she thought of her good fortune.

"Ah, Kyra," Rafael said reassuringly, "I believe there are no accidents in life, and you were *absolutely* meant to be here today. The Universe provided you with the opportunity, and you were brave enough to take it. This is true for all of us."

Kyra looked into Rafael's eyes and melted. "You are exactly right. I asked the Universe to help me find the answers about what I should do with my life—and I ended up here," she said, confirming again how important it is to follow the signs. "I've been thinking of pursuing at least part-time work in the healing arts after I return home," she continued. "I think you've further inspired me to do just that. Thanks so much for sharing your aspirations with me. It feels like we were destined to meet."

Rafael nodded in agreement, and Kyra pictured him in the future being very successful and happy in his new career. She felt, once again that a friendship would blossom long after their class ended.

After allowing time for the students to continue their bonding process, Jonathan led a group discussion on the core values of a Reiki Master. He next asked everyone to do a practice session by giving each other attunements—which was one of the key skills of a Master Teacher. Last, he covered the use of distance healing, in which one doesn't need to physically be with a person to send them Reiki. Kyra was fascinated by the idea of sending Reiki to anyone through her thoughts via meditation.

She recalled from her high school physics class why that may be possible. All living things are made up of atoms, and each atom is made of smaller particles called protons, neutrons, and electrons—which are constantly in motion. *We are all basically energy fields*, she concluded. Even now, she knew that scientists could measure the human energy field using sophisticated equipment. *If that's true, we really are all connected across this dynamic energy field that we live in—so distance healing makes perfect sense!* A goofy grin spread across Kyra's face. *I'm such a geek. Nana used to tell me that too.*

With that last thought, she was also reminded of the times when she would suddenly think of Nana—and a phone call would come through from her grandmother almost instantaneously. How could Nana know she was thinking of her when they lived so far away from each other? *I'd like to think it's because my love traveled across the energy field, and Nana felt it too.* Kyra felt her heart swell, then her thoughts returned to the class lecture.

It was late afternoon when Jonathan dismissed the group. "I'd like to thank each and every one of you for a truly remarkable day," he said in parting. "I'm very excited about your accomplishments. Feel free to ask me any questions before we meet back up for dinner tonight at six thirty. I will see you soon."

As everyone gathered their belongings, Kyra turned to Zoé with whom she'd started a discussion about intuitive experiences during the mid-afternoon break. "It's been nice getting to know you better. I'd very much like to continue our conversation when you have time."

Zoé responded in her heavy accent, "*Merci!* It has been my pleasure, dear Kyra." She stood up with her camera in hand. "I'd love to take a few photographs in this magnificent garden. Would you join me? We can talk after."

Kyra didn't hesitate. "Of course! That's a great idea."

A few others from the group joined them as well, including Rafael, Sophie from New Zealand, and Nicholas from Singapore. Photos were snapped, and lively conversation was exchanged. When the group walked back inside, they met up with several more students gathered in the downstairs hallway.

"*Excusez-moi!*" Zoé exclaimed. "May I take a group photo of everyone? Come, come! Let's assemble, and I will take a few photos. Yes?"

About fifteen students obliged by forming a single line in the dark hallway. Zoé stood with camera in hand and said, "Squeeze in closer so I can fit you into the picture." She then yelled, "Smile! *Ouistiti!*" and she took several pictures. "Wait, don't move," she said, stepping back to examine the photos on her digital camera. "This old house is very dark inside. Let me make sure the flash worked and none are blurred."

The group hung tight, and Zoé let out an unexpected gasp. "Oh, my goodness! We seem to have some visitors in our photographs."

Kyra and the other students waited for an explanation.

"My dear Kyra. If you look closely at this picture, you'll see three orbs just above your head."

As Kyra stepped closer to exam the photos, her thoughts raced back to Mary's comment that orbs were common occurrence inside the house.

"I'll send you a larger photograph so you can see it more clearly," Zoé offered, "but there they are!" She pointed to the small screen.

Kyra squinted at the picture. Sure enough, she could clearly see three tiny round balls of light just above her head. A shiver went down her spine.

Zoé noticed the look of concern on Kyra's face as the other students gathered around to examine the photograph. Isabella from Brazil, whose native tongue was Portuguese, spoke first. "*Nossa!*" she exclaimed, her eyes intense. "Orbs are a good thing. It means that loved ones are close by. Do you have any loved ones, Kyra, who may be around you?"

Kyra felt her knees go weak. She took a moment to gather her thoughts. "Actually, yes, Isabella. I lost my grandmother recently—and I've been thinking a lot about my mother and father lately, too. They passed away several years ago." The students all looked surprised, but

Kyra calmly added, "I have a funny feeling it may be them in the pictures, and they are with me even now . . . at least that's what I'd like to think."

Vicki stepped forward and gave Kyra a hug. "That does make perfect sense, *darlin'*—and, yes, I believe with all of my heart that you are right."

Kyra appreciated the warm assurance, but silently thought back to many of her strange experiences thus far. On the way to dinner later that evening, she filled Gabby in on the unusual occurrence. Her dear friend was not at all shocked.

Afterward, they retired to the downstairs library and spent time preparing for their next day's lessons. Both women went to sleep early, and Kyra drifted off when her head hit the pillow. She recalled her last thought just before she fell asleep: *Thank you, Nana, Mother, and Father for visiting me today. I can't wait to see you again.*

The next morning, Kyra was awoken by the 6 am alarm. She was shocked that the blackbirds had not roused her with their morning song. Groggily, she hit the snooze button a few times before propping herself up in bed and then heading down the hallway to get ready for her day.

At breakfast, Gabby generously heaped the eggs, fruit, and crumpets on her plate, only returning once for a second helping. Inspired by her friend's appetite, Kyra ate a hearty breakfast as well. Afterward, the women made their way to the sitting room for their class agenda and morning meditation.

Once the students were seated, Jonathan made his morning announcement: "Today we will begin the *final* phase of our Master Teacher training!"

A few of the students applauded, and Jonathan raised his hand to acknowledge their excitement. "Tomorrow evening we will travel to Stonehenge for our Master Level attunement. It will be an extraordinary ceremony, and I have a small surprise for you." Jonathan's face lit up. "As you may be aware, this prehistoric monument is roped off—and visitors are not allowed to walk among the stones. However, we have special permission to have our ceremony *inside* the stones after the visitors leave.

Once we finish our meditation, I'll fill you in on the rich history of these sacred grounds."

The students exchanged excited looks before closing their eyes to prepare for the morning meditation. After grounding their energy with a few deep breaths, Jonathan took them on a delightful guided visualization along a pathway that eventually led to a hidden treasure box. Kyra could vividly picture in her mind's eye the trail winding through a forest and up into the hillside.

Once she had the treasure box in hand, she examined it. It was an ornate box with crushed red velvet and gold filigree around the edges. *A box fit for a king*, she smiled. *King Arthur to be precise!*

Next Jonathan instructed the students to visualize opening the box to see what lay inside for each of them. "It will be a unique gift just for you and something of special meaning," he explained.

Kyra squeezed her eyes tighter and suddenly saw the crushed red velvet box pop open. Inside lay an ornate golden key. *Oh! Like the statue of the Japanese foxes with the keys in their mouths.* she realized with excitement. The key glistened, and she visualized rolling it over in her hand. *What meaning do you have for me?* she asked the key.

The words she heard were simple, "Unlock yourself."

*How strange.* she reacted, trying to gain clarity on the meaning. After thinking it through for a few more minutes, it suddenly came to her. *You want me to unlock my potential! Yes, that's perfect . . . and thank you so much for the message.*

Kyra vowed she'd pursue her metaphysical interests wholeheartedly upon returning home to San Francisco—no matter what any of her former colleagues or friends might think.

After finishing the meditation, Jonathan went on to describe the amazing history and significance of Stonehenge. "You may have read up on Stonehenge before arriving here, but let me fill you in on some of the more unique historical and spiritual significance of the area—which we'll be visiting tomorrow evening."

The students were on the edge of their seats.

"Stonehenge was built over five thousand years ago in a variety of stages and took around fifteen hundred years to complete! The largest stones weigh up to *forty-five tons* and were moved more than nineteen miles. Even to this day, we have no idea how all of this was accomplished."

A few students murmured in wonder, and Jonathan continued, "The site is one of the most unique stone circle structures of any prehistoric people on Earth, both in terms of the design, construction, and sheer size of the stones here. The location also has great spiritual significance due to the ley lines that cross here. Because of the ley lines, it's believed the area has powerful healing energies."

Jean, whom Kyra knew was from New York, raised her hand and asked, "What is a ley line exactly? I've never fully understood the concept."

"That's a great question, Jean," Jonathan answered. "Ley lines are thought to be geographical alignments on the earth that connect both natural sites and prehistoric manmade structures together. Ancient monuments and megaliths often mark the lines. Some people believe these lines may correlate to magnetic energy fields on the earth."

Jonathan took a deep breath, allowing the students to absorb what he'd told them thus far, and then he continued, "But the most important significance is *where* the ley lines cross—or intersect—as these intersections are believed to be great energy points on the earth. Stonehenge and the Egyptian pyramids are both great examples. It's also thought that these intersections have important spiritual significance and healing powers."

Many of the students nodded to indicate that they understood, and no further questions were asked regarding the ley lines. Jean expressed her appreciation for the clarification.

"Let me give you some additional thoughts on why Stonehenge is spiritually significant," Jonathan said, moving about the room. The students were listening carefully, their eyes following Jonathan as he continued his monologue, "It specifically sits on the largest ley line in England called Saint Michael's ley line. This ley line also passes through Glastonbury, which I'll talk more about tomorrow. We'll also visit the town of Glastonbury in the afternoon too. Saint Michael's ley line passes through Avebury in England as well—and just so you know, Avebury is the largest stone circle in Europe. It's another famous Neolithic henge monument and prehistoric site."

"That's very cool!" Elsie said loudly, and the other students laughed with her at her outburst.

Jonathan gave her a smile. "Before we digress too far, let's get back to Stonehenge specifically," Jonathan said, returning to his seat. "Stonehenge was designated a World Heritage Site in 1986. And while Avebury is the largest site with three stone circles, Stonehenge is the most architecturally complex prehistoric stone circle in the world. The stones were cut using very sophisticated techniques and erected with interlocking joints—unseen in other similar stone monuments at the time. The stones were in continual use for more than *two thousand* years. They were used in both Neolithic and Bronze Age ceremonies—even for burial practices," Jonathan added, pausing for any questions, none of which came.

"There are many theories on the origins of Stonehenge," he continued, a glimmer of humor crossing his face. "These include a Druid temple." He paused. "An astronomical computer that recorded eclipses and solar events—the summer and winter solstice are examples—and an ancient site of worship for the celebration of births, deaths, weddings, and even rites of initiation into priesthood."

Jonathan leaned forward, as if what he had to say next required full attention. "But, more importantly, as I mentioned earlier, the stones are thought to have great healing power due to the energy associated with the ley lines. As Lightworkers, we understand the importance of healing and helping others. We are very privileged to have private access to the center of the stones for our ceremony, and I look forward to taking you there tomorrow evening."

Kyra couldn't sit still in anticipation of what their experiences would entail. Gabby caught her eye from across the room and mouthed, "We are going to have a blast!" Kyra's return smile indicated she had no doubt her friend was right.

Jonathan concluded by giving instructions for the day's workshop, and then moved the students outside to enjoy the magnificent weather.

Today, they formed smaller groups in the gardens to practice giving attunements.

Kyra's group included Benjamin whom she recalled was from South Africa, Henry from Germany, and Carolyn from Canada.

The students each took turns giving and receiving attunements to refine their skills.

Kyra couldn't help but feel the amazingly positive energy of the Abbey as they practiced. After finishing one session and preparing for the next, she took a moment to admire the powdery blue sky. Cotton-candy clouds gently drifted across the horizon. She glanced down at the vibrant green grass, which felt like suede carpeting. *Mother Nature is truly amazing*, she straightened her shoulders, feeling blessed to be there.

Magnificently large English oak, bay willow, and lilac trees hugged the ground with their huge roots, lifting their wonderful branches up to the sun, drinking in the nourishment. A warm summer breeze swayed the branches of a Copper Beach tree, which added a bold splash of coppery red to the landscape. Wild flowers added touches of color, including patches of corn chamomile with bright yellow centers and daisy-like white petals, which contrasted nicely with another flower with big pompom-shaped blooms in deep lilac hue.

When they finally took a fifteen-minute break, Kyra struck up a conversation with Carolyn, whom she sat next to while enjoying some tea. A serious yet sweet-looking woman, she had long blond hair and bright blue eyes. Kyra guessed she was about her age. Carolyn volunteered that she worked for a major consulting company—similar to Gabby's career—and traveled extensively for work.

"I'm curious, Carolyn. With your busy career, how did you become interested in Reiki and in pursuing the Master Training level?" Kyra asked. She took a sip of iced green tea and awaited her classmate's response.

"That's a very good question—especially since my eighty-hour workweek makes my personal life challenging, to say the least." Empathy etched itself across Kyra's face, as Carolyn continued, "A friend suggested Reiki to me to help reduce my stress level. I was having difficulty sleeping and my mind was always racing with what I needed to do next." Carolyn crossed her legs and leaned forward. "I didn't give it much thought at first, but eventually I found a Reiki practitioner in my hometown of Toronto. I was *totally* amazed after my first session. I slept like a baby that night!" She closed her eyes with a dreamy expression and smiled. "My mind wasn't spinning with worry. I also felt more grounded and centered. It was like a massage for my soul."

"A massage for your soul," Kyra repeated. "I like the sound of that. Seems like we share a lot in common—I used to work crazy hours, too, and travel constantly." The memory of her old travel schedule made her shudder. "But I've left my corporate career recently—and I am enjoying the time to myself." Her face brightened.

"Oh, then you do understand how difficult it is for me to squeeze a Reiki session into my life! I talked to my local practitioner and he informed me that once you're trained, you can give yourself a treatment. The light bulb went off, and I took the first two levels of training on my first available weekend."

"That's so fantastic," Kyra said, her tone confirming she was impressed that Carolyn had chosen to make time for herself.

Her new friend smiled appreciatively. "This week is a real treat for me, Kyra—a whole week's vacation! I unplugged my cell phone, and hopefully, I won't get fired when I return to the office for not being available." Carolyn laughed, but Kyra knew that a corporate career was often viewed as a 24/7 commitment. "I can't wait to see what I may do with this training," she continued. "You never know what the future will bring."

"I totally agree," Kyra replied, once again recognizing the amazing synchronicity of the Universe. "I learned Reiki in grad school, but then I kind of forgot about it after I started my career. Recently, I've had some major shifts in my life—including the death of my grandmother—so here I am taking the Reiki Master class thirteen years later. I wish I hadn't waited so long." Her heart swelled and tears threatened to fall, but she held them back.

"I have a very good feeling that many new adventures are in store for us," Carolyn said. "I think we should arrange to take a future seminar together—Sedona, Arizona, has always been on my bucket list! What do you think?" she asked in all seriousness.

Kyra jumped at the invitation. "Sedona? Yes, that would be wonderful!" She reached out to embrace Carolyn, feeling proud of herself for no longer hiding her feelings. *I am so blessed to have met yet another awesome person here in Glastonbury*, Kyra thought with both reverence and excitement. *Thank you, God, for introducing me to all of these amazing people!*

By the look on her face, the hug had clearly surprised Carolyn, and she reached up to rub her eye. "There must be a speck of dust in my eye," she said composing herself. "You know, Kyra, I have a lot of business acquaintances, and they are great and all, but now I feel like I've made a friend who I can share my spiritual interests with. . . . Life gives us exactly what we need—*when* we need it—if we just learn to trust and open our eyes to the possibilities."

Kyra happily agreed and patted her new friend's hand. "I couldn't have said it any better myself Carolyn."

# 40

The next morning, Kyra sat straight up in bed when the alarm went off. A snore from Gabby made her giggle. "Our big day has arrived!" she exclaimed, but Gabby kept right on sleeping. Excited for their upcoming adventure, Kyra jumped out of bed and flung open the shutters, letting the warm sunlight kiss her face. In the ancient tree across the way, the blackbirds sang their morning praise to the rising sun, delighting her heart with their sweetness.

Kyra offered a silent prayer of gratitude: *Ah, what a glorious day, God! Thank you for allowing me to be here.*

After her shower, she rubbed Gabby's back to wake her. "Come on, Gabby! It's our big day. Put some pep in your step!"

Gabby pulled the pillow over her head and mumbled, "I will find some pep, even though I've cut my *café con leche* way back for the baby." Peeking out from under the pillow, she added, "My body is telling me this baby wants to rest. Five more minutes? *¿Por favor?*"

With playful anticipation, Kyra gave her a wake-up call five minutes later and stood over her until she got out of bed. Gabby's eyes flickered with amusement over Kyra's childlike excitement. A short while later, the women were enjoying a tasty breakfast in the dining hall with Kyra practically bouncing in her seat.

"Welcome students to our final day of training," Jonathan announced. "You've all worked very hard, and I'm so proud of each and every one of you!" He looked at each student in turn, meeting their eyes, making everyone one feel special. "Today's schedule will be a little different. We will start as usual in the sitting room for our meditation and final preparations, but after lunch, we'll take a group tour of the town of Glastonbury. If you get separated from the group, you must return to the Abbey no later than five thirty pm. Our bus to Wiltshire leaves at six o'clock sharp, and we need to be on time for Stonehenge."

The students shifted in their seats, clearly excited. Kyra saw Vicki and Carolyn, who seemed to have become close, squeeze each other's hands, and she caught Miguel's eye from across the room. His shoulders straightened as a look of exhilaration crossed his features, indicating his readiness for the final ceremony. Kyra felt ready too.

"After the visitors leave for the evening," Jonathan went on, clearly energized by the excitement in the air, "we will be given instructions for entering the center area for our ceremony. This is sure to be an evening of enlightenment—and one that you will not soon forget."

"I am so excited!" Gabby whispered perhaps too loudly, giving Kyra a shoulder hug.

Kyra felt electricity pulsing through her core. *This will be an incredible experience for us both. I can't wait to see what happens!*

~

In the sitting room after breakfast, Jonathan reviewed the agenda with the students for their final half day. "This morning we will do our coursework inside since we have a light rain shower," he explained. "We'll finish reviewing several important techniques and additional information on attunements, as well as the use of the sacred Reiki symbols. After lunch, we'll depart the Abbey House at one thirty pm to explore Glastonbury. Remember to be back here no later than five thirty pm if you get separated, but better yet, be sure not to wander too far."

"*Eu prometo não me perder!*" Isabella exclaimed. "I promise not to get lost!"

Thinking back to when she'd gotten lost in Spain, Kyra laughed, but quickly realized that she hadn't actually been lost . . . it was all divinely planned.

~

When it was time for the tour of Glastonbury, the group walked a few short blocks to the one of the main avenues in the city center called

High Street. Brightly colored shops and pubs lined the sidewalks, just as Kyra had expected—but her eyebrows arched at some of the more mysterious-looking storefronts.

*The Goddess and The Green Man?* she read, curious to see what lay inside.

She recalled her conversation with the young couple in Bristol. The woman had laughed saying that Glastonbury was "a *smashing* town with Wiccan and New Age shops." Kyra could now see that her comment was most accurate.

At center of town, Jonathan gave the students basic instructions and encouraged them to tour the local shops. Kyra formed a smaller group of friends that included Carmelo, with his delightfully heavy Italian accent; Kevin, whom she noted had a strong Southern accent being from Georgia; and Di Di, who had the delicious English accent she had so come to adore.

Kyra noticed that Di Di blushed when she met Kevin's eyes. The reaction was adorable—and quite natural—Kyra thought, given Kevin's good looks and Southern charm. She appreciated how his dimples accentuated his smile, and so did Di Di, it would seem.

As the friends strolled the streets of Glastonbury, Kyra likened the experience in some ways to being in a Charles Dickens novel. Wrought-iron street lamps gave the area a turn-of-the-century charm, and many of the buildings were three stories tall and made of traditional dark red brick or stone. But that's where the turn of the century seemed to meet the twenty-first century. Intermingled among the traditional buildings were lively pubs and an assortment of colorful metaphysical shops—and compact cars buzzed loudly through the streets. Tourists and locals alike enjoy their leisurely stroll up and down the stone-flagged pavements, as Kyra learned *sidewalks* were called locally.

"*Che fortuna!*" Carmelo said loudly as they turned a corner. "There's a pub named Ye Queens Head. We must come back tomorrow night after dinner and celebrate our rites of passage with some ale. Are you agreeable?"

Kevin responded, "*Yes-sir-ree*!"

Di Di replied with a big smile. "A pub? *Twist* my arm."

Kyra added, "Absolutely, Carmelo. Sounds like fun!"

The friends continued their walk, and Kyra became fascinated by the more unusual stores. They visited the Goddess Temple, which had a nice selection of artwork, books, music—and an oracle card deck for connecting to the deeper mysteries of the Isle of Avalon. Next they stopped at The Cat & Caldron, which Di Di said *fancied* crazy witch costumes—but also offered incense, dowsing rods, herbs, and other Wiccan paraphernalia.

While the Mystic Garden Gallery focused on fairy and fantasy-inspired original works of art, The Crystal Man shop offered new age enthusiasts an overwhelming selection of polished and raw crystals and minerals. It also had an array of beautiful handcrafted jewelry. The crystal and stone pendants caught Kyra's eye. She examined them carefully before deciding to purchase a larimar pendant. The shop owner explained that larimar was found only in the Dominican Republic and was associated with the lost continent of Atlantis.

"I have a feeling I'm not in San Francisco anymore," Kyra joked, as they left the store. "They don't have shops like this back home." She held up the bag with her treasure inside.

"Well, you know what they say, *darlin'*—when in Rome, *shop* as the Romans do," Di Di joked. "But I'll let Carmelo defend himself on that statement since he's from Italy!"

The friends burst into laughter, and as they walked on, bantered back and forth as if they had been friends for years.

Down one of the alleyways, Kyra's eyes stopped at a tall red brick building that had an old-fashioned straw broomstick leaning up against the doorframe. The name on the sign read The Wonky Broomstick, which gave her a moment's pause. *Does that shop sell broomsticks . . . to witches?!* she wondered, realizing she had, in fact, seen many a broomstick outside the doorways of several shops.

Seeing the puzzled look on Kyra's face, Di Di clarified, "The broomsticks indicate that the stores are 'witch friendly.' A little British *humour* perhaps, but they have become much more popular since the Harry Potter novels arrived on the scene." She guffawed.

"It's a good thing I'm friendly to witches," Carmelo joked.

Kyra giggled. "It feels like we're making our way down Diagon Alley!"

Kevin interjected, "We should be *shoppin'* for our school supplies for Hogwarts School of Witchcraft and Wizardry." His lips broadened into a dimpled smile. "I've read the entire Harry Potter series."

"Me, too!" Di Di exclaimed.

Although neither Carmelo nor Kyra had read the books, Kyra knew from the movies that Diagon Alley was where the wizards purchased all of the items on their Hogwart's supply list.

"Let's be careful *not* to transport ourselves to Hogwarts." Di Di quipped.

*I've enough transporting for a lifetime at this point*, Kyra thought with a grin, recalling her strange, mystical experiences in Spain.

Later in their room at the Abbey, Gabby and Kyra prepared for their 6 pm bus ride to Stonehenge and shared the highlights of their time in the town.

"I had an amazing time today, *Chica!*" Gabby finally concluded. "I made even *more* friends. I feel like I've known our classmates for my entire life—not just a few days."

"I feel exactly the same way," Kyra echoed. "I feel so comfortable with everyone—like they're my family—or *familia*—I should say."

"We are amazingly lucky, and now we have an even larger network of Reiki practitioners," Gabby affirmed.

With that, Gabby took Kyra's arm, and the women headed to the bus for the culmination of their studies with their new friends.

The bus left slightly past the hour, heading east toward the county of Wiltshire. Kyra chatted with a few of the students she hadn't had an opportunity to spend much time with and became so engrossed in the conversation that when the bus rolled to a stop, she was surprised to discover they had arrived at the main parking lot near the Stonehenge Visitor Centre.

The students filed off the bus, and when the last person stepped foot onto the lot, Jonathan exclaimed, "Welcome to Stonehenge! I know you are excited, but let me first fill you in on some important details for this evening. We'll enter the main area shortly as a tour group, and then spend some time exploring the grounds. You don't have to stay with our group—so have fun exploring. Once the grounds close for the evening and visitors leave, a custodian will greet us and give us instructions before we enter the center of Stonehenge. Let's regroup at eight o'clock sharp on the sidewalk in front of the stones. Enjoy yourself, and I will see you soon."

Kyra walked beside Gabby, who bubbled with such excitement that Kyra could actually feel her energy. A few of the other students joined the women to form a small group. This included Dimitra from Greece and Elsie from Florida, as well as Arjun from India and Daniel from Israel.

The group chatted enthusiastically as they walked the perimeter of the ancient stone monument. A roped fence along the interior of the huge circular sidewalk securely kept visitors from touching or being close to the stones. Kyra noted there were security personnel standing by to take action if the rules were broken.

Sounding scholarly, Arjun said, "There are two types of stones here at Stonehenge." He pointed across the way toward the center of the stones as he spoke. "The larger ones are called *sarsens* and the smaller ones are *bluestones*. The sarsens were erected in the large outer circle but also in an inner horseshoe shape. It's a little hard to see from here."

Kyra squinted her eyes to look, but Gabby grabbed her hand indicating that she was ready to check it out. She noted that Arjun's accent was barely perceptible as he spoke again and perhaps he even sounded a bit British.

"The bluestones on the other hand form a double circle," Arjun continued, pointing to another area of the stones. "Jonathan talked earlier about the theories on *why* and *how* the monument was constructed, but I thought it would be fun to share some of legends about how the stone came to be. Does anyone have one they'd like to share?" he asked, shifting to a more playful tone.

"I've done quite a bit of research on Stonehenge, but the one I like the best is the Arthurian legend. It may not be historically accurate, but it warms my heart the most," Dimitra answered in a soft, sweet voice. Kyra noted she also spoke English quite well with almost no Greek accent.

Elsie encouraged Dimitra to continue, and Kyra ear's perked up since the legend of King Arthur fascinated her.

"The legend came about in the twelfth century when an English writer claimed that these stones are healing rocks. He said giants first brought them from Africa to Ireland." Dimitra chuckled, but she continued in all seriousness, "Merlin, a powerful wizard, was then asked by the King of England—Arthur's father, Uther Pendragon—to bring the stones from Ireland to England. Stonehenge was said to have been *magically* constructed by Merlin as a memorial to the king's brother, Ambrosius, who had been killed in a battle against the Saxons. Anyway, that's my favorite story . . . or perhaps aliens just put them here to let us know they visited our planet."

Despite Dimitra's serious delivery, the group broke into a fit of laughter.

"I prefer the idea that Merlin constructed Stonehenge," Elsie said, turning to Arjun. She thanked him for the information he'd shared, then added teasingly, "Hopefully we won't run into *any* aliens tonight."

In his heavy Israeli accent, which warmed Kyra's heart, Daniel chimed in, "Vicki told me that the Brits do enjoy a good alien sighting from time to time, and crop circles aren't uncommon."

"What exactly is a crop circle?" Elsie asked. "I've heard the term but never gave it much thought."

Daniel seemed happy to explain. "A crop circle is an elaborate pattern mysteriously left in fields of corn or wheat—supposedly by aliens, though there are many skeptics. The crops are flattened in such as way that a pattern can be viewed only from a high altitude—like from an airplane. The Brits claim that it would be impossible for human beings to create a crop circle due to their sheer size. Crazy-sounding, don't you think?"

Kyra didn't know what to believe and, in all seriousness, said, "The last thing we need are aliens attending our ceremony tonight!"

This was met by more laughter, and the banter continued until it was time to assemble near the front entrance to the stones. At 8:00 pm, Jonathan and the students waited for the custodian to offer instructions on accessing the grounds.

A stout, dark-haired gentleman dressed in tan pants and a white shirt arrived to make his announcement. "Good evening, all," he said in a voice loud enough to be heard by everyone. "My name is Oliver." He welcomed Jonathan back, and to all the newcomers, he told them to listen very carefully to the rules. "Okay, *mates?*" he asked, ensuring the group was listening.

"Once I pull back the black rope, you will have access to the grounds for your ceremony. However—and this is very important—you are *not* allowed to touch or step on any of the stones. This site is of great historical significance. If anyone is caught touching or stepping on a stone, they will be *immediately* removed. Do I make myself clear?" He looked very serious, and again, his eyes searched the crowd to take note of their willingness to comply. "Please enjoy your privileged visit here tonight," he said, and then to lighten the mood, he added, "*Cheerio!*"

When Oliver stepped away, Jonathan took his place. "In fifteen minutes, we'll meet up in the center, but in the meantime, feel free take some photographs. You're welcome to sit directly on the ground or on a small mat. We'll form a circle in the center, and start with a grounding meditation. I'll then perform your Reiki Master attunement. See you shortly and have fun."

Kyra gave Gabby a wide-eyed look when Oliver swung back the black ropes and the students began to rush into the center of Stonehenge.

Gabby said in a playful voice, "I'd better be careful tonight. I don't want to get expelled before I become a master!"

Kyra smiled, but her smile quickly faded when her foot lightly touched a small surface stone and panic set in. She paused mid-air, teetering off balance in an effort to obey Oliver's instructions.

"*¡Ay—ay—ay!*" Gabby grinned. "I can't take you anywhere."

With muffled laughter, the women stepped forward.

Under Oliver's watchful eye, the students skipped among the stones in childlike wonder, clearly thrilled to be given this opportunity to explore the ancient grounds. Photos were being snapped from all directions.

Gabby handed her camera to Kyra, as a mischievous look overtook her face. She whispered, "Take a photo of me over here," pointing to one of the large sarsen stones. "I'm going to touch the stone for two seconds! Just keep an eye on Oliver."

"You crack me up," Kyra whispered back. Nervously she agreed to take the shot. "Let's do this quickly so we don't get thrown out and miss our ceremony."

Gabby rolled her eyes, and Kyra quickly snapped the photograph.

When Gabby dared her to do the same, Kyra shook her head no. *I'm definitely loosening up*, she smiled as Gabby snapped a picture of her in front of the stone, *but I'll never be as crazy as my dear friend Gabby.*

The sun was still strong in the late-evening sky, and bold shadows cast their way to the ground from the massive stones forming the outer circle. Kyra took a photograph of her "shadow self" on the ground, feeling proud for having released many of her negative thoughts—the "darker" side of her personality, so to speak.

The students soon began gathering in the center, placing their small mats on the ground in a circle. Gabby sat on Kyra's right side and Vicki sat on her left. Jonathan took his seat among the students once everyone was settled and began the Reiki Master Level attunement ceremony.

Kyra bowed her head for a silent prayer as they prepared for their meditation: *God, thank you for allowing me to be here today with all of these amazing and kind people from all over the world. Thank you for the friendships that will continue long after we leave. Thank you for allowing us to be a divine instrument of your healing. And last, but perhaps most important, thank you for this perfect day and all the blessings coming our way. Amen.*

Kyra looked up as just Jonathan began to speak. He asked the students to inhale deeply and close their eyes. He led them on a soothing visualization through a magical forest, asking everyone to envision they'd stepped inside a tree. Kyra could feel the sensation of strong sunlight nourishing her branches and leaves, while her tree roots ascended deep into sweet Mother Earth, anchoring her to the ground.

As the meditation came to a close, Jonathan asked the students to keep their eyes closed. He made his way around the circle to conduct the Master Level attunement on each student. When he slipped silently behind Kyra, she felt his hand gently touch her shoulder. As he began the attunement process, Kyra's thoughts drifted and she tried to imagine what it must have been like at the ancient grounds eons ago.

In her mind's eye, she went back a hundred years, then a thousand years, and then three thousand years. She could see ancient men and women, dressed in primitive-looking robes. *Druids?* she wondered.

The robed ones were dancing among the stones, performing what Kyra instinctively knew was a rite of passage. Strangely the stones looked much less worn than they did now, and the structure itself was complete—no stones were missing or broken. Kyra also realized she could *hear* their voices as they gave praise to the Goddess, Mother Earth. Though they spoke in a language she did not recognize, she could still somehow understand their words. She could hear the ancients offering their praise for the abundance of water, food, and life. The ceremony grew louder and more vivid in her mind as she watched.

She could now tell that it was springtime. *They're celebrating birth!* she thought. The ancients, some with flowers in their hair, gave thanks to God, holding their babies up. In joy, they danced around the stones.

Springtime soon turned to summer, and Kyra witnessed the celebration of the Summer Solstice—the longest day of the year. The ancients danced in the hot summer sun, honoring the divine feminine, Mother Earth, asking to be blessed with life-giving rain.

Summer turned to fall, and now Kyra could see the ancients harvesting their crops. They sang among the stones, offering gratitude for their bounty. Then fall slowly faded into winter. In the icy coldness, the ancients celebrated the Winter Solstice—the shortest day of the year.

With curiosity, Kyra also witnessed a celebration of death in which these people burned the bodies of their deceased loved ones atop funeral pyres and buried the remains at Stonehenge. They did not weep at their love one's passing. They instead *celebrated* life and the wondrous journey of returning home, Kyra noted with amazement. She watched the men and women dancing around a fire and listened to their rhythmic drumming. Their voices chanted joyfully in the celebration of their loved ones' lives.

Kyra was lost in her thoughts, when unexpectedly, she felt herself lifting *up* just like she had experienced at first in Spain and then in Japan. But this time, when she looked in front of her, she saw her spirit guide, Arianna, waiting for her. She was dressed in the same flowing ancient gown she'd seen so many times in her childhood dream.

*Dearest Kyra. You have come so far, and I am very proud of you.* Arianna reached out her hand to Kyra. *Will you join me?*

Kyra looked at the tender love in Arianna's sparkling eyes and replied, *Yes, Arianna, I'll join you. I have missed you, and I look forward to our journey together.*

She took Arianna's hand and gently felt herself drifting up. They seemed to be moving toward the night sky and then out into the universe. Kyra could see a million twinkling stars against a black velvety backdrop, and off in the distance, there was a great ball of white Light. Kyra looked at the light, and it felt incredibly *good* and *loving*—and with all of her being, she raced toward it.

But Arianna abruptly interrupted, *No, dear one—not just yet.* She turned, taking Kyra's hand. *Let's return and first finish your work on this Earth—as a Lightworker.*

Kyra felt herself falling gently back down toward the earth. She saw herself going through the earth's atmosphere, and then further down, until she slowly was back inside her body. She could once again feel her legs crossed on the straw mat beneath her and realized that Jonathan was just finishing her master attunement.

He stood up and moved on to Gabby.

Kyra remained in meditation, not consciously thinking about the mystical experiences she'd just had, but rather just basking in the afterglow of being part of something much larger and beautiful.

When every student had received the attunement, Jonathan quietly spoke, "I will now conduct a final grounding meditation. Once we are finished, we will discuss our experiences and then head back to the Abbey for the evening."

After they all partook in the grounding meditation, which helped to return them fully to the earthly plane, Kyra listened as her classmates, many of whom she now considered good friends, describe their experiences during the attunements. Some saw bright swirls of colors, while others simply felt warmth and love. Still others had visions of significant events that sounded somewhat similar to her own experience. Kyra concluded that everyone had experienced exactly what they needed to experience and, for everyone, that was an overwhelming feeling of love.

After boarding the bus to head back to the Abbey House, the students were noticeably quieter, speaking in soft tones and reflecting further on their experiences that evening.

"*Chica*," Gabby said, her voice much lower than usual, "I saw my deceased grandfather during the attunement; he looked so young and happy . . . but it was so brief that I didn't mention it to the others." She wiped away a tear.

"How beautiful," Kyra replied, thinking of how lovely it would have been to see her grandmother. She felt a warmth lightly touch her heart and realized that Nana was with her every moment, even if she couldn't see her.

Gabby went on, "I also got a glimpse of my future as a Lightworker, performing healing work. And my baby!" She scrunched up her face. "I saw my baby, but oddly it almost looked liked *two* babies. Ha! *Mamá* would be thrilled."

Kyra hid her shock as she gazed lovingly into Gabby's radiant face. "Thank you for inviting me along on this trip, Gabby. You are such a dear friend and you deserve the best . . . even *double*, I should say."

# 41

Even before the alarm rang the next morning, Kyra was out of bed and standing at the window, watching the sun slowly ascend. The light grew stronger with each passing minute, and she felt the rays warm her face. She listened reverently at the sweet sound of the blackbirds as they gathered in the tree for their morning song.

*You do sound like angels*—she thought dreamily, listening to their voices grow louder. *Thank you for singing your beautiful praise for this wonderful day and all its blessings.*

Folding her hands over her heart and closing her eyes, she offered gratitude to God and the Universe for all that had transpired thus far in her life. Then she lovingly glanced out across the magical landscape that had once been called the Isle of Avalon.

*Surely, I lived a previous life here*, she thought. *I feel so connected to this land.* Then she let out a sigh. *Or maybe it's only my imagination.*

Though her heart told her it was true, she still had difficulty believing it because she couldn't assign any specific details to the feeling. She dismissed the thought and simply enjoyed the morning sunrise.

This was her last full day in England, and she felt some regret that she couldn't stay longer. "I am going to miss this enchanting place," she whispered, trying not to cry. Then she reminded herself that the day ahead would be a glorious one. Turning away from the window, she went about getting ready.

Later, at breakfast, Kyra had the opportunity to become better acquainted with Sophie, who had introduced herself as a "*Kiwi* from New Zealand." Kyra thoroughly enjoyed Sophie's dry sense of humor. With her other ear, she overheard Gabby deep in conversation with Tom and D'Lisa from Arkansas. Gabby's distinctive Spanish accent sharply contrasted with Tom and D'Lisa's Southern drawl, which reminded Kyra that we are "all one" in this big world of ours.

Once breakfast came to a close, Jonathan stood up. "Good morning, everyone!" his said enthusiastically. "It's been an extraordinary week filled with hard work and fun. Many of you will be departing for your homes tomorrow morning very different from when you arrived: you are all now officially Reiki Masters."

The group buzzed with excitement, exchanging pleased expressions.

Jonathan's face beamed with pride as his gaze met the eyes of each of his students. "Congratulations to each and every one of you. Please, take a moment to congratulate your fellow classmates too."

The group members exchanged hugs with their neighbors and some gave each other high-fives. After a couple of minutes, Jonathan continued, "I'm pleased you have all bonded and become friends. I've made a list of everyone's contact information, so feel free to stay in touch." He handed out a sheet of paper to each student. "Now, on to today's agenda."

The student's listened as Jonathan described the various sites of importance they would be visiting in the Glastonbury area that day. Both Gabby and Kyra were particularly interested when he mentioned the Earth's seven major chakras. "It is believed that there are seven major energy sites on the Earth—or chakras—each residing on a different one of our seven continents," he explained. "For Europe, the heart chakra is thought to be located in the geographical area of the counties of Somerset, Dorset, and Wilshire, right here in England—which includes Glastonbury! It's believed that by immersing yourself in these energy fields, or energy vortexes, your own physical electromagnetic field becomes aligned with the frequency, helping you to heal. Just keep that in mind as we visit the area."

"*Y'all* have my attention," Kevin interjected, clearly interested in the energy fields.

Jonathan acknowledged Kevin's good-natured comment before resuming his discussion of the itinerary. "We will also visit several sites that fall on the Michael ley lines, including the unique Glastonbury Tor. As you may know, the Tor has ties to both Christianity with the ruins of

Saint Michael's Church located there, but also to the Arthurian legend and the old Isle of Avalon. More to come on that topic." He winked. "Let's meet out front at ten sharp."

When the group assembled outside, Jonathan led the way to Chilkwell Street and to their first destination of the day. "Welcome to the Chalice Well," he said with a lightness in his voice. "Here on the *old Isle of Avalon*, we have two famous springs: The White Spring and the Chalice Well, also known as the Red Spring. Both are considered to contain healing waters and lie in close proximity to each other. Today, however, we will only have time today to see the Chalice Well—but perhaps you will visit the White Well on a return trip. I will note that the White Spring has a heavy calcite concentrate, which makes the water a milky white, while the Chalice Well has a heavy iron ore concentrate, giving it a unique blood-red color."

"*Whoa*, red water," Sophie murmured.

"I wonder how it tastes," Zoé added.

Jonathan went on, "There are many legends surrounding the origin of the Chalice Well. One legend says the red water represents the blood of Christ. This same legend says the well miraculously sprang forth from the ground in the very spot that Joseph of Arimathea buried the cup from the Last Supper." He paused, building suspense. "Yes—The Holy Grail."

Elsie gasped. Rafael moved closer, the expression on his face indicating that he was fascinated by the whole concept.

"All legends aside, let me tell you the *facts* that I do know about the well," Jonathan said. "Archeologists have concluded that the well has been in continual human use for more than two thousand years—or around the time of the birth of Jesus. This spring produces an amazing *twenty-five thousand* gallons of water a day. It maintains a constant temperature all year round. But more interesting—and perhaps unique—are the special symbols here at the Chalice Well."

Kyra looked over at Henry as he scribbled notes on a small pad of paper. Benjamin, who stood beside him, listened intently, even stepping closer as Jonathan continued.

"The cover to the Wellhead is composed of wood and metal. It's in the shape of a Vesica Piscis, a sacred symbol." Jonathan held up a photograph of the two interlocking circles. "You can see in this photograph that the center of the two interlocking circles form the symbol of a fish. In Roman times, Christians used this symbol to identify each other during turbulent times."

Jonathan made sure everyone had a chance to get a glimpse of the photo. "The Vesica Piscis symbol is sacred to several religions. It's thought to represent the duality of heaven and earth, the masculine and feminine, but these are just a few examples. . . . Notice also that the Sword of Excalibur pierces right through the center of the Vesica Piscis on the cover to the Wellhead."

Some students craned their necks to see the photo, and Jonathan allowed them to pass it around. "Incidentally, did I mention that one legend says the Sword of Excalibur is buried on the grounds of the Glastonbury Abbey?"

With those words, a chill raced up Kyra's spine and goose bumps of excitement broke out on her arms.

"But I digress," Jonathan said lightheartedly, returning to the subject matter. "The same Vesica Piscis shape is also found in the pool bearing the same name near the entrance, so make sure you look for it there. Just past the Vesica Pool, you'll see a beautiful garden protected by the Guardian Yews. There's also a meadow close by that's a tranquil place of healing that's excellent for meditation. I've heard that you may see elemental spirits there, *including* fairies," he said in all seriousness, then added, "if you look hard enough."

"I love fairies!" Sophie shouted. She laughed at her own silliness, eliciting a few chuckles from those around her.

"The red well water that flows across this property is located where two powerful ley lines intersect—the Michael and Mary—hence, part of its healing aspect. After the meadow area, you'll see the Healing Pools and the Lion's Head fountain, where visitors are welcome to drink the ancient spring water to partake of their healing powers. So, yes, Zoé. You'll get to find out how it tastes. Bottles of the water are available for purchase at the gift shop or you can fill your own bottle if you'd like to take some of the healing home with you."

"I'll be taking a few bottles back with me," Jean interjected.

Zoé looked pleased that she would get to taste the water.

"Lastly, please take notice of the tree located above the Lion's Head," Jonathan said, wrapping up his talk. "Legends say it was grown from a graft of the original Glastonbury Thorn. The original tree sprang up in a location close to here when Joseph of Arimathea thrust his staff into the ground. Sadly, the tree was destroyed, but several graftings prior to its demise have allowed the tree to live on. It's also believed that our tree here at the Chalice Well is associated with miracles. Not only does it flower once in the spring—but it also said to bloom once in the winter, too—marking both the *birth* and *resurrection* of Christ. This occurs because, remember, the well water is warm all year round."

"That's *amazin'*," Ella said playfully. "We don't have any trees like that down under."

Ivan added, "It is quite amazing. We have extremely cold winters in Russia—but no trees bloom there in winter, I can assure you of that—unless you've had too much vodka."

A few students laughed, and Jonathan finished. "If there's aren't any questions, let's get started! Check your watches. Let's meet at the front gate in two hours. Then we will head to our next destination, the White Spring."

Gabby took Kyra's arm, and they stepped inside.

"It feels awesome to act like a child again," Kyra teased, racing ahead.

"I couldn't agree with you more!" Gabby responded as she ran to catch up.

Within minutes, they arrived at the Vesica Pool. The pool was indeed shaped in double interlocking circles, just as Jonathan had described. Red well water flowed abundantly into the pool and then spilled out, forming a smaller stream that flowed across a soft beige cobblestone pathway. The stones beneath the water had turned a bright coppery red, likely from the many years the iron-rich waters had been flowing over it.

Kyra bent down, letting the cool water flow through her fingers. "Isn't the color so unusual."

"It's thought to represent the blood of Christ," Gabby said with reverence. Gabby made the sign of the cross, feeling it was appropriate, and Kyra bowed her head out of respect.

Following the map, the women next ventured to the Guardian Yews. The two ancient trees were perhaps fifty feet tall. *Enormous* was the word that sprang to Kyra's mind to describe them. "They do look like Roman Centurions protecting the entrance to the garden sanctuary," Kyra said, confirming what she had read in the brochure.

Gabby motioned for her to follow, and both stood beneath the huge trees.

Kyra felt as if she were connecting to the energy of one of the trees, sensing a regal presence. *Am I feeling the tree's spirit?* she asked herself. Closing her eyes, she placed her palm on the rough bark. *It feels as if the tree knows I'm standing here! He feels protective—making me feel both safe and loved.*

Gabby closed her eyes as well, communing with the tree in her own way. After that peaceful moment, the women continued along the pathway into the garden where they met up with Ella, Vicki, and a few others.

"Hi, friends! We're *plannin'* to meditate in the meadow just off to the side here. You're welcome to join us," Ella offered, pointing across the way. "It's where the Michael and Mary ley lines meet. . . .maybe we'll summon some *fairies*."

Kyra felt childlike anticipation welling up inside.

"That's the spirit, Ella!" Gabby said. "Let's get real quiet and see if we attract any of those tiny creatures."

The small group deviated from the main pathway and made their way to a large open meadow. Soft, luscious grass carpeted the ground, and various types of trees, some quite tall, offered shady areas—especially over the concrete benches scattered about.

They chose a bench that would seat eight people. Vicki sat on one side of Kyra and Jean sat on the other side. Ella sat beside Gabby, and then came Nicholas. Henry sat on Vicki's opposite side with Kevin rounding out the group.

Once they were settled, Nicholas took the lead. "Ella, would you mind if I conduct the meditation? I'd appreciate the practice . . . but only if that's okay with you."

Nicholas's command of the English language impressed Kyra. She knew he was a native of Singapore, but she also knew that he taught English. His students had a very good teacher indeed.

When Ella assured him that she would be happy for him to take the lead, a pleased look crossed his features. He instructed the group to put their feet firmly on the ground, close their eyes, and take three deep breaths. They all did as he instructed. In a soft, mesmerizing voice, he led his fellow classmates on guided meditation that took them to a magical garden.

Kyra's lids rested softly on her cheeks, and she soon began to visualize a magnificent but mysterious garden. In her mind's eye, the tall trees protected the surrounding flower garden. She could feel the energy of the trees as they drank in the sunlight. *Almost like the Guardian Yews!*

Next she spied small creatures that lived in this imaginary place: squirrels scurrying about playing with each other, cardinals chirping loudly and dotting the trees with their stunning red feathers, and bright-yellow butterflies dancing in the soft summer breeze.

A bumblebee flew toward her, but instead of being afraid, she looked at it adoringly. *Yes, I know that bumblebees are an animal totem for overcoming the impossible . . . plus, you pollinate our flowers.* She giggled, wondering if the bee could understand her thoughts. *Thank you, Mr. Bee, for visiting me today.* The bee stayed a moment longer before flying away with a joyful buzz.

More animals appeared in the garden, and Kyra squinted in her mind's eye to see them clearly. She gasped when a white unicorn bowed its head as it galloped past her. All the animals were incredibly happy living in this magical place.

She kept her imagination flowing as she followed the path deeper into the trees—and suddenly was taken by surprise. A tiny purple orb flew up to her, tickling her arm. It moved quickly like a hummingbird, and then stopped in front of her. With a gentle blink of its light, Kyra knew it was saying hello. *Oh my!* Kyra thought, *it is a fairy!* The tiny creature blinked again before darting away. Kyra watched the fairy zigzag across the magical landscape.

*It's just like in my childhood dream,* she realized. She took a moment to cherish the feeling she'd once had as a child—the feeling that everything was possible. *I am the co-creator of my life,* Kyra confirmed, realizing she could manifest anything she desired—even silly mythical creatures. She knew in her heart that from this moment forward her life would have an element of enchantment—and be totally different from anything she'd experienced in her past.

Kyra was ready to come back when Nicholas guided them through a grounding exercise to finish the meditation.

Jean spoke up first. "That was a most wonderful meditation. I think you do have the *juice*, dear boy!" she exclaimed.

The rest of the group agreed and offered Nicholas their compliments. Kyra thought she noticed him blushing when she offered her admiration of his humility and authenticity.

Henry suggested that the group remain together to visit the Healing Pool to partake of the waters. They gladly assembled on the grassy area near the concrete ledge of the pool. Kevin immediately flung his shoes off to the side and rolled up his jeans to step into the rust-colored, ankle-deep water. "Last one in is a *rotten egg*," he yelled as he jumped into the spring.

"*Bugger!*" Vicki complained as she wadded in. "I always forget how cold this water is!"

The 52°F water chilled Kyra's legs to the bone. She felt the healing waters swirling around her ankles and half-expected to feel miraculously rejuvenated . . . but she didn't feel anything other than cold. *Ah, expectations!* she chided herself, remembering that the Universe works in its own ways and when least expected something incredible would happen.

She next decided to splash water on Ella, who in turn splashed Gabby, and soon the whole group was splashing water and laughing at their childlike behavior.

Following a group photo, they visited the Lions Head Fountain, where they met up with several more of the now-Reiki Masters. The water flowed steadily through the mouth of the carved-stone Lion's head.

Gabby stepped up with cupped hands and caught the fresh spring water in her palms. She raised the water to her lips, took a sip, and let out a satisfied *Ahh.*

Not feeling as bold as Gabby, Kyra held her bottle out and partially filled it. She cautiously took a sip—she enjoyed the cool, crisp clean flavor, noting it didn't have a metallic taste.

Everyone began commenting on how refreshing the water was. Those who'd brought bottles with them filled them up to the brim and tucked them away for later.

Finally, the entire group made their way to the last destination, the Wellhead, the point at which the spring originated. Kyra ran her fingertips delicately across the wrought-iron design in the Wellhead's wooden cover. It was just as Jonathan had described and her arm tingled with excitement.

"I see the fish shape and Excalibur's sword!" Ella shouted, marveling at the clever design. The students each took a turn at admiring the Wellhead up close. Several stared down deep into the well itself, seeing the sunlight fade away into deep, dark shadows of the narrow opening.

"It's time for us to go, fellow Reiki Masters," Jonathan announced to the group once everyone had had a chance to view the Wellhead up close. "Next stop is the Glastonbury Tor, but first we'll enjoy a lunch at a nearby pub."

After their bellies had been filled, Jonathan resumed his lecture on the area's highlights. "*Tor* means 'hill' in old English. The Glastonbury Tor—or hill—is the highest point here on the Isle of Avalon. We have about a half-mile walk to our destination, so I'll fill you in on some of the more interesting legends and historical information as we go."

The group readily followed their guide, listening carefully as he spoke.

"This area was once filled with seawater, but was later drained in the fourth century, turning it into dry land—back around the time of King Arthur." Jonathan grinned. "One legend says that King Arthur visited the Glastonbury Tor while searching for the Holy Grail. There's even the school of thought that the Cadbury Castle—which is only eleven miles away—may have been Camelot. But, even more entertaining, is the belief that Merlin, the Wizard, still resides *inside* the Glastonbury Tor."

A couple of the students glanced sideways at each other, but Sophie shouted her enthusiasm for the idea.

"Of course, none of this can be proven," Jonathan added with a wink.

"Still, I adore hearing these legends! I find them so fascinating," Isabella chimed in. "*Tão engraçado!*"

"Thank you, Isabella and Sophie—I appreciate your zeal. Let me share a few more facts about King Arthur. I'm sure you're all aware that we don't know if King Arthur actually existed."

Jonathan's voice rose as he spoke, which fully captured Kyra's attention. She moved closer so she wouldn't miss anything.

"In the year eleven eighty-four, a fire broke out destroying many of the Glastonbury Abbey's buildings—including the church that sits directly across from where we are staying. But during the rebuilding of the church, an *important* discovery was made at the Abbey."

He paused for effect, and a few members in the group, including Kyra, urged him to continue.

"Sixteen feet below the earth . . . a double oak coffin containing the remains of a man and woman was discovered. On the outside of the coffin was an inscription written in Latin, which translated read: *Here lies buried the famous King Arthur with Guinevere his second wife in the isle of Avalon.*"

"I *knew* it!" Isabella gasped.

"Not so fast," Jonathan said, wagging a finger playfully. "No one can verify the accuracy of the inscription. However, about a hundred years later, King Edward I had the bodies reinterred at the abbey in a black marble tomb. Today, only the sign remains."

Kevin, who seemed to like facts, raised his hand to ask a few additional questions, but everyone else seemed satisfied with the information Jonathan had shared.

"I thought you'd find that fascinating," Jonathan confirmed. "Now let me get back to the Glastonbury Tor," he said in a more serious tone. "The Tor is has roughly seven symmetrical terraces and their formation remains a mystery to us even today. The number seven is often associated with luck, and spiritually it also corresponds to the seven major chakras—an interesting synergy. The Tor is both a sacred site to Christians and Spiritualists. It's a place of pilgrimage for many Christians because it's believed that Saint Patrick visited the Tor and may have lived in this area before moving back to Ireland. We know with certainty that monks lived on the Tor as early at the ninth century and enjoyed the hill for solace and reflection. It's also the former site of Saint Michael's church."

"What happened to the church?" one of the classmates asked.

"It was destroyed in an earthquake in the year twelve hundred seventy-five, but a smaller church was built to replace it. We'll see the ruins of Saint Michael's tower shortly—but nothing beyond that remains today." Jonathan faced forward and continued on, his voice loud enough for all twenty-six in the group to hear.

"From a spiritual standpoint, the Tor also falls on the Michael ley line, making it a sacred energy point on the earth. Again, it's thought to be a part of the earth's heart chakra. We will see the tower shortly after we make our ascent up the steep hillside. Please follow me. Feel free to sit and enjoy some quiet self-reflection once we reach the top."

Jonathan fell quiet as they approached the terraced walkway at the base of the hill.

"I can already feel the intense energy of this mystical place," Kyra commented. "Can you feel it, Gabby?"

"What I feel is *drained* of energy. I can't wait to sit down and meditate," she said, although she was grinning. "This baby is taking it out of me!"

Watching her step and walking carefully up the uneven stone terraced walkway, Kyra was even more amazed than she expected to be by the spectacular view once they gained attitude.

*This is the most beautiful summer day I've experienced in England to date,* she thought, appreciative of the nearly picture-perfect weather.

After stopping so that Gabby could have a quick break, Kyra peered up at the crystal-clear blue skies to fully absorb the beauty. Not a single cloud appeared above their heads. The late-afternoon sun beamed brightly, casting its light down for all of Earth's inhabitants to enjoy. Kyra's playful imagination envisioned the trees thanking the sun for nourishing their leaves. A small deer appeared just at the edge of forest, capturing her attention when it blinked its large black eyes at her. The whole scene felt peaceful and sweet—like a perfect moment in time.

Soon, however, the wind began to blow, growing stronger as they continued their ascent. They were now above the tree line, and Kyra's hair swept wildly across her face. She caught it with her hand and gently tied it back. Once they reached the top, the wind was blowing furiously. There was no protection on the treeless hilltop, but Kyra choose to embrace the wind's power, enjoying how it felt as it rushed across her face. The grassy area looked flat, and only the small crumbling tower of Saint Michael's Church remained.

Several members of the group crowded inside the tower, but Kyra and Gabby decided to sit down to rest. *What an incredibly beautiful place this is!* Kyra thought with awe. *I feel like I've stepped into a magical storybook.*

The view was indescribably breathtaking—a panoramic extravagance that Kyra felt blessed to experience. The English countryside lay directly beneath her, and the Chalice Hill was just off to the West.

Gabby pointed out she could see Penn Hill just to the east of them; she'd been reading up on the area's geography that morning.

After a quiet moment of reflection to give thanks for all the blessings in her life, Kyra opened her eyes and looked back at the tower. It appeared empty now with most of her friends sitting atop the hill, enjoying their own moment of solace and peace. She stood up, but Gabby indicated that she still wanted to rest, so Kyra walked toward the front entrance.

Saint Michael's Tower was small in size, appearing to be only about fifteen to twenty-feet wide, but very tall. The ancient weathered stone on the arched doorway felt cold to her hand. She peered into the shadowy darkness and stepped inside. Noting there were no windows, she stopped for a few moments to allow her eyes to adjust to the dimness.

Standing still, she absorbed the energy of the tower.

*It feels very good . . . as if it were a happy place in the past*, she thought with a strange knowing. She took another step forward and noticed a simple inscription on the wall. Using her cell phone to shed some light, she read a brief history on the Glastonbury Tor. It described that the origin of the Tor was unknown and mostly based in legend. The earliest reference was back in the mid-thirteenth century when Saint Patrick was thought to have returned to Ireland after living at the Tor for a while. The sign went on to say that later excavations had shown that Christian monks had likely lived there even earlier during the tenth century or so—some 400 years after King Arthur was thought to have ruled the land.

Kyra felt an odd tingling sensation overtake her body; it was subtle at first but then quite powerful. "My goodness!" she said aloud, anticipating what might happen next. Rather than allow fear to grip her, she calmly closed her eyes and began to use her intuition for information. Unlike her experiences in Spain, the feeling this time was very faint, like a *whisper* of a memory. She could see in her mind's eye a male monk—but she quickly realized she *was* the male monk. She glanced down at her clothing and saw she was wearing a plain dark brown wool robe. The fabric was tattered and worn—and not very clean. Her hands were weathered and chubby with grimy black fingernails.

*These are the hands of a man who tilled the earth for his food*, she thought, her intuition delivering the information into her consciousness. She felt pleasure at her next thought. *But more amazing, these are the hands of someone very kind and giving—as if he touched many people's lives*. Kyra felt her heart melt at the sweet, glowing sensation. It was as if she could feel his heart—her own heart in that lifetime.

She turned her hands over and continued to study them. *My hands are surrounded by Light!* she realized, stunned by the vision. She could also *feel* a healing sensation in her hands, as if she had used them to comfort and heal people, similar to Reiki.

The faint flashback lasted only a few moments. Kyra opened her eyes, feeling the goodness of the Tor, not the dark shadowy impression she'd expected before she stepped inside. *Now I understand my connection to this land!* It had not been at all what she'd expected—a romanticized vision of living in King Arthur's court. She relished the delicious joy she felt having lived a simple life and being of service to others.

Kyra stood there a few minutes longer enjoying the sensation, and then moved toward the opposite door. The bright wonderful sunlight awaited her, but just as she stepped through the archway, a sparkling object on the ground caught her attention. Curious, she stooped down to look closer. The earth was dry and hard, but she could see it was pale pink in color, and partially buried in the dirt.

Kyra took her keys from her purse and gently scraped dirt away to free the object. Astounded, she picked up a small heart-shaped piece of rose quartz. She held the unexpected discovery in her hand. The stone seemed to radiate a soft presence of its own and a flurry of emotion overwhelmed her, bringing tears to her eyes.

*How long has this stone been in the ground? Where did it come from? And why did I find it here to day?* Her intuition searched for answers, but none came. *It really doesn't matter,* Kyra concluded. The Universe had simply provided her with a gift on her journey—a replica of her heart.

*Yes, Uncle Saul I did find my heart.* She smiled, recalling her dear uncle's advise in Jerusalem. *Thank you, Nana, Mother, and Father, too. I truly appreciate everything you did, and tried to do, for me. I love you.*

For the first time in her life, Kyra felt that her heart was completely open. She was open to receiving *all* the love she had desired as a child but never fully received. She was open to the love of her friends, recognizing the opportunities she'd missed in the past. Her heart was also now open to receiving the love of her soul mate, whenever the Universe deemed it was time to meet him. But, most important, Kyra felt she was open to receiving the love of the God. *I am a perfect and divine child of God. I deserve love exactly the way I am now*, she affirmed, *but I also vow to continue bettering myself too.*

Kyra could hardly contain her excitement. She took a calming breath, her heart beating rapidly, and decided to share her incredible gift with all of her friends. Walking to each small group on the hilltop, Kyra made sure to share her rose quartz heart she had unearthed with everyone.

"This area *is* known as the Heart Chakra," Jonathan reminded her. "You have received a very special gift indeed. And that, dear Kyra, is because you are a very special person."

The tears welled up all over again, as Kyra thanked Jonathan for his kind words and profound reminder.

A bit out of breath, Kyra finally sat down beside Gabby, who was the only friend she hadn't shared her newfound treasure with.

"You were so excited walking around to everyone, *Chica.* I didn't know what was going on! I thought you were Christopher Columbus and had discovered America . . . *En serio!*" She giggled. "What's the commotion? You already know how much I love you."

Kyra gave Gabby a *muwahhh* on both cheeks, before telling her about her discovery. When she was finished her story, the friends wiped away tears and sat beside each other arm in arm.

"I am looking forward to starting my new life as a Lightworker," Kyra commented, gazing off into the distance.

"And I am looking forward to seeing Alejandro! I miss *mi amor*," Gaby said honestly, rubbing her tummy.

Kyra looked at her friend in amazement, realizing how much both of her babies would be loved.

After enjoying the splendid view for a while longer, the group reassembled and walked down the hill, making their way back to the town of Glastonbury. After a delicious dinner of fish and chips, amidst a party-like atmosphere where their bonds were further forged, Kyra and Gabby returned to the retreat house, feeling full of life and love.

A pleasant look played upon Kyra's face as her head hit the pillow. She and Gabby had grown so close during this time and rekindled their sisterly relationship. But tomorrow, Gabby would be heading back to Spain to Alejandro, who was surely impatiently awaiting his fiancé's return—and Kyra would return home to her beloved San Francisco to begin her new life.

# 42

Kyra tossed back her bed covers and tiptoed to the window. The bright sunlight streamed in through the fully open shutters and gently warmed her face. One last time she enjoyed the sweet melody of the blackbird's morning praise. Then, with overflowing love in her heart, she glanced at Gabby, who, mid snore, opened her eye a sliver. "Too early," she groaned and turned over. Apparently, Gabby was not quite ready to enjoy the sunlight on this glorious morning.

After showering and preparing for departure, the women made their way down the flight of stairs with their suitcases. Kyra took her time inching down each step until she reached the bottom. She let out a loud, "*Whew!*" and wiped her brow dramatically. "I will do a much better packing job for my next trip!"

"When you come back for my wedding *Chica*, don't pack a dead body in there again . . . We don't want you getting arrested," Gabby said with a sly look on her face.

"Don't worry, I think I've learned my lesson. Maybe I'll just bring a backpack *a la Raquel* . . . But most important, I can't wait to see you and Alejandro tie the knot!" Kyra said with laughter as they entered the dining room for breakfast.

The crowd was smaller as a few people had said their goodbyes the evening before, but Kyra was glad to see Vicki one last time.

"*Luv*, I enjoyed last night's *proper* English dinner of fish n' chips with you—and that pint of ale was the best! . . . *Blimey*, Kyra, I don't know how you managed to leave half of your ale behind!" Vicki's luminous eyes flashed as she joked affectionately.

"Thank you, Vicki, for your *lovely* stories this week," Kyra said, accentuating her words to sound like a Brit. "I know we'll remain friends even though we live across the ocean from each other. I look forward to seeing you again."

It became a bittersweet morning of goodbyes. Everyone hugged and kissed each other, expressing that they looked forward to staying in touch.

Toward the end, Kyra was nearly in tears. "I feel like I've known everyone here . . . well, forever!" she told Gabby.

"I feel the same way . . . and you're making me tear up." Gabby replied. "Stop that . . . I have to look good for Alejandro today!"

The women walked to the front of the Abbey House arm in arm. Gabby spied the limo that would be taking her to the Bristol Airport for her flight back to Barcelona.

"Lucky you, a limo," Kyra said good-naturedly. "I'm driving my rental car to the Heathrow Airport this time for a direct flight home to San Francisco . . . if my drive goes smoothly, and I don't get lost." She chuckled a bit, hoping her drive would be uneventful.

Gabby gave her a big hug. "Everything will go smoothly, I promise. You will do incredible things when you get back home . . . as a *Lightworker*," she said, her eyes glistening with unshed tears. "I love you."

Kyra returned the hug and finished with a *muwahhh* on each cheek. "I love you too."

When the limo driver came around to the back to hold the door open for Gabby, she said, "I have to run now, *Chica! ¡Ciao!*"

As she slid inside, Kyra waved goodbye, and the limo drove away.

"I hope I'm ready for my journey," she said under her breath.

Mustering up her courage, she inhaled deeply and hoisted her suitcase into the trunk of the car. She successfully got a full tank of *petrol*, then set her GPS for the Heathrow Airport.

As she took her final journey across the English countryside, she reflected on all that had transpired on this trip, all the amazing people she'd met, and the mystical experiences she'd had. She felt incredibly light and blessed.

After dropping her car at the Hertz Car Hire, Kyra took the shuttle bus to the airport terminal. It was Saturday mid-morning so the airport was filled with travelers preparing for their next destination. She made her way through security and located the gate for her flight. The airport was now quite crowded and she surveyed the area for an empty seat. Much to her dismay, every seat appeared to be taken, and several passengers were standing in the isles.

*I guess I'll have to stand*, she thought resolutely, but then spied an empty seat facing the window across the way. She dashed over, nearly tripping over another passenger's suitcase.

She came to a complete stop to regain her composure, took a deep breath, and asked, "Is this seat taken?"

A handsome man beside the empty seat looked up and said, "Yes, I was saving it just for you."

Kyra blushed and simply stared back. *That's a strange thing to say*, she thought, not knowing how to respond at first, but then she did something she had never done before. She confidently extended her hand and said, "Thank you. I'm so glad you were holding my seat. My name is Kyra."

"Hi, Kyra. I'm Michael," the man responded, his blue eyes twinkling.

Kyra blushed a second time as their hands met, and he stood up, revealing that he was tall and even more handsome than she first thought. She quickly surveyed him and noted his dark brown hair and pale skin. His complexion was flawless and his slightly ruddy cheeks accentuated his strong cheekbones.

Kyra asked, "You aren't by chance Irish, are you?"

"Why actually *yes*, I am part Irish," he responded a bit surprised, sitting back down and indicating that Kyra should do so too.

"My mother's side of the family came from Limerick, but I'm also English and Dutch too. A mutt if you will!" His lips curved into a broad smile, and Kyra laughed. She stared straight into his sincere eyes as he spoke again. "Are you heading home to San Francisco, Kyra? . . . Oh, if you don't mind me asking."

"Yes, I'm heading home. I've been on quite an adventure for a couple of months now," she explained. "Before I left San Francisco, my position had just been eliminated, and I lost my grandmother too." She paused feeling at peace with the knowledge that both events were meant to be.

"I'm so sorry about your grandmother," Michael said immediately, his voice sympathetic and caring.

"No, Michael, please, don't be sorry. It was just her time," Kyra offered bravely. "I do miss her terribly . . . but truthfully, the changes I've been through recently have really opened my eyes. I've taken some time off for the first time ever and just joined a dear friend of mine for a Reiki Master Training course in Glastonbury . . . that may sound strange to you, I realize," she said, her voice trailing off, not knowing how he'd respond.

Michael's eyes widened, and he paused before responding. "Reiki, hey?" he said raising his voice. "Actually I've been interested in learning more about Reiki. I'm a doctor. Oncology is my specialty, and I was just attending a medical conference in London this week. We had a session on complementary alternative medicine—CAM for short—and the speaker covered various modalities of energy healing."

Kyra face lit up, and she nodded to indicate that she was familiar with the term.

"I've had an interest in approaching medicine a little differently. I'd actually like to integrate into my practice more holistic healing techniques for treating my cancer patients, in conjunction with traditional Western medicine. I'd enjoy hearing more about Reiki."

Kyra couldn't contain her excitement, and for over an hour, she and Michael talked non-stop about Reiki and other natural healing modalities. Time flew by until they were interrupted by the overhead speaker: "Delta Flight 2555 to San Francisco will begin boarding in just a few minutes . . ."

"It's been so wonderful talking to you, Kyra. Here's my business card. I'd love to touch base once we're both settled back home in beautiful San Francisco. Does that sound good to you?"

Kyra shot the handsome man her most brilliant, heartfelt smile and said, "Yes, Michael, I would like that very much!"

## Part 6

# Journey Home

# 43

Kyra woke up and looked at the clock on her nightstand. It was 6:40 am, but the alarm was not set. It was Saturday morning in late April, nearly nine months after her return home from England.

Rubbing the sleep from her eyes, Kyra glanced across her bedroom toward the east-facing bay window. The morning sun had just begun to rise on this glorious spring day in San Francisco. She watched as the sunlight gently drifted across her bed, slowly growing in intensity. Her lips parted in a joyful smile when the light replaced the darkness and brightened the entire room.

A flash caught her eye, and she glanced down at her left hand, almost in disbelief. The gorgeous princess-cut diamond engagement ring on her finger twinkled in the early morning sunshine, shooting brilliant flecks of colored light across the white ceiling. The specks of light danced above her head, reminding her of the stars in a black velvety sky from the shoreline of her dreamscape. Kyra's eyes swept across the ceiling, and she let out a giggle—just like she did when she was a child.

A moment later, she turned on her side and snuggled up to the man beside her. Softly kissing him on the lips, Kyra whispered, "The morning light looks amazing on your face, Michael." She giggled again as she gazed down at him, his dark brown hair messy and his eyes tightly shut. Kyra rubbed his shoulder. "I love you," she said, trying to rouse him from his deep sleep. "And you're missing the beautiful sunrise!"

Michael moved slowly and opened his eyes. With a shout of surprise from Kyra, he quickly turned over and rolled on top of her—gently pinning her to the bed. Looking deeply into her eyes he tenderly said, "I love you too, Kyra. But, my darling . . . you *are* the Light."

# Acknowledgments

I wish to thank the following special people, who without their help, I couldn't have written this magical tale.

First, I'd like to express my gratitude to Lisa McCourt and Deirdre Abrami for their inspirational writer's workshop. You sparked my imagination and gave me the courage to begin my writing journey.

Through Lisa, I met my outstanding editor Carol Killman Rosenberg. Carol, it's truly been a pleasure working with you—your advice and help has been immeasurable. I can't express in words how much I've appreciated your loving guidance and friendship.

Next, I wish to express my gratitude to Lisa Pagola Rivers for her intuitive guidance. Lisa, your guidance from my spiritual team helped me stay on my path, even when I doubted and questioned myself.

I must also thank Reverend Kevin Lee, who gave me so many incredible resources through his extensive network. Each time I needed help, you offered just the right person.

I'd like to offer a sincere thank-you to my beta readers: Pamela Kirkpatrick, Reverend Tim Jack, and Kelsey Merritt. Each of you offered your unique perspective. I'm so appreciative of your valuable time and feedback.

Finally, I must express a heartfelt thank-you to Carolyn Harvey for being a dear friend and travel companion for some of the adventures in this novel. I have appreciated your friendship over the years—more than you will ever know.

*Please join Shari on her socials:*

 Shari A. Hembree

 Shari A. Hembree

 Shari A. Hembree

Shari A. Hembree

Shari A. Hembree

www.shariahembree.com

Sign up for Shari's newsletter and special promotions on her website: **shariahembree.com/contact/**